Praise for *Blackmail, My Love*

"Have you ever felt the ghosts that swirl down San Francisco's Tenderloin streets and North Beach alleys? You'll meet them face-to-face in Katie Gilmartin's noir trip down a very queer stretch of Memory Lane, to a Frisco of corrupt blackmailers, rough cops, intrepid homos, and pre-Stonewall constraint, connection, and possibility. Complete with guns, fedoras, bribes, José Sarria at the Black Cat, chest bindings, Coit Tower, retired showgirls from the Forbidden City, and a bruise shaped like St. Francis—Katie dives so deep (and convincingly) into the still-somehow-familiar details of the City's hidden past that you'll feel like you've time-traveled."

—Carol Queen, author of *The Leather Daddy and the Femme*

"Gilmartin's magisterial command of her historical period ensures that the reader will be effortlessly immersed in the instant paranoia, mistrust, and betrayal so typical of that pre-liberated gay era. A darkly entertaining mystery, *Blackmail, My Love* also grounds us in why the Stonewall Revolution would shortly afterward happen—as well as why it had to happen."

—Felice Picano, author of *Like People in History*
and editor of *Best Gay Romance 2015*

"This is Katie Gilmartin's first work of fiction, and she clearly drew on her academic work: interviews she conducted with lesbians about their lives in the 1940s and 1950s. That work paid off. Her future in fiction is bright."

—*New York Journal of Books*

"Honestly, I haven't read anything so dark and vibrant in a really long time."

—Louise Barros, of Bookshop Santa Cruz

"This intriguing noir novel captures a cultural moment, set in 1950s San Francisco at a time when gays and lesbians established a strong sense of community, despite being harassed and often arrested by law enforcement simply for congregating. *Blackmail, My Love* will entertain fans of the noir genre, but its social themes and messages about love and redemption will also appeal to a wider audience."

—*Foreword Reviews*

"Although it is a dark tale of a harrowing time—the queer world in San Francisco in the early 1950s—the narrative voice in *Blackmail, My Love* is fresh, keenly observant, and even charming. I highly recommend Katie Gilmartin's wonderful debut novel and I am eager to see what she does next."

—Michael Nava, author of the Henry Rios mysteries

"A hard-boiled homage and detailed, nostalgic romp through post-WWII San Francisco, *Blackmail, My Love* reveals and revels in the City of 1951 through a GLBT lens, and the history is spot-on."

—Kelli Stanley, award-winning author of *City of Dragons*

"Nancy Drew meets Leslie Feinberg."

—Animal, of lesbian punk band Bitch and Animal

"*Blackmail, My Love* is a throaty noir mystery with enough heat to set a coffee-soused Beat poet aflame—but it's also a novel about tenacity and community and the forces that hold us together when the world really does conspire to tear us apart. The writing is rich in style and soul, and surprises by insisting on laughter as a source of redemption."

—Alex Algren, editor of *Soaking Wet*

Blackmail, My Love
A MURDER MYSTERY

M

WRITTEN AND ILLUSTRATED BY
KATIE GILMARTIN

CLEiS
PRESS

Published in the United States by Cleis Press, Inc., 2246 Sixth Street, Berkeley, CA 94710.

Printed in the United States.
Cover design: Scott Idleman/Blink
Cover illustration: Katie Gilmartin
Text design: Frank Wiedemann

First Edition.
10 9 8 7 6 5 4 3 2

Trade paper ISBN: 978-1-62778-064-3
E-book ISBN: 978-1-62778-076-6

Library of Congress Cataloging-in-Publication Data

Gilmartin, Katie.
  Blackmail, my love / by Katie Gilmartin. -- First edition.
     pages cm
  Historical note at end of volume is a brief summary of lesbian, gay, bisexual and trans-gender history in the United States and California in particular.
   ISBN 978-1-62778-064-3 (alk. paper) -- ISBN 978-1-62778-076-6 (e-book)
  1. Gay private investigators--Fiction. 2. Brothers and sisters--Fiction. 3. Extortion--Fiction. 4. Police corruption--Fiction. 5. Gays--Violence against--Fiction. 6. Gay bars--Fiction. 7. Gays--History--20th century. 8. San Francisco (California)--Fiction. I. Title.

  PS3607.I452145B53 2014
  813'.6--dc23

                    2014001498

foreword

H istorian and practicing artist Katie Gilmartin has outdone herself with *Blackmail, My Love*. This gripping and beautifully written detective novel is actually a well-researched piece of historical fiction, illuminating San Francisco's post-World War II era, when bars were the primary mode of queer socializing and police raids really did ruin people's lives. Gilmartin has an eye for detail—as detectives and historians must—and she sets her story at a time in San Francisco's history when queer communities, often segregated by race and class, matured into new modes of political consolidation and resistance. Taking seriously the idea that queer social movements emerged out of bars rather than formal homophile organizations, Gilmartin's novel charts the lives of a cast of characters (some right out of history) who work together to trap the entrappers. As a bonus, Gilmartin supplements the text with illustrative prints that enliven her already vivid prose. *Blackmail, My Love* is a must-read for anyone who enjoys queer history!

—Nan Alamilla Boyd,
author of *Wide-Open Town: A History of Queer San Francisco to 1965*
and Professor of Women and Gender Studies
at San Francisco State University

chapter one

I don't go for swanky joints. I checked my shoes for scuffs, my gabardine jacket for lint, shrugged off a passing memory of worrying if my stocking seams were straight, and straightened my tie instead. Then I grasped the knob of the hefty oak door and turned. My hand slid, but the doorknob didn't budge. I knocked. No response. I knocked again, louder and longer, and waited. Silent as God when I'm praying. I took a step back and considered the reticent brass plate: "Dollar Bill Delivery Services," with a miniature dollar bill engraved neatly below. I stared at that bill awhile. Thought, *queer as a three-dollar bill.* I knocked again, three distinct raps. The door opened inward.

A wide guy in a wider suit looked me over as I stepped inside. We were in a cramped office, brightly lit, with a metal desk, a couple file cabinets, and an antiseptic smell. I looked at him inquiringly, trying to make the look brash. He grunted and stepped aside. Behind his glacial bulk was another door and another brass plate, this one marked PRIVATE. The door opened reluctantly, like a vault, its tight seals giving way to smoke and muffled music. When my eyes adjusted to the darkness I saw a thick curtain inches from my face. Red velvet, heavy enough to knock your hat off as you push your way through, in case you forget to take it off yourself. I bent to pick it up, and the haze hit me full force when I stood. These bars are twice as smoky as the rest of them. People here twice as nervous.

The sleekly paneled room was lit by tiny brass sconces and a glittering chandelier centered in the low ceiling. Through the haze I saw an elegantly curved bar, dark mahogany. The massive mirror behind it let everyone check their nonchalance. That surprised me: these places usually avoid mirrors. Too much like photos. No one lets themselves be photographed in a joint like this unless it's cops busting up the place or politicians arriving for a press photo after the dust has settled. The mirror hanging there in its ornate frame said *confidence*. The mirror said *Ain't you pretty, and not so afraid. No need to be afraid here.* I noticed no one was looking in it.

Flanking the mirror were rows of bottles diverse as the asses crowding a beauty parlor on Saturday morning: skinny ones, squat ones, ones that bulged out here and ones that bulged out there. A whole shelf devoted just to gin. No Schlitz in sight. Opposite the bar sat six booths plushly upholstered in leather of the same dark red as the curtain that took my hat for me. Between the booths hung brocade curtains, voluptuously swagged, so each booth became an intimate room, a private dell. The drapery extended across the ceiling to the bar, and together with the plumes of smoke lent the room the look of a vast, elegant opium den. At the far end, across a compact dance floor, stood a tiny stage all of six inches high. Three musicians strained to avoid one another's elbows. Another breach of the law: unlikely they had a cabaret license. Someone paid big to put this place together, and someone kept paying to keep it together.

In the far corner I could see a dark hallway. Even a fancy gin collection and a sax player on a six-inch stage didn't eliminate the need for a back door. I'd case it later. Everybody did: the obligatory bathroom run, to find out whether the window was large enough to climb through. Just in case. I headed toward the bar, which was as crowded as double-Ds in a C-cup. The men were all of the fuzzy sweater set: neat cashmere, no pills under the arms, and spiffy shoes without heel-taps to extend their wear. The ladies were of two species. The severe skirt set, hair short but coiffed, just enough fluff to pass for a profes-sional: schoolteacher, nurse, or librarian. Butch, but pansies next to the butches in other bars. The femmes were fuller all over: full hair, skirt, lipstick, heels. Full but not excessive; they'd catch your eye but not raise your eyebrows. Pearls, real ones, where dive bar femmes wore rhinestones.

I knew a drink would rival the cost of my dinner but decided, this time, to skip the bartender and focus on the guests. I'd need a drink in hand for that. A petite brunette—two strands of pearls—caught my eye as I approached. I ordered, the bartender set me up, and I looked around for Miss Double Strand. She smiled archly at me. I was butch of center in this crowd, but her eyes seemed to approve. I relaxed a bit. Her off-the-shoulder taffeta dress swirled across her curves.

"Don't think I've seen you here before," she said.

"First time. Nice place. What do they deliver?"

She laughed, a light, bright sound. "Oh, the usual: smoky intrigue, heartbreak, the occasional romantic triangle."

"Nice to know I don't have to go out for my heartbreak anymore. Can have it delivered right to my door. That'll save all kinds of trouble."

Her eyes flashed. "You go in for heartbreak often?"

"Whenever I have the time. Does take time, you know. Dedica-tion too. All that melancholy. All that black coffee. Walks in the rain with damp cigarettes. And then if isn't raining, you've got the glorious weather to contend with. Hard to pull off heartbreak when the sky's as high and cobalt as it was today."

"Well, then, time to order in a romantic triangle."

"A ménage à trois," I said, smiling. "Now, that's an all-weather activity."

Her deep brown eyes, with tiny flecks of gold, held mine. So I asked, "You come here often?"

The flecks lost a bit of their luster. "Now and then," she said, shrugging. "I'm not really a bar person. But my friend—" She hesitated, then continued, "My friend Charmaine, she told us about this place. What brings you here?" she asked coyly.

"I'm looking for my brother. He disappeared."

The movement was smooth and sudden, like a windup toy: she swiveled. Instead of sparkling brown eyes I was looking at the clasp of the double-stranded pearls. It was delicate, white gold to match the pearls. She jumped rather shrilly into conversation with her friends, and I saw the bartender's eyes buck, then ricochet from her to me. He continued washing glasses, his towel-enrobed hand twisting back and forth inside each one before he set it on the shelf.

I moved down the bar. The cashmere-clad torsos ranged from champagne to taupe, with the occasional navy for a splash of color. Halfway down I caught the eye of a tall, balding man in camel. "Haverford Huntington," he offered, along with his fleshy hand. I asked whether he came here often.

"I'm not much of a bar person," he replied with a shake of his jowls. "But I like to stop by on the way home from work on a Thursday or Friday. Occasionally I'll pop in Saturday for a pick-me-up on my way to the opera. Oh, and Sundays"—he brightened—"Sundays they have a lovely brunch, with canapés and mimosas."

"Perhaps you've met my brother, Jimmy O'Conner. I'm looking for him."

Haverford's neck was claspless, but his fleshy back rolled over his sweater in a generous, stubbly fold. The bartender's eyes were drawn by the sudden movement, and flickered again from its source to me. I pretended to be considering my gin options, then nodded to an elderly gentleman with a burled pipe curving from his mouth. He removed it briefly to smile and introduce himself as Frederick Kitterington the Third. The pseudonyms here were at least three syllables longer than any I'd encountered, so I said I was Joseph O'Conneringtonville and we settled into a discussion of the furnishings. I'd idly begun to wonder what the scruff of his neck would look like, when a large hand wrapped itself around my elbow. A grimly smiling face asked Frederick, "Would you kindly excuse us for a moment?" and with the slowest of movements the hand steered me toward the back of the bar.

I asked why.

A voice low in my ear replied gravely, "You're disturbing our patrons."

"I am a patron," I countered.

"Patrons are those who maintain the genteel atmosphere of this establishment." The grip on my arm tightened, propelling me to the rear hallway. He patted me down with no lingering at the usual lingering spots, then rapped on a door. After a murmur from within we entered a windowless office. He released his hold, but not his proximity.

A large desk dominated the room, one cushy leather chair behind it and a wooden one in front. For no particular reason it occurred to me that the wood chair was perfect for tying someone up: sturdy, stiff-backed. No sign of rope, though; the desk was bare. Behind it was a handsome vitrine flaunting a few expensive bottles and four glasses lined up an inch apart in the center of the shelf. Nothing else there. Except another door, and a slender man in a suit so crisply starched you could cut your chin on the crease running down his trouser leg. A silver streak in his jet-black hair created an elegant highlight above his temple. Perfect posture: upright, shoulders back. I thought of a coil, under intense pressure. But his voice was surprisingly soft.

"Jack Chantry," he announced, smiling genially. "How may I help you?"

"Joe O'Conner. I'm not sure. I didn't come here of my own accord."

He smiled apologetically and gestured courteously toward the stiff chair, then settled in the cushy one. A vein at his temple throbbed, but he spoke with a sympathetic smile.

"We noticed your conversation distressed our guests. Would you care to share it with me?"

He could find out easily enough by having his bartender eavesdrop. The hand could have steered me out the door, with an assist from the foot. Apparently he wanted to hear it from me.

"I'm looking for my brother, James O'Conner. Jimmy."

"I don't think I know him," he replied vaguely, apologetic.

"He disappeared."

"I'm so sorry," he said, and seemed to mean it.

"The cops don't care. Just another fleck of social detritus. One less pervert for them to keep away from the good citizens of this town."

He nodded slightly, noncommittal. "I'm sorry for your trouble." The pause was long, considerate. "However, our guests find this a sanctuary from precisely those attitudes. Questions about the disappearance of a man disrupt the climate of safety we've established. I must ask you to stop your inquiries." He waited, then prompted, "I trust you understand."

I nodded, unprepared for his apparent sincerity.

"I'll ask my staff if they know your brother. Jimmy O'Conner, you said?"

Defeated again, this time by a velvet glove, I gave Chantry the number of Jimmy's hotel and wondered whether I'd find him before I started thinking of it as my hotel. As I stood he rose, graciously thanking me for the visit, as though it had been voluntary. The hand piloted me to the door. When I looked back Jack was tapping his cigarette on a silver lighter. Watching me go.

Two weeks earlier I'd lurched, stiff-legged, off a bus in downtown San Francisco and staggered to police headquarters. From its front steps I saw an imposing granite edifice, but inside it was all chipped veneer and sour linoleum. A cop with too much hair pomade presided over a colossal desk. He looked at me with the enthusiasm a drag queen affords a pair of brown wing-tip brogues. Size six.

"This is the police department, lady. Etiquette complaints go to Emily Post," he squawked, returning to his paperwork.

"But my brother *always* calls me on my birthday. Even when he was in Korea he called me!" I was too exhausted for logic.

Without looking up, he pointed. "Missing Persons that way."

I grabbed my suitcase and stormed out of the office, but my sensible pumps reduced the stomps to snippy clicks. Doors with windows you couldn't see through lined the long, stale hallway. At the far end a man mopped the floor. Murky puddles stretched between us. Department of Vice had a puddle. Homicide had two.

The cop behind this desk had a pimply face and vague eyes that couldn't find a missing person who was washing him behind the ears. He took his time looking me over, with a desultory detour in the vicinity of my chest. "I need to report a missing person," I announced.

He inquired jocularly, "Who's missing?"

I dropped the suitcase. "I'm Josephine O'Conner. My brother, Jimmy O'Conner, is missing." His eyes, which had wandered to my legs, shot back to my face.

"He used to be a policeman here," he blurted. "Who're you, his sister?"

"The manager at his hotel says he stopped coming around a month ago."

The cop looked momentarily stricken. Then he leaned back in his chair and a slow smile spread across his face. "You sure he isn't off on a bender?" he asked, insinuating. "You know he was in a fight a while back. Got him kicked off the force. That brother of yours, he couldn't handle his liquor." He shook his head and the smile stretched to a leer.

"My brother never drinks."

"Maybe your brother used to never drink, but when your brother drank he wasn't so good at stopping."

Sometimes I didn't hear from Jimmy for a few weeks, even a month. But when he didn't call on my birthday I knew he was in an alley somewhere, blood clogging his nostrils, or worse. In the wilds of Korea he'd managed to finagle his way to a phone call, his voice dim and echoey

across the line, saying, "Hey Josie, happy birthday! I'm so grateful you were born." In that way he had of pouring his heart into a goblet and holding it to the light so it shimmered and let you know that, no matter what—even if you were sixteen and the world was expecting lemon chiffon pie and yielding smiles and all you had were sharp angles and confusion, even so—there was a place in it for you.

I gathered my fear and fury and plunked it on the desk with my purse. "I just traveled two thousand six hundred miles in a rank Greyhound bus in August. I want to file a missing person's report on James O'Conner."

He took his time sliding a drawer open, selecting a form, placing it on the blotter. He picked up a pen. Then he put it down.

"You know," he said, his eyes relocating to a spot ten inches south of my face, "I really think ol' Jimmy's sunning himself on a beach down south right now, drying out. Santa Monica, maybe. I see it all the time! Family's worried and he's just working his way through a hair of the dog that bit him. Why don't you hold off for a coupla weeks? He'll be embarrassed enough without his buddies knowing Little Sis filed a Missing Person's on him. That's mortifying for a cop, you know. Even a *former* cop," he added.

"James O'Conner. O'Conner with an *O*."

He tipped his chair back, laced his hands behind his head, and settled his feet noisily on the desk. "You know," he began, reflectively, "you remind me of my sister. She's just like you. Perky as a daisy on a summer's day. What say you and me get together for a drink and I show you the town? Exciting town, San Francisco, but we got a lot of lowlife and degenerates. Might be a bit much for you to handle. I get off work at five."

"I feel as perky as a dishrag after a burnt spaghetti dinner and an evening with you sounds about as glamorous." I snapped the form out from under his foot. His heel scuffed a black mark across the page. I clicked my damn snippy pumps to a chair, jerked off my gloves, and filled out the form. Then I clicked back, picked his foot up off the desk, slid the form underneath, and dropped it. He was very effective as a paperweight. "I want to talk to someone who worked with him."

"Why don't you come in for a chat with Sergeant Fitzpatrick?" he asked with an oily smile. "I'm sure he'll be delighted to meet you. Fitz's not really a leg man, after all," he sneered. "He'll be in at nine on Monday."

"But that's three days away!"

"Monday at nine. Ish."

I gathered my things, slammed the door behind me, and slipped in a puddle outside Vice.

The stretch of town my brother lived in was called the Tenderloin. I couldn't see anything tender about it. It had seen seedy come and go, fondly recalled disreputable, and waxed nostalgic at grim. Storefronts that hadn't been boarded up were painted out with blunt, irregular strokes. Cadwick Ams Hotl read the sign, with dusty smudges where letters had gone missing. The building's peeling paint had long ago given up any aspiration to color. The front door had stories to tell, but you've heard them and they were tedious the first time around.

In the dim foyer a gaunt man looked up slowly and with suspicion, his face furrowed by years of failing to accurately assess bad character. "Yeah?" he inquired.

"Mr. Wilkinson?" He nodded. "I spoke with you on the phone. My brother Jimmy lived here. You said he left without taking his things."

"Or paying his last week's rent."

"Is his room still available?"

He squinted at me, skeptical. "You sure this is the place for you?"

"Staying here will help me find him."

He turned to an unlocked key safe. The brass discs jingled mirthlessly. He passed me one with "4B" embossed deeply in the scarred metal. "I haven't needed it, so I left his things as they were," he said. He paused and looked at a bug-filled light fixture on the ceiling. "Your brother was a nice boy. I didn't believe any of the things they said about him."

I left that remark—and the past tense—for another day, and mounted the stairs. Jimmy's room was in the back, behind a door with alligatored paint. A spindly bed, neatly made, sheet turned down over the wool blanket. Mismatched chairs flanking a small table with a riot of rings left by damp glasses. The papered walls looked like someone had flung faded bouquets against them randomly and furiously. Dropping my suitcase and purse, I peeled off gloves that hadn't been white since midway through Iowa and sent the pumps flying.

The closet held shirts and trousers, a lightweight coat, and a pair of black wing tips. Pockets yielded a car key, a handkerchief, half a movie stub, and lint. Jimmy's suitcase, wide strap doubled around it, sat on the closet floor, empty save the sewing kit Mother had tucked inside a sagging pocket. On the shelf above the clothing rod was his fedora. I reached for it. Underneath was a small bottle of whiskey, white paper seal intact. I froze. I dropped the hat.

On the bureau with my gloves was a half-full glass of swampy water and another key, this one dangling from a medallion that pictured a narrow tower on a hill. Forming an arc around the fob were three acorns, caps bright mossy chartreuse. I stared at the acorns a while. Then I checked the bureau drawers: boxer shorts, undershirts, socks, a stack of neatly pressed handkerchiefs, and some gangly black sock garters. The bottom drawer held dirty laundry.

I walked to the table and pushed open the window above it. Weights clanged behind the plaster but the sash held. A haphazardly shaped lot sprouted brown grass and drooping fennel. My pulse quickened when I saw the sunflowers. The rows he planted at home every year would lean this way and that, over the front fence, back toward the house. He'd announce with a grin when the first one passed his own height. By early August he tied cheesecloth over the heads, puffy veils to discourage birds. Our kitchen table always held a bowl of cracked shells. These sunflowers lacked veils, and I could see from the third floor that birds had disrupted their geometry.

The day cooled and became dusk as I sat at the window. When I woke from my reverie, I undressed and laid damp cheeks on Jimmy's pillow.

The orange-gray murk of the city night infused the room. I watched shadows for a while, bulbous forms cast by the radiator, stripes the bed's spindles threw against the wall. I wondered how much time Jimmy had spent watching these shadows, and what he was looking at now. I unpacked my suitcase. There wasn't much; I'd left in a hurry. I put on a tailored dress that had been Mother's, dowdy enough to ward off unwanted attention. I piled Jimmy's laundry in my suitcase and slid it into the closet. I'd wash his things so they'd be fresh for him when I found him.

I headed back toward the bus station, keeping to the darker streets and watching for nervous men. A certain kind of nervous: driven by hunger, dismayed by its hypnotic urgency. Drawn against reason and every ounce of self-preservation. I knew their kind because I was one of them. So I smelled his fear before I saw the furtive looks he cast over his shoulder. I followed him from a distance as he passed the bus depot. He walked intently, slowed for a while, then suddenly sped up, all the while throwing cloaked glances at any man he passed. He traced the block again, veered off onto a side street, then disappeared down a dark stairway at the side of a dejected hotel. I found a shadowed doorway and waited. About twenty minutes later the stairwell swallowed another man. Then a lone figure emerged from its darkness and skulked away. The second-story window of the next building shed bright yellow light and jagged sound, a rockabilly recording drowned out now and then by raucous laughter. The glare made the dark stairway darker, but as men came and went it briefly lit their faces. My feet grew numb as other figures disappeared down the stairway or rose from its hollow, always alone.

I crossed the street and descended. No sign above the door, but it yielded to my touch. A low-ceilinged room, poorly lit, with scattered tables and an improvised bar of boards on bricks. Twenty or so men

sat here and there; all faced the door. They lifted their heads briefly to stare. The talk was hushed, the room alert. The bartender was broad, mustached, grim. He stared at me without welcome.

"I'm looking for my brother," I began. He shook his head conclusively and turned away. "No, I—my brother disappeared. I'm afraid something's happened to him. Maybe you know him."

"I don't know anyone."

"His name is Jimmy, Jimmy O'Conner." The face was impassive, focused on the bucket he doused glasses in. "I know he came to places like this. It's not about that."

He continued to ignore me. I started toward the tables and he turned sharply. "No one here wants to be bothered by anyone looking for someone. It doesn't matter why. Go away."

I scoped the room again. There was an acrid scent, the sweat of fear. I knew he was right. I fled. Next door the party on the second floor continued, rowdiness spilling from the window.

Back in Jimmy's room I was too agitated to sleep. The floor squeaked under the faded carpet as I paced. Three steps, squeak, four steps, turn. Four steps, squeak, three steps, turn. A long gray stripe in the carpet matched my path. Jimmy had paced too. And decades of previous occupants. I wondered about their worries, hidden in the tuftless weaving. The fretwork.

In cities you hear sirens all night long, crisscrossing the town. Here they didn't cross: they stopped abruptly, usually across the street. I continued pacing, and eventually the squeak became a comfort. Then the heat pipes exploded with sound. Downstairs, someone was pounding on them. I got into bed.

The next morning Mr. Wilkinson was slumped behind the front desk. Showing him the keys I'd found, I asked whether Jimmy had two cars.

"Only one that I know of. He gave me a ride to the bowling alley down in Pacifica once. There's a lot around the corner. '41 Ford, maroon."

"Do you know where he spent his time?"

Mr. Wilkinson shook his head slowly. "I'm used to respecting people's privacy."

"But I think my brother may be in trouble."

He pondered this, then said laconically, "Some people don't want to be found. That's why it's hard to find them."

"But what if he's hurt? What if he needs help?"

"He'd let you know. Drop a crumb somewhere."

"He told me he was working as a private detective. Did he have an office?"

Mr. Wilkinson shifted his attention to the far corner of the ceiling. He studied it carefully. I waited. He watched it still. I checked it myself; it wasn't doing much.

"Mr. Wilkinson, perhaps a bit of remuneration might help you remember."

He perked up like a damp paper bag. "Well, now that you mention it"—his eyes followed my hands as I set my purse on the counter and opened the latch—"I do recall him going to an office now and then. He'd call over, ask if there were any messages, and when there were he'd trot right over. I was on my way to lunch one day and walked with him. That old gray building on Eddy. Between Leavenworth and Hyde."

"Thanks, Mr. Wilkinson," I said as he slid the bill from between my fingers. But he wasn't finished.

"There's a diner down on Market, near Jones. He ate there most mornings."

"You said you didn't believe the things people said about him. What did they say?"

"Your brother's life is his life. You should be careful about poking around in it. You might find out things you don't want to know."

Eddy between Leavenworth and Hyde was a long block, and all the buildings on it were old and gray. Two story mostly: auto repair or glass cutting on the first, establishments three weeks shy of defunct on the second. I stepped inside the lobbies to check nameplates. Emerson Elevators. Golden Gate Secretarial School. A-1 Rubber Stamp Company. Acme Professional Services sounded sufficiently oblique. A self-service elevator took me to the second floor. I knocked. A voice said, "Come in," but didn't sound enthusiastic about it.

The office had seen too many divorce cases. A short wooden balustrade guarded a metal desk and two battered file cabinets, each flanked by a door with an etched glass inset that said OFFICE. They were creative types. The woman behind the desk was dressed for a classier set. Pretty as a doll, and about as warm. She slammed the carriage of her typewriter back and turned to me impatiently.

"I'm Jimmy O'Conner's sister," I said.

I was relieved by her nod.

"Jimmy's missing."

Her eyebrows began a tête à tête.

"He's been missing for about a month."

The eyebrows conferred. They were delicate, artfully tapering at the outer ends.

"I'd like to see his papers."

The eyebrows rose like a row of pigeons abandoning a telephone line.

"I'm sorry, that's confidential," she said, only she pronounced it *confi-den-she-all* and sounded sorry as a priest refusing to share the sacred mysteries.

"But this could be a matter of life and death."

"We deal with life and death matters every day," she said loftily, then pulled out a gold compact and flipped it open to check her lipstick. Satisfied, she returned her attention to me. "I'm not just a secretary, you know. I am"—she paused for effect—"Guardian of the Records."

I went for broke: "If something's happened to Jimmy, I'm his survivor, and his records belong to me."

"We would need to see the death certificate and proof of your kinship," she replied primly. Her acquaintance with the requirements sobered me; untimely death could be a fringe benefit here.

"I need to speak with the owner."

"That would be Mr. Foster. He's away on biz-e-ness." I wondered if he paid her by the syllable.

"Please have him call me."

She wrote a note and put it in a box. "Saturdays we close at noon," she announced, looking pointedly toward the door.

The diner was typical, but everything erred on the side of dingy. Instead of black and white the checkerboard floor was black and gray. Their lemon meringue pie was tinged green. My waitress, Thelma, erred on the side of ample. Monumental breasts, full hips, and a peroxide bouffant that barely cleared the frame when she came through the kitchen's swinging doors.

"Jimmy O'Conner? Haven't seen him since—let's see, almost a month ago. It was a Monday or a Friday, 'cause we were refilling ketchup bottles. I remember lining them up over there and thinking, Hey, Jimmy didn't come in today. And he wasn't here yesterday neither. I wondered about it. He hadn't said anything about going anywheres. He wasn't looking so good. You know,"—Thelma lowered her voice—"he'd started drinking. You could see that. Like with some people it's an all or nothing thing. Was that with him. He came in with bloodshot eyes and one day a big shiner. Took a long time for that shiner to fade, went through the yellow and purple stage for a whole week." She crossed her arms and settled them on her colossal bosom. "It wasn't like him—he's a regular kind of guy. I never needed to take his breakfast order because it was always the same: two eggs over easy, rye toast, cuppa joe."

"Do you know any of his friends?"

"He didn't come in with buddies but a few times, and I didn't know them." She frowned, scrunched her lips up together like she was getting ready to kiss a baby, and slid into the booth. She rearranged the salt, pepper, mustard, and ketchup. Then, with a gesture so elaborately nonchalant it wasn't, she picked up my spoon and began polishing it with her apron. "You know," she said, philosophically, watching some-one settle at the counter, "some of these spoons get bent. They're still fine, nothing wrong with them. They just don't nest with the others quite the same way. So they tend to fall off to one side in the drawer." She eyed me close. "Know what I mean?"

I eyed her back and nodded. "I do know what you mean."

She exhaled, satisfied, and leaned back against the Naugahyde. "There's a bar in North Beach I heard him mention, bohemian place called the Black Cat. I'll bet they have a lot of bent spoons there."

"North Beach?"

"That's the I-talian neighborhood. North of downtown. Follow Columbus Avenue."

I left a good tip.

The parking lot around the corner from Jimmy's hotel was a square of cracked asphalt with crabgrass heralding the return of wilderness to the Tenderloin. The guard dog, mangy and diffident, looked at me, sniffed, and dropped his head back between his paws.

"I'm Jimmy O'Conner's sister," I said to the grizzled man in the shack. He nodded skeptically. I pulled the two keys from my purse. He peered at them, lifted a tired arm, and pointed in the direction of a Ford. "Do you know what the other key goes to?" I asked him. He shook his head.

Speckled dirt from the grille to the fins reduced the deep maroon to a dull brown. The doors were unlocked: he hadn't planned to be gone long. A few cracked sunflower shells littered the front seat. The glove compartment held maps, flares, and a book of postcards from someplace called The Mystery Spot. Nothing but an old newspaper and an empty Coke bottle under the seat. The trunk revealed a spare tire, jumper cables, and a quart of oil. The key without the fob fit the ignition. The engine coughed, then turned over. I ran it for a few minutes, cut the gas, locked the doors, and left. I spent the afternoon asking at corner stores and diners. Nobody had anything to tell me, except that they were free that night. The pumps rubbed my feet raw. I went back to Jimmy's room and watched the light fade. Then I headed downtown.

chapter two

C olumbus Avenue cuts through the grid of downtown, creating complicated six-point intersections. One of these anchors a soaring flatiron structure with a copper tower weathered to bright green, as if Cinderella decided to homestead in the Emerald City. Below the verdigris castle stooped women argued over vegetables and drunkards shouted their momentary bliss to the heavens. I made for the side streets and watched for peculiar characters. Trouble was, peculiar characters thronged the place, and they were all kinds of peculiar.

I followed a stocky man with thick black glasses, hands jammed tight in the pockets of a pea coat, muttering as he looked over his shoulder. He led me to a smoky café with only one thing on the menu: coffee, made seven different ways. Another man in thick black glasses read aloud, grandly, like he was reading poetry, while off to the side someone banged on a drum, just now and then. The men all had bushy, untrimmed beards, like myopic Paul Bunyans in their Sunday best. A pixieish woman in a white blouse and black stretch pants leaped erratically around the room, thrust her arms in the air, and shimmied wildly. I was the peculiar character here, in my blue flowered shirtwaist.

East of Columbus the skyscrapers gave way to low brick buildings crowded along narrow streets. Sure that the bar for bent spoons would be hidden here, I probed shadowed hollows for a door or passageway. Then, rounding the corner where Columbus begins, I stopped in my tracks: thrust out into the intersection hung a sign, BLACK CAFE, with a sinewy feline posed proudly between the words. No one could enter or leave without being seen from six directions. Four men entered convivially, like they were walking into a greengrocer—no whiplash checking for surveillance. I thought Thelma must be wrong about this place, but I followed them in.

Dapper men in flannel suits crowded the bar alongside lumberjacks, flaming queens, dour butches, black-clad poets, sandaled bohemian types, and sailors. The crowd reminded me of a tavern back east: in a town too small to support a homosexual bar, all the marginal flora and fauna found their way to one seedy locale and managed, edgily, to get along. But never as if, given the choice, they would opt for the company. Here, they seemed to: the room buzzed with conviviality. And they were serving spaghetti, all you could eat for fifteen cents. A longshoreman was making eyes at a queen, a bohemian was getting cozy with a suit, and a waiter in a tutu pranced through, smiling at appreciative catcalls, then burst into operatic song. My heart pounded. If this place existed, Jimmy would have found it.

With the return of hope a sudden hunger gnawed me. The spaghetti came with pungent garlic bread and I devoured it, studying the crowd. I was mopping up sauce when everything stopped. Lights flickered, the room froze. I poised to sprint toward what I hoped would be a back door, but nobody moved. Two policemen swaggered in, sneering. One was tall, the other taller, and both walked like they owned the place. Their belts, oversized charm bracelets, dangled nightsticks, handcuffs, and holsters. As they strolled to the bar, those on the first few stools decamped hastily. The bartender pulled an envelope from under the cash register. The tall cop slid it into his breast pocket, then ordered two beers. The taller cop pointed to a spot high on the wall and said loudly, "*Our* glasses." The bartender reached for two tumblers set apart on the top shelf and poured their drinks. The room was subdued and tense while they drank. Then they swaggered out like they'd swaggered in. The entire place exhaled as the bartender bellowed, "Time to wash '*our* glasses,'" and a stampede ensued. By the time I reached the alley a crowd circled the two tumblers sitting on the pavement. I peered between shoulders. Six men, flies unzipped, peed into the glasses as urine spilled over like frothy champagne.

Back inside, the bartender greeted me warmly, but when I explained my purpose he turned sullen as the others. I thought he flinched when I spoke Jimmy's name, but then he insisted he'd never heard of him. When I pressed he growled, "Listen, girly, no one in this place is going to help anybody find anybody. That's not how we look out for each other around here."

I moved on to the patrons. When I said Jimmy's name the air seemed to chill, but they claimed they didn't know him. As I left I sensed whispers and glances in my direction. The city towered over me, empty office windows looming, bright apartment windows mocking. Behind one of them was someone who knew Jimmy. Behind one of them was someone who knew what happened to him.

A voice blared from a darkened doorway and I jumped.

"Do you know my brother, Jimmy O'Conner?" I asked desperately.

"Ah'll be your brother, you can call me Jimmy if you want," came the slurred reply.

I fled back to Jimmy's room.

Slamming the door, I hurled my pumps into the closet. The zipper on my dress stuck halfway down. I tried to slide it off over my head, and a claustrophobic panic descended. I tugged frantically. Finally I heard a tear, and the sound unleashed me: I split the back in two ripping it off. Huffing, I jerked at garter tabs and dug fingernails into my last good

23

pair of hose. Unhooked my bra and threw it across the room. Pulled my underwear off, opened the window, and flung it into the night with an angry bellow. It floated delicately down to the trash-littered lot below.

I paced, naked. Four steps, squeak, three steps, turn. I veered toward the closet, picked up Jimmy's hat, and grabbed the whiskey. Tearing the bottle's seal, I remembered the horrors of home, the promises Jimmy and I made to each other. I put the bottle back, then reminded myself that he'd broken those promises, succumbed to its narcotic promise, and poured myself two fingers. It burned going down. I wiped sputtering lips with the back of my hand and paced some more. Earrings pinched my lobes and I snatched them off. They clattered on the thin veneer of the dresser. I crossed to the window and, belatedly, pulled down the shade.

Returning to the closet, I grabbed a cream-colored shirt off its hanger and slid my arms through. The sleeves were long, bunching above the cuffs. I buttoned myself in and checked the mirror. The shirt pushed out where it should lie flat. Still, I was grateful for the long torso and wide shoulders Mother always tsked about. I pulled off the shirt and dragged Jimmy's suitcase out of the closet. Slid the strap off and worked the buckle loose. Starting under my arm, I wrapped the strap three times around my torso and tucked the frayed end under my armpit. I fished one of Jimmy's undershirts from the top drawer, pulled it on, and then slid the shirt over it. The mirror told me I was on my way.

I stepped into Jimmy's boxers, then his black wool trousers. His tangled sock garters reminded me of a sanitary belt and were about as comfortable; I let the socks slouch. Jimmy's black wing tips were much too big. They clopped when I walked. I'd need to get a pair that fit. I could do that. I looked down. Tightening his suspenders didn't stop the trouser cuffs from pooling around my feet. I flipped open his suitcase and felt along the back wall for the sagging pocket. The sewing kit held thread, needles, buttons, and a small pair of scissors, the blunt

kind they give kindergartners. I sat at the table and took the pants up two inches while I finished my drink. When I put them on they no longer pooled. They were heavier than the dungarees I'd worn for chores: I felt sturdy in them.

I checked the mirror again, grabbed the blunt scissors, scooped my hair into a ponytail, and cut. I had to hack at it for a while, but it was too late to lose my nerve. The hair came off thick and limp in my hand, and I threw it on the dresser, scattering acorns. I did a lousy job trying to clip up over my ears, then put Jimmy's hat on my head. I clopped over to the mirror and stood with my legs wide apart. I'd always resented my angular face and broad shoulders, but now, suddenly, they pleased me. I looked like Jimmy at nineteen. With a very bad haircut.

That's when it hit me, right in my bound-up chest: Jimmy could be dead. I felt loosed, abandoned by gravity. I gasped, reached my hand toward the dresser, leaned on it for support. It slid on spindly wheels and slammed against the wall. The mirror shattered explosively—a waterfall of flashing light, jagged fragments cascading to the floor. I stumbled back to the bed and stared at the scattered shards, panting.

When I could breathe again I got the metal wastebasket from the bathroom and set it among the mosaic of reflections. Picked up a shard, looked at myself in it, and tossed it into the container, where it jangled loudly. I did it again. The third one cut me across the thumb, smeared blood mixing with the sliver of my image. I tossed it, got the torn dress from the corner and soaked up the blood. Locating the kindergarten scissors, I hacked my way through the lower seam twice, then tore a strip of cloth from hem to waist. I poured myself another couple fingers of whiskey, dipped my thumb in, felt the sting, wrapped the strip tightly around my finger, and tucked in the end. It wasn't pretty.

I reached for another shard, looked, threw it in the container, listened to the clang. Another and another. I cut myself again. Whiskey and another strip. Eventually my hand resembled Dorothy's scarecrow. I didn't care. I did it some more. Then I was done. I got a broom and dustpan from a closet down the hall, swept up the remaining shards, fishing out the acorns but not the earrings or hair, and slid it all into the container. I dumped the whiskey, cloudy from my blood, down the drain, and poured myself one last finger. I swallowed it, took off everything but the boxers, and climbed into bed.

When I woke, the window behind the shade was bright. I stumbled to the bathroom and washed my face. My fingers stung, but none of the cuts were deep. Looking in the mirror, I remembered seeing Jimmy in myself and realizing he might be dead. I didn't want him dead: I was going to find him alive. I dressed slowly, his undershirt, his pants, his shirt, his too-big shoes. I took the dark suit jacket off its hanger and slid it on, ignoring the sleeves that came almost to my knuckles. I added the hat. I crossed to the window, gave the shade a sharp tug, and let go as it sprang up.

Clopping my way down the stairs, I realized I'd need to pass the one person in town who knew me: Mr. Wilkinson. On the third flight, I figured: he's having a hard time filling the place, he won't hassle me. On the second flight I decided: he'll kick me out, maybe even call the police—impersonation! Last flight: nothing to do but go forward. I reached the lobby. I tried to clop quietly past. He looked up, looked me over, hat to oversize feet. "San Francisco changes people," he said drily, and returned to his paper.

I headed for a one-chair barbershop I'd passed the previous day, but veered off the sidewalk when I saw a pawn shop: shelves of suitcases and coffeepots, telephones, and typewriters. Hair dryers with enormous hoods, guitars, a burnished brown saddle. Movement behind the counter startled me. The man's long gray face was adorned with a tiny mustache and alert eyes. He cleared his throat and stood up, which put him hardly taller than the counter.

"May I help you?" he asked, studying me intensely.

"I'm looking for a pair of shoes," I said, realizing too late that I should have practiced my voice. I tried lowering it and continued. "Size—um..." What was a ten wide in men's? This was going to take some thought. A memory crowded my mind: the day Mother decided I was old enough to wear a brassiere. The bra was just a start. Stockings and a garter belt to hold them up. A purse and nylon underpants to replace the flowered cotton ones I'd always worn. Bobby pins to keep my hair off my face. Lipstick, a shade close to my lips' natural color so I'd learn not to wipe my mouth on the back of my hand all the time. I may have been born female, but the five-and-dime sure helped.

His voice brought me back to the pawnshop. He was peering at my foot, muttering, "seven, seven and a half." He heaved a large box onto the counter and announced, "maybe eight with thick socks." I settled on a pair of brown wing tips with heels still level. He reached to take Jimmy's shoes from me.

"I'm gonna need them back," I said protectively. "When I find my brother I'm gonna need them back."

"One month?" he asked.

I nodded, filled out a manila tag, and paid. My hand was on the doorknob when he said, "Wait." He had something in his palm that looked like a small brown turd. "Open your hand." He nestled the turd just where the fingers meet the palm. It was surprisingly heavy, made of soft leather, worn and stained, with what felt like lead pellets inside. He pushed my fingers closed. "Keep that in your pocket," he said. "Grab it if you need to punch someone." I tried to pay, but he waved me away and returned to his perch behind the counter.

When I saw the red-and-white pole I walked on past and went once around the block, clearing my throat in ever-descending registers. Then I pushed open the barbershop door. The barber gestured me into a chair and I watched his face in the mirror as he examined me.

"Do this one yourself?" he asked.

"With kindergarten scissors."

"Kind of spur-of-the-moment?"

"Drunk too."

"Any tattoos?"

"No, I stayed in."

He nodded thoughtfully. At least he wasn't throwing me out.

As most of my remaining hair fell to the floor I lost another two years. I looked like Jimmy at sixteen, before he'd been shipped off to the army. I'd missed him so. He wrote full, reassuring letters every week. I know he felt awful about leaving me with parents living in that fractured, alcoholic world of surface and depth. That was the first year he called me on my birthday.

The buzz of the electric trimmer ceased. The barber leaned toward a chrome contraption, and hot foamy shaving cream filled his hand. He patted it where my sideburns would have been if I'd had any, and along the hairline at the back of my neck, then took a razor to those areas. He reached for the Slickum and persuaded the remaining hairs above my forehead to stand straight up. Pulling off the cape with a bit of a flourish, he dusted me carefully with talcum powder. There I was. I stared. I'm not sure how long. He waited. I fished money out of my pocket, thanked him, and pushed open the door to head to the police station. The thought of it made me turn back.

He looked at me inquiringly. "Sonny?"

"Do you... Did you..." I fumbled, not knowing how to ask. "Two days ago I was wearing my mother's hand-me-downs. Now I'm wearing my brother's."

He nodded. "I think you should get some clothes of your own."

I wasn't sure whether he was answering my question.

"Those look mighty big on you," he clarified. "They attract attention. Other than that I might not have noticed right away. 'Course, as a barber I did see your hairline. And we're somewhat accustomed to your kind in this-here part of town. Mostly they're going in the other direction: the men come in wanting me to take their sideburns right off and cut up close around the back. But the ladies, they all want the butch. That's how I knew you would too. Good thing you're tall." He gestured to my suit. "Not as tall as your brother, though. Or as broad. No pun intended."

I looked down. I didn't want to have Jimmy's suit taken in. He'd need it back.

"Head to the Miracle Mile. They've got every kind of suit you could want to find. That's Mission Street, after it turns. Don't forget a hat." He gravely wished me luck. As though I'd need it.

The Miracle Mile lived up to its name. Block after block of shops with grand trapezoid plazas flanked by plate glass and mannequins posing as happy people. Four movie theaters, names in neon high above the sidewalk. In between were haberdasheries, record shops, and soda fountains. I walked the entire mile searching for the store I wanted to walk into to ask for a suit.

I chose a small one, dim and quiet. Two salesmen stood sentry behind the counter and a third adjusted a mannequin's tie. I strode nervously once around the store, past ties, suspenders, and cummerbunds. Approaching the cufflinks I heard a guffaw, then a loud whisper, "Whatever it is, I bet he wants it in pink." I considered bolting, but I could work my way down the whole mile without finding the Miracle Salesman who wouldn't hassle me. At least they thought I was man, if a nancy boy.

I headed for the clerk attending to the mannequin and said firmly, "I need a suit." My voice rung out in the quiet store, a register too high.

I ignored the sniggering behind me as he asked, "Blue, black, brown, or gray?"

"Which can you wear most of the time?"

"You want gray," he said. I nodded.

One of the countermen appeared at my elbow, a little too close. "I'll measure you," he commanded, steering me to a mirror against the back wall. His buddy joined us, grinning, as he stretched the tape across my back and announced the measurement. Then he took his time wrapping the tape around my chest. He lingered over my breasts.

"I don't think you need that measurement," I said.

"Oh, but I do," he replied, smarmy. I was a dandy no more. He crouched in front of me, his head at my crotch level, to position one end of his tape at my ankle. Then he slowly extended it up my leg, taking his time from calf to thigh to crotch. Once there, he slid his hand around.

"Does he dress right or left?" his buddy asked, snorting. I shoved the hand away.

The assistant returned with a suit coat and two pairs of pants on a hanger. "You shoulda gotten something double-breasted." He took the suit and handed it to me with a smirk. "Put this on and we'll continue the fitting." He and his buddy strolled away, conferring.

The assistant hovered near, then said low, "You should go."

"I need a suit," I hissed back.

"You *don't* want to go into the dressing rooms," he whispered darkly. I followed his gaze and saw the other two heading toward us from the front of the store. "The Goodwill, Market Street," he whispered through clenched teeth. "Focus on the shoulders, take in the rest. Now get *outta* here."

"What's going on here?" the counterman demanded.

"I decided to take my business elsewhere," I said, thrusting the hanger at him and moving toward the front door.

He grabbed me by the arm and dragged me toward the dressing rooms. I swung around fiercely, knocking over two mannequins headed for a picnic. As they crashed to the floor I pulled free and bolted toward the entrance, lunging against the door. They'd locked it. I heard footsteps behind me. I grabbed an ashtray stand with both hands and spun around hard, spewing cigarettes and sand into my face. The marble base added heft as I swung back and forth wildly, blinded. Through my coughing I heard menacing taunts. "Is that your big prick?" "Come on, girly, lay it down and take a look at a real one."

"Unlock the door or I throw it through the front window," I threatened. The taunts continued. "Unlock the door!" I bellowed, preparing to hurl it.

I heard the sound of keys. "Okay, okay, settle down, freak." I dragged the stand with me through the door, dropped it to the side-

walk, and ran. I heard them shouting after me but didn't try to make out the words. Women enjoying their Sunday morning window-shopping snatched small children out of my way. I was chilled and sweating both, wiping ash from my face. I didn't slow down until Market Street. Unsure which way to turn, not ready to look for help in the faces of strangers, I headed downtown. Images of what might have been bloomed in my mind, lurid flowers. Behind one of them appeared the sign promising an "Army of Salvation."

The place was huge, cold, and spare. The smell of ammonia pierced even the stench of cigarette ash. But there were racks and racks of suits, trees of faded hats, stacks of ties, and no one paid any attention to me. I found several suits narrow in the shoulders. Some were shiny at the elbows and the knees, some had pockets worn through by too much change, but a couple fit and one wouldn't require too much taking in. I chose a hat and shirts, paid, and counted my steps back to the hotel.

Tending to the evenness of stitches steadied me. I transferred my wallet and my little brown turd from the pockets of Jimmy's suit to my own. When dusk fell I stayed in, watched the shadows, and thought about him.

We used to play "church" together. I was about six, Jimmy thirteen, and the seven years between us more consequential than ever. I'd experienced what, in my mind, I called the God feeling—in the woods sometimes, when a hush fell over me and the light slanted and I heard the breathing of the bees and the thoughts of the trees. It gave me a feeling of turning inside out, so that I was part of everything and everything part of me, the sap flowing in the trunks the same as the blood that pulsed through the web of veins at my wrist. I thought it would be mighty fine to have that feeling reliably, once a week, just by walking into a building.

Mother said, "No."

"But why?" I asked.

"Because we're not churchgoing people."

"Why not?"

"There are different kinds of people in the world," she said definitively. "There are Negroes and whites, there are rich people and poor people, and there are churchgoers and church-shunners. We're church-shunners."

I pointed out what seemed to me a flaw in her logic: "Rich people can get poor, and poor people get rich. Can church-shunners become churchgoers?"

"Yes, they can," she replied. "But none of them ever want to."

Jimmy and I were out by the creek when I told him about the conversation. He sat and pondered a while. Then he said, "We can make our own church." My face must have brightened, because he smiled and asked, "Do you want to be the pastor or the flock?"

"Flock," I said, thinking I'd get to feel the God feeling settle on me.

He marched to a spot in the woods where Father had felled a hefty tree shattered by lightning. He hadn't yet split the logs, and Jimmy rolled one to the center of a clearing. Then he chose a bigger log and together we pushed it about ten feet from the smaller one and gruntingly upended it. Jimmy told me to sit on the little one and climbed on the big one. He stretched his hands out, palms down, as though he was shining some kind of light on me. Then he said in a booming voice, "Let us pray." In a normal voice he added, "That means put your hands together and bow your head." Continuing in his pulpit voice, he said, "Our sermon today is from first letter of Harry to the Olympians. Dearly beloved, we are gathered here today to celebrate God. God is great, God is good, let us thank Him for our food."

I looked up at Jimmy. He reddened, then said defensively, "I'm warming up." I put my head back down.

"Dearly beloved," he began again, "God loves us like the trees love the light. Like bears love honey. Like worms love mud. He sends angels to look over every one of us, and every living thing. Every blade of grass has an angel looking over it, whispering, 'Good little blade of grass, beautiful green blade of grass, grow.'"

Right then I got that God feeling. Not as much as sometimes, just a little flush, but I figured maybe you have to practice. When Jimmy came down from the stump I thanked him and told him I wanted to play church every Sunday morning. He looked plagued but agreed.

A few Sundays later, after the sermon, Jimmy said, "Next Sunday you're the pastor and I'm the flock." I thought about it all week. Maybe the pastor walks around with the God feeling all the time. Even when he's just drying the dishes after dinner. I decided to try. While I was drying the dishes I thought about bees breathing and the sap in the trees. I dropped a plate; it broke into six pieces. Mother inhaled sharply, held her breath a moment, then let the air out with a big sound. "No dessert for you tonight, missy." I sat on my bed wondering if pastors got in more car accidents than regular people.

Jimmy and I played church for a few seasons, then the game faded. But we played it together one more time, years later, when something I didn't understand exploded around me, filling the house with shouts and whispers. At the dinner table Father announced that Jimmy was leaving to join the Marines, and Jimmy's face turned white. When we were alone I cried and asked why he was going. He cried too, said he'd explain it to me someday, and promised to write every week. Sunday morning I woke to his hand on my shoulder, shaking me gently. "Get up," he said. "We're going to play church." I'd outgrown that and started to protest, but Jimmy looked anxious. Maybe, I thought, he needs to feel that God feeling one last time before he goes.

We walked to the clearing. The logs were long gone, and being spring it was boggy, but Jimmy strode to where the biggest log had been. I sat on the ground where the flock belonged. His sermon that day was fierce.

"We never look at a flower and say, 'That's the wrong petal for this flower.' We don't look at a squirrel and say, 'That's the wrong tail for a squirrel.' Flowers and squirrels were made by God and they are perfect just as they are. The same is true of you: God made you, so you are perfect. Your arms and your legs do all the things they're supposed to, and do them perfectly." I looked at my slender arm, the downy hair golden in the morning light, thought about how it enabled me to climb trees and build forts, and was grateful for my perfect arm.

Then he spoke like he was figuring out each word just before he said it. "Every kind of hunger you have is perfect, because it was made by God too. You know just what you need, and your wants and needs are perfect." This seemed an odd line of thought to me, but I considered that when I ate my oatmeal in the mornings I knew when I was full, and that fullness almost always carried me to lunch. So yes, indeed, my appetites were perfect; the thought surprised me.

"No one else can know what is right for you. What's right for you might seem wrong to someone else, and that's okay, because maybe it's wrong for them. But if your heart wants it, God put that desire there, and it is the right desire for you."

My mind turned immediately to peas, which I'd hated since I was a baby. Everyone was astonished that I could dislike such a delicious vegetable. They tried to persuade me that the texture wasn't mush and the taste wasn't yech, but I knew it was, and Mother allowed me this one aversion. Consequently I never ate them, except when one snuck onto my fork, riding piggyback on a carrot, and those occasions consistently confirmed my disgust. Sitting there in the warm sun, I felt a sudden rush of pride in my ability to know mush from not-mush, yech from not-yech. I felt wise to have recognized these distinctions and adhered to them with such commitment. It gave my ten-year-old self, tender and green as the leaves emerging around us, a sense of sturdiness; instilled in me an awareness of some bedrock kind of knowledge that I knew without knowing, that I could depend on to divine what was right for me and what was wrong.

As I surfaced from this revelation I saw Jimmy watching me. I admired his ability to weave squirrels, oatmeal, and peas into divine revelation, into a shift inside me that I couldn't articulate but felt as surely as the dampness seeping through my jeans from the boggy earth beneath. It was years before I understood what his sermon was about. He'd already seen the signs.

I'd worn Jimmy's old clothes for Halloween once. With a porkpie hat and charcoal on my face, I became a bum. Everybody saw the bum, and saw me inside the bum. But putting on a suit I bought for myself, a suit that fit me, a suit I wore to become a man: this clothing revealed me, and I felt naked in it. Exposed. I thought of the Miracle Mile and rode a wave of nausea. So I put my mind to how the snot-nosed cop had treated me, the way men on the bus from New York to California had behaved, and gathered enough resolve to look at myself in the bathroom mirror the next morning.

It was hard to know what people would see. As I watched myself draw my shoulders back I remembered how Father carried himself. His body didn't move much when he walked; it was all in his legs. In town he didn't smile, like Mother did, at everyone he passed on the street. He didn't comment cheerfully on the weather. He'd nod curtly, maybe touch his right hand to the brim of this hat. If he met a pretty lady he'd reach his hand to the crown of his hat and lift it half an inch. Otherwise he'd just nod and walk on. I practiced pacing across Jimmy's room with a stern face and a long stride. I focused on planting my feet solidly as I walked. I said "Hello" to nobody in the deepest voice possible. It came out all Vincent Price. I tried less deep. I practiced saying, "Joe O'Conner," earnest and authoritative, like Sergeant Joe Friday. I put change in my pocket and jingled it, like Jimmy did.

Still, my heart pounded as I stepped onto the sidewalk. I felt a klieg light tracking me, drawing all eyes. But most eyes in the immediate vicinity were too drunk to focus properly. They like to get an early start in the TL. It was commute time, so I headed for Market Street, where a crush of bodies was surging downtown. I plunged into the stream, heart pounding, but a block later realized no one was actually seeing me. I turned abruptly, heading upstream. Startled eyes met mine, jolted by a body moving against the tide. None lingered.

Because there was nothing to see, or because they were rushing to work? I needed to know.

I fought my way to an eddy of people waiting for a streetcar. Joining them, I asked the woman in front of me where the approaching streetcar was headed. She looked me up and down, seemed to linger at my mouth, and said, "Glen Park—here it comes." The driver accepted my dime and waved me on. I felt eyes survey me as I walked the aisle. A middle-aged man with a sharp nose studied me as I approached, so I sat next to him. He snapped his newspaper and resumed reading. Eyes shifted, avoiding mine. When the bus got crowded I gave my seat to an elderly woman, who said, "Thank you, young man." I stood with my hand on a strap, swaying, dazed. Two teenage boys jostled each other in the backseat as they stared at a lithe young woman beside me. Then the eyes of one of them shifted to me. He gaped, nudged his friend, and whispered in his ear. The friend's eyes scanned the bus, sliding over me, and his face turned quizzical. The boy leaned in and whispered furiously. I sought his friend's eyes, touched my right hand to the brim of my hat, and nodded. The two of them guffawed loudly, drawing stares, which ricocheted to me. None lingered; they returned to their newspapers, their worries, their daydreams. I was, mostly, passing. Jubilation mingled with relief. Then it struck me that perhaps the greater danger was here.

By the time I transferred and rode back to the Tenderloin, the klieg light had dimmed. I headed to Jimmy's diner. Thelma stared a few seconds, then demanded, "Are you having as much luck finding your brother as you are becoming him?" But there was a smile in her voice, so I ordered two eggs over easy, rye toast, and a cuppa joe.

She laughed, warm comfort, and as she poured my coffee I asked, "You know those spoons you mentioned?"

"Mmm-hmm."

"Any ideas where else they spend their time?"

She considered, tapping her pencil against her teeth. "I heard there's a place in the Mission, but I don't know where. I'd look along Polk, instead."

"How about spoons like me?" She smiled again.

"There's a place called Pandora's Box that I heard about. Quite sure it's in North Beach." She winked. I was grateful, as much for the friendliness as the information.

I decided to warm up for Sergeant Fitzpatrick with another visit to Acme Professional. Skipping the elevator, I took the stairs two at a time and didn't knock. I bounded over the balustrade, slapped my hands flat on the desk, and demanded, "Who's in charge here?"

Fingers poised over her typewriter keys, the Guardian of the Records replied querulously, "Why, that would be me."

"Then it's you I need to talk to." I took up residence on the desk and gave the back of her chair a sharp twist, turning her in my direction. I watched her face as she took in mine: no sign of recognition. "I need to see the files of Mr. James O'Conner."

She straightened her spine, pulled her skirt down over her knees, and rallied. "Those files are confidential," she announced, extra syllable at no additional charge. Then she stared haughtily at a spot on the wall.

I gently grasped her chin and tilted her face toward me. "Not when it's a matter of life and death, they're not. Where are his files?"

Her eyes moved back and forth like a windup toy with a jammed gear. Then they stayed to the right. I released her chin, strode to the file cabinet on her right, and jerked open the top drawer. It flew out, empty file hangers swinging wildly. Only five or six had anything in them. Inside the one labeled O'CONNER were eight or nine curt messages—all with check marks next to "Urgent" and times they planned to call again. None had phone numbers.

"These are his messages. Where are his files?"

Her eyes grew large. "Like I told your sister, we don't have his files. We just take his messages and he comes here when they call back."

I slammed the drawer shut and jerked open the next: another choir of barren hangers, and another, and another. The office door revealed a desk, a telephone, and a pencil stub. This place was all bluff. Battered bluff. I needed a new tactic. I turned toward the Guardian and gasped.

"What?" she cried, eyebrows on alert.

"Why, I just realized... It's *you* my brother was raving about. He said he worked with a woman with the most gorgeous hair—'a waterfall of chestnut tresses.' He was talking about *you!*"

She blushed. "Well, it is my crowning glory," she acknowledged. "Aside from my legs."

"He mentioned them as well," I murmured, "but I didn't want to embarrass you." She pulled on the hem of her skirt. "Sweetheart," I said. "Sweetheart." Her eyes fastened to my face. "My brother's in trouble. I need to know everything you know about him. *Everything.*"

Her eyebrows conferred. "It's not much. He does private detective work. His ad says 'Blackmail' and gives the number here."

"Ad?"

"He runs an advertisement in the *Chron* and the *Examiner.* It just says 'Blackmail,' like that's his specialty."

"Okay. What else?"

"Most of our clients meet their clients here. He never did, not once. Just spoke with them on the phone, arranged meetings somewhere else. We take his calls, but most of his callers won't even leave a number. I tell them he'll be in at four, then call him, and he's here at four when they call—if they call. Some don't. His clients are skittish. He always closes the door when he speaks with them, but one day it opened a crack and I overheard them. Your brother had to talk him into meeting."

"Where?"

"I don't remember," she wailed. "It was weeks ago. Somewheres in Albany, I think. Oh!" Her eyebrows rose like a high-board diver launched into the sky. "It was a tree street. Like Elm or Oak or Spruce."

"Very good. What else?"

Uncertainty lined her face.

"Go ahead."

"Well," she began. "Well, I don't know this for sure. It's just something I suspect. I was out with some friends one night, walking back from a restaurant, and I saw him come out of a café. One of my friends said, well, he said that…"

I nodded encouragingly. She took a breath and the eyebrows committed. "He said it was a place for queers. He'd read about it in the paper. Some court case about homosexuals or something. It's a café right near where Columbus Avenue begins. That's all I know. I'm not saying that's what your brother is. I'm just saying that's the café he was coming out of."

The Black Cat. They did know him there.

Police Headquarters was quiet. Another hunched-over man was mopping the floor, moving the grime from one place to another, leaving dank speckled swashes in his wake. The same guy as before was seated behind the counter at Missing Persons. "How's your sister?" I asked.

He looked confused. "I don't have a sister."

"I'm here to see Sergeant Fitzpatrick."

He jerked his head in the direction of a door. I knocked.

It was a deliberately imposing office: desk the size of a small warship, framed photographs of himself with important-looking people, an expensive pen in a gleaming gizmo made just to hold expensive pens. Sergeant Fitzpatrick had a five o'clock shadow that made an appearance before noon and a jaw gentle as Mount Rushmore. Centered in the jaw was an astringent smile.

I remembered to drop my voice as I stuck out my hand. "Joe O'Conner," I said, squeezing firmly. "I'm Jimmy O'Conner's brother. He used to be on your force. He's been missing for about a month."

His eyes narrowed as they studied my face. "O'Conner never mentioned a brother."

"Okay, so I'm his sister."

A flicker of surprise. His scrutiny moved to my mouth, then up to my eyes. "I don't meet many kid sisters dressed like that," he said, lifting his head and pushing his jaw out to indicate my suit.

"Next time I'll wear a prom dress. Pink or yellow?"

His face curdled. "I could throw you in jail for six months for impersonation," he growled.

"I'm trying to find out what happened to my brother. Given the circles he moved in," I explained, watching his eyes, "I wasn't getting very far wearing heels." He didn't snap handcuffs around my wrists, so I continued. "The department didn't so much as put out a missing persons on him."

"Is that an accusation?" he asked, hostility lacing his voice.

"It's surprising."

"Not at all: O'Conner assaulted a fellow officer. He was relieved of duty."

"I'd like to know the story behind that."

"Not a very original one. He drank too much and picked a fight."

"With who?"

"That's internal departmental business."

"That's doublespeak for 'I won't tell you.'"

"If you'd like to file a request for information," he began brusquely, then paused. "Look, Joe—JoAnn, Jennifer, whatever your name is— your brother was a good cop. Unless he drank. And after three years on the force, Jimmy began to drink. I'm sure he's off somewhere drying out. Wait a while, give him time to get himself together."

"That's the party line, huh? Jimmy's on a beach in Santa Monica, sleeping it off."

"That's not such an original story either. Happens all the time."

"Sergeant Fitzpatrick, our parents drank. They drank a lot more than they should have. Jimmy swore he'd never touch the bottle. Something must have pushed him, pushed him hard. Any idea what that was?"

"I don't know anything about his personal life."

"Jimmy's a gregarious guy. People like him. Who were his buddies on the force?"

"I'll look into it for you."

"Thanks," I said, with no conviction.

"Listen, kid." His voice grated. "I could book you right now on four different charges. I'm gonna leave you alone on account of your brother having been an officer of the law. But I warn you to lay off this little investigation of yours. You might find out things you don't want to know. And you might just get hauled in for impersonation, vagrancy, lewd conduct, no-visible-means-of-support, or any combination of the above. A vag-lewd charge'd cost you twenty days in this town," he added menacingly. Then he seemed to relent. He rose, reached out his hand, and said in a conciliatory tone, "Give it some time. Come back day after tomorrow; we'll run some routine checks. But I'm sure they're unnecessary. He'll be back. I have no doubt he'll be calling you on your next birthday."

I felt the skin on the back of my neck prickle. I watched him watching me and saw no provocation in his eyes. When I reached the sidewalk my hands were still shaking. There was more to this story than they were letting on. They were in on it.

chapter three

When I turned down the alley the crowds vanished, the side-walk crumbled, and streetlights gave way to furtive shadows. A blunt, dead-end passage broke off to the right, and I saw the entrance just beyond it. Pandora's Box. Advertised by a dim seam of light seeping through the edges of its doorway. I pushed open the door.

The place was crowded but motionless as a plastic nativity scene. All eyes were locked on a body on the bar, a slim figure in a striped, cream-colored suit, hips slowly gyrating as she sang, "According to the Kinsey Report, every average man you know"—her hips reversed direction—"much prefers his lovey-dovey to court when the tempera-ture is low—." Dipping on that last word, her voice climbed with the temperature to "sizzling hot." She offered a low growl as Mr. Pants forwent romance, then rose to strut the chorus.

Her voice could coax you into believing in your wildest dreams. She strode the length of the bar as Cole Porter cooed and wooed, fell to her knees to plead, "Sister, you'll fight my baby tonight," then rose with shimmy and shake. Rounding on the finale, she distilled every drop of innuendo from "the marine, for his queen," then paused, a silence to gather force. Her head snapped back like the cover of a lighter and she wailed, "too...darn...hot" as though she'd never need to do anything again. When the applause came she hopped nimbly off the back of the bar and began pulling beers. The frozen tableau became a roiling crowd, lifting drinks, lighting cigarettes, carousing.

When I got through to the bar she was wiping it down with a dishrag that hadn't been washed since before the war. Her dark hair, slightly damp, was swept into a loose chignon at the base of her neck. I asked for a ginger ale. She served it with a maraschino cherry and a sly smile. "A buzz cut takes five years off a girl," she said with a grin, and turned to her next customer.

I retreated to the only available barstool. Beside me was a severe butch whose greased hair met in a precise duck's ass above the nape of the neck. The femme on her far side wore a vermilion halter dress elegantly set off by her dark-brown skin. The way she filled out that halter ensured that the D.A. was all I'd see of the butch that evening. On my other side was a stout older femme.

"Who's she?" I asked, gesturing toward the bartender.

"That's Lily Wu. She owns the place, along with Madge Collins."

"She sure can sing."

"Livelies up the place, don't she? Oh, that's Madge there."

Lily was joined by a dark-haired butch with a dour expression: Rosie the Riveter gone bad. She and Lily exchanged a few words, then Lily flipped up a segment of the bar, stepped through, and headed toward the back door. I followed.

She was leaning with her shoulders against the wall, one heel against the brick, lighting a cigarette. The flame flared as I arrived.

"Mind if I join you?"

"*Mi* alley *es su* alley. I'm Lily."

"Josephine—Joe," I replied as I leaned against the building beside her. The space was narrow and our bodies touched lightly along the shoulders. She warned, with a slight tease in her voice, "Anyone catches us like this, they'll be calling us kiki."

"Would you care?"

She looked over to see how serious I was, then looked ahead again, across the alley, considering. "No."

Silence for a while, till she asked, "You don't go for femmes?"

"I do, sometimes. If there's something butch about them."

She laughed, a low rumble. "How about butches?"

"Same thing. The ones that have something soft about them, something vulnerable they're not afraid to show. Say, the butch suit with the soft sweeping hair. The femme with the fuck-you attitude and solid stance. I've even—" I paused to consider whether this revelation was wise, and proceeded anyway: "I've even fallen for a drag queen."

"Hm," she commented, curious. "Did it go anywhere?"

My turn to laugh. "No. But it sure was educational. Never knew there were so many uses for tape. Kind of makes me a queer queer, if you know what I mean."

"I've got some idea of that," she said.

"I hear this place is yours."

"Mine and Madge's."

"If you can sing like that, why do you bartend?"

She blew out smoke and looked at me skeptically, as though gauging her answer. "Coupla reasons. I've heard 'This is a gay bar, not a chink bar' too many times. And I got tired of being the Dragon Lady."

"Who's the Dragon Lady?"

"Red satin dress, tight, stops just below the knees, but slit up to here. High collar with diagonal buttons running to there. Narrow bow lips, bloodred. Controlling, manipulative, deceitful." She tilted her head, as if considering. "Actually, it was fun for about a minute, as a stage persona. I camped it up. But it got tired quick. I'd introduce myself as Miss Vera Scrutable," she continued, her voice caustic, "but nobody in those audiences got it. The only other option was a China Doll. Delicate maiden, mysterious instead of inscrutable. Things were better

47

in the Fillmore, at places like Bop City and the Blue Mirror. But I can see which way the winds are blowing. They don't like neighborhoods where the nationalities mix. And the Negroes prosper." She scowled. "They're tearing it down. 'Urban renewal,' they call it. Renewing their wallets is more like it."

"So you opened your own bar to have a place to perform?"

"Madge had been talking about it for a while. Only way either of us could bartend: females have to own at least a third of a bar in this town to tend it. They assume we're chippies otherwise, would slip a mickey into every john's drink and roll him. Then when the law changed—you know about that?" I shook my head. "Friend of mine, Sol Stouman, owner of the Black Cat, they tried to shut him down. He took the case all the way to the California Supreme Court. They ruled that cops can't bust bars just for having homosexuals in them. So now it's harder for the cops to lean on us. They used to be able to raid us whenever they felt like it. 'It's Wednesday and my shiny black copper shoes are fittin' too tight? Let's go bust some queers.' They can still do it, of course," she added, her voice thick with anger. "Just have to work a little harder at it. Anyway, Madge and I decided it was time."

"So now you sing whatever you want, whenever you want."

"Not quite. We need a cabaret license for that, and haven't managed to pull one yet. They don't like to give them to female bar owners, much less females with eyes like mine. But eventually we'll get it. In the meanwhile I do numbers on the bar. Now and then, no regular schedule, so as not to make it too easy for them to bust us." She turned toward me. "You're new in town."

I nodded.

"What brought you here?"

"My brother. He's missing. As of about a month ago."

"Maybe I know him. What's his name?"

"James O'Conner. He went by Jimmy."

She turned sharply. "Jimmy O'Conner?"

"Yeah."

There was just a moment's pause, not enough to really be sure there was a pause at all.

"Never heard of him." She brought her foot down, pushed with her elbows off the building, and turned. "Sorry, gotta get back to work." And she disappeared into the deeper darkness of the bar's back door.

I stayed there awhile, watching the shadows, too disappointed to try again. Then I started walking. Walking soothes me. A hill appeared, so steep it had stairs instead of sidewalks, and at the top was a tower with art deco lines—the tower on Jimmy's key fob. I walked around it, then down the other side of the hill, till I reached the bay. It was wide and black and cold before me. I stepped out into the darkness on a floating dock. Waves lapped gently against it, and the dock sighed as it lifted, whined mournfully as it fell. The lights across the bay shimmered, dense by the waterfront, extending upward in glimmering folds. The bay reflected them dimly, then became inky, silent. I tried not to think of Jimmy in the pitch-black water as I listened to the sigh, the whine. A wind came up, rousing the waters and raising the pitch. Suddenly, I knew where Jimmy's files were.

I walked across the floor, listening for the squeak, then threw the carpet back and knelt. The nail file slid easily between the planks. The squeaking board lifted. In the space below it was a handgun. Cradling the gun, nestled neatly in the gap between the joists, was a fat curl of files.

"My name is Joe O'Conner. I'm calling for Mr. Peter Dunham."

A furious whisper: "What did you say your name was?"

"Joe O'Conner. I'm Jimmy's brother. I'd like to speak with you."

"What kind of a detective is he, disappears in the middle of things?"

"I'm very sorry, my brother *has* disappeared. I'm trying to find him. Can I come speak with you?"

The whisper grew frantic. "No, no, I don't want any trouble. I've already paid. It's over now."

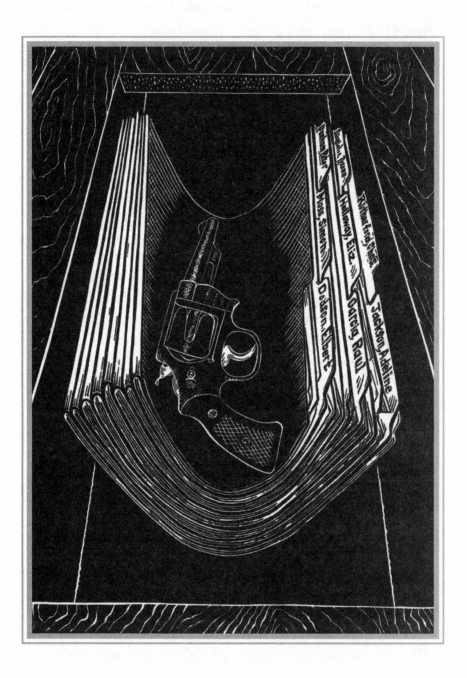

"But they may—"

"I'm telling you it's *over*. Don't call me again. Ever."

"Hello, my name is Joe O'Conner. I'd like to speak with Mr. Tyrone Singleton."

"There is no Mr. Singleton here."

"I'm calling regarding a private matter my brother, Jimmy O'Conner, was looking into."

"There is no Mr. Singleton here."

"Is there...anyone else in the household?"

"There is no Mr. Singleton here."

"Hello, my name is Josephine—I mean Joe—Joe O'Conner. I'm calling for Mr. Elbert Dodson."

"This is Mr. Dodson."

"I'm Jimmy's brother. I understand he was looking into a personal matter for you."

"Oh! Oh, my! Your brother—oh!"

"My brother has disappeared. I'd like to speak with you."

"I—I know nothing of his disappearance. We were merely...acquaintances."

"I'm trying to find out what happened to him."

"I don't know anything about it. I was waiting for him to...that is... I hadn't heard from him in some time."

"Mr. Dodson, may I please come speak with you this afternoon?"

"This afternoon? I, I—"

"Please. I need your help to find him."

"Well...if you must. Three o'clock." He gave me an address in Albany. On a tree street. In a quiet suburb buzzing with the gentle sounds of insects and children.

He opened the door with an expectant smile, but when his eyes took me in his round face drooped. "Oh, dear, I see that you are one of us... Do come in," he continued, as his eyes made a surreptitious sweep of the street. His rather large head sat atop a slender body, and this contrast, together with the thinning of his sandy blond hair, gave the impression of a highly intelligent but undernourished child.

An alcove set in the foyer wall held a statuette of a tree stump engulfed by vines with extravagantly intricate pink blossoms. A halo of purple eyelashes ringed each center profusion. "Purple passionflower," he offered, pleased that I noticed it. "Named for the passion of Christ—not the other passions," he added. "A native, you know, and quite a fascinating story of coevolution... But do come in. The water just boiled, so I'll only be a moment with the tea—you do want a cuppa, don't you, dear?" I nodded, and he nodded back with satisfaction. "Make yourself at home, Josephine, er, Joe."

Heavy drapes the color of pea soup lined the windows, creating a dark oasis of cool. Mr. Dodson reappeared with a large tray and poured two cups. "Sugar or cream?" he inquired quite formally. Then he leaned back against the flowered chintz and eyed me with apprehension.

I knew that what I had to say wouldn't diminish his unease. "Jimmy was involved in several investigations, which may be the reason for his disappearance. You can help me, and I hope I can help you. You are, I believe, being blackmailed?"

His teacup rattled dangerously in its saucer, and it took some moments for him to navigate it safely to the table. "Why, my dear..." he stammered, "I, I, I..." His mouth opened and closed several times, like a fish, before he continued. "It was only with the greatest reluctance that I called your brother. And it is only—it is desperation, my dear, desperation that forced me to meet with you."

"Please tell me about it."

He gripped the arms of his chair tightly, knuckles turning white under the strain. "Four months ago I received an envelope in the mail. It contained a photograph of me leaving a bar—a homosexual bar. There was nothing else, just the photograph. But my heart raced upon seeing it. I am a schoolteacher. I have been for thirty-two years. A revelation of this sort would sever my livelihood, and it would, it would..."—his face scanned wildly, searching for the extent of the catastrophe—"destroy my reputation, turn my life's work to filth! The friendships I've treasured with my students, held so tenderly sacrosanct, would appear as hideous, calculated efforts to ingratiate myself for the most sordid of purposes. I would have to leave here—and my garden!" He gasped. "I would lose my garden. Not only would my past, all that I have ever done, be sullied, defiled—my future would be extinguished. Who would care for my rare clematis, my Passifloraceae, the *Datura wrightii*?" His eyes no longer saw me or the beige walls. He was staring into an abyss.

"Mr. Dodson," I urged gently, "can you tell me what happened next?"

His eyes settled on my face, and only then did he appear to hear my words. "Well...nothing. Nothing at all happened next. I waited. Each morning I woke and tended the garden and went to school—several times I took the photograph out from where I'd hidden it to confirm that it was real. Because nothing at all happened. I studied it—the photograph. It was very dark, poorly lit, slightly blurred, nothing at all really, nothing—if you don't know the address to be that of a homosexual bar. A putrid place, anyway." His voice became an urgent whisper. "They consider themselves quite sophisticated, quite pleased with themselves—but really! I've only been there twice, when desperate loneliness drove me to it. The photograph was taken on Christmas Eve. I had no plans at all for that evening or for Christmas day. A colleague had invited me to his house, promising a genial group of friends, but I suspected they would all be homosexuals and I—well, I suppose they might be a better sort than one would find in a bar, but there are those homosexuals who consider it a fine thing to be, who even, well, flaunt it—and I couldn't bear a roomful of that. On top of which, there have been remarks made at school about this particular colleague. Among other things, he is quite friendly with Miss Portman, the school nurse. She's an obvious one—coaches the woman's softball team and lives with her 'cousin'—who, from what I've heard, bears no familial resemblance." He gave me a pointed look and shuddered slightly. "I'm quite sure other faculty suspect her, and with the two of them such good friends—for all I knew she and her cousin would be there as well. So for me to spend Christmas Eve with him—why, it was too great a risk." He laughed bitterly. "So instead I find myself photographed outside a den of homosexuality."

"And—no letters since?"

"Oh, yes, eventually I received another envelope. Thirty-one days later. The same envelope, the same photograph—only a close-up: just my face, right below the address. This photo was blurry, because of the enlargement, but there was no mistaking my face, or the numbers. And then—again nothing. I counted the days. I thought: another thirty-one days, then what? I was sick with worry—I had to arrange for a substitute that thirty-first day, I couldn't possibly have gone in to school with my hands shaking the way they were—they'd have thought I'd been drinking! I sat in this room, waiting for the postman. I heard him come down the walk and mount the steps. A momentary pause as he sorted. The flap of the mail slot lifted. I heard the letters slide through, saw them fall silently on the carpet there. I made my way to the door. And— nothing! There was nothing! Just the water bill and a circular from the hardware store. For a brief moment I felt jubilation. A reprieve! Then I realized: the wait wasn't over. It had just begun. Now the letter could come *anytime*. Would they wait another thirty-one days? Or would it be arbitrary? I'd come home from work one day and there it would be. I felt the most profound regret. Regret! That the letter had *not* arrived. I'd been consigned to a purgatory of waiting with no idea what my tenure might be." He sighed heavily, unclenched and reclenched his hands.

"And then?"

"It was another twelve days. I came home to an envelope with the photograph again, the original one, and this time a letter. Nine words: 'Your principal might find this to be of interest.' That's it. No demand for money, nothing but that: 'Your principal might find this to be of interest.'" He was rocking slightly in his chair, gripping the arms, moving forward and back in time with his breath. Suddenly he exhaled heavily and held himself still, as if by force.

"Forty-six days before the next letter. Demanding five hundred dollars. A large sum, but I gladly paid it. Left it in a crevice in a rock. In the Rose Garden, of all places! They promised the negative, and indeed it was there, a day later. I rushed home and melted it at once. I felt myself to have emerged, at last, from a harrowing tour of war, astonished, elated, to find all my limbs, my life, intact! I fell in love with the world again—my students, my Passifloraceae, the extraordinary wonder of it all. I was ecstatic—indeed, I'm afraid I got quite carried away with myself; Mrs. Turnbull, in the principal's office, asked me whether I'd at last fallen in love." He blushed at the memory. "Rather embarrassing. In any case, short-lived. Another letter arrived, with the photograph again, demanding two hundred dollars. They had made multiples of the image, of course. I...I...I...oh, that was the worst. I saw it all stretch out before me, a lifetime of this uncertainty, never knowing when another would arrive. I'd have to sell the house—lose my garden!—and what explanation could I give my colleagues for moving to a shabby room near the highway? I'd certainly have ended my life if it hadn't been for the garden. Who would care for it? Some new owner might overwater to the point of fungus or rot—or uproot them entirely and pave the whole yard! It's a collection of very rare plants, you understand, plants I have nursed for years. When I saw your brother's ad in the newspaper, I thought it was divine intervention. The word glowed on the page as though lit by phosphorescence: 'Blackmail,' with a question mark. It was a leap off a cliff, something I'd never have considered a few months earlier. Hire a private detective? But now it seemed a godsend."

Mr. Dodson reached for his cup. Most of the tea sloshed into the saucer as it made its way to his lips. He sipped, maneuvered the cup back to the table, then continued. "I was greatly reassured when I met him. Your brother is a good boy. One of us, but careful and respectful. No swashbuckling, no saber rattling, and not flamboyant in any way. He'd been a police officer! Quite respectable. He had several cases following the same pattern, terse messages and long waits. We met, and he said he would call again—but I never heard from him. I thought perhaps I'd been swindled—but I couldn't really believe I was such a poor judge of character. So when you said he was missing..."

"Do you know if he'd made any progress on the case?"

"None that he told me about. He only came the one time."

"And since then?"

He sighed deeply, released his grip on the chair, and carefully folded his hands together. "Two more letters. I've paid them another three hundred dollars. I have about that much left in the bank. After that, I'm prepared to sell my car. I have a small phonograph collection, but it won't fetch much. Then there's nothing left but the house. I've considered taking in a boarder, but the rumors *that* would encourage... Truly, my dear, I don't know where to turn."

"Tell me about your visit to the bar. Did you talk to anyone?"

"A fellow named Tom—that's the name he gave, anyway. A very sympathetic fellow. We commiserated on the loneliness of the holidays. But... I became disgusted with myself—with the place—and left rather abruptly." He paused. When he resumed his voice was doleful, his eyes wary. "It's a terrible life, m'dear. I would warn you away from it if I could. But I see you're not a casual interloper." He shook his head and added bitterly, "They think we recruit—recruit! To inflict such suffering..." Bending his head forward, he grasped his temple and squeezed.

"Do you have the letters and photographs?"

"I burned them! Each time I thought it was over I burned them. I have only the most recent."

"May I see it?"

The letter was typed. I looked closely. The bottom of each "e" was slightly fuzzy. Mr. Dodson fetched a magnifying glass. A fracture ran through the tail, where the type was cracked. Clipped to the back of the paper was a grainy photograph of a man exiting a building. The street was dark, the building looming, its only detail the numbers: 840.

"Mr. Dodson, do you think it's possible the photograph isn't entirely...damning? It is merely a picture of you on a dark street. It could be any street, any street at all."

"By itself the photograph is quite innocuous. But were they to send it to my principal, identifying the street name and the type of establishment, the school would—quite rightly—investigate. Patronizing such an establishment is clear grounds for dismissal on the basis of moral turpitude. In truth, my principal is a kind man. I suspect he would try to keep the details under wraps. But dismissal it would be, without question."

"Let's go back a little. Tell me everything you remember about that evening."

He sighed heavily and closed his eyes. "I was feeling quite despondent. Christmas eve, and I was desperate for some human contact that didn't feel shallow and cheap as that flimsy tinsel they sell. All this false brightness, this supposed festivity, when I was alone in my life, alone in this world, except for my plants. It was too dark to spend time in the garden, and I decided, with great ambivalence, to go to a bar. Actually—I didn't mention—I went first to another place." His lips compressed briefly in a sardonic line. "Rather a queer place, hidden behind an office. You must knock on the door just so, to be let in by a burly mountain of a man. I entered the bar and"—shock washed over his face—"saw someone I knew. I left immediately! I know you will say that if he was there he must be a homosexual and would wish me no harm. Might even provide friendship, the companionship of a—a fellow inmate! Yes, I've been through that in my head. Perhaps. But he works at the local post office, and he's one of those flamboyant types—effusive, like *everything* that happens is an astonishment. I could see him flashing that horrid grin as I asked for stamps. Congratulating me every time I received a package. I'd be mortified to go into the place—who knows who might see him being so familiar with me, and what conclusions they might draw. No, I couldn't risk it. I turned right around and left." He shuddered. "I drove to the other bar. That's where I met the supposed Tom. We spoke. I had a drink. Then I went home, no less lonely than when I'd left."

"If you do receive another letter demanding payment—"

"If, you say. If!" He gaped at me. "The question is when, my dear. I can see that now."

I couldn't think of any reason to contradict him. "Well, when you receive another demand for payment, I want to watch the place you leave the money."

"Oh, no, my dear, absolutely not."

"But Mr. Dodson—"

"I won't consider it! I couldn't put you in that kind of danger. Out of the question."

"Please, at least think about it." His face was unyielding.

We sat for a few moments. Then he clapped his hands and his face brightened. "Time for a tour of the garden!"

The late-afternoon sun blinded me as we stepped outside. The yard was a riot of color and texture. He turned to see the expression on my face. "Yes, it is glorious, isn't it?" I was staring at a poinsettia, a plant I knew from my grandmother's coffee table; this one dwarfed me.

He led me from plant to plant, pointing out their particularities, and on occasion tenderly stroking a leaf. Around the perimeter a fence was laden with startlingly intricate flowers.

"You recognize it from the foyer?"

I nodded. I'd assumed his statue exaggerated the color and detail of the plant, but the opposite was true: here was a Technicolor version, with shimmering lashlike periwinkle tendrils. The blossoms gave off a heady floral scent, like a divinely drunk, overperfumed drag queen. Next he showed me a plant with pointed leaves and long, erect buds, art deco in their curving elegance.

"Ah, the twilight crown of my garden, *Datura wrightii*. You must come by some evening, Josephine, when its flowers are open. White, with a purple tint along the margins. Just a few of them perfume the entire garden. It's moths they're trying to seduce." He chattered on about pistil and stamen, coevolution and long-tongued moths, as he drew me down a path to the center of the garden. A small bower of

58

young plum trees, branches woven together, formed a room of dappled light, and we settled in the wrought-iron chairs beneath.

"I always wished to bring my students here for tours—in groups, of course—perhaps even get them engaged in growing. Who knows, one might go on to study botany, or open a nursery. But I shudder to think"—his delicate body trembled despite the mild air—"what they'd make of that now. I have been scrupulous, my dear. Absolutely scrupulous in my role as a teacher. I know that a moment's lapsed vigilance could lead to the development of particular affection for one student over another. I've weighed every word before I spoke it, considered every act before I performed it, to be certain that no fault could be found in any of my pedagogical relationships. But if I am exposed as a homosexual, every parent will scour their memory for any hint of misbehavior, any whiff of undue affection toward their child..."

His shoulders collapsed inward, like a fallen leaf beginning to curl. He shaded his eyes with one hand as though shielding himself from the future unfolding in his mind, and his voice dropped to the merest whisper. "I never touched any of them, boy or girl, not once in all those years. Our sort do prey on children, but I'd as soon fondle a young student as"—he looked around wildly, eyed a fat bud encased in green—"as tear off that bud and peel it open, petal by petal. Children are delicate kernels of possibility. That someone might blight them horrifies me. I watch with care other teachers I suspect of harboring similar tendencies. And I watch myself scrupulously—we must, you know—for the slightest impulse."

"Mr. Dodson," I began hesitantly. "Do you think it's possible that maybe we aren't all that way?"

He was still eyeing the dense bud. For a moment he shimmered—his entire being seemed suddenly transparent—then froze. His eyes deepened into round pools, and in them I saw all the horror of hell. "Yes," he whispered, hoarsely, "but what if we surrender our vigilance—and it turns out we are?"

chapter four

It was just a hunch. The next day, I entered the Albany post office at twelve fifteen, thinking long lines would buy me time to case the employees. He was as difficult to locate as the yolk in a fried egg. Six one, broad brow, green eyes, and enthusiasm as unrelenting as an uncapped fire hydrant. Reaching the front of the line before he could burst into song, I requested stamps.

"Oooh, you've got letters to write!" He beamed with a riotous smile. I saw his pupils expand momentarily as he took me in. "Got a girlfriend somewheres?" he whispered conspiratorially.

I tried to look hangdog. "I have a dear Jane letter to write." Perking up, I added, "And I'm looking for a girlfriend closer to home. Know where I can find one?"

His eyebrows did calisthenics. "Have I got a place for you! Meet me outside at five fifteen."

He strode out the door, giving coworkers a farewell worthy of an ocean liner bound for Tokyo. When he saw me he stuck out his hand. "I'm Aaron!"

"I'm Joe."

"I want to hear all about it!"

"Cuppa coffee?"

"I know the perfect place!" I knew he would.

We slid into a high-backed booth, he put a dime in the mini-jukebox, and Rosemary Clooney sang "Come On-A My House." The waitress sloshed coffee into his cup and brought me a glass of milk. When she left he leaned forward, expectant.

"Whaddya do, Joe?"

I braced myself. "I'm a private detective."

"A shamus?!" His eyes flashed like thunder on a muggy afternoon and a hailstorm of questions followed. "How'd you get to do that? What kind of cases do you have? Any *murders*?"

"I specialize in blackmail."

Horror and delight duked it out across his face. Delight dealt a knockout blow. "*Blackmail?* Oooh, *black*mail! Do they have *photos? In fla-grante delicto!?* Tell me all about it!"

"Aaron, detective business is delicate. Requires a soft shoe, if you know what I mean."

His face became deferential as a mortician discussing casket costs. "Oh, I understand," he whispered, "my shoes are soft as, soft as…" I thought of Boris Karloff in *The Bride of Frankenstein* as he concluded triumphantly, "Butter! And my lips are sealed," he continued, "but we can tell my friends, right?" He nodded insistently.

"Some people are scared off by my questions."

"Not *my* friends!" he persisted. "They'd love to talk to you. How'd you become a private *dick* anyway?" he demanded, extracting maximum pleasure from the word. His eyebrows had a field day complete with three-legged races and a greased watermelon.

I weighed the question. Jimmy's name was the one thing that might cap the fire hydrant. It made people clam up as effectively as a noose at its fall point. But if it didn't silence Aaron, I might find out why. "My brother disappeared. He was working on several blackmail cases. I think his disappearance is related to them, so I started investigating too."

"Who's your brother?"

"Jimmy O'Conner."

His body recoiled like Senator McCarthy chancing upon freedom of association down some dark alley of the Constitution. I kept talking. "This is the part where everyone shuts up. My brother apparently did something heinous, but no one will say what."

Aaron hunkered, his lips compressed, and glared at me. "Are you working for the cops?" he spat.

"Do I look like someone the police would hire?"

He chewed the side of his lip. I waited. Someone whose pleasure in hearing gossip was exceeded only by his pleasure in sharing it was my best bet.

"Your brother was a lousy snitch for the police! He was a regular cop when he first got into town. Kept his private life secret, visited the bars, but very careful—fake name, all of that. We were friends, a bunch of us. Good friends, *we* thought. Then his boyfriend Bobby got beat up in jail, beat up bad. Bobby died and your brother lost it. Went on a two-week bender. Fought with everyone—his friends, the bartenders, the police. Got thrown off the force, or so he *said*. Suddenly he stopped drinking, got real quiet, and hung around the bars all the time, just watching. He'd sit in a corner, not talk to anyone. Like a snake." The corners of Aaron's mouth twisted.

"At first we thought he was waiting to get picked up in a raid himself. Was gonna let loose on the cop who killed Bobby. But a coupla raids happened when he was around, and *he never ever landed in jail*. Lotsa other people we know did, but somehow he disappeared at just the right moment every time. That's how we figured out he was working for the coppers still, undercover. They must've known that we knew because all of a sudden he was gone. He's probably in Los Angeles somewhere, snitching on queers, pretending he isn't one himself. Lousy bastard. That's what happened to your brother. Go look for him in LA."

My hands circled my glass of milk. It was thick glass, the kind that curves in and out. My mouth opened and closed a few times. Eventually, I spoke.

"When I was ten years old Jimmy left home all of a sudden, to join the Marines. He was only seventeen. He loved school, played basketball and ran track—was going to get a sports scholarship to college. He had lots of friends—my big brother, who knew everyone and did everything. And then suddenly he was gone. He wrote to me every week. Things were rough at home—Mother and Father drank too much, and fought, hard. He felt terrible about leaving me alone there and stayed in touch as much as he could—but I couldn't understand why he left so all of a sudden. All I had were his letters. And a phone call on my birthday." Aaron was eyeing me, distrustful.

"I heard whispers and jokes around school. People asked me, 'How's your sis-terrr,' drawing it out like that, singsongy and taunting. It didn't make any sense—he'd just joined the Marines, why was everyone calling him my sister? I didn't find out till years later, when he came back to visit. I was sixteen by then, and I'd told him, with a lot of confusion, that I thought girls were more interesting than boys. Then he told me the whole story. Said he'd known for years that—well, for him, boys were more interesting than girls. That's how he put it, to let me know he understood. He said he had a couple of special friends in high school, friends who felt the same way. One of them liked to wear ladies' clothing. He'd tried on his mother's clothes when he was little, but now his mother was tiny compared to him, and he desperately wanted to see himself in a dress. He just wanted to know what he'd look like. So one night these two friends broke into the high school to raid the theater's wardrobe closet and find him a dress he could fit into. The principal came by, saw a light on—the boys took off, one of them still in the dress—ran like hell and got away. But the principal swore that one of them was my brother."

Aaron was still listening.

"Jimmy could have gotten out of it, easy. All he had to do was turn in his friends. But he wouldn't. Said it could just as easily have been him. 'They didn't really care about the break-in,' he said. 'Kids broke into school all the time—all they got was a couple of days suspension. It was the pervert they wanted, and I'm as much of a pervert as either of them.' So my parents, who thought he was guilty 'cause he wouldn't say he wasn't, made a hush-hush deal with the principal and Jimmy got shipped off to boot camp. Then he was sent to Korea. It was the end of college for him, the end of everything. *That's Jimmy.* There's no way he'd rat on his friends. No way. Not Jimmy."

"That doesn't explain why he never got picked up in a raid," Aaron replied bitterly. "And it doesn't explain where he is right now." He stood up, concluding sourly, "I sure hope you're a good detective."

"Aaron, wait!" I begged. "Please, I need your help. No one will talk to me. Can you tell me who his friends were?"

He dropped down on the bench, glaring. "I don't trust your brother and I don't trust you. But I'll tell you what I'd do." He leaned forward and lowered his voice. "I'd start with Lily Wu. She and Madge own Pandora's Box. If Lily believes Jimmy was a snitch, everyone else will too. News like that travels fast—one glance from a bartender and you know to be careful. There was a court case that changed everything, see. Now the cops have to observe lewd behavior before they can raid us. And their weekly envelopes from bar owners have gotten a whole lot lighter. They're pissed about it. So they're sending out undercover cops, like your brother. They lurk, they lure us into anything they can call lewd behavior: a hand on a knee, a smooch on the cheek. So now it's the bartender's job to keep everyone in line—and to warn us about anyone who might be vice squad, fishing. If the bartenders believe Jimmy's a fink, all the regulars know it, and you won't get any help from them. Lily and Sol—he owns the Black Cat—they share word of undercover louses. Lily's the ringleader. So you've got to start with her. Persuade her to believe your little story," he said with disgust. "If you don't, nobody in the bars is going to talk to you." He stood, threw a dime on the table, and stalked off.

Walking on Hyde Street back to Jimmy's room, I saw a dark bundle writhing on the sidewalk, like an overstuffed package trying to unwrap itself. It ripened to a man wrestling turbulently as mutters, squawks, and fierce whispers rose from his body. I was turning to cross the street when I heard him splutter, "The sky is falling, the sky is falling. No more pennies from heaven! The sky is *falling!*"

I looked up. A few stars pierced the deep blue-black directly above.

"How do you know?" I asked.

The writhing ceased. "I heard them talking. I heard them! They wouldn't say it but I heard them." The writhing resumed.

"Maybe they're wrong. It's still up there."

The bundle froze again. It shuddered, and a face appeared, square, grimy, and tormented. "Wrong? Wrong!" He stared at me like I was deranged. At least I had company. "They're never wrong," he insisted furiously. "They make the sun rise and set in this town."

"How about the stars?"

"Them too."

"Well, they're still up there."

Haunted eyes moved from my face upward. He stared in stunned silence at the twinkling stars. I joined him.

All at once one bright light lost its hold. As it fell it seared a brief white arc in the darkness.

"There they go," he said, voice hushed with awe.

The next morning I returned to Police Headquarters. Fitzpatrick greeted me all hale and hearty, reporting cheerfully that the bad news was good news: no match with unidentified bodies from the morgue. He reminded me that Jimmy just needed a few more weeks to finish drying out, but if I wanted to pass the time he'd found a friend of Jimmy's: Sergeant Eric Weiner, two flights up in the personnel department.

The door said PERSONNEL. I pushed it open and there she was: crimson bouffant towering to improbable proportions, green peepers enhanced with enough eyeliner to stripe 101 from here to Los Angeles, cavernous cleavage, hips generous as a cherry tree in June, and a derriere that defied gravity. She looked up from her typing, gave me a good once-over, then tilted her head to take another gander over her rhinestone-encrusted cat eyes. She raised her right eyebrow inquiringly.

"My name is Joe O'Conner. I'm looking for Sergeant Eric Weiner."

She pressed a button, murmured into a box, then gestured toward a door to her left. He came out swaggering with the wide-legged stance of a man with a two-by-four up his ass. On posture alone I could tell he wasn't a friend of Jimmy's. Our conversation confirmed it. He recapped the high points of Fitzpatrick's beach hypothesis and urged me to relax, see the sights, and wait for Jimmy's return. No comments about my appearance; Fitz must have briefed him. I didn't need more enemies, so I thanked him for his time.

She was there at a bank of file cabinets, manila folder in one hand and cigarette in the other, pluming. Her glasses were off and I looked right into those emerald eyes. "I need your help," I said quietly.

"I'll bet you do," she agreed, in a voice that leached whiskey and cigarettes. She slid the drawer shut with a thrust of her hips and sailed majestically toward the desk. Her breasts preceded her like the prow of a ship. I wondered how that ass could be so high and firm without can-tilevering. Settling it in a chair that was surely the envy of most cops in the city and a good number of the robbers, she indicated another. I sat. She began drumming her fingers on the desk.

"My brother worked here. Then he didn't. Then he disappeared."
She nodded.

"His name is James O'Conner. He goes by Jimmy."

She nodded again, more slowly. "What do you need to know?"

"Who was in that brawl with him, the one that got him kicked off the force? And when did he stop working for the police?"

She looked doubtful but sailed back over to the cabinets, pulled a

file, flipped through it, and piloted back. I wondered how many idle questions she got in a week from people who just wanted to admire her ass while she looked for the answers.

"His employment was terminated on April thirtieth." She lowered her voice. "There's nothing here about the fight. Disciplinary files are kept in Sergeant Wiener's office."

"There must have been some talk when it happened."

She was drumming her fingernails again. "I wasn't privy to the details."

I stared at her hand making that rhythmic sound on the desk. Her fingers were long and plump, her nails crimson, just a shade or two away from her hair. Two of those nails were shorter than the others. The last two in that drumming line. Distinctly shorter, filed back below the tip of the finger. I looked up. Her green eyes met mine, followed my gaze to her fingernails, then traveled back to my face.

"I need to find him. *Please, can you help me?*" I whispered. She glanced in either direction and picked up a pen. Her plump fingers scribbled on an envelope and slid it across the desk. Just then a door to the right opened, a hand appeared, and a voice commanded, "Miss Locket, the file of Officer Michael Miller."

"Right away, sir." She turned to me and said crisply, "Glad I've been of assistance." Then she soared back to her filing cabinets.

I left clutching the envelope. Outside the building, I uncrumpled it: "Black Cat, 6:00. Lucille."

"Start from the beginning," she commanded. She listened closely, and when I was done asked, "You file a missing persons?" I nodded. "Nothing's turned up?" I shook my head.

"I made an excuse to look at the disciplinary files. There wasn't much. He assaulted a fellow officer, unnamed in the files, and it didn't say what sparked the incident. Usually they include that. Another officer involved in the dispute was dismissed at the same time, a Gabriel Bambino. Residing on Franklin Street."

"I'll find him."

"Let me look around a bit more. It'll take a few days, a week at most. I'll call you. Try to stay out of trouble in the meanwhile." I nodded. Then she leaned forward, bringing her mouth close to my ear. "Shave," she said quietly. I turned my head in surprise. "Those fine hairs on your chin are a dead giveaway," she said gently. Then she smiled, winked, and departed. I wasn't the only one watching her go.

I sat for a long while, watching the crowd, eavesdropping. The waitressing chanteuse flitted by, eruptions of laughter in her wake. I was surprised to hear she went by José. I heard a snippet of her banter at the next table.

"Miranda has a friend who calls himself 'a professional artist.' Isn't the *point* of being an artist that you don't *have* to be a professional? Where's the wild abandonment to the muse—grabbing life by the balls and *wrestling* into existence through the act of creation!? 'Professional artist,'" she scoffed. "That's sadder than a frigid tart."

As José and her red stilettos waltzed on, I listened to a formidable butch holding court at the next table. "I ran into the widowed Mrs. Henderson the other day, in the lobby of our apartment building. She moved several flights up, so I asked how she liked her new home. 'Well!' she said,"—the butch sucked in her gut, adopting a querulous tone—"'there is a *hom-o-sex-sual* living next door!'" The butch widened her deep-set eyes in alarm. Leaning forward conspiratorially, she asked in a loud whisper, *"Male..., or female?"* Returning to a high trill she replied, "'Male.' As we stepped into the elevator I said with enormous relief, 'Well, thank God for that!' Mrs. Henderson looked startled. 'Why, they're *very* good decorators,' I told her, nodding knowingly. 'If you need help deciding where the couch belongs—or which pair of earrings goes better with a dress—they're *very* opinionated, and invariably correct. Far more reliable than a husband! You're a lucky woman to have one right next door.' I smiled strenuously. The widow Henderson looked confused, but then the fog cleared. 'Why, of course,' she replied brightly, 'how fortunate.' The elevator stopped, I disembarked, and we waved goodbye as the doors closed."

A young butch leaned in to ask, "But what if the neighbor had been a *female* homosexual?"

"I'd have said *exactly* the same thing, only the opposite! How useful one can be when you need that couch moved, or a dress zipped." She launched her authoritative neighborly voice again: "They can be rather brusque, it's true, but you mustn't take it personally; it is their way. And they offer all *kinds* of services useful to a woman without a husband," she concluded slyly.

I shifted my attention to the table on my right, where a slender Negro walked that razor's edge between "distinguished gentleman" and "queen" artfully as an acrobat. His companion walked the equally treacherous line between lumberjack and bum: plaid flannel shirt patched with contrasting plaids at each elbow, dungaree trousers boasting an overly wide cuff.

"...at least we're seeing work that deals *openly* with the subject," insisted the gent.

"Is that all we can hope for?"

"*The City and the Pillar* is a positive portrayal: the protagonist is a successful, virile man, and he doesn't die in the end."

"What a high bar we've set for ourselves. Does it matter what he does instead? *Drifts* through the entire novel, aimless, unmoored, from sea to land, hoping to run into his boyhood love. When the golden boy finally appears, all this ennui makes the final scene all the more stark: *finally* a deed, finally he acts! And what does he do? *Murders his boyhood love!*"

The gentleman conceded ironically, "But it *must* be a positive portrayal: the *New York Times* won't even advertise the book."

"Oh, he'll never be reviewed again."

The gent rallied. "I think we should put our hope in the poets, who can circumvent narrative constraints," he announced, creating an eloquent swoop in the air. "We need a Whitmanesque refusal of nothing but refusal, an embrace of Hughesian improvisation, however coded. It is the poets who will..."

Hubbub continued around me. The trio to my left was replaced by a boozy drag queen in a puce capelet, two middle-aged men with the sartorial flair of insurance agents, and one of the leaden-spectacled creatures I'd seen in the coffee shop.

"...so I finish my drink, call for the check, and the sniveling waiter delivers it with a little engraved card. The light's dim enough that I need my reading glasses, and while I pat my pockets I'm thinking it's a nice little thank-you, a complimentary drink card. I get my glasses on and it says, 'The Management of the St. Francis no longer appreciates your patronage.'" The speaker's face flushed deeply.

"My friend Sylvester got one too. The gall! *We* make the place fashionable and then our money isn't good enough for them."

"I don't know why you went there to begin with: if the clientele was any stodgier they'd need to call a taxidermist."

"It's the kind of place men take their wives," snarled the queen.

"But one of the few that's never been raided. *That's* why I went there—but only later in the month. Every raid I've been caught in was at the end of the month, when cops need to fill their quotas."

The queen snorted disparagingly. "Yeah, only late in the month. Or when the moon is full. Or when the humidity's high. Or when their girlfriends aren't putting out. The truth is they raid whenever they damn well feel like it."

"What's it like?"

"You mean you've never been caught?" Astonishment all around.

"Mary, you're a charmed one!"

"Well: if you're lucky someone sees them coming and flashes the lights—you have about two seconds before the cops arrive. They burst in with these bright lights shining right in your face so you can't see a thing as you rush for the back door or the bathroom window. If you don't make it—or you do but they're out there waiting for you—they throw you in a paddy wagon and take you downtown. Then they toss you in a cell with toughs, which makes for quite a night. In the morning they slap you with a fine and a record and let you out around noon—"

"Just in time to pick up the afternoon paper with your name, address, and occupation on the front page. I lost a good job that way. Finished. Can't show my face in the industry again."

"Couple of times I got off before I was booked. I always keep a fifty in my left shoe. Been rolled for it more than once. But it's insurance."

"A friend of mine was thrown in the paddy wagon and dumped off in some dead-end part of town."

"Yeah, but not without first spending some time on his knees." Grim laughter.

"Maybe that Kinsey book will change things—there are so many of us."

"The situation's *worse* since the Kinsey thing. Used to be I could come and go in the world as I pleased—there was a place for the confirmed bachelor. Now they get suspicious if you're over thirty-five and single. I'm going to have to get myself a beard."

"I agree. I always minded my business and my neighbors minded theirs. Now I get suspicious looks when I crack the door in the morning to get the milk."

"It's harder at work, too, always having to bring someone to office parties. I persuaded Katherine to get a studio portrait done, paid for it myself, so I can keep it on my desk and tell people she's my fiancé. Now they keep asking when the wedding is."

"But you've got to admit, Kinsey's woken everyone up. How abnormal can we be if almost forty percent of men have found happiness in the hands,"—he smirked—"I mean the arms, of another man?"

Back in Jimmy's room, I eyed the acorns he'd left on the dresser. Their caps were velvety, not hard and bumpy like the ones back home. I undressed, took one in my hand, and crawled into bed. Watching the shadows, I thought about growing up. Most of the time it felt like the four of us were barreling down the road in a car with nobody at the wheel, nobody watching the road for a curve or a stop sign or a cow. Mother and Father brought out the worst in each other, and were so busy doing it they had little time for the road or for Jimmy and me. Huddled in the backseat, I'd look over at him, and he'd tilt my head up so our eyes met, and that was the only time I wasn't scared.

Our farm was one of those you pass that has six cars out front, only one of which runs. The others are parts cars, but three of them have parts for a car we no longer own because Father wrapped it around a telephone pole one night coming home from the Grange Hall. He was drunk enough to walk away without a scratch. Neither of them was cut out to be a farmer. The barn roof never got patched last year so the hay molded and here it is February and there's no hay for the animals. The canning hadn't gone well and half the lids popped up, so we eat pickled cauliflower, breakfast lunch and dinner, for a month straight. They're both too tight to milk the cows, so on our way home from school Jimmy and I hear the cows bellowing from half a mile away, their udders are so swollen. Most winters we ran out of firewood around March and had to cut and haul wood in the wet spring snow. The fire would hiss and smoke with the damp logs, and then one night we'd hear a sudden roar. Lucky for us the VFD was good with chimney fires. "Unseasoned wood builds up creosote," I heard the chief say to Father as his men climbed ladders to the roof and Jimmy and I huddled in our pajamas in the backseat of a parts car.

When you're zooming down the highway with no one at the wheel, you figure out ways to make life feel less precarious. We used to take turns describing the room to each other down to the smallest detail, the color of the petals in the flowers in the curtain on that window, so we wouldn't hear Mother and Father screaming, or worse, a sudden silence. Every color and shape and texture put in its right place instilled order when there was none that could be relied on.

Weekends were the worst. Jimmy could tell by Thursday if a real bad one was on the way, and he'd take me camping. The first time, as dusk fell, I was scared. Of the impending dark, of animal eyes staring at me from the edge of the clearing, of bogeymen and strange rustlings. Jimmy said, "Hey, Josie, it's okay. We just need to make a magic circle. Then you won't have to be afraid anymore. Where are those acorns?" I reached into my pocket and pulled out three acorns I'd collected, charmed by their little brown caps. Jimmy placed them in an arc on one side of the tent, then helped me collect a few more to close the circle. I walked the inside of the ring, brow furrowed. Then I walked it again, stooping at each nut to turn it so the sharp little tip pointed outward. As darkness fell I felt safe in our charmed circle.

The next morning I decided a stronger circle was an even better idea, and it had to encompass the tent, the campfire ring, and the rocks we sat on to eat. I spent the day roaming the woods like a demented squirrel that just realized winter starts *tomorrow*. We circled the entire camp with acorns, their pointy tips, like spears in my mind, warning the baddies to stay away. After that, every camping trip began with the creation of our magic circle. Before bed I'd walk the loop, checking on the tips with a devotion that cast the spell. When we headed home I'd slip a few acorns in my pocket, in case things got scary there. When they did I placed them in an arc around my bed to keep the future, hurtling toward us, at bay.

The next morning, I stared at myself in the bathroom mirror, Jimmy's shaving soap in a froth on my cheeks, his razor in my hand. Shaving with his kit felt more intimate than wearing his clothes. The scent of the soap was the scent of him.

There was one Gabriel Bambino in the phone book, but the number was disconnected. The listing led me to a tired apartment building on Franklin. Judging by the painted ceiling in the Moorish-style lobby, it had once been elegant. The manager smelled of whiskey and talked too much, which in this case was just enough. He waved a pungent cigar around as he spoke.

"Gabe Bambino? Disappeared about a month and a half ago. All of a sudden like, left most of his things behind. He was a cop, but you wouldn't know it. Opera records, etchings, you know the type," he sneered. "Usually I sell abandoned property but I just threw it all out, didn't want any of them sniffing around here. Got too much of that in this town. We need to kick out that filth, make room for decent, upstanding citizens like you an' me!"

"No forwarding address?"

"Nope, nothing. One less fairy, nothing to cry over." Some dim awareness washed over his face and he tried hard to focus on mine, demanding, "Hey, whaddya want him for, anyways?"

"Just a friend of a friend."

"Miss Holloway, my brother, Jimmy O'Conner, was looking into a private matter for you."

"Yes," she whispered.

"Jimmy disappeared. I've taken over his investigation. I'd like to speak with you."

Her voice was a thin thread of despair. "It's too late."

"You've already paid them?"

The whisper collapsed in a sob. "She's gone."

"Gone?" I asked dumbly.

"Dead. She killed herself. She was just too afraid."

"I'm so sorry." I held the line as, gradually, the sobbing subsided. "Miss Holloway, may I speak with you? Please."

Her voice was weary and resigned. "You may as well. It's over now anyway."

Buena Vista Avenue winds recklessly around a steep hill, bordered by extravagant Victorians. A guild of exhibitionist architects outdid each other in a mad rush of turrets, towers, widow's walks, pitched peaks, and porticoes. Among these peacocks, Miss Holloway's home was austere as an egret: a marble mausoleum that seemed to disdain its neighbors with a silent, seething chill. Doric columns presided over cypress shrubs bent by an eternal gale.

A slender woman in her forties ushered me in. She dabbed her eyes with a handkerchief and gestured for me to sit. "I'm sorry to greet you like this," she began, "but it's only been three weeks." She settled herself on the couch. "I can't cry at work—Anne was supposed to be just a spinster friend I shared the rent with—so when I get home it's like a dam breaks."

"I'm so sorry for your loss," I said, inadequately. "Should I come back another time?"

"No. It would be a relief to talk about it. I've only told a few friends, and they were so horrified—the suicide, and then when I told them why—well, I haven't seen much of them since." Tears found uneven pathways down her cheeks. "I don't blame them, really. It's like leprosy, blackmail. They fear it's contagious, and it may be; the funeral was cruel enough without the haunting fear the blackmailer might be there, scouting fresh victims. I know some friends took circuitous routes home. The brave ones who came." Her chin buckled, and she shook her head. "Two months ago we got a letter in the mail: unsigned, no return address. It just said, 'We know about you.' That was enough. It brought back all the horror. We talked about moving, taking only the clothes we had on our backs and going somewhere, anywhere. But Anne was afraid they'd follow, and we'd be in some cheap hotel in the desert with *them* lurking outside the door. At least here, we're home. She insisted we stay. And I thought, what's the worst that can happen? We lose our savings. Our jobs. Our friends. We'd still have each other. But—but she couldn't bear it.

"We met in the Women's Army Corps. She was a nurse, like me. We never would have found each other without the war. But when it ended they began these investigations. None of us saw it coming—saw that when they no longer needed us they'd slice us off like a gangrenous limb. Some girl we knew mentioned our names. I don't hold it against her. They'd pull you out of your bunk any hour of the day or night, suddenly you're in a cold bright room with five of your superiors firing questions at you. 'Where were you March twenty-third at two in the afternoon? With whom? Why?' Another time they'd take a different tack. 'We know about you.' *Those same words.* 'We know about you. We have proof. Name some names or we'll tell your hometown newspaper.' Witch hunts: they throw you in a lake and if you float you're a witch and they burn you at the stake. If you sink, you're not a witch but you drowned: oh, well. Those who floated—confessed, named names—got thrown into the brig, then dishonorable discharges. And they told the hometown newspapers anyway. Those who sank, well, they got off the hook in their own way. Hung themselves in a closet. Slit their wrists. One friend went AWOL, back to Wyoming where she grew up. She got drunk, stole a car, and drove twenty-four miles on the wrong side of the road in the dead of night, waiting for a head-on. Only it was such a backwater, she never met another car. They caught up with her in Cheyenne and brought her back here. Two weeks later she was in a psychiatric hospital. Still there today. I visited her every week for a while. But she was distressed by my visits, they upset her so much, I thought it wasn't right. Now she's utterly alone in there."

When Miss Holloway spoke again her voice was low, drained of anger. "That's where Anne landed. She was so frightened by the interrogations—terrified she'd crack, and give them names. Couldn't sleep, wouldn't eat. After three weeks of it, them picking her up any time, she went mad. She was changing the sheets on a bed at the hospital, and just *wouldn't stop.* Kept making up the bed, then stripping it and getting another set of sheets. Another and another. The supply room assistant finally realized something was wrong when she'd given Anne her twentieth set of bedding—the hospital only has sixty-five beds. It took three nurses to get her to the psych ward. She kept on there, with her own bed, putting the same sheets on, taking them off. Of course the higher-ups didn't admit she'd been under investigation, so it looked like she just suddenly cracked, for no reason at all. War's over, we're all supposed to be celebrating and finding husbands, and Anne won't stop changing the sheets.

"She was in for three months. Drugs didn't help. She was paranoid, they said. Of course she was! So they moved on to shock treatments.

Those left her limp and confused, but they called it a cure and released her. By that time I was out—dishonorably discharged, so no benefits and no work prospects. I got us a cheap place and nursed her back to health. When she was better we eventually found work by lying about our discharges. We made ourselves a home. We had our lives, modest but happy. But when that letter arrived it brought it all back for Anne. She was wild with fear. Oh, god, I didn't see it coming—I should have but I didn't. I didn't want to, I guess. Because I couldn't stop it. She's a nurse, it was easy for her to squirrel away enough pills. And she did it at work. I know that was for me, so I wouldn't find her, here, alone, in our home. A coworker found her slumped in a supply closet. It was too late."

Miss Holloway reached for an envelope on the low table. "Here it is. Not much to see. I expect I'll get another one, any day now. Maybe," she added caustically, "they're waiting a decorous period before they demand money. I don't care anymore. They can tell whomever they want. It's over anyway. Anne's gone."

I opened the envelope and pulled out the letter. The tail of the sole "e" was cracked. "Did you and Anne ever go to any bars? Gay bars, I mean?"

She shook her head definitively.

"Do you have friends who go to them?"

"No," she said vaguely. "Oh—one does. She's in bad shape, always drunk. Anne would meet her for dinner once in a while. I think she might go to those places."

"When did Anne last see her?"

"About three months ago. You think that's how they found us?"

"Possibly. Or maybe they tracked down dishonorable discharges."

"We always made a point of doing things separately, to make sure people saw us as roommates. We were never obvious."

"Could you talk to that friend, ask her what bars she frequents?"

"I'd rather not. It's been difficult..."

"Of course."

She planned to move as soon as she was able. She promised to forward her new address. The chill of the mausoleum haunted me the rest of the day.

When Jimmy was shipped off to the Marines, I felt like I'd been torn up by the roots. My loneliness was vast. Mother and Father never let us treat any farm animal as a pet, knowing its eventual slaughter or demise would become a tragedy. But seeing my desolation, they allowed me to adopt two rabbits with the expectation that I breed them and sell the kits. Flopper and Bopper became my closest companions. A black doe with drooping ears and a brown buck with a smoky plume of a tail, they thumped their feet impatiently whenever I came near and made me feel loved again. Soon Flopper began burrowing a nest in the hay of their hutch, lining it with fur from her belly. I stayed with her the night she gave birth to three kits, watched her lick her naked, blind, mewling babies clean. When I woke in the mornings I missed Jimmy and then wondered how much the kits had grown since yesterday.

But it wasn't only loneliness that made those years harsh. Jimmy had been popular at school, and when he left under a cloud of rumors other kids turned to me with the viciousness reserved for those who've fallen from grace. A bully named Mac focused his attention my way, taunting me at recess, following me after school. One afternoon he and his sidekick, Ollie, pinned me down and sat on me. I struggled till I was exhausted while they talked, one of them on my back and the other on my bottom. Mac's monologue focused on the intricate ways he enjoyed tormenting various creatures. He was well beyond pulling the wings off flies. He showed Ollie the exact distance to hold a magnifying glass from an ant so the sun's rays would crisp it to most dramatic effect, and how to attach a firecracker to a frog so it couldn't escape before being blown apart. He moved up the animal kingdom to squirrels and cats, offering torture techniques that ensured they didn't die before the grand finale.

A few months later, when my sweet kits were old enough to be parted from their mother, Father announced he'd already found a home for them: I was going to sell them (at a very favorable price) to Mac. I howled, but Father said he'd given his word—and Mac's father owned the bank that gave farmers loans to tide them over from planting to harvest. When I told him about Mac, Father scoffed and said he was a fine boy. When I begged and pleaded, he made a lesson of it, insisting I had to learn to treat farm animals as farm animals: he'd be taking the kits to Mac tomorrow. I couldn't stop my mind from seeing Mac do to my kits what he'd done to squirrels. I didn't know what to do—how to save them. They were domesticated bunnies; if I set them loose they'd die in the wild, and not peaceful deaths. I tried desperately to get Mother on my side, to get Father to change his mind. Everything I said increased his resolve to teach me this lesson.

That night I crept out to the barn and filled a bucket with water. I took my sweet kits, held each one gently, rubbed it in its favorite spot behind the ears or under the chin, felt its impossibly soft fur, whispered in its ears, and then plunged it under water. One by one they struggled furiously, surprising me with the strength of their small bodies, the power of their hind legs. Then, eventually, they went limp. I drowned three small creatures that night. Knowing that my next litter would be promised to Mac, I took Flopper in my lap and whispered in her ears. I tried to explain, and then as I submerged her and held her there, I sobbed so hard I choked and had to fight for breath myself. Poor Bopper huddled in the hutch, like me, suddenly alone.

I put the soft bodies in a burlap sack and carried them to the place in the woods where Jimmy and I had played church. By the light of a flashlight I dug a hole far deeper than necessary, taking my fury out on the compacted earth. I buried them there. The next day Father beat me with his belt, but I'd already cried all my tears. That's when I knew that love is the tenderest thing there is, and also the toughest.

chapter five

Mr. Wilkinson crooked his finger at me and turned to the wall of little boxes. "A message for you," he said, handing it over. He watched me expectantly. It read: *7:00, 1095 Shotwell Street. Lucille.* "That's in the Mission District," he offered helpfully.

When six o'clock rolled around I put on the suit with the least shiny elbows and slid Jimmy's blunt scissors in my pocket. Empty bottles, rusted bedsprings, swollen books, and discarded clothing festooned the path to the sunflowers in the rear lot. I had to hack with those blunt scissors, but cut enough to make a respectable bouquet.

Her address was just a few blocks off the Miracle Mile, but I avoided that thoroughfare in favor of side streets. Shotwell Street was lined with stately Victorians, hers on a corner. She oohed over the flowers. Then I got to follow her up a steep flight of stairs. She wore a fitted sheath of black lace over red satin, pretty outrageous with that crimson hair of hers, but my eyes weren't troubled.

Lucille led me to a living room painted gold and draped with bur-gundy satin, gestured toward a velvet couch, and offered me a drink. When I declined she left briefly, then returned with the flowers in a vase. Placing them on a side table, she settled herself in a brocade chair, took a sip of her drink—a tall one—and started talking.

"I looked through the unidentified body files. Those are files on any bodies that come into the coroner's office without definite identi-fication." My brain was already struggling to catch up with her. "Each generally contains two reports: a cover report written by the officers who brought it in, describing when, where, and under what circum-stances the body was found. A coroner's report identifies the cause and approximate date and time of death." She was watching me with soft eyes.

"I checked the files starting with the date the hotel manager last saw your brother. None fit your brother's description. I decided to read them through more carefully. There was a body found about a week after your brother was last seen. On the cover report, the one by offi-cers, the body was described as a white male, five foot one. The coro-ner's report said six one. Could have been sloppy handwriting—the difference between a five and a six isn't much. But it means the body wasn't flagged for your missing persons report."

She paused, and asked again if I wanted a drink. I said no. She swirled hers a bit, then continued. "The coroner estimates the date of death as June twenty-ninth. The body was found in a field by the edge of the bay. The description roughly fits your brother: brown hair, about two hundred and ten pounds, muscular. But the coroner's report didn't have a photo of the face attached." She hesitated, then spoke very slowly. "This usually means that the face was unidentifiable. The coroner's report says he was beaten beyond recognition." She was quiet a moment. Then she continued gently, "The only way to get a definite I.D. would be dental records. I'm sorry, honey," she added. "I'm sorry even to suggest this."

My mind was moving back and forth between the possibilities:

Jimmy sleeping off a hangover on the beaches of southern California, or beaten beyond recognition and dumped in a field by the bay. "His dental records?" I asked numbly. She nodded. "I don't know whether he saw a dentist here. I could get them from back home, but they'd be from when he was a teenager."

"That would help. Tell them to send the X-rays."

"Who were the cops who brought it—who brought the body in?"

Lucille sighed heavily. "That's troubling. The report wasn't signed. There's no name attached to it. They're *always* signed." She paused, then said, "Someone didn't want to be connected to that body."

She asked if I wanted to stay for a while, and I said yes. She put on a record, some slow mournful blues, and we listened to it in the near dark. When I left she kissed me on the cheek, patted me on the back, and said she'd keep looking.

I returned to the Black Cat. I knew I wouldn't find any welcoming faces, but I didn't want to be alone, and it was a crowd I could easily get lost in. I sat at the edge of the bar, nursed my ginger ale, and watched the evening unfold. On my left a pompadour butch was deep in debate with a longshoreman, and on my right a poet caroused with a hooker. José wove through the crowd in a strapless brocade cocktail dress. Every now and then she'd extend her hand to a handsome dark-skinned man, who with debonair grace guided her to the top of a low table. There she delivered an aria in a gorgeous high tenor. Far into the evening she encountered some favorite from among the black-clad poets and hushed the crowd for a recitation. Afterward the bar remained silent, all eyes upon José. She casually lit a cigarette and blew out smoke, then began.

"The other day I realized the essential difference between us and normal people. When they look back over their lives they're liable to say, 'Oh, that was after we had little Richard, just before we had Betty.' Whereas a gay person will say, 'Hm, that was when I was with Richard, just after I'd divorced Betty.' And for some of us," she continued coyly, laying a delicate hand across her décolleté bodice, "that was when I *was* Richard, just before I *became* Betty.'" An amused murmur rippled through the café.

"Speaking of *gay* people, the newspapers are full of talk about Kinsey's sex studies. Everyone's scandalized by what he has to say about homosexuals, of course, but there are other shocking items in there. For example, I read that cunnilingus—you all know what cunnilingus is, don't you?"—merriment all around—"well, the report declares that cunnilingus is a frequent occurrence among married couples. Of the married men interviewed, four percent of those with a grade school education had performed it, fifteen percent of those with a high school education, and forty-five percent of those who had attended college. What I want to know is, what *are* they teaching in the schools these days?" Raucous laughter erupted across the room.

"Do you know that before he studied sex in *Homo sapiens*, Kinsey was *the* expert on a particular species of insect called the gall wasp? Perhaps *that's* where he got the gall to ask perfect strangers whether they'd performed cunnilingus on their wife last night." This time the room groaned, but José continued, undaunted. "Seems he's a workaholic, this Kinsey, working fourteen-hour days. Also an insomniac, so he works many a night. They interviewed Mrs. Kinsey, a mousy woman, rather homespun. You won't believe what she had to say about it." José pulled a clipping from the left side of her bustier with a flourish, then assumed a querulous tone: "'I hardly ever see him at night anymore since he took up sex.'" Another wave of laughter.

"And you know society is in an uproar over his research. People are shocked, just shocked, to hear homosexuality discussed on the radio. 'The children!' they say, covering their delicate ears. 'Mustn't let the children hear about homosexuals!' They seem to think that if children so much as *hear* about homosexuality they're all going to cross over to our side! Is being normal really *that* bad?" Hoots and hollers rang out.

"Yes, the newspapers have been *very* interesting lately. Negroes fighting back against discrimination! I think this is a wonderful thing.

What I want to know is, what will it take to get the homosexuals to fight back? Some event of towering proportions—some *absolutely cataclysmic calamity...* They'd have to ban mauve." She'd touched a nerve. The crowd chuckled uneasily. "And of course, there has been endless debate about the causes of homosexuality. Experts cite as possible causes"—José pulled a clipping from the right side of her bustier and read in a bored monotone—"excessive masturbation, appetites jaded by normal means of sexual expression, oversolicitousness by the parent of the opposite sex, abusiveness on the part of the parent of the same sex, emotional instability of the parents, homosexual seduction during puberty, the Oedipus complex, castration anxiety—" Stopping short, she looked up from her clipping and asked, "Has anyone considered the possibility that we simply like it?" A few shocked laughs erupted, but she'd cut too close to the bone. Stuffing both clippings into her décolletage, she clapped her hands together and said, "Okay, friends, now it is time to sing."

José raised her arms, and everyone joined in. The cacophonous assortment of drunken voices was hard to decipher. The tune was familiar, but I first made the words out to be "God save us jelly beans." Then I realized it was "God save us nelly queens." Everyone was singing—butches and longshoremen, poets and hookers, odd ducks and pimps—like the finale of a play in which every bit player returns to the stage in full regalia. I felt my face flush, felt an anguish of emotions I couldn't sort out and didn't understand. I forged a quick path through the maze of humanity and bolted.

The next day I tracked down Jimmy's dentist back east and arranged for his records to be sent. Then I drove to Colma, a small town south of San Francisco where they'd moved all but two of the city's graveyards. Lucille had told me where to find the potter's field. Rows and rows of white wooden stakes, each marked only with the date of death and a number. Two graves were sunken the way new graves are, like a sigh, an exhalation, had come directly out of it. I found the one with the right date, stood at the foot of it, and tried to decide whether I felt Jimmy there. I couldn't say. The rolling hills nearby were all graveyards except for one. It had rows and rows of gently curving streets branching like grape vines into cul-de-sacs. Each street had driveways set off at regular intervals, but nothing more. Just the streets and the driveways, barren, waiting for houses, hedges, and tilted tricycles. When I gave up on deciding whether or not I felt Jimmy was there, in that grave, I drove those desolate curving streets to nowhere.

That night I called Lucille and asked if I could come by again. She said, "Sure, honey," and when I arrived settled me on the couch with a cup of tea. We sat in near darkness, only the gold-fringed lamp in the alcove lighting us. She was already in her nightclothes, a robe of black chiffon with feathers at the collars and the cuffs, a hint of red lingerie peeping from beneath. I knew I was keeping her up, but the words needed to come out of me, and needed someone to hear them.

"Last night, at the Black Cat..."

"Yes, honey?"

"I stuck around for a while. There was that waitress, José, making everyone laugh." She nodded. "At the end of the night she got everyone singing. They sang, 'God Save Us Nelly Queens.'"

Lucille smiled. "Yes, I've been there for that."

"I couldn't stay. I hightailed it out of there. I'm not sure why. It— they—I felt so many things, tangled together."

"Tell me about it," she commanded, sliding to the side of the overstuffed chair and stretching her arm over its curved back. Her robe slipped a little off her right shoulder, and in the shadowy light I saw that her negligee was cut deep.

"My first thought—it was all confused, but my first thought was that God sure as hell has other things to attend to. I mean, Buchenwald. Hiroshima. All those boys who died in the trenches. Nelly queens should be the least of his worries." She nodded, sympathetic.

"But that wasn't the heart of it, what made me run away. I don't believe we're all neurotic, or unstable, or morally depraved—*sick*, like they say. But I felt—so ashamed." My face flushed, heat spreading to my ears.

Lucille sat quiet awhile. Then she nodded, smiling sadly. "Shame. Seems there's always more where that came from." I felt naked. "I know it's a shock, honey, learning who you are," she continued, gently. "It takes a while. We want to shut up the ones who are farther out there. We think maybe if we can just get them under control, we'll be okay too." She sighed. "Somehow they won't notice we're freaks if the freakier ones are gone. But they will. And the freakier ones, they barrel through like a bulldozer, widening the path for the rest of us. But don't be too hard on yourself. Shame is like a bulldog that's caught hold and won't let go. Even when we think we're beyond it."

We sat in near darkness. A car passed, its light sliding across the far wall. Some carousers lingered, euphoria drifting in through the window. When Lucille continued, her voice was soft, more tentative. "About this God thing. I don't know any more about it than anyone else. We're plunked down in a mystery, and if we didn't know it before, the war made clear that those in charge don't know any more than the rest of us. I had an uncle, my Uncle Terrance, who was a traveling preacher. He was also a drinker, a gambler, and a womanizer, but he always repented in time for Sunday morning's sermon. He said his own shortcomings in the sin department helped him better understand his flock. I don't think he was a bad man, or even a bad preacher. I think he was simply just as kind, generous, and forgiving toward himself as he was toward everyone else. So when he sinned, he brushed himself off, repented, and started over again. Doing this weekly didn't seem to trouble him." In the dim light Lucille looked older, probably closer to her age. To me she was luminous.

"Uncle Terrance was my primary authority on the subject of God. When I was very young I asked him what God looked like. We were out on the front porch. He leaned back in his chair, chewing on some tobacco, and said, 'Well, that's a mighty fine question, Lucy. Mighty fine. The Bible tells us God created us in his image. So he must look a bit like us. But I'm here to tell you something else: I think we also create him in our image. We think of all the attributes that are good and fine, all the things we would like to be, and that's what we make God out to be. A finer version of ourself. And then that's what we strive for, what we strive to be ourselves. So build yourself a beautiful God to guide you.'"

Lucille leaned forward to adjust the flowers in the vase. "A few years later I asked him about prayer. It seemed to me God must be pretty stingy if he sat around waiting for people to pray to him and only helped those who prayed the most. What a chintzy God! 'Lucy, my girl,' Uncle Terrance said, 'that's a profound insight you're heading toward. Here's what I think: God doesn't need our prayers. We need them. When we pray, we conjure up in ourselves the things we're calling on him for. When we pray for protection, the part of ourselves that knows how to protect us comes alive. The part of ourselves that believes we are *worthy* of protection. When we pray for love, the part of ourselves that knows how to love and to be loved comes alive.'"

Lucille sat for a while, silent. Then she continued. "I think Uncle Terrance was right about that. It seems to me, when I've hit rock bottom and turned to prayer because it's the only thing left, calling on God was actually more like...invoking him in myself. Not locating him out there, or up there, wherever his throne is. When I pray, I find the strength, or the faith, or whatever it is I'm in need of, here," she touched herself just below her throat. "So calling on him is really summoning him in myself."

We sat with those words between us for a while. When the contours of the room around me returned to my gaze, I saw that Lucille looked tired around the eyes. I haven't mentioned that she had Robert Mitchum eyes—always at half-mast, like she just pulled herself, reluctantly, out of bed. They were looking more weary than sultry, so I roused myself and began to apologize for keeping her up. She placed a finger—one of those short-nailed ones—on my lips and shushed me. Then she sent me off into the night.

"I'd like to speak with Mr. Charles Rutherford."

"Speaking."

"My name is Joe O'Conner. I'm following up on a private matter my brother, Jimmy O'Conner, discussed with you. My brother has disappeared. I am pursuing his cases, and also trying to locate him. I'd like to speak with you."

"Hmm. Sounds sketchy, but you might as well come by," he said breezily.

Market Street cuts a diagonal swath through the flat heart of San Francisco, then abruptly winds its way up the hills of Twin Peaks. Mr. Rutherford lived at the foot of those hills in a sleepy neighborhood resembling a small town. An enormous theater marquee dominates the strip, spelling out the name of the main drag, CASTRO, in orange and blue. This neon flight of fancy is quelled by the surrounding domesticity of greengrocers, dry cleaners, butchers, and bakers. I couldn't locate a candlestick maker, but if there's one in town, he'd surely settle in that dull enclave.

Rutherford's home, a towering Edwardian, was on the peak of one of the smaller hills. Anchored by an enormous turret with a witch's cap, it was a gorgeous blend of mauves, pale greens, and dusty ochers, tipped in gold. Enormous tree ferns curved like eyelashes above the rounded windows of the turret. I climbed the wide front stairs to an alcove adorned with arabesques and spindles, and stopped to catch my breath. Turning, I gasped at the expansive view of the city, spread out over jutting hills, nestled into a glittering bay.

The door opened and out stepped a tall, trim man with the cheekbones and jaw of some rugged adventurer from *Man's World* magazine. His hair was perfectly coiffed to appear not to have been coiffed at all—with one overweening tumble of auburn above the forehead. His soft brown flannel suit set off the pink paisley tie, a handkerchief of matching paisley peeked from his breast pocket, and a pinky ring winked from his smallest finger. I wondered whether the blackmailers bothered with photos.

"Lovely, isn't it," he said, gesturing expansively toward the view. "My family thought I was quite insane, settling in this backward boondocks. They're all solidly ensconced in Pacific Heights; the only bohemia they care to recognize is Russian Hill, next mound over. They acted like I was pioneering the Wild West, homesteading among savages! But then, in a way, I am: I wanted to be where no one knows me as Charles Henry Rutherford the Third. Chas, to you." He winked and led me inside.

We entered a large foyer, bounded by a flight of stairs curving to a second-floor balcony. He invited me into "the drawing room," where long-fringed Persian carpets in jewel tones created a surface soft as the duff under a pine forest. Violet damask drapes garnished the bay window, framing a fainting couch of crushed velvet. The dark walnut sideboard anchored a colossal gilt mirror with swags of silver and gold. The room was large enough to hold all this plus a divan, two couches, an enormous split-leaf philodendron, and a vast brass tray serving as a coffee table. Chas was fussing with lemonade. The ice tinkled.

"A swig of something to lively it up?" he asked, belatedly checking his watch. "Thank goodness it's after noon, a respectable hour for beginning the gentle inebriation that is sometimes necessary to carry one through the day." I declined the lively version, but the iced lemonade was deliciously tart. Chas splashed a bit of vodka into his, then settled on the divan, languorously extending himself till his head rested on one arm and his feet dangled over the far end. He took a sip of his drink, set it aside on the tray, and turned his attention to me, looking me over from head to toe with a slow particularity that suggested a vast list of improvements was being formulated. I did hope he'd fund them. When his inventory was complete he cocked his head to one side, smiled, and asked, very mildly, what it was that I wished to discuss.

"I believe you're being blackmailed."

Chas rolled his eyes, then nodded. "I can tell you this much: they are *entirely* devoid of imagination. They send a couple of barely incriminating photographs, and then a letter stating, 'Your family might be interested in these.' In truth, given a choice, my family *wouldn't* be interested. They'd far rather ignore it. No one wants secrets to be revealed—they tend to breed like bunnies! *J'accuse!* That affair my brother-in-law had with cousin Jennie. The torrid background of that woman my brother Harold married. Let's not forget the love child begat by my father upon the housekeeper. Or the spring my younger sister suddenly had to go to France, for almost a year. What's a little polymorphous perversity mixed in with that? In my family, lusting among those related to you is worse only than lusting among those not related—by the promise of a vast inheritance."

"So...you're not worried about the blackmail?"

"Oh...I am, on and off. I contacted your brother on a lark. Thought it would be rather daring to meet a detective. But really, the whole business is quite tedious. I'm concerned, certainly, about the negative effect on my finances. But I'm only able to take it seriously some days, and today is not one of them. There are far more charming topics; I try to divert myself with those." He examined his fingernails blithely, but his left eye twitched.

"So, your family," I began hesitantly. "Do they... Is there any chance that they might already have an inkling that..."

"Do they suspect I am a"—Chas puckered his mouth and spoke with a nasal twang—"*homosexual?*" He threw up his hands and laughed breezily. "Why, of *course*, they do, darling, have from the time I was six, when I appeared for Christmas dinner as an angel in my sister's pink satin robe and marabou slippers, with a tutu around my head in lieu of a halo." He laughed. "The *point*, though, is that the word has never been spoken—never uttered within the four, no, twelve walls of our family home, and I daresay never voiced within the confines of Pacific Heights. The family knows what I am, but it's of the utmost importance that it never be acknowledged. Once acknowledged, you see, disinheritance is necessary, and that would demand that I defend myself by raising the various and sundry lapses, indiscretions, and improprieties of others." Roused by the subject, he got up, strolled to the win-

94

dow, and gazed pensively at the view. "I could get by, perhaps, on the yearly allowance allotted by my trust. They'd have trouble retrieving that. I'd need to get a job, dear God, join the unlucky bucks who slog through the week in some godforsaken skyscraper downtown, toeing the line, attending to matters, wearing a blue striped tie. I could get by. But,"—he brightened—"I'd rather not. Hence, your brother, and now, for reasons I fail to fully understand, you."

"Jimmy disappeared about a month and a half ago. He was investigating a number of blackmail cases. I think they may be related: to each other and to his disappearance."

"Hm," he replied, blasé. "A month and a half *is* a long time to be gone. Your standard binge generally lasts no longer than three weeks, plus one to recover and find your way home. Possible extension if, say, opium is involved. Or heroin." He arched a questioning eyebrow. I shook my head. "Even the most dedicated degenerate usually returns home before six weeks have passed—if only to replenish the wallet. Any leads?"

"One, relating to his former employment as a police officer."

Chas nodded. "Yes, I found that impressive. Well, how might I be of assistance?"

"Did you visit any bars in the months before the letters began?"

"I don't go to bars much—as those in my social set like to say, 'I'm not a bar person.' Hah! We love to say that." He wrinkled his nose, thrust it high in the air, and repeated, shaking his jowls with withering disdain, "'Oh, no, I'm really not a baaaaaar person.' We say we prefer private parties because it allows us to avoid the seedier element, the riffraff. Hah! What we fail to disclose is that our little soirees always include a fine sprinkling of rent boys and other carefully selected representatives of the proletariat. Otherwise no one would attend! The truth is, my set aren't bar people because we're terrified of associating with anyone too outré. Too limp-wristed, too temperamental, too flamboyant. Myself, I'm on the razor-thin edge of acceptability, sashaying that fine line. Shall I wear this pink paisley tie with that yellow suit? Better not, might be ousted. They look down their long noses and say, 'Chas, good fellow, don't you think that combination is a wee bit, well...Gertrude?' That's their favorite adjective: 'Gertrude.' A summation of everything blatant—everything fabulous. And why do they abhor everything Gertrude? They've got more to lose! All those investments, stocks and bonds, vacation homes, *inheritances*. We gather at each others' homes because we can—because they're big enough—and because we're terrified of getting caught." He collapsed on the divan, deflated, adding glumly, "And now I am. So, to answer your question, no, I don't frequent the bars."

"You haven't visited any in the last few months?"

"Wait. I did pay a visit to this odd little spot in the Mission District. I'd heard about it through a friend of a friend, they said it was quite solidly outside the law. Allowed men to dance with one another—outrageous, really—and yet, I was assured, it was very safe. Very well *protected*."

"When were you there?"

"Some time around... Now that I think about it, it was shortly before my birthday. Which means it was shortly before their first letter arrived." He looked at me with surprise. "Do you think it's connected?"

"Too soon to say. But they have to find their targets somewhere."

"It's a queer place in more ways than one. Funny little routine when you arrive. Very elaborate setup, for this town. I suppose it's designed to reassure the well-heeled clientele."

"Did you talk with anyone there?"

"Oh, a little chitchat, but I never use my real name when I'm in those places."

"Remember anything about your departure?"

"No. I left alone, if that's what you're asking."

"Any chance you were followed?"

"I certainly looked left and right before I stepped out. But the alley was empty. Someone might have seen me leaving the alley, of course.

But I try not to think about it. It's so—*Maltese Falcon*," he said, jerking his head to flick that auburn lock of hair from his eyes. Still standing, he smiled at me, slipped off his jacket, and turned it inside out. There, just beneath the shoulder pad, was a concealed pocket. From it he extracted a twenty-dollar bill. "For minor infractions." Then he flipped to the other side, where a pocket held a hundred in twenties. "For your more serious indiscretions." He turned it right side out and slipped it on as he continued jauntily, "Your best insurance against the law. Everyone wins: the cop takes his girl out to a nice dinner, and you don't have your life ruined. I know a tailor who'll put 'em in for you, no questions asked."

"So, the blackmailers: I take it you haven't paid them."

He looked at me in astonishment. "Of course I have!"

"But why?"

"It seemed like the simplest solution. Pay them and they'll go away." He flitted his hand around in front of his face like he was shooing a gnat. "Of course, they didn't. They came back and asked for more."

"And?"

"I paid that as well. It's easier than fretting over the thing at night! It's...a worthwhile investment in my peace of mind," he added haughtily. But then he sighed. "Now they've asked for still more. It's making a dent in my monthly allowance. Soon I'll have to economize, for God's sake. Not a skill I've acquired in my life." He grew fervent. "Believe me, I respect the rest of you for possessing the capability. It's an admirable accomplishment. But I'd prefer to be admired for my generosity, my largesse! As Will Rogers said, the money's all been appropriated for the top so it can trickle down to the needy, and I've created my own special little rivulet. I throw a vast party once a month, and invite plenty of riffraff—those to whom it should be trickling!" He suddenly abandoned himself to the couch, threw his head back, and swooned. "Ah, parties, now there's a better topic of conversation! We always have a theme, to get the fun going—and costumes! The last was 'Marlene Dietrich.' *Everyone* arrived as Marlene! Well, not everyone—I had a gaggle of dresses for those who can't don a frock till they've had a few, you know? We have to make allowances for those who'd never"—he adopted a shocked expression and clutched nonexistent pearls—"be a broad in broad daylight! But we have a marvelous time. Indeed, I hereby invite you to attend the next one—you and a friend or two. You look like you could use a little pick-me-up, my dear, if I may be so bold." He sprang out of his chair and began to fiddle with the silk ropes restraining the drapes. "That's if I can afford to host it now that the trickle has been diverted to those unimaginative bores!"

"How did you pay them?"

"They don't take checks, if that's what you mean," he replied petulantly. "They identified a rock, in Duboce Park, under which I would find an envelope containing the negatives. I got them, but of course there were others, more incriminating. They sent photos from *those* negatives along with their subsequent demands. Me strolling arm-and-arm with another man into a thicket. God knows what else they have in store for me." He shuddered. "Sex is most definitely not a spectator sport. Those absurd positions, those horrid grimaces, those disconsonant grunts. It's all delightful enough when you're engaged in it, but it isn't meant for viewing."

"Do you have any of the letters?"

He roused himself, strolled to the massive sideboard, and opened a small drawer. Reaching in, he pressed something, and a panel slid back to reveal a hidden compartment. He eyed me with a pleased grin. "Very Sherlock Holmes, yes? I bought it for that. Never imagining I'd actually have a use for it."

The letters were typed. I looked closely at the "e"s. "Definitely the same blackmailer."

"Well, that's delightful," he replied. "So reassuring to know they are an established outfit, boasting a substantial clientele." He cocked an eye in my direction. "Anyone as well-heeled as I?"

I shook my head. He shrugged. "I paid them about two weeks ago.

No doubt another photograph and another demand will arrive in a month or so."

"Will you let me know when it does?"

"Certainly." As I left he made me promise to attend the next party.

"My name is Joe O'Conner. I'd like to speak with Adeline Jackson."

"This is she."

"Miss Jackson, my brother was looking into a personal matter for you."

"Yes, he was," she said, her voice leery.

"Jimmy has disappeared. I'm pursuing his cases and trying to find him. I'd like to speak with you."

"You are speaking with me."

"I'd like to speak with you in person."

"Hmph."

"Please," I said, and waited.

"Hmph. Tonight. Seven o'clock. And no more of this 'Miss Jackson' business. Everyone calls me Tiny. But don't think that means you're my friend. Even my enemies call me Tiny."

She inhabited a Victorian with a steeply pitched roof, leaded windows, and paint faded to gorgeous reds, violets, and blues like an aged burlesque dancer whose wrinkles and drooping feathers only add to her mystique. The door opened just a crack. Tiny was tiny, no more than five foot one, a squat, compact woman who rumbled with energy the way a stove crammed with hardwood trembles with heat. Her short hair was touched with silver, but her light-brown skin was nearly unwrinkled. She wore tortoiseshell glasses and a dove-gray suit well tailored for her proportions. After looking me up and down she opened the door and led me wordlessly to a room almost four times her height. Scattered throughout on a variety of tables and a gleaming baby grand were framed photographs with Tiny beaming from within.

She didn't waste time. "Nasty business." She poked me into an overstuffed chair low enough that she towered over me. Placing her hands on her ample hips, she eyed me fiercely. "You know that I know there's a good chance you're in on it, right? Blackmailers pull that all the time, send someone who's in on it with offers of help. The outraged uncle of the violated young woman, the indignant mother of the spoiled boy—relying on their victim to be so terrified he'll cough up some green. So let me say right now, I'm not coughing up. I don't know what you've got going on with this disappeared-brother business: maybe the two of you think an old lady can be more easily swayed by you than by him; maybe you plan to play good cop, bad cop. I don't know what your game is, but I can tell you that I'm not paying hush money. I am what I am and I don't care who knows it. I've got nothing to be ashamed of, nothing to hide, nothing up my sleeve, and no skeletons in my closet." She glared at me, looming.

"You're right," I replied, "get someone scared enough and stay in proximity, chances are they'll offer you something to make it go away. But in this case, I'm not in on it. My brother really has disappeared. I'm afraid that he's hurt, or worse. So I'm not here to offer help so much as to ask for it. I need your help to find the blackmailer."

She folded one arm across her stomach, balanced the other elbow on it, gripped her chin, and glowered some more. Her eyeglasses steamed as her eyes made the trek down my trousers to my shoes, up again to my shoulders and my hat—which I belatedly remembered to remove. I wondered how she managed not to care, how spending nights with a woman in her arms didn't constitute a skeleton in her closet. I wondered whether her lack of shame was bravado, marshaled to deflect an extortionist, or whether it was real. I wondered whether the springs in her chair broke all by themselves or whether she removed them for times like this when she wanted to tower.

"Hmph," she announced. Then she turned and marched out of the room. I heard dishes rattling, cabinets slamming, and her voice muttering. I wondered if I should go. I looked at the pictures on the table beside me, nightclub photos, each depicting a line of glamorous people

in every shade from deep ebony to glaring white, all in beaded gowns or evening suits, Tiny invariably wearing the latter. The women in dresses had crimped hair in perfect, undulating waves, with feather or flower adornment. Smiling solo from a large silver frame was a dark-skinned, tuxedoed woman in a fancy studio shot in which her freckled skin was gorgeously shadowed. The flowery signature in the lower corner read, "Bricktop."

I heard footsteps and got to my feet, but she grumbled and told me to sit my ass back down as she set a tray on the table between us. She poured coffee from a tall porcelain coffeepot with pronounced angles. "One lump or two?" she demanded.

"Three."

Suddenly she smiled. "Too much of a good thing can be wonderful," she pronounced as she handed me the cup. Then she sat and scowled. "There are two possibilities: either you're telling the truth, or you aren't. One way or another, truth will out. So we might as well begin. We'll start with you. After I've heard your story I'll decide whether to tell you mine."

As I spoke, she listened intently, nodding now and then, interjecting an occasional question. Some seemed idle—what color house, how many floors—like she was testing me. Others were more substantial: how many files; were the pictures taken from the same perspective; were the letters typed on the same typewriter? She retrieved hers. Cracked tails.

When I was done, she sat drumming her fingers on the arm of her chair for about a minute and a half. Then she began. "Letter came out of the clear blue sky. Went to pick up the mail one day, second Tuesday in April, and there it was. No return address. Had a bad feeling as I opened it, and that feeling was confirmed as I read it. 'We know about your liaisons,' the first one said. 'They may have accepted them in France, but they won't here.'" She shook her head. "So they knew a bit about me. They'd done their research. My career, that I played trumpet in Paris and moved in those circles. That's not hard to figure out, long as you know some French. I appeared in pictures in the papers there, my name spelled out in black and white." She gestured to the photographs. "They couldn't prove anything from those pictures, but they could imply plenty." She picked one up, admired it, then put it down.

"I just sat on it for a while. Waited for the next letter. Didn't scare me. Not much they can take from me: time's taken most of it already. Of what remains, none of my friends and few of my acquaintances don't know everything there is to know. I was curious, mostly: what was it they thought they could hold over me? They had a little old lady with a scandalous past. They believe they can coerce her into forking over a pile of money to stop them from—what? Telling her landlord? I own this house. Telling her church? Nobody I care about gives a damn. Telling her employer? These days I only work when I want to and they're begging me to come out of retirement. So how would they goad me: that's what I wondered." She thought for a while, then continued.

"They took their time about it. The second letter, and the third, all innuendo. Trying to spook me. I don't spook easy. Been through too much to spook easy. I know what's what, what's important to me and what can fade away. Would they threaten to go to my home town, tell my old pastor that I'm a deviant? He's long gone, and the one who replaced him doesn't know me from Eve. Same with everyone else back home. But here's the thing: it wouldn't have mattered anyway. When I was a girl coming up, they all knew me to be me. 'That Tiny,' they'd say, 'she's got her ways.' Every town has room for a few eccentrics, and they didn't trouble me much about wearing my hair short, playing the trumpet, tooling around in trousers. 'That's Tiny,' is what they'd say—a little proud, truth be told, that their town had a few who did things differently. Because there were others, some before my time and some after. Bobby Jefferson covered every inch of his car with bottle caps. Mary Jean Stone insisted on walking around town with her favorite chicken roosting on her shoulder. Kept things lively, rather than the same ol', same ol' every day. They weren't troubled; *didn't read too much into it*. As for relatives, I've got just a few of them left. Two nieces. One lives in Oakland: I visit with her and her two children every holiday, the big ones and the small. They'd sooner shoot their dog than care who I love. So those blackmailers, they couldn't touch me."

She was breathing heavily, and when she spoke again her voice slowed. "Then they mentioned my niece's job. Seraphina, she's a cook in the prison out on Alcatraz. Federal Pen. They're cleaning house at those places, ever since that lunatic Senator Joe McCarthy started around with his list, 'Communists In Government Service.' Now they're giving the boot to anyone who ever in their entire life said anything about workers not being doormats. And somehow he's got homosexuals tied up in that. Pretty soon won't be anyone left to work for the federal government. They'll have to let the prisoners out, or let 'em starve. So that's what those blackmailers are threatening me with: telling Seraphina's boss that her aunt, with whom she spends New Year's, Christmas, and every holiday in between, is a known homosexual. That girl has two children to support. She's got a good job and a need to hold onto it! That's why I called your brother." She leaned forward to pick up her coffee, but continued before she had a chance to sip from it.

"Honestly, that scared me. Both ways: that they're threatening my niece's job, and that they know about her job. How much do those miscreants know about me if they know where my relatives are getting their paychecks? That's mighty close to home. Made me feel like eyes were peering in these windows all hours of the day and night." She shivered, and gathered her elbows together. Then her eyes blazed and she slammed her cup on the table. "Nefarious scoundrels! Trying to profit off someone else's misery. Letter after letter, leaving you time to sit and stew and wonder in between. They're getting more than money out of it: they're getting pleasure, too. Got a jones for making someone squirm. No one sends letters like that without enjoying their fellow man's suffering.

"So that's my story. Received that letter on the fifth of June. I'd seen your brother's ad in the paper before then, took notice of it but never thought I'd need it. When I read the letter about my niece's job I didn't so much as stop to straighten my tie: I marched up to the corner store, bought myself a paper, and called him. He was here the next day." She looked me over again, glaring. Then her face softened. "I'm sorry your brother is missing," she declared with a tenderness that evoked in me a fresh flush of grief. I'd been holding it at bay, turning my attention and my fury to the search. Just that morning I'd called Jimmy's dentist and lied: said he needed a root canal, and the new dentist insisted on seeing records before proceeding. There in the phone booth, for a few brief seconds, I inhabited the lie. The threat facing Jimmy was a simple root canal, nothing more. Not this knot of alcohol and violence, blackmail and betrayal, doubt and depthless venality. This void of not knowing.

Tiny's voice returned me to the room. "What do you know about the blackmailers?" she prodded, leaning forward.

"Not a lot so far," I acknowledged. "They're well situated, not in a hurry for the money. They have plenty of resources, their research is thorough."

"None of that's news to me. What angles are you working?"

"I'm hoping to figure out where they're finding targets. Whether there's some location in common. Do you go to any of the bars?"

"Been to every one of them. Nighttime's when I live. Habit developed from when I was in Paris. Any bar I hear about that caters to our kind, I visit." Her voice became caustic. "A few of them were less than welcoming. Like that one behind the office. *That* place. I'd heard about it—the whole rigmarole at the door, the tony setup, the little stage. Hah! That pathetic stage wouldn't fit a timpani and a contrabass without damage to one or the other. Yeah, I went to that place," she growled, her face taut. "No doubt they wouldn't have opened the door for me but I arrived same time as two white women. Cold shoulders all around from the moment I got there. Nobody said one word to me. I know what it's about: they look at me and see everything they're afraid of seeing in that mirror. Damn bartender mixes me a watered-down drink with the wrong gin and his eyes track me like a hungry dog. Soon it wasn't just his eyes. A six-foot-three, two-hundred-pound chump hovered over me like dots on dice. I was just preparing to douse him with my drink and leave when one of the musicians recognized me. He didn't see my mood, pulled me on stage and put his horn in my hand. 'Show 'em, Tiny!' he bellowed. So I showed 'em. Blew the wildest version of 'Strange Fruit' you ever heard. Played that last note high and discordant like Billie sings it. Then utter silence. I handed the trumpet over, cut through the crowd looking neither right nor left, straight out the door. I shook the dust off my shoes. Hmph!" Tiny pretended to spit on the floor. "That's what I think of that place. The Dollar Bill indeed." She grimaced. "A couple of the others tried to turn me away. Treated me like a redheaded stepchild. They realized quick what they'd be up against and backed off. Then I didn't want to be there anyway."

"I heard about things like that from a friend in New York."

"New York, Chicago, San Francisco, Los Angeles. Only place I haven't been treated like that was Paris, France. It was a shock to come back here—I had to return, when the war broke out. Then I had to wonder exactly what kind of democracy we were defending. Wouldn't surprise me a bit if that bartender was behind the blackmail. Only I'd call it whitemail, based on who's sending it."

"Have you decided what you are going to do about it?"

She bristled. "Are you asking whether I'm going to pay them?" Without waiting for a response she released a "hmph" so ferocious it spilled her remaining coffee and a photo on the side table shuddered and collapsed. She regarded me with fury.

I put down my cup and held my hands up. "I want to find the blackmailer. If you're going to pay, I want to stake out the place you leave the money. See who picks it up."

Her eyes gripped mine. "If you're in on it, that's feeble cover," she spat.

Then the steam rising from her fury swayed like the flame of a candle when a door is slammed shut. "If you're not, that's perilous."

chapter six

I was at Jimmy's office, Acme Professional, only it wasn't his office, just an empty room. The jangled blinds were there, but other than that, nothing: not a desk, not a chair, and certainly not a typewriter. In spite of that I sat down at a typewriter and though I'd never learned to type I lifted my hands, they settled on the keys, and I typed. I wrote a letter to Jimmy, telling him what was happening and that I missed him and needed him, and please would he come back soon? Then I leaned forward and pulled the top of the page taut—and the words there were all wrong: *We know about you...*

It went on from there, in ugly, lurid detail. I'd tell you but you know it already: cheerless corners of seedy bars and sulky alleys, sordid motel rooms with mattresses sagging like hope, steamy cars invaded by sudden glaring lights, heads ducked, hands up, cringing, and photographs that captured it all in black and white. I tore the page out of the typewriter, crushed it, and hurled it across the room. I got another sheet from nowhere and jammed it in and started over, telling

Jimmy that I needed him and missed him and please would he come back soon? Halfway through I leaned forward to read it and again it was *We know about you* and the ugly details: grim theater with sticky floors, silent phone with a sudden click, stranger behind us on the street, the inconsolable night and the longing, the longing that I knew was underneath and behind and throughout, permeating all the ugly, treacherous detail.

I put another page in vowing to watch it closely: to keep my eyes on the keys so it came out just the way it went in. I bent forward to hunt and peck and that's when I saw it: the typewriter keys, all thirty-one of them, were blank. Perfect little ivory discs with nothing at all written on them. One just the same as another. There at the top of the typewriter it said Corona, the word spelled out in fancy lettering clear as day, but beneath it every key was barren as the morning after.

I don't know if that's when I started to sweat or if I'd been sweating all along, but suddenly my collar was tight and my skin damp and the angles of the room all wrong. I reached my hand out and set a finger on a key. I hesitated. Then I hit it. I hit it again. And then again and again, the same key. The key clacked just like it should, and I leaned forward to check which letter it was that I'd typed ten or twelve times on the page, and what I saw there made the air too thick to breathe: *We know abou...*

That's when I knew that the room wasn't empty. With the light that seeped in through the jangled blinds skulked the fetid stench of hatred. It permeated the air. Everywhere. It was there when the postman tramped through rain and snow and sleet and hail. It was there when children placed their hands on their chests and pledged allegiance to the blackboard, when mothers pinned their laundry to the line, when senators leaned forward and spoke into microphones and flashbulbs popped. It was in the air we drew into our bodies and filled our lungs with.

With that knowledge, I woke.

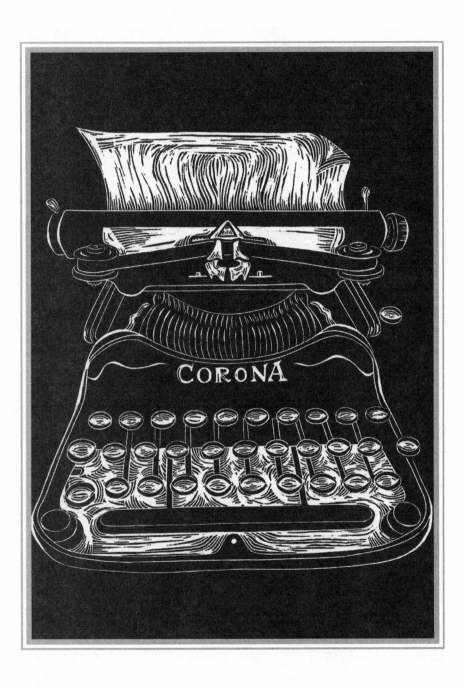

The dream haunted me throughout the day. The stench was with me when I set out for Mr. Dodson's house. He had invited me for dinner: "My *Datura wrightii* has been blooming—I'll take you out to the garden after we eat. The most remarkable scent..."

That evening, we hadn't yet gotten to remark on it when he broke down and told me another letter had arrived.

"Three hundred dollars, tomorrow night."

When I broached the idea of watching to see who came for the money, he eyed me with utter astonishment. "Absolutely not, Josephine! That is far too dangerous." But he was so alarmed by his financial situation that he gave way, agreeing on one condition: that I not follow whoever came for it. I explained that this entailed all the risk with little reward, but resigned myself to just glimpsing whoever picked up his envelope. I doubted it would be the blackmailer—he could afford to hire someone for his dirty work. Still: a glimpse, and I'd have someone to scour the town for.

Mr. Dodson was to deliver the cash at eleven sharp to a tree stump in San Francisco's Buena Vista Park. Early the next morning I borrowed the mangy dog from Jimmy's car lot and tromped the hillside to find it. A weary fern fronted the stump, near a park bench with broken rails and chipped paint. This depressing tableau sat in a gentle hollow, surrounded by woods. I located a tree nearby, broad enough to shield me from anyone on the trail that bisected the hollow. There was no way to hide from the many informal paths that threaded the woods, so I had to hope the pickup would use the trail. The mangy dog, who'd perked up considerably during our woodland exploration, was defeated to find himself back at the lot. He slumped beside the shed and covered his face with both paws. I returned to Jimmy's room and did the same.

A bus to the Haight-Ashbury District deposited me at the base of Miss Holloway's Street at nine thirty. I followed its rogue curves as fog settled, so dense that the demented Victorians drifted in and out of sight. An enormous turret emerged, then a rococo porch with nothing but fog to support it. The mist muted the streetlights, reducing each to a wan halo. Sounds were muffled, voices indistinct. I watched for flying monkeys, but the street was nearly empty. No poppy fields to soothe my nerves.

As the steep street turned steeper, my steps slowed. Jimmy's gun was heavy in my pocket. A car door slammed in a muffled hush. I didn't see the park till I'd reached it: no bright green patch on the hill, beckoning; just the sudden, silent presence of shrouded trees, looming. A wind rose and the world became unstable, the trees animate, whole limbs emerging, then retreating. The fog sucked color, leaving only shades of gray and indistinct boundaries, permeable, hesitant. I entered the park on steep steps, slippery with moss, which gave way to a narrow dirt trail. I found my way to the broad tree, relieved that the fog didn't entirely obscure my view. I leaned against the trunk, searching for a position that I could hold. Then I waited, bark jagged against my cheek.

A tall, stout man in a dark overcoat strode through the clearing. His footsteps quickly faded. Half an hour later a shabby man with a dog passed through, muttering. The dog was eager, the leash taut. Their sounds ebbed as they lurched into the fog. Mr. Dodson was early. He approached quickly, nervous, tentative. Without looking for me he settled on the bench, hands palm-down on either side, then jumped up, reached into his coat, and pulled out a thick envelope. He slid it into the stump behind the fern, turned, and staggered away. A few moments later I heard, or imagined, a car cough to life in the distance. Then silence.

The fog churned. The clearing expanded to include the sloping limbs of surrounding pines, then narrowed to a small room of grass, bench, fern. I tensed as I heard voices approaching. Not soft murmurings, but clear, confident voices that boomed after hours of hush. Two policemen entered the clearing, walking with intent. The taller one was well built, in his mid-forties, pale skin, and a curl of black hair escaping from his cap. The short one looked like he'd just smelled a bad odor.

They stopped in the center of the clearing and turned slowly, surveying the surrounding vegetation. Then they began tromping in circles, widening with each round. Eventually one stopped short, elbowed the other, and pointed.

"You," he said, surly. "What are you doing? Step out here."

I walked as casually as I could from behind the tree. "Good evening, officers. Just enjoying the night air. Quite a fog, isn't it?"

"This fog's here every night. You new in town? Got some I.D.?"

"Matter of fact, I am new—"

"Let's see it buddy, quitcher stalling."

"With all due respect, officer, is there a law against a citizen enjoying a local park?"

"There's laws against loitering in the parks, and it looks to me like you were loitering. Look that way to you, Homer?"

"Why, matter of fact, it does, Arnie. You got a purpose for being in the park?" He examined my face, my shoulders, then returned to my face.

"Just enjoying the night air. An insomniac, you see," I continued, hoping for a change of direction.

"We got a real good place for insomniacs," Arnie snarled. "And you still haven't produced any I.D. Looks to me like you're resisting arrest." His hand shot out, grabbed me by the collar, and pulled me close. He sneered. I reached into my pocket, then felt his fist crash into my jaw and I fell back into the underbrush.

"We'll do the reaching into pockets, buddy," he growled. "Get up and put your hands on your head. Move it!"

"If you wanted me up, why'd you knock me down?" I asked as I lumbered to my feet.

"Oh, we got a wise guy here," Homer said, scrutinizing my face some more. Suddenly he grinned. "Why Arnie, I'm not sure it's a guy at all. Take a look at this mug." He grabbed me by the chin, squeezing hard. "I think we can add impersonation to the charges. What do you think?"

"Well, now, I'm not sure," Arnie drawled. "Not sure at all. I think we oughta be certain, don't you? Damn certain. Turn around, hands on the tree!" he barked. "Spread 'em." He drew the words out slowly, and as he chuckled I felt his breath against my ear.

I turned quickly, lifting my right elbow and aiming for his jaw. Contact. I heard him gasp, then curse, as I ran hard. Branches scratched my face, roots tripped me, but I sprinted, hands straight out in front to protect my eyes. I heard their voices barking behind me, and the thudding of their boots. Then I must have veered off the path: my feet crashing through the bushes made too much noise for me to hear how close they were. My breath came gasping and filled my ears. I tripped, landed hard, and pain exploded in my knee. I heard pounding just behind me as I dragged myself up. Limping, I passed a low stump with a rotten core and dropped Jimmy's gun into it. Then I ran smack into a tree, and they were on me. Homer threw me to the ground, grabbed my arm, and twisted it behind my back, wrenching it hard. Arnie shoved my face into the dirt. They wrestled my other arm back and I felt handcuffs snap around my wrists.

"Get up, you fucking pervert!" I rolled on my side to try to stand without the use of my hands. Pressure on my knee made me gasp. One of them dragged me roughly to my feet, then pushed my face into a tree. I felt hands on my body, patting me down, but they were more like punches. Then a hand shoved my legs apart. My face ground into the bark as I tried to regain my balance. The hand grabbed my crotch, squeezed hard, and I heard laughter. "We've got a perv on our hands, all right. The chief's gonna love this, Homer. Turn around sweetheart, let's feel your titties." They rolled me around, four hands grabbing at my chest. The bindings infuriated them and released a confused string of epithets. "Think you're a man, you bulldagger faggot? You lesbo! You're sick, that's what! You're a sick homo dyke. Now walk!" The big one shoved me from the side. I caught myself and began limping in the direction he'd pointed. My shoulders ached and my knee bellowed. My face announced it was full of cuts and scrapes. But my mind was focused on what was going to happen next.

At the station Arnie and a guard entertained themselves patting me down again. They took my little brown turd and booked me. Then they removed the cuffs and steered me through two sets of heavy doors to a corridor lined with cells. The guard stopped midway down, rattled a ring of keys, and began to unlock a gate. In the near dark an inmate in a plaid suit slid down from the upper bunk of a bed. He strode to the bars, sharp, quick eyes darting from the guard to the cop to me and back again. Arnie sidled over and said "Hey, Roscoe, we got some company for you. Consider it a present from the chief."

They began a tête-à-tête, and I saw Roscoe's eyes on me as a smirk lit his face. He turned to say "Welcome!" in a leering drawl.

Arnie and the guard laughed. Then they shoved me inside. I tripped, fell forward, caught hold of an upright on the other bed. A man exploded out of the upper bunk, face scowling, fists whirling. "Awright, you bastard, get 'em up, get 'em up, awright, you bastard, get 'em up!" he shouted, executing a roiling boxer's dance with me as his partner. I let go of the bed and backed off as Arnie, the guard, and Roscoe cackled.

"Take it easy, Floyd," said the guard. Floyd's scowl became a resentful glower. As the gate clanged and the guard disappeared down the corridor with the cop, I kept one eye on each of them. Floyd was a pudgy guy with a sallow face and a handful of hair combed over a bald pate, but he moved like a self-contained cyclone. Roscoe's chest was puffed and his shoulders back and his crotch preceded him wherever he strode in all of the thirty square feet the cell allowed. He was slender but tough, like an old bird with one eye on the younger ones and the other on the stockpot.

I stood my ground, what little there was of it, as Roscoe came close to inspect me. "What's your name, *girly*?" he sneered.

"Name's Joe," I announced, aiming for a tone that reached confident but fell this side of defiant.

"Welcome to our little club, Joe. My name's Roscoe, and this here's

Floyd. Whatcha in for, Joe?" he asked, his voice oily, his mind elsewhere. Mine was too, but I tried to keep him talking.

"Taking a walk in the park. How about you, Roscoe?"

"Oh, we're asking the questions right now, Joe. We want to know aaaaaaaall about you." He slid his hand down to his crotch, and stroked it as he spoke. Floyd, who hadn't taken long to catch on, laughed.

"Afraid there's not much to tell, Roscoe, except that I'm looking for my brother."

"Those your brother's pants you wearing, Joe?"

He was close enough that I could smell his sweat and the liquor on his breath. "No, matter of fact they're mine. So's the suit." A lot depended on how they played it. I could maybe fight them off if they came at me one at a time. But if they got together I didn't have a chance.

"Not bad, that suit," Roscoe conceded. "Sharp cut. But I'm more interested in what's underneath it." His lower lip hung out a little. "Whatchya got underneath, girly?"

He moved closer, his hand rubbing the bulge in his crotch, and in that moment I didn't feel the icy chill that later spread through me when I realized this was the jail, maybe even the cell, where Jimmy's boyfriend, Bobby, was beaten to death. I might have gambled differently; might have realized more acutely, as I weighed one kind of injury against another, that in the balance between them what I was gambling with was my life.

Instead I stared at his crotch and crooned suggestively, "You're excited, aren't you, Roscoe?" His hand froze and his eyes narrowed. "Look at that bulge you've got. You're hot for me, aren't you?" One kind of injury doesn't necessarily preclude another. But I thought it might, with a rooster like Roscoe.

He shook his head from side to side. "You really are a freak, aren't you, girly." His voice hardened. "Sounds like you want it." His hand resumed its slow slide up and down.

"Your thing is hard, isn't it, Roscoe?"

"Yeah, it's hard, girly. Soon you'll know how hard it is."

"You see how hot he is, Floyd? Roscoe's got a hard-on for me," I purred.

Floyd gloated, "Yeah, he's hot for you, girly."

Roscoe kept rabid eyes on me as he spoke. "Floyd, grab hold of her arm from behind." I wrestled with Floyd. Soon enough he had me, my left arm twisted back so he could keep me wherever he wanted.

I kept talking. "You're so hot for me, Roscoe, even Floyd can see how hot you are, how you can't wait to have me." Roscoe was weaving his head from side to side, like a snake considering its options. "Know why he's so hot for me, Floyd?"

"Shut up now, girly. It's time for you to shut up," Floyd said softly.

I met his whisper. "He can't wait to get into this suit of mine, Floyd. Can't wait to unzip my trousers and reach inside. Can you, Roscoe?" I asked in a low taunt.

Roscoe's eyes were glazed with lust. "Shut up, girly," he hissed.

"Know why he can't wait, Floyd? Know why he's so hot?" I kept my eyes glued to his face as I heard him unzip his trousers. "Wanna know why he can't wait?"

"Awright, girly, shut up now," I heard Floyd mutter, near my ear. He twisted my arm upward and pain seared my shoulder.

"He can't wait to unzip my trousers because he's got a little secret. Don't you, Roscoe?"

I felt his hot breath on my face. His voice was thick as he said, "Yeah, girly, I'm going to unzip them—"

"You can't wait to do it because of your little secret. That's why you're so hot for me, Roscoe, so hot that Floyd can see it. Know what that secret is, Floyd?"

Roscoe reached toward my neck with both hands. I tried to rear back, but Floyd held my arm tight and the movement sent pain flaring up my shoulder again. Roscoe grabbed hold of my shirt, one collar with one hand, one with the other, and yanked. I heard buttons bounce around me on the concrete floor. He leered at the tee shirt underneath, through which the lines of my binding were visible. Then his eyes moved downward to my crotch.

I said it seductively, without venom. "That's your little secret, Roscoe, why you're so hot for me: what you really want is a man. You're all excited because you can finally unzip a man's trousers and reach inside for his cock—that's it, isn't it Roscoe, what you really want is a cock, and even though part of you knows there's no cock inside these trousers you're all hot because you're going to pretend there is and that's what you really want, even Floyd here can see that's what you really want, you're all hot and ex—"

The first blow caught me hard across the jaw, slammed me back into Floyd, who fell against the wall but didn't lose hold of me. Pain shot across my face and neck. Then the pain of the second superseded the first and spread like agonizing heat, and soon there was a third lower down against my ribs, and another, and then he began in earnest and the sounds of the blows were loud in my ears, louder than his words, "You sick fuck you pervert you goddamned lesbo sicko," and I felt my body jerk to the right and then to the left and I bounced back against Floyd but the blows kept coming. I heard something in my chest crack and then I heard Floyd shouting, "Awright!" and then I heard him shouting again, "Awright, Roscoe, now awright!" and he released my arm and tried to push me off him but the blows kept coming, sending me hard back against him, and the sounds of my body being pummeled and my face becoming soft and pulpy drowned out his voice. I felt him shove hard from behind again and that shove met Roscoe's fist and I heard another crack and the pain pulsed and flared like light in my head, billowing and spreading with each blow.

Floyd started in with his awrights again. I heard him yell, "Roscoe, that's enough already. Ya kill the punk, you're gonna have a tough time findin' an alibi!" There was a loud slap that didn't coincide with a burst of pain anywhere in my body. Then Floyd spoke again. "Roscoe, this punk ain't worth the noose."

I think that's when it stopped. I drifted in and out of consciousness through what was left of the night. The floor was hard, but the pain too great to be bothered much by that. The cold, though, the cold came up from the floor like death seeping into me. One of the times I surfaced I thought of Bobby, and the chill that spread with the realization that it was here he was murdered was colder even than the concrete. Another time it seemed like I was far away from my body, and all the nerves in me that led to memories of Jimmy ached. Those nerves were everywhere—not just in my brain and heart, but in my gut, my fingers, in the knee that was gashed open when I fell out of a tree and he was there to catch me but I was too big already to catch and we both went crashing to the ground. My body became a map with points here and here and here, each point a memory, the map all that was left of him and the only thing holding me together.

The raucous rattle of a tin plate across the bars of a cell woke me, the guard's alarm clock, answered by grunts and groans and shouts up and down the corridor. I felt Floyd lift my wrist to feel for a pulse, then drop it. Then a lot of cursing as the guards found me and rattled keys and opened the gate and hauled me off to the infirmary in an agony of tugging and lifting.

I don't know how many days I spent there. A week, probably closer to two. I expected them to arraign me next, but instead they bandaged me, dressed me in someone else's clothes—a stained shirtwaist, torn bra, and worn pumps—and put me on the street. I wandered till I found my way back to the hotel. Mr. Wilkinson exercised an eyebrow when he saw me. I asked him what day it was, and when I realized how long it had been, I knew Mr. Dodson would be frantic.

I tried calling, but he didn't answer. They'd taken my best suit, and the strap from Jimmy's suitcase that I'd been using to bind myself. But they'd wrapped me in a long medical bandage, for the cracked ribs, and when I raised it a bit, it served the same purpose. I put on my second-best suit, then tried his number again. Still, no answer.

I wanted to drive myself; in Jimmy's car I could pull right up his driveway and have only a few steps to go. I knew how sensitive he was, how hard it would be for him to explain the visit from a slow-moving man with a bandaged face and a limp, but between the ribs and the gauze over my eye I wasn't up to driving yet. When I got in the cab, the driver studied me in his rearview and then asked, "How many?"

"Two," I said.

He shook his head. "One of 'em musta been a truck."

"No, a rooster."

"Some rooster," he scoffed, and headed for the bridge. He left me standing there in the middle of Mr. Dodson's street, so I made my way to the sidewalk, across the sidewalk, up his walk, up his stairs, to the front door.

No answer when I rang the bell. I tried the narrow side gate to the garden. It opened. I knocked on the back door. Then I banged on it. Then I tried the knob. It was unlocked. "Mr. Dodson?" I called as I went in. "Mr. Dodson?" I called as I walked from the kitchen to the living room, then again as I made my way up the stairs, feeling more and more scared for him as I neared the top. A hallway with one door at either end and two in the middle. The near door opened to a bathroom. I was spooked as I pulled back the shower curtain, but there was no Mr. Dodson with bloody wrists in the tub.

I'd stopped calling by this time, knowing that if he could hear me he'd already have heard me. The next room had a bed in it, and lying in the bed, neatly dressed and very still, was Mr. Dodson. A heavy, drowsy scent filled the room. Where a shaft of light came through parted curtains, dust motes hung, expectant, in the air. On the bedside table a tall, slender, orange vase held several stems of his *Datura wrightii*, some of the extravagant blooms collapsed to a pulpy, twisted mass. His face was pale, waxy, his features relaxed as I'd never seen them in life. I bent close and listened for his breath. I heard nothing.

I reached for a wrist. The limb was limp, heavy, cool. I felt for a pulse. My fingers curved around the wrist and, finding none, I squeezed tightly—angry with him, angry with the world, angry with myself for having precipitated his death. I realized, as I grasped, that I'd never touched him before. And as I stood with the surprise of that thought, my hand tight around his wrist, I felt the faintest flutter of movement beneath my finger. I believed I'd willed myself to feel it, so I released the wrist, then gripped again, and it came, a faint thread.

"Mr. Dodson—Elbert," I said, "Elbert, my friend. Please stay with me. Stay." I gave a moment's thought to calling for help, but if he lived the scandal would be, for him, worse than death. I dragged a chair to the side of the bed and sat beside him, his hand in mine, willing him to live. The light from the window moved across the foot of the bed, then the room melted into darkness. The scent intensified. His pulse continued, slow, discernible only if I pressed against the wrist.

I must have dozed, because birds were twittering boisterously as they do just before dawn, when his arm jerked, then fell back again. I felt his pulse resume, then strengthen. By the time light flooded the room I could feel it without gripping the wrist. I began to hear his breath, shallow at first, eventually deeper. When his voice broke the silence it was surprisingly steady.

"Josephine. I thought you were—I was afraid you were gone. I heard them take you. I followed them to the station. I was afraid to go in at first, but then I asked to see you. I said I'd post bail, and *demanded* to see you. They said you weren't there. They said they had no record. I went back every day. But after six days—they continued to deny—I was sure you were gone. I thought they had...made you disappear, like your brother. I felt so responsible, Josephine—I'd allowed you to take such a risk for me. I never should have agreed. I..." When he opened his eyes and saw me he trembled, then began to shake so violently I knew the dust motes across the room were churning. "Oh, oh," he said, shaking his head. "Josephine." He studied the bruises and the gashes on my face, the bandaged eye, the shattered lip. "You're alive," he said finally.

"I'm alive," I agreed.

He tried to sit up, failed, then leaned back and asked me, "But are you... Are you okay, Josephine?"

"I'm okay, Mr. Dodson. I am."

"Oh, you're okay," he said, sighing with relief. "Tell me how it happened."

So I told him. He trembled throughout, clutching my hand tightly. When I finished he said, "Josephine, that was a gamble you took." Then he thought for a while and nodded and said again, "A gamble, Josephine," squeezing my hand.

"Tell me about you now," I said.

He sighed. He was pale as a paperwhite, and still shaking, but he offered a wan smile. "Datura is poisonous, I may have mentioned that. I couldn't find any reliable account of the mechanism or lethal dosage in my books, so I lay here for over an hour, terrified, not knowing what to expect. I heard the children in the neighborhood called inside for supper, and suddenly I smelled her scent. I plunged down her roots into the loam, thick with worms—which winked at me!—then burst through the hard crust and was swimming in fire."

He squeezed my hand gently, closed his eyes, and continued. "In that swirling liquid fire an enormous face appeared, the face of that boy—that hideous, harmless boy—from the post office. When he saw me he laughed maniacally, the laughter rolling like thunder till my body trembled with it. Vines sprouted from his teeth and its tendrils reached out and lifted me up, up, into the branches of a large basswood tree— *the* basswood in front of my childhood home in Minnesota. Looking down, I saw my friends playing—I mean I *really* saw them, Sara Jensdatter and Carl Swan, Mary Beth Larsen and that fellow, something Ditmeyer—Peter! Peter Ditmeyer!—flesh and blood they were, right there in front of me! I climbed down to join them, but they ran off behind the house. When I followed, the whole house began to flutter, like a flag, and I realized it wasn't a house at all but a massive curtain. I reached for its edge, and just then felt a weight on my shoulder—barely there, just the slightest pressure. It was a moth, an enormous hawkmoth—*Manduca sexta*, lovely creature, brown and pale yellow—but rather frightening at that size. It startled me by speaking in a deep, sonorous voice.

121

'Don't pull back the curtain if you still want to believe in the Wizard.' Then it cackled, rather rudely, and fluttered off.

"I stood there with my hand on the hem of that huge curtain wondering what it meant to believe in the Wizard, and what it would mean not to. But I wanted to see my friends! So I pulled it back, and there before me were all the people from my life—not like a dream or a hallucination—*as real as you or me!* And yet so strange... Mother and Father stood with a pitchfork between them, and as I looked horns sprouted from their heads, flickering tails whisked out behind them, and I saw that Father was fondling Mother's buttocks with his free hand. I've never seen them so much as kiss, so you can imagine—and then I saw my teachers, all of them from first grade on, right there in front of me, cavorting with each other in the most obscene way! As I watched, their faces changed: they became my colleagues at school, the principal and all the faculty, carrying on in a way I won't describe to you, Josephine, but most indecent.

"I backed away until I bumped into something, and it was an altar, and on it was the boy from the post office, there with a priest dancing the samba, surrounded by naked little cherubs like you see in a painting, only they had the faces of my students. The priest and the boy were calling for me to dance with them—there in front of my parents and my colleagues and my naked students! I turned to run but I was in a church, so I staggered to the end of the pew and began to creep away down the aisle. I saw my parents a few rows behind me, weeping for the grandchildren I hadn't given them. I averted my eyes but somebody pulled me into the confessional, and the priest asked for my sins.

"It was all so real, Josephine—the confessional with its screen, the priest there demanding my sins—so I confessed that I coveted the samba, that I'd wanted to dance it there on the altar with him and the postal boy. He told me to say a thousand Hail Marys and ten thousand Our Fathers. I got on my knees and began, but the words that came out were the words of the letters, the letters from the blackmailers—'Your principal might be interested to know'—and the words took shape as

122

they came out of my mouth, the letters forming a chain that snaked through the pews and flowed over the altar and began to wrap around the giddy postal boy and the priest. I tried the Our Father instead, but the words kept coming out of my mouth all wrong, slithering till they had them in a tangle, and the priest called for help. The cherubs tried but couldn't free them—the words were choking them like a snake. Then postal boy began to laugh his maniacal laugh again, so loud and so wild that his body shook, and the words shook loose of him, just fell to the ground, and he was free! And then I heard you calling my name, Josephine, and I remembered the curtain, the curtain that was a house, and I turned to run back through it to the other side, but it was solid as a brick wall. I crashed against it and fell flat on my back, and as I fell I remembered the moth and heard him cackle again, his mocking voice, and that bit about the Wizard... And then I was lying here, and I felt you near, and I was in bed, back home, with you."

He sighed heavily and opened his eyes. "So, here I am. Must make a note of that: eight seeds not sufficient to kill a man of a hundred and eighty pounds." He tsked a bit, gently withdrew his hand from mine, and slowly sat up. I reached out to help him as he turned and put his feet on the carpet. He stood up, swayed a moment, then regained his balance and turned to me. "Tea, Josephine? My mouth is quite dry. I think we need a good hot cuppa."

Later Mr. Dodson led me to a spare bedroom. "Not very cheerful, I'm afraid, but I'd feel so much better if you spent the night."

I slept around the clock, and when I appeared the next morning he was on his knees in the garden, muttering under the Datura, apparently none the worse for wear. He peered at me intently, then announced, "Josephine, m'dear, I'm going to ask Miss Portman, the school nurse, to come over tomorrow and take a look at you. I'm worried about that cut near your eye. It seems more angry around the edges since you arrived." Then he beamed at me from under his broad-brimmed hat. "Toast and a soft-boiled egg under the plum tree?" There he had little trouble

123

persuading me to spend the week. My ribs still bellowed whenever I took a deep breath, and if I tried interviewing Jimmy's clients the bandages would surely scare them off.

We played scrabble that evening and began to develop an awkward intimacy. As he handed me tea, he called me "Joe" rather than "Josephine." Later he stumbled as he said "Josephi—" He sighed. "I'm sorry, m'dear, I had the best of intentions."

"Thank you for trying."

"Hardly, m'dear, it's what I should have called you to begin with."

"You know, Mr. Dodson, Jimmy always calls me 'Josie.' I wonder if you might try that instead. It would be comforting. Familiar." He glowed, and I was Josie thereafter.

When I woke up Monday he was gone. I browsed his books and napped until he returned. With him was a woman in white with short hair and the manners of a drill sergeant. Miss Portman examined me disapprovingly. "*All* of your cuts should be bandaged, and your bandages *must* be changed daily to allow the wounds to weep," she barked. I nodded. The dull aches flared as she washed and dressed them. She demanded I take deep breaths despite the pain. "Ten, on the hour, throughout the day, or you'll develop pneumonia," she warned.

By the end of the week I was ready to return to the City. The bandages were reduced to two, leaving me presentable. The pain in my ribs when I took a deep breath was bearable. And Jimmy's disappearance was three weeks colder.

chapter seven

The mangy dog perked up soon as he saw me. I thought it was time to stop thinking of him that way, so I asked the grizzled man for his name. Then Grimace and I spent a couple hours tromping around Buena Vista Park, searching for the stump I'd dropped Jimmy's gun into. Looking for something that may not be there is harder than looking for something that you know for sure is. Fortunately, no one had found the gun and kept it for their own. I brushed off some dirt, watched a spider crawl out, and slid it into my pocket.

"May I ask what this is pertaining to?"

"My brother, Jimmy, was working on a personal matter for you before his disappearance."

"Hm. Yes. Well. I will meet you"—his voice dropped to a murmur—"at the Arboretum in Golden Gate Park. There is a bench in the redwoods section. Tomorrow morning, ten o'clock."

Raul García knew his benches. It was far from the main path and backed by a dense thicket; our only eavesdroppers would be four-legged or avian. The cracked ribs still limited my pace to a stroll, so I'd left extra time and arrived early. The air was cool in the shade of the redwoods. He arrived with a briefcase in one hand, *The Examiner* in the other, a robust man in his late fifties sporting upswept eyebrows, an understated silk tie, and cufflinks. He settled at the far end of the bench before saying, "Good day."

"Thank you for meeting."

"Please understand that if we encounter a passerby, I will focus on my newspaper." He was studying my face, my bandage, my attire, as he spoke.

"Of course."

"The question necessarily arises whether I should trust you. You could be aligned with the blackmailers. You could *be* the blackmailer. I wondered as much about your brother when he ceased returning my calls." He looked at the sprays of fern across the path, then continued, courteously, "But I find it unlikely that a blackmailer would make himself as vulnerable as you have, dressing as you do, and..." he trailed off, gesturing vaguely toward my bandages. "At the same time..." He stroked an eyebrow. "Enough: I will, for the time being, trust you. If you're involved in the sending of the letters, you already know about them. The first envelope arrived at my office in early June, marked 'personal and confidential.' Just a photograph of myself in a car with another man. Not a compromising photograph, but the intent was immediately clear. The next letter, three weeks later, indicated that my employer as well as my wife would find certain information to be of interest. It made no demands." He spoke calmly, but his face paled as he continued. "The third letter arrived at my home. That shook me, deeply. It included a considerably more compromising photograph, and a demand for five hundred dollars."

He gazed up at the towering trees, shot through with shafts of dusty light, and smiled slightly. "This is rather like confession. While it's a glorious cathedral, please don't take offense if I say you make a rather inadequate priest." His eyes swept the glen, then he lowered his voice and continued. "They are no doubt aware that I am conservator of the Art of the Americas Collection here. The museum world is small. To be terminated for such reasons... But more disastrous is the threat to my family. It's not my wife who concerns me most; Anna grew up in Mexico, where it's understood that a virile man may, on occasion, use another man for gratification. But my children were raised here, grew up with these American notions—that such men are psychologically disturbed, that we have an unnatural interest in children." He retrieved a handkerchief from his pocket to blot beads of sweat from his forehead. "My grandchildren are the light of my life. Should my children learn of this... At Sunday dinner my son-in-law was speaking with admiration of that Senator McCarthy and his so-called Pervert Inquiry. These American ideas are pernicious. Losing my family would..." He fell silent, gazing into his clasped hands. After some time, he roused himself. "I haven't paid them. I'd gladly give that amount to have this problem disappear, were I to believe the matter would end there. But payment implies culpability, and the stakes only rise."

"Do you know where the pictures were taken?"

"Outside a bar in the Mission District. I rarely visit bars and I'm exceedingly careful when I do: I don't use my real name, and I strike up acquaintance only with men of character. Cultivated types, with an interest in the arts. I've had several friends over the years, gentlemen with whom I shared a great deal, intellectually as well as otherwise. We've always been superbly circumspect. I prefer men who, like me, have a great deal to lose: families, careers. We balance each other, respect each other's lives. We have too much to—"

I heard footsteps, and Mr. García's newspaper snapped to attention. The footsteps neared, then receded. We listened to the birds scold one another. After a time the newspaper descended.

"The bar you'd been to when the photograph was taken: did you enter through an office, ostensibly a delivery business?"

"Yes. The bar itself is quite sumptuous. Those who go there have money to spend."

I nodded. "And few of them visit the bars regularly, so they're unlikely to talk about the blackmail with other patrons. Others being blackmailed have visited that bar."

"Have you found other patterns?"

"He or she is patient. Enjoys the tease, or knows he can get more from people who've lain awake night after night worrying. He has the resources to get to know his victims, and he isn't doing this to turn a quick buck. He views blackmail as a business."

Mr. García's upper lip curled in distaste. "I see your point, ugly as it is." He looked at his watch and rose. "I must return to work. I trust you will keep me apprised of your progress."

I hadn't finished thanking him when the redwoods engulfed him.

Judd Nestle agreed to meet at a record shop on Powell Street. "Look for Adonis," he said cavalierly. "That's my professional name. You'll know me when you see me."

He was right. He had the vast forehead, thick neck, massive chest, and tapering waist of a Greek statue. The clerk and other customers glanced surreptitiously in his direction. He was clearly accustomed to the attention and sauntered around at ease. His skin glowed like it was lit from underneath. Only when I was next to him did I see the fine dusting of bronze powder.

"Judd Nestle," he announced, jolting my ribs as we shook hands. He pulled an album from a case and motioned to the clerk, who took us to a glass booth at the back of the store. Adonis settled himself on the bench as Johnnie Ray began to croon, "If your sweetheart sends a letter of goodbye..." He looked me over and concluded, "You're pretty young, kid."

"Not as young as I look."

"What happened to you?"

"Run-in with a roughneck."

"What happened to your brother?"

"I don't know. I think it may be related to the blackmail."

"Whaddya know about the blackmailer?"

"He's not in a hurry. He gets to know his victims. And he's got a sadistic streak."

"In other words, not much. You sure you're bright enough for this, kid?"

"I only just got started."

"What kinda qualifications you got to be a private dick?"

"I got a missing brother."

"What angles you working?"

"Trying to figure out where the blackmailer locates his victims."

"Any candidates?"

"He'd choose a bar with well-heeled clients. You ever been to the Dollar Bill?"

"Never heard of it."

"How about the Black Cat?"

"Nah. They got a lot of fruits there."

"What bars do you go to?"

"The St. Francis was my mainstay, till they started handing out those cards. Now I go to the Top of the Mark."

"The blackmailer sent you pictures?"

"Yeah. Me and another guy in a car. We weren't tuning the radio, if you get my meaning."

"Were you coming from a bar?"

"Dolan's Supper Club."

"Tell me about the letters."

"First one arrived two months ago. 'The Public might be interested to know.' Creepy. I'm a model, see? Been on the cover of *Grecian Guild*, *Olympians*, *Vim...*"

"*Vim?*"

"Yeah, *Vim*. Like vim and vigor. These magazines, they cater to a particular audience, if you get my drift. Only they can't say so, otherwise they get shut down. They gotta be all squeaky-clean. Bob's real particular about who he photographs. They turn that picture over to the police, my career's history."

"Did you pay them?"

"Sure I paid 'em. Five hundred dollars. That's a lot of dough. Now they want more."

"You got the picture or the letters?"

"I burned 'em. Creepy, like I said. What are you gonna do if you find the guy? You gonna go to the police?"

"That depends," I equivocated.

"You'd need someone to go with you. Someone willing to say they were being blackmailed. Not me. Police knowing is worse than blackmailers knowing. You got anyone willing to go to the coppers?"

"Not yet."

"Sounds like you're all dead ends, kid."

Him saying that, me missing Jimmy, Johnnie Ray singing over and over "Give Me Time": my head was going to burst.

"You don't look so good, kid."

"I don't feel so good either. Think I'll head out."

"Keep in touch, kid."

I pulled the door shut clumsily, and the large window, meant to contain sound, trembled alarmingly.

I walked, for hours, remembering to breathe deeply. By the time I neared Jimmy's hotel the streets were barren, but a large figure lumbered around the corner, heading my way. His coat bulged with layers, and several scarves fluttered at his neck. The rope belted tightly around his waist gave him that look of an overstuffed package. As we passed, his arm looped mine, and his greater weight swung me around.

"Hey!" I shouted, in a burst of pain, trying to disentangle myself. Muffled laughter, high-pitched, somewhere between giddy and maniacal. The laughter continued as he grabbed me by the shoulders, shook me, and brought his face close to mine. Reeling from the shock to my ribs, the stench of liquor and delirium hit me full in the face, and for a moment the edges of my vision grew dark.

"The Queen has spoken!" he shouted, then threw his head back and bellowed to the sky, "Dum-da-da-daaa!"

With his hands firmly clenching my shoulders, I decided to play along. "The Queen has spoken," I roared, matching his abandon.

His eyes were wild, incredulous, outraged. "She speaks to you as well?" he demanded.

"No, never," I whispered conspiratorially. "I await your word. What has she proclaimed?"

Confusion clouded his face for moment, then he leaned in and whispered, "It's a secret proclamation."

"Aaaah," I replied, nodding wisely. "For your ears only."

He looked at me with pity and agreed. Then his features clouded with a terrible bewilderment. He closed his eyes and steadied himself on my shoulder. When he opened them his face was suddenly eager. "She says I can share one secret!"

Mock enchantment lit my face.

"The secret is..." he whispered hoarsely, rough skin scraping my cheek. "The secret is... There's a dragon!" He reared back to peer at my face in delight. "I've been chasing the dragon!"

"A dragon?" I asked with exaggerated surprise. "And is there a damsel in distress?"

Astonishment lit his face. "A damsel, yes, a damsel in distress!" His voice broke in a shrieking, anguished laugh, his body convulsed by it, releasing me. He nearly toppled, reached to steady himself against a wall, missed, and fell heavily to the ground. I heard a crack as fabric gave way, but his lumbering body rolled with the fall and the laughter continued, more mirth in it now.

He splayed his legs out, and his arms, and looked up at the sky. I leaned into his field of vision and asked with a flourish, "And you, my lord, are you the knight in shining armor?"

The lunatic laughter stopped abruptly. He turned from the sky to me and snarled, "Knight in shining armor?" A sudden, jarring lucidity shone in his eyes as he carped raggedly, "No such thing as a knight in shining armor!" He rolled back and forth, jeering. "Knights on white horses?" Sarcasm bloated the words. Then he fluttered his arm and muttered, "Away with ye."

Mr. Wilkinson beckoned the next evening. A friendly message from Jack Chantry inviting me to pay a visit. I'd been putting off my return to the Dollar Bill, not sure how to play it. I knew Chantry could be the blackmailer. I knew it could be one of the bartenders, or any of the patrons. When I pushed my way past the heavy velvet curtain, everything seemed staged, everyone suspicious, play-acting for my benefit. The arm appeared. He didn't pilot me this time, just accompanied me to the office. Chantry greeted me genially, gesturing toward the chair.

"Turns out, one of my bartenders knows Jimmy well." Chantry glanced over at the arm, which returned a minute later with a man sporting a white jacket and a black bow tie. Chantry introduced him as Frank Sedge, then excused himself.

Frank smiled warmly at me, his eyes beaming gently under bushy brows.

"I can see the family resemblance," he said, nodding as he studied my face. He didn't ask about the bandage. "Jimmy spoke of you often." Then his face grew grave. "I'm sorry to hear he's missing. How long has he been gone?"

"A little over two months."

"Then I saw him just before he disappeared, around the fifteenth of June. We'd been friends for, oh, about six months. We didn't meet here of course—he's very discreet. It was at a haberdashery on the Miracle Mile—Tyrone's, I think. We struck up a conversation, both dropping hairpins. He asked if I was a friend of Dorothy's, and I said she was practically a sister to me. But he was...not at his best, as you probably know. He was deeply shaken by Bobby's death."

"Did he say which cops were involved?"

Frank shook his head sadly. "He told me that's how it happened, of course, but he didn't give names."

"Did he mention the fight he was in?"

"Yes, it got him kicked off the force."

"Who did he fight with?"

"I'm sorry, Joe, he wouldn't tell me how it came about."

"He did say he was kicked off the force, though—that he stopped working for the police?"

"Yes, certainly. Was there any question?"

"Well, there's been some... Some people say he turned coat. Went undercover for the cops. Then was transferred to Bay City."

Frank looked troubled. "If that's what happened, he didn't tell me about it. But then he wouldn't—I'm a bartender here. If he's down south though, why wouldn't he get in touch with you?" Shaking his head, he continued, "Those people, the ones who say he went undercover. Are they connected to the bars—the Black Cat and that other one, Pandora's Box?"

"Yes."

"Jimmy was...concerned about them, Joe. Said they'd all turned on him. He was afraid that they were after him. They're very protective of their taverns and their little circles."

"You think *they* made Jimmy disappear?"

"I know for sure he was worried about them. He has valuable information he could provide to the police, knowing their world from the inside. Some of those bar people are real thugs. When I heard he'd disappeared, that conversation was the first thing that came to mind."

My mind was reeling from the thought of Lily, Madge, José, Aaron— threatening Jimmy. And yet it made sense: I'd seen their animosity. I'd been blind not to consider it. What else was I blind to? Maybe Judd was right: maybe I wasn't bright enough for this.

Frank's words brought me back. "I wish I could tell you more, Joe. That's all I know. Sorry not to be of more help."

He walked me out to the bar. I nodded my thanks to Chantry and left, hurrying from the alley to a better-lit thoroughfare. I stepped under a streetlamp, took off Jimmy's fedora, flipped it over, turned till I found the label. TYRONE'S HOUSE OF BETTER HATS. The ground slipped out from under me. My mind grasped for other explanations. The blackmailer would have wanted Jimmy's files as much as I did. He could have searched Jimmy's room, noted the label on his hat. Frank could be another made-up friend, working for the blackmailer or the cops—or both. But I couldn't be sure.

I was in Jimmy's office again, with the jangled blinds and the emptiness, but this time instead of a typewriter there was a table fan. An old one, with brass blades like enormous petals, tarnished in the center but shiny along the edges. I recognized the stiff wooden chair I was in as Chantry's chair, and that's when I realized my ankles were tied to its legs, my torso bound to its back with heavy rope, thick and coarse like you'd find on a ship: the kind of rope you toss from the boat to the shore so you don't float out to sea. My left arm was caught under it, pinned to my side, but my right arm wasn't. I wondered how hard it would be to untie the knots with just one hand, but before I had a chance to find out three men entered the room, all in sleek suits, luxe ties, and shoes that didn't so much creak as sigh when they walked toward me. Their masks conformed closely to their faces, so I could see their features, but it wasn't the face I was seeing, just the smiling mask. Then I heard a click and couldn't see their suits or their ties or their masks, couldn't see anything at all because of the blinding light.

They told me to tell them everything. When I said I didn't know anything they said quit stalling and start squawking. I insisted. They said if I was going to play it that way they knew how they'd play it, and the way they said it made my blood run cold. One of them laughed, a sound with no humor in it at all, and I heard the whirr and felt the breeze of the fan, felt it against my face, there and gone, there and gone. Someone must have turned off the oscillator because then the breeze came steady. And I felt a hand grasp my right wrist.

It took forever for the news to travel from my hand to my brain, but when it did I knew what the fan was for. Another hand joined it so there were two hands moving my fingers toward that whirring sound, and my hand with the wind on it felt like it did when I was a kid in the car with the window down, riding the currents of the air: I'd tilt my hand down just a little and it would dive like a bird, then lift and swoop, and I'd wondered how birds felt soaring through all that space, that boundless unyielding freedom. But I wasn't in the car, I was in Jimmy's office tied to Chantry's chair, my arm gripped by two hands moving my fingers closer to the whirring blades. Feeling the blast of air against them, I suddenly knew why the edges of the blades were shiny while the flats were tarnished: someone had taken a file to them, honed them the way Father took a whetstone to the axe, and with a sudden ocean of pain consuming me, I woke.

I was in Jimmy's room, the sun streaming in on me. My right hand was clenched and aching and my body was covered in sweat. I found some aspirin behind the bathroom mirror, but my hand ached all through that day and into the next.

This time she wore satin. Fitted on top but flared at the waist, a sea of robin's-egg blue that, in the murk of the bar, glowed like neon. She strode across the gleaming wood in slingback pumps and a top hat with a thick band of the same searing blue. "This one's for my friend Yukiko, who spent three years in Manzanar," she announced, before launching into "Don't Fence Me In." She sang it slow, drawing out the melancholy like saltwater taffy, but in place of the barnyard twang of Roy Rogers she brought dark sardonic wit. When she was done she hopped off the bar and started slinging beers. I elbowed my way to her.

"Lily, I need to talk to you." I lowered my voice. "I know what they're saying about my brother and it's not true. I'm going to prove it."

She scowled. Then her gaze eased and she studied my face. I was beginning to feel like the *Encyclopedia Britannica*; everyone was looking up Jimmy. But she turned away. "I've got nothing to say."

"I do. Please?"

She adjusted the left shoulder of her dress, lining it up with the strap of her brassiere. She scrubbed a spot on the bar. She emptied a couple of ashtrays, banging them loudly in the trash, a look of faint disgust on her face. Without changing the look she said, "I've got a break coming in forty minutes. Meet me out back."

This time we didn't get cozy. She stood in the middle of the alley, feet apart, smoking. Despite the satin I imagined that a Mack truck trying to knock her down would drive off with a battered grill.

"What happened to you?" she asked.

"I got beat up. I'm better." She was silent. "Please, Lily, my brother isn't a rat." She said she'd heard the story from Aaron, so I told her more recent news. "Jimmy was investigating a blackmail ring. I watched a drop to see who came for the money, and got picked up by two cops sweeping the area. Whatever happened to Jimmy involves the police somehow, but not in the way you think. They're trying to cover up something, I'm sure of it. I need your help. You know who he spent time with. Please, ask them to talk to me."

"How do you explain the fact that Jimmy was there when bars got raided but his ass never landed in jail?"

"I don't know. But if he was working for the cops they wouldn't have blown his cover that way. They'd have hauled him in too, just for show."

"Not if they were getting ready to transfer him down south." She took a long drag on her cigarette, blew out smoke, looked me in the eye, and spoke in a torrent.

"I wouldn't say there's much reward to being in the life. But you do have a chance to find out what you're made of. When you realize your longings are contrary to everything around you—every movie, every song, every story you've been told—when you realize you don't fit into that happily-ever-after life the world's been telling you is your reason for living, you have a chance to become real. Those rules you learned, all that morality and etiquette, you realize that was just training wheels. Now you've got to figure out what's right and what's wrong for yourself. Every knot you get tangled up in, every thorny situation where you need to cover for a friend even if it costs you—each of those decisions you make stacks up, one on top of another, and eventually you turn around and find you've grown a backbone: *you know who you are*. You know what you believe in. And you're living your life rather than letting it live *you*." She threw the butt of her cigarette down and ground it out with her shoe. "There are plenty of us who never get there because they spend all their time hiding it. Some are delighted to discover a lower rung in the social order: instead of staring up at the 'normals,' figuring out how to blend in, they amuse themselves disdaining those who can't—or wouldn't even if they could. So some of us get it overtime. If we're smart we start to see how it all works. Who's on the front lines catching the brunt of it, who gets to stay further back, cushioned. Who crosses over and aids the enemy while covering their own ass. The higher up the ladder they are and the more they can blend in, the bigger their reward for crossing over."

She whipped off the top hat and ran her hand through her hair, agitated. Then she bent down and started picking up butts, hurling them into a trash can. In the silence I heard a rat squeak and rustle inside the hollow metal bin. She heard it too, and laughed mordantly. When she spoke again her face was in shadow and her voice taut, grim. "As far as I can see, that's the one reward we're offered. Some of us get it. Some of us don't. It all depends on whether or not we grow that backbone. Your brother Jimmy may have been on the way to one, but that spine of his got twisted."

She turned back to me. She exhaled sharply, shook her head, and put her hat back on. "Okay. You're young. You need to find out what happened to your brother. Maybe finding out will help you grow a backbone of your own. I know someone who can tell you what was happening with him, before, when Bobby was murdered by the cops. All of us pulled away from him later, so nobody'll be able to tell you about that—except maybe his copper friends." She slapped her hands

together and dusted flecks off her satin bodice. "The name's Pearl. Black Pearl. She'll talk to you. Come back in a coupla days." She looked up to the orange-rimmed sky for a moment, then headed into the building. Stopping suddenly, she turned.

"I didn't know your brother well. He was a cherished friend of cherished friends of mine. I didn't want to believe it about him. But it wasn't just me I had to consider: it was everyone who comes into this bar. I hope for your sake that you prove me wrong." She paused, then added, "But I'm not bettin' on it." Just before she spun and disappeared into the gloom, the dim light caught shine at the outer corner of her eye.

I saw that robin's-egg-blue satin dress one more time. Only it wasn't blue at all. It was black and white: tiny little dots of black and white. Lily's crumpled body was sprawled across page three of the *San Francisco Chronicle*. One of her slingback pumps lay just to the side of her shoulder, the heel dangling off. The angle of her left leg was terrible. The headline screamed, "Lady Tavern Owner Dead."

chapter eight

The day of the funeral was obscenely beautiful, the light indifferent to grief. Lily's mother and her aunt, a sturdy butch named
Marie, moved with aching slowness through the crowd, shock and
grief freshly etched on their faces. Tiny was deep in conversation with
a graceful Oriental man, his long, lithe body bent to hear what she was
saying. I saw many faces I recognized from the bar. Two or three in
the crowd were drunk in their grief, and when they became tragically
boisterous Madge nodded and they were hustled off to a car. Aaron
avoided my eyes. Only a few outliers hovered, like me, on the margins.
An imperious middle-aged matron in dark glasses and dahlia-trimmed
hat, two men dressed like undercover cops collecting dirty looks, a
fey man who startled like a fish when anyone drew near, and me in
my second-best suit. Everyone else knew one another. Everyone spoke
about how brave she was, and how beautiful. Everyone said that the
world wasn't yet ready for her kind of beauty and her kind of courage.
I wondered if it ever would be.

We got in cars and drove a long way to where she was to be buried. It was one of the cemeteries I'd seen in the distance in that godforsaken land of empty cul-de-sacs. The casket was lowered into the ground, and chunks of soil made hollow thuds as Lily's mother wailed amid a murmur of compassion like doves roosting.

When I arrived at Pandora's, Lily's mother and aunt were there, seated with Madge and a tall, elegant Negro woman. José, in a dark suit and somber tie, stood like a priest with one hand raised, the other over his heart. His face had the gaping look of a car that's lost its headlights. "We gather in deepest sorrow, sharing the grief of Lily's mother and Aunt at the tragic loss of their beloved daughter and niece, our cherished friend. Lily was loved and respected by so many. I invite you to tell the story of how she touched your life."

The long silence was interrupted by a chair scraping loudly as a stocky old butch with weathered cheeks rose. She swayed a moment, till someone reached out a hand to steady her. She cleared her throat.

"I'm not one for talking, those of you know me know that, but I have to speak about Lily because of what she done for me. I been in this life many years and most of them were lonely. I went home every night after work and sat on the couch, or went out and sat alone on a barstool. But then one night I came into this place, expecting the night to be like all the other nights, except that it wasn't. Lily announced that it was story night and everyone had to play. It was a silly game: we passed around a sheet of paper and each person as they got it added a word. The paper went all the way around, each one reading the words others had written and writing in one more. After the piece of paper passed you couldn't help but talk to the person on your left because they had written the word before yours and you wondered what they were thinking of when they wrote it. Then the person on your right jumped in because they were wondering why you wrote your word. And pretty soon you were talking with them both, and then when the paper went around a few times Lily took it and hopped up on the bar, right there"—she pointed—"between Gladys and Flo, and she read the whole story to us, acting it out as she read. We all listened and laughed at the funny thing we'd written, and I listened for my words and Lily read them with the rest of the words and I heard how it became a story we'd written together. When she was done we clapped and had to talk more with each other about the story, and pretty soon everyone was talking with everyone and even I was talking with this person and that person and..."

Here she broke down, the big old butch, her voice faltering, but she persevered. "I'm sorry, I never talked to so many people at once, especially never when I was so sad, but I have to finish this so you know what Lily done for me." She turned and put her hand tenderly on the shoulder of a diminutive femme with tears forming rivers in the wrinkles below her eyes. "Lily brung so many new people into my life, and she brung Evelyn into my life, and Evelyn has just been everything to me. Now when I go home at the end of a lonely day at work, I go home to Evelyn, or we come here to see friends, and instead of sitting lonely we talk to each other. That is what Lily done for me, and I didn't say it well enough, but I hope you got a little picture of what it means, and I'm so sorry for Lily's mama and for her aunt, and for all of us that lost her." She sat and took Evelyn's hand and looked around, dazed, and everyone in the bar nodded their heads as tears streamed down their faces.

A middle-aged man with a three-inch pompadour stood. "I just want to say that Miss Lily welcomed everyone in her door. There wasn't anyone too this or too that, too old or too down at the heel, too swish or too ugly, that she wouldn't welcome you in her door. Some of these bars, if your wrist is limp or your tie splashy, why, they'll be serving you warm beer and making sure none of the regulars talks to you, so you won't want to come back again. They're all high-toned about it and say they do it in the interest of 'the community,' but all I know is their community never provided me with shelter from the storm. Miss Lily and Miss Madge were never ones to say 'this one is in and this one is out.' Everyone is welcome in their door. And I am so torn up that she's gone."

The tributes went on for hours. At the end of the evening José led the crowd in a tear-stained rendition of "God Save Us Nelly Queens." This time I sang too, my voice merging with the ragged cacophony of grief.

The next day an outsized, weighty envelope arrived. Jimmy's dental records. I held the X-rays up to the light and saw ghosts of his jawbone. For a moment I had the horrifying sensation I was looking at Jimmy's skeleton. Then I realized I was.

After I took the packet to Lucille's, I headed west. San Francisco spills toward the ocean in a rush of pastel stucco houses, each fronted by a miniscule lawn and bushes pruned so severely they bear a closer resemblance to poodles than shrubbery. I turned south and drove along a ribbon of road perched high above the sea. The houses continued undaunted by the steeply rolling hills, the sudden plunges to eternity.

I drove till I found a spit of land jutting out into the water. Then I parked, walked out onto the spit, and sat. The waves crashed around me, the gulls screeched above me, the spray washed over me, and I found comfort in feeling my utter desolation mirrored in the world.

Mother and Father took us to the county fair one evening when I was five. I wanted to wear the cowboy outfit I'd gotten from Jimmy, but Mother insisted I put on a yellow dress with a fluffy organza overlay. I felt like Roy Rogers and looked like Tinker Bell.

They gave Jimmy a pocketful of change and we wandered through the carnival dazzled by the lights and the sounds. He let me carry the thin paper cone of cotton candy as we picked at its sticky threads. When he won at the arcade he let me choose the prize: a set of tin spurs that attached to his boots and jingled as he walked. Then he rode the teacups with me, no doubt a mortifying prospect for a twelve-year-old. I held his hand tight as we whirled round and round, the plunky music in our ears. He sat me between his knees in the bumper cars. Then we got on line for the climax of the evening: looming above the fair was an enormous Ferris wheel, radiant with glittering lights. I couldn't wait to feel myself lifted and swaying high above the world. When we got to the front of the line and the wheel stopped for us to board, I saw our car: bright blue with red swirls and a yellow seat. I ran toward it—into the arm of the pimply-faced man in charge of boarding. He pointed to a sign and shook his head. I was too short for the ride—I might slip out from under the chain that held riders in place. I told him I'd hold on tight! I told him Jimmy would hold me tight! He shook his head and gestured for the people behind us to get in our blue car with the red swirls.

I was devastated. I wanted to see the people below us become tiny as ants, to be up there twinkling with the stars. Jimmy tried to hug me, but I was inconsolable. I sobbed as the wheel turned and other people got seated for their ride to the glittering lights. I wanted to forget there'd ever been a carnival, ever been a Ferris wheel. I kicked the pimply-faced man in the shin and ran.

Jimmy was just behind me as I reached the parking lot, a dusty field bordered by woods. I sat in the weeds, glad that my stupid dress would get dirty, not caring that I'd be punished. I cried as only a five-year-old does, for everything wrong with the world: rides that keep little kids out, parents who don't understand that a cowboy wouldn't ever go to the fair in a fluffy yellow dress. As my tears wound down, I noticed Jimmy doing something with the hem of my dress, then darting off into the darkness at the edge of the woods. When I looked up, the lights from the carnival reflected off the parked cars and renewed my heartbreak. Sobbing again, I was only dimly aware of Jimmy running to the woods and back, over and over. Finally he peeled my hands from my face and said to me, "Josie, stand up."

"I don't wanna."

"Josie, I have a surprise for you!" I wasn't ready to relinquish my misery, but his face was shining with anticipation.

"Where is it, in the woods?" I asked.

"No, it's right here. Just stand up." I shook my head, but a glimmering green light caught my eye and then disappeared. Another light sparkled, right there in my lap, then vanished. Mystified, I stood up. My skirt, as it flared out around me, was full of light—lights that winked at me for a few seconds, only to be replaced by another and another. I turned slowly, and the lights turned with me, a cascade of glittering radiance.

I lifted my tear-stained face to Jimmy. He smiled. "Lightning bugs. I put lightning bugs under that top layer of your skirt." They blinked, on and off, better than any Ferris wheel, my own magic carnival of lights.

The next evening, another crooked finger from Mr. Wilkinson. A message from Lucille.

You could say I knew from the moment she opened the door. But then how far back do we have to go? To my birthday, when I stayed up for hours waiting for his call, then finally calculated the hour on the West Coast and realized that California, too, was on to a whole new day: he had missed the day I entered the world, the day, he'd told me, he first saw my bald head and wrinkled skin and felt the world was whole. I knew then that something irrevocable had happened. Maybe if it had turned out differently, maybe I wouldn't be looking back at that moment and seeing myself so certain. But when Lucille told me the dental records matched, it felt more like she was confirming a horror I already knew than giving me the worst news of my life.

Oh, I tried to find my way past what she was telling me. I asked her whether it wasn't possible that some other brother of some other sister happened to have the same cavities in the same teeth, the same slight overbite that made him look always a little eager. Lucille was kind. She nodded gently and her lips moved, saying, "Certainly that's possible," but her eyes kept saying, *I'm sorry, I'm so sorry he's gone.* And after a few minutes of that, of denying what I already knew, I toppled over on her velvet couch and howled. I howled for everything I'd lost. The floor that supported me wherever I walked. The walls that assured me I had a place in the world. The windows that affirmed my vision was true. The mirror that confirmed that what I was, was meant to be.

I don't remember Lucille coming to sit with me. I only recall, as I drifted in the abyss of loss, that she was there rocking with me, holding tight to me as I held to her. She murmured wordlessly, offering comfort with her sounds as I was bellowing grief with mine. I cried till I was exhausted. She insisted I spend the night there on that couch. When I woke up, the world around me was changed completely, the light a different color than I'd ever seen. It took a few moments to recall where I was, but I already knew, I woke with the dread knowledge, that Jimmy was gone.

Lucille was utterly kind. She sat with me. She fixed me eggs with Cheddar cheese and good strong coffee. She'd taken the morning off, and she said I could stay as long as I wanted, even after she left. But by the time the sun was high above the windows I knew I needed to find my place in a world without Jimmy. I went, briefly, to his room; lived through the harrowing knowledge that it was now my room. I collected a few things and told Mr. Wilkinson I'd be gone for a couple of days. I overlooked his suggestive smile and picked a road and drove till the pavement ended, kept driving till the gravel ended, walked till the trail ended, and then sat high on a bluff overlooking the ocean. At some point the bluff called to me, but I didn't answer. The steadiness of the surf comforted me. I missed his steadiness, his sure, even ways. I knew I'd have to make that for myself now: lay my own bedrock. Preach my own sermons.

I drove further north, to where I'd heard there were entire forests of those towering redwoods that formed a cathedral above my head when I spoke with Mr. García. I sat and watched the shafts of light move through them, illuminating miniature gardens of fern and sorrel. Saplings encircled vast stumps, forming intimate, sacred circles. I sat, for three days or four, watching, the grief too great to seek, or even remember, the God feeling. It was the solid things that comforted me. I lay for hours in the dense duff under a circle of vaulting trees, staring up to where their branches met above me. The enormousness of the trees reestablished the field of gravity. The soft spring of pine needles underfoot, the dampness, the scent of decay and of growth returned me to the world.

I drove back to San Francisco along the curving coastal road, across the towering burnt-orange bridge, knowing two things. The first: I needed to talk with Aaron. At 5:01 I was outside the post office, watching the good citizens of Albany come and go. He stopped short when he saw me, then started again on his way. I matched my pace to his.

"Aaron, I know you're mourning Lily. But I need your help. Jimmy's dead too. Beaten beyond recognition. The cops tried to cover it up. They're involved." He turned to me, his mouth forming a perfect "o," no sound coming out. Then he nodded, realigned his face, and we fell into step.

We claimed the same booth in the diner, and the waitress poured us coffee. His eyes were cautious, unbelieving.

"A friend of mine works at police headquarters," I began. She's one of us. There was a—" I faltered, then began again. "There was a body found shortly after Jimmy disappeared. The height was recorded wrong by the cop who brought him in, so it wasn't flagged when I filed my missing persons. I ordered Jimmy's dental records from back home. They matched."

His eyes met my sorrow. That brought on tears I thought I could control.

"I'm sorry," he said thickly. Tears were wetting his lashes too. "You know, I thought I knew Jimmy pretty well. Before. That's why it hit so hard when he betrayed us. Not just everyone who goes to the bars, but us, individually: the people who thought of themselves as his friends." He shook his head. "We were all so shocked, so hurt, when he crossed over." He paused, then moderated his conviction for the first time: "If that's what he did."

"I thought his disappearance had to do with the blackmail. Now I'm not so sure. Something was going on with him and the police. Maybe it's what you said, but I don't think so. Why would they kill him if he was working for them, if he was still useful? Why would they cover up his death if they had nothing to do with it? Maybe he knew something. I need to find out." I paused. "I spoke with Lily the night she was murdered. She was going to introduce me to someone who knew Jimmy, someone named Pearl."

Aaron's face grew red with anger. "The cops are saying it was a sexual assault, just a random thing, because Lily was out on the streets late at night, alone. They're saying it had nothing to do with who she was, nothing to do with how she was fighting the coppers. Nobody buys it," he spat.

"I think my friend might be able to help. She can find out what's in the files on Lily's murder."

His forehead almost met mine across the table. He looked me hard in the eye. "Black Pearl was Bobby's best friend. She and Jimmy were tight. She can help you. Pearl was hurt, hurt real bad about Jimmy, who he became. But I'll talk to her. I'll let her know you need to find out, one way or another."

"Do you think it's too soon?"

"It'll always be too soon. You should talk to her." His face broke out in the shadow of a smile, muted, like the setting sun reappearing beneath low clouds. "And you should see one of her shows. The curtain rises and center stage is an enormous glittering pink oyster shell." He moved his hands to show me how huge it was. "It's made of this gorgeous moiré with a shimmer you can see from the back row. On either side are mermaids in pink chiffon, fins bigger than a Bel Air's, swaying to the rhythm of the billowing taffeta waves. The oyster shell opens just slightly, then closes, opens and closes like it's breathing. You keep watching and the music swells and the top slowly lifts and inside is this gorgeous queen dripping with rhinestones and feathers and iridescent black satin, an ebony pearl in the pink shell. She belts out her songs in this huge voice, so gorgeous you're sure she really is a girl."

His smile faded with the vision. "She'll talk to you, I know she will," he concluded soberly.

The second thing I knew: it was time to start carrying Jimmy's gun. That night I hacked two of his sock garters to pieces and made a holster to secure it under my arm. I rolled back the worn carpet and lifted the floorboard. I took out the gun and the clipping about Lily's murder I'd put with Jimmy's files. I studied the grainy photographs. That shoe up by her shoulder was stuck in my mind. There was a second photograph: a close-up of her face covered by someone's handkerchief, its contours evident, the shoe inches away. I stared at it awhile before I realized what that shoe was doing up there. Lily had used it to fight. I smoothed the crinkled newsprint and peered closely. There was a small tuft of something, fuzz or hair or fabric, dangling there on the end of the heel. The photo was too grainy to see any more than that. But that tuft—it belonged to whoever had killed her. There was no way of telling what it was from the photo. But the police would know. If they cared.

Aaron left me a message: I could meet Pearl the next evening at her apartment. It was on Divisadero, not far from Tiny's place. She opened the door in a turquoise and brown kimono and stared at my face for a full thirty seconds. Then she flung her arms wide and folded me in them. "You look like him," she whispered as her cheek pressed against my ear. "He told me all about you. He loved you so much." When she released me and stepped back, our faces were slick with tears.

I recognized her as the woman who'd sat with Lily's mother and Aunt after the funeral. Standing protectively behind her were two men. She introduced Luther first, caressing his dapper shoulder. Tall and slender, his hair crimped in perfect waves, he nodded gravely when she spoke my name. Then Hugo stepped forward to shake my hand. His large bulk filled the doorway, and none of it jiggled when he walked.

They ushered me into an apartment awash in satin, sequins, and lamé, with plumage to rival a flock of flamingos. Pearl had colonized the upper regions of the twelve-foot-high space: a row of stilettos stretched the length of a wall, heels held in place by the picture molding. Just beneath, a narrow shelf held a line of mannequin heads bearing platinum, auburn, and ebony wigs. On the opposite wall a metal rod just below the ceiling curved under the weight of gowns arranged by color from magenta to sable. Underneath this finery resided a small table with a sewing machine. Scraps of fabric and thread littered the floor below like confetti.

Hugo gently guided Pearl, still weeping, to the center of the room, where she curled her graceful six-foot frame into a plush damask loveseat. Luther brought crystal goblets and a bottle of wine.

"First Bobby. Oh, god, then Lily. And now Jimmy!" Pearl rocked back and forth, shaking her head. Hugo knelt beside her, soothing her knee with his hand. "And Jimmy... So estranged. We couldn't understand who he'd become. Now there's no chance for him to explain." I felt my grief rise like water on the verge of boil. "You're Jimmy's brother-sister, I can see that in you. I'll try to help you, honey. Maybe you can help us *all* make sense of it." She pulled a handkerchief from her kimono and blotted her cheeks. Then she slid deeper in the loveseat, resting her head against its curving arm. Hugo settled at her feet, his hand moving gently against her calf.

"It started with Bobby. Dear, sweet Bobby was a brother to me. We'd both run away, him from New Jersey, me from Missouri, neither of us seventeen. We met on the corner of Polk and Bush, and we always kidded about that. We were both getting by in the usual way of runaway kids, and we pledged to be the family each of us had lost. Kept that pledge, too. When the war came we got called up, then they wouldn't take me; took Bobby, but spit him back out after four months, blue discharge. That made it hard for either of us to find work, with people suspicious of any man not doing his part for the war effort. We were lucky: San Francisco was thronged with soldiers, so the bars and nightclubs were booming. Finocchio's was off limits to servicemen, which ensured that every man in uniform paid a visit. They had four shows a night, six nights a week, and we got hired together. They call us 'female illusionists.' In my case it's not an illusion, but that's okay. We'd been working at Finocchio's five years when Bobby met Jimmy and they fell in love. Oh, those two were so tender together, so sweet—they were what all of us hoped for: love that would make the world right, regardless of how wrong it is."

Pearl couldn't speak for a while, so Hugo filled in. "That's how we all got to know Jimmy. He was extra careful, kept his head low, being a cop and all. But Bobby'd bring him here, or to parties, and we all got to be friends."

Pearl resumed, "They adored each other, Bobby and Jimmy. You could *see* the delight in them when the other one appeared. No coyness, no hard-to-get games. There was no hiding how in love they were." Her voice was ragged with grief. "Then Bobby got picked up in a raid. He's like me: couldn't hide his light under any basket. That's why we got along so well: we'd say what we believe and *damn* what anybody thinks," she declared, her voice defiant. Then it fell. "They didn't pull me in that night, so I came here, changed into the man's suit I have for such occasions, and went back to the station to wait. Usually they keep 'em till morning, but I kept asking for him. I was worried, for some reason that night I was so worried, I *knew* something was wrong and I kept asking and asking, and they kept putting me off, till it was getting light outside. Finally..." Her voice broke, and she continued in a hoarse whisper, "Finally they told me, 'His body's been released to the coroner.' That's how I found out. That's how they told me my sweet brother-sister Bobby was gone."

She shuddered. "Internal injuries. They said he fell while he was getting into the paddy wagon. But I was there—I saw him climb into the back of that wagon! He extended his hand, elegant as you please, and waited, just waited, till one of the boys stepped forward and held it so Bobby could climb in with dignity. He was like that when he dressed—wasn't full-time like me, only dressed for performing, but when he was *en femme* he was the perfect lady. Of course, when they got

154

to jail they threw Bobby in with the men—and not the ones he came in with. We don't know if it was them that beat him, or the cops. But even if it wasn't the cops, the guards must have heard him screaming and ignored it—Bobby wouldn't have gone down without a fight.

"I'm the one who told Jimmy. Oh, god, his face when he heard. Something snapped in him. He went...crazy. I tried to calm him, to keep him here, but he was wild, just *crazy* wild. He went to the station to find the guards who were on duty, got in a fist fight with a cop who tried to hold him back, got beat up pretty bad himself, and spent that night in the same jail where Bobby'd died. Oh, god," she moaned, "that must have been hell, just hell." I shuddered with my own memories. "They kicked him off the force the next day. That's when he hit the juice, and hit rock bottom *fast*."

"I've seen a lot of people lose it, but I've never seen anybody drop that fast—like a preacher's daughter out on her own," Luther added.

"He'd always been so steady, such a rock, and suddenly he was so far gone. We tried to help, but he pushed us away. Fought with *everybody*. That went on for a couple weeks, and then suddenly he stopped, quick as he started. But he didn't come back to us." Her voice was wounded, wondering still. "He'd come to the bars every night, but wouldn't hardly speak to us. Every night he'd show up and just...lurk. Real quiet, real tight, real tense, watching. Like one of those air raids during the war, a siren and then sudden silent waiting: every second you think something's gonna happen but it doesn't and the dread just builds and builds. There were several bar raids and we noticed *he never got pulled in*. Disappeared just in time. *Every* time. That's how we figured out he'd crossed over." Grief, rather than anger, suffused the words. "I couldn't believe it at first. Not sure if I ever did, if I do right now. But it was too dangerous not to assume it was true. Especially with it all heating up—the court case, Lily trying to stop the payoffs. See, Jimmy knew it all from the inside. On *both* sides. And there's a mayoral race not far off, you know how politicians like to clean up the town with elections on the horizon. Make a lot of noisy busts, get their picture in the paper shaking hands with the chief of police—no matter how much graft they're taking from him with the other hand, no matter that the money came from *our* pockets. The whole thing was a conflagration just waiting for a match." She paused, exhaled heavily. "And then he disappeared. Just up and disappeared. People said he got moved to Tinseltown, I don't know. I've got friends down there, I asked around, but no one'd seen him."

"Did Jimmy tell you about the fight he was in, with the other cops?"

"No. That's when he pulled away from us."

"Did he have any friends on the force, anyone he was close with?"

"Not far as I know. He kept to himself there. I'm sure there've been other gay cops, but not many. It's dangerous." Pearl smiled mournfully. "Bobby told me Jimmy said he sometimes felt like a 'male illusionist,' impersonating some kind of ultrabutch man, so cold, so tough. Of course, in his case, his cock ratified the performance. But he wasn't actually like that, cold and distant, till after Bobby's murder."

"Was there anyone he spent time with then?"

"No." Pearl straightened suddenly and put her glass down. "When he was at the bars, just lurking, there *was* someone else—we noticed another guy who started coming in at the same time. They didn't sit together, but he was always there when Jimmy was. We guessed they were both undercover. He was built—big, you know, like Hugo."

Hugo nodded, adding, "He looked Italian, dark hair and lots of it."

"We stayed away from him," Pearl continued. "And he disappeared when Jimmy did. But I don't know anything else about him."

"Did Jimmy talk to you about his detective work?"

"No—but remember, he hardly talked to us after Bobby's death." A fresh wave of tears crested. "Oh, I miss them so much. And now Lily... You met Lily, right?"

"Just twice."

She shook her head. "Oh, I wish you'd *really* known her. Lily was a spitfire. I can't believe *anything* could quench that blaze. We did some shows together, her and me—oh, god, they were wild." Luther and Hugo murmured assent. "Being the Black Pearl, my signature entrance involves a huge oyster shell: the top lifts up and there I am inside. But I have this *other* shell, one Lily and I made together. We wanted to do a show for the girls, *just* for the girls, so we built this shell that's turned the other way, opens out like a door. When the curtain rises, all you see are the glorious undulating edges of the shell, flaring out slightly in the middle, all glistening pink and brown." She caressed the words with innuendo. "When it opens, there I am inside, in this fabulous robe, all fluttering dark rose and mauve and brown, edged with sequins cascading from the top of my body to the bottom. On my head is a pink globe, hooded with fabric and lit from inside, so it almost throbs. Above it there's a pouf of curly brown coq feathers. And I stand on a settee in the shape of lovely little rosebud." She watched to make sure I was getting the picture, and laughed as the tears continued to stream down her face. Hugo leaned forward, pulled out his wallet, extracted a photograph, and slid it across the table. There was Pearl in the center of the vulvic oyster shell, smile radiant as the sun.

"When I first unveiled it, my ladyfriends were shocked that I could make something so—so accurate. That's 'cause Lily helped! She pulled off her clothes and spread her legs for me! I couldn't believe how gorgeous it was—I'd always heard they were damp and smelly!" She wrinkled her nose, and then wonder blossomed on her face. "I didn't know they could be so ornate! She showed me the parts, and said we had to have a globe up there, a glowing pink globe. Lily insisted"—Pearl raised her arm and pounded the back of the loveseat—"*No moving forward without that globe!*" Then she added coyly, "The rosebud was my idea. But"— she shook her head sadly—"it was too much, actually. Some of the girls just laughed, but some of them got mad. They said it was vulgar. They said it was crude. I think they were just...shocked at how beautiful it was. Maybe they couldn't see that, you know?"

Pearl hiccupped, then shook her head. "Never was a partner in crime like Lily. She was up for anything. Try to hold her back, you'd just make

her want to do it more. Hah!—you ever tell her she was tall?" I shook my head. "Damn good thing! 'You tall for an Oriental.' *Whoooooooo*, she hated that. Her favorite answer: 'You smart for a white person.'" Hugo and Luther chortled while Pearl roared, her face drenched, her kimono darkening beneath her chin. "Yeah, she got her nose in it. Wouldn't take much." She sobered suddenly, and her voice turned harsh. "Those bastards. She wouldn't pay their goddam hush money. They decided to make an example of her. I know that's what happened!" Her bloodshot eyes looked around the room wildly. "They're never gonna solve the case, because they're in on it. They killed her, or had her killed. Bastards."

"Did she tell you what was happening with the cops?"

"She was planning to cut back to nothing, but I don't know the ins and outs of it. Madge would, you should talk to her."

"What were things like between Lily and Madge?"

Pearl gave me a sharp look, then said firmly, "They loved each other like sisters. And they fought like sisters do. It's true they fought like *sailors* over Lily's games and special events. Lily wanted to bring people together, to create a community. Madge figured people could create their own community: what they go to the bars for, especially the men, is to find pickups. The whole game thing spoiled that mood. Sidelong glances, subtle body language, the heat of the night: try and do *that* in the middle of charades. Madge was sure they were driving away good business. Lily insisted that over time, when there was more community, that would build business. And of course, it would be good for all of us."

"Who was right?"

"Both of them," she replied with conviction. "Neither of them was wrong, that's for sure. They worked it out. Friday and Saturday nights, the main business nights, no games or dress-up events or anything else. Those nights it was just a bar. Earlier in the week, and on Sundays, games and events. So there was room for both."

Pearl looked tired, and I realized it was time to leave. I thanked her,

159

and Luther and Hugo. She held me again, rocking with me in her arms. Then she told me not to be a stranger.

Madge was a bulldog of a butch, short, squat, and ornery. Wore her dark hair slicked forward in a pompadour, shorn on the sides, and tapered to a sharp D.A. There was nothing about passing in her butchness: she was a mannish woman and didn't care who knew it. Her weathered features suggested she'd earned the right not to give a damn.

Me, she didn't like much. For so many reasons. Definitely because of Jimmy. Possibly because I was new in town, and like any good bulldog she trusted only those who were familiar. No doubt because I was a brazen butch too foolish to know I needed to earn the right to be brazen; as such, I was a danger to myself and those around me.

I got to Pandora's before the evening crowd. Madge looked up and her face twisted to chagrin. When I walked over to the bar she put down the glass she was washing, but didn't extend her hand.

"I'm Joe O'Conner."

"I know."

"So you know my brother's body was found."

"I'm sorry."

"And I'm very sorry for your loss." She nodded silently. Her face said she'd seen every kind of trouble there was but didn't doubt my ability to invent some new ones. "I know Lily believed Jimmy was a snitch, and I know you do too. You may be right. I hope you're wrong. I'm trying to find out, one way or another."

She nodded, noncommittal.

"I believe the cops were involved in Jimmy's murder. I know for sure they tried to cover the tracks of whoever killed him. I know a lot of people think the cops were involved in Lily's murder too."

"Look," she began, her face flushing, "I don't know what your theories are, but I'm grieving for my friend and your conversation isn't helping any."

I tried to keep my voice from sounding urgent. "Madge, I'd like to

160

know what was happening with the payoffs to the cops—what Lily was doing. That may be why she was murdered. If it is, the cops aren't going to find the murderer."

"Of course that's why she was murdered," she snarled, furious. "But I don't know whose side you're on, and I have no interest in talking about it with you."

"What about the tuft on her shoe—have the cops said anything about the tuft?"

"The tuft?" she asked, startled. "The tuft?" she repeated, her voice growing incredulous. "What the hell are you talking about? No—I retract the question. Just. Leave. Me. Alone."

I wasn't ready to let it go. "The tuft, that little knot of thread or hair on Lily's heel, the one she was fighting with. You can see it in the photo. Are they following up on it?"

She faltered for a moment, then rallied. "Get the hell out of my bar. Go! Go away! And don't come back!"

It hadn't gone as well as I'd hoped.

I was surprised to get a message from Madge the next day. More surprising, she asked me to meet her at Pandora's that afternoon.

Her face was an anguished mix of emotions. "Thanks for coming," she said, indicating a barstool. I sat. She avoided looking at me as she spoke. "I'm sorry I kicked you out. This whole thing is a nightmare. Lily—Lily was such a friend to me." Madge's voice grew thick, rough. "I saw the tuft. It was awful, awful to look at. But you're right: Lily was using that shoe to defend herself. Of course she was—that's Lily, fighting to the end." Angrily, she wiped away the tears collecting at her chin. "The cops were here last night, asking questions. I asked them about the fluff." I winced. "They acted like I'd asked them what the moon's made of. So," she concluded abruptly, "I'm ready to answer your questions."

"What was happening with the payoffs to the cops?"

"Lily was livid about them. Since that court ruling she insisted we shouldn't be paying at all. I persuaded her to put something in an envelope, less than before, but something. You know, let them save face. That's what cops are all about. Needless to say they weren't happy. They kept leaning on us."

"Did they know it was Lily pushing to pay less?"

"Yeah, and they probably knew she was talking to other bar owners about it. They'd have heard *that* from your brother," she added bitterly. Then she closed her eyes for a moment and shook her head. "But here's the thing. Two days before she was killed, the cops came by for their money. I was at the other end of the bar. I saw Lily fish the envelope out of her purse. It was *thick*. Puffy. I asked her about it later, but she kept mum."

"You think she gave them a bunch of money for some reason?"

"No—it was *too* thick. No way she'd be giving them that much. I think there was something other than cash in that envelope. But I have no idea what."

"Do you know who the money goes to?"

"Maybe the head of vice gets it, but more likely it goes straight to the top: Gafferty, Chief Gafferty."

"And who picked it up that day?"

"Hagerty and Olsen. I'm sure of it. Sometimes two of them come in together, sometimes just one. That day it was Hagerty and Olsen."

"What do they look like?"

"Hagerty looks like he sounds: curly red hair, face full of freckles. Mid-forties, tall and skinny. Olsen is stout, blond. Big ugly nose like he got in a fight when he was a kid and they never set it right."

"They still come in, since her death?"

"Same ones," she replied grimly. "Same routine: they stride in like they own the place, hands on their guns, throw their crotches around a bit, leer at whoever's behind the bar, and settle on a stool down at the end. Hagerty harasses anyone in earshot. Sometimes Olsen announces, 'I gotta take a leak.' Five minutes later he's back, they drink up, and leave."

"When do they come?"

"Monday afternoon, around four."

"Mind if I come by next Monday?"

She squinted at me. "I don't want no more trouble."

"No trouble," I agreed. She nodded.

chapter nine

How's water twelve feet deep more dangerous than water ten feet deep? I asked Lucille if she could get a look at the file on Lily's murder.

The news was shocking. The coroner found a pair of red satin panties stuffed in her mouth. Red satin with a dragon embroidered on them, right on the part that invites the most attention when panties are worn to invite attention. This seemed to support the cops' contention that she was murdered by some sicko sex maniac. But I hadn't heard about it from Pearl. Or Madge. Or even Aaron. The police were keeping the panties to themselves.

Lucille found no mention of a tuft of thread or hair dangling from Lily's heel. "That's a tough one. The evidence closet is under lock and key to prevent tampering. There's never been any call for me to go in there. It would be hard to make a case for it." She sipped her coffee and drummed her fingers on the table for a while. Then she said decisively, "Give me a week."

Three days later, Lucille sat me down in her kitchen. "The pump with the broken heel was in the evidence box. It had an evidence tag attached, but no bit of fluff. I pulled everything else out, and there it was in the corner of the box. No tag attached. Hadn't even been noticed." She shook her head darkly. "Two kinds of thread in it. A turquoise wool, very curly and rough. And a chartreuse mohair, more refined. They were tangled together with one white hair. About three inches long, and fairly coarse." She sat back and crossed her arms. "And the panties: red silk with a dragon—but old."

"Old?"

"Yeah, old."

"You mean, worn?"

"No, I mean old. The thread on the seams is rotten—coming apart on one side. At least a couple decades old."

"Old panties."

"That's right. Old panties."

"Anything else?"

"That not enough for you?"

"How did you manage to get into that closet anyway? You said it was under lock and key."

"I was at the office sifting through possible pretexts, none the least bit persuasive, when in walks my six-foot-three solution: Dennis Holland. Deputy Inspector Dennis Holland. He had three things going for him. Been leaning on me for a date forever. He's a heavy drinker. And he's got a key to that closet."

She pulled a cigarette out of her purse, I lit it for her, and she slid back in her chair. "Just as my lips were telling him no dice, my brain starts humming. I hold out a little longer, then relent. Thursday night, I say, an early dinner. He's delighted when I agree to a restaurant in my neighborhood; I can see he's already working out potential scenarios. So, we have a nice little dinner, bottle and a half of wine between us, and I suggest we head back to my place for a drink. Martinis. Olives are good at masking the taste of the stuff I slip into his. Ten minutes later he's out cold. I take off his shoes, make him comfy on the couch, find his keys, and hightail it to the office. Tommy Rollins is on night shift, a cute young rookie. I tell him I've got a hot date and left my best lipstick in my desk." She mugged an expression of utter tragedy. "He lets me upstairs. He isn't supposed to, so I know he won't be mentioning it to anyone in the morning. The evidence room is, unlike the rest of headquarters, nice and tidy, boxes arranged by date of the crime. So I find your fluff, wave a lipstick at Tommy on my way out, and catch a cab home. Dennis is still out cold on the couch."

Lucille inhaled heavily on her cigarette. "The rest was easy," she continued, waving away the cloud of smoke. "I undress him, and myself. I scatter our clothes around the room, along with a couple near-empty liquor bottles. I wrap myself in a robe, and then wrap myself in his arms. I pretend to be asleep, and eventually doze off. When he rouses me an hour or two later, I'm *very* understanding. 'I had a delicious time *anyway*, Dennis—don't make a big deal out of it. It happens now and then. Nothing to be ashamed of, just a fluke, I'm sure of it. A little too much to drink, that's all.' Not a nice trick to play on the guy, but I wanted to make sure he wouldn't be expecting seconds this weekend."

"Jesus, Lucille. You should have told me what you were planning."

She blinked at me. "You'd have tried to talk me out of it?"

"No, but I'd have hung around to keep an eye out. What if you'd been caught? What if Dennis woke up before you got back—noticed his keys missing and headed to the station?"

"I'd have worked something out."

"How?"

"Balance of power," she said flatly.

"What?"

"Balance of power." She seemed to consider, then continued, "I'm going to tell you something that may be hard for you to hear, honey. I didn't get these digs"—she gestured to her apartment—"filing papers.

Given my personal attributes, I receive a fair amount of attention at the office. Flirtation, innuendo. Invitations. One day some big mucky-muck stops by, leans over my desk, and describes a little scenario he's just dying to play out with two redheads. As it happens, I know two redheads—well, one's a brunette, but it won't take long to remedy that and I can make it *really* worth her while. So I tell him I know just the ladies to make his dreams come true. I mention that they liked to be treated well—oh, all of that. Long story short: I become a madam. Catering to big wheels. Top brass in the police force, politicians, that kind. I've had the asses of several senators and one rather well-endowed bishop high in the air, begging for pleasure. And the higher that kind goes in the world, the more perverse his proclivities." She drummed her fingers on the table, pondering. "I'm not sure whether power makes them perverse, the perverse ones make it further, or they're less inclined to hold back as they move up. In any case, I've seen enough deviance to make the two of us look like girl scouts. And I have discreetly, very discreetly, ensured that there is a record of these events as crisp, clear, and incontrovertible as the wrinkles on Franklin's forehead. It's a kind of insurance: if I find myself in a tight spot, at an impasse, I'll have the assistance of a well-placed ally. Or half a dozen. To balance the power. So I can afford a few risks." Like other things Lucille had told me, it came as a surprise and it seemed like I'd known it all along.

She waited patiently.

"Are you always just the madam?"

"I'm more than that when the need arises, but it doesn't arise often," she replied crisply.

"What's it like for you?"

"You mean having sex for money, having sex with men for money, or answering questions about having sex with men for money?"

I nodded.

She got up and clattered around, assembling her percolator. Added water, measured coffee, lit the burner. Got out cups and saucers, sugar and cream, and sat down again. The aroma of coffee was suffusing the air when she spoke again.

"Having sex for money is sometimes pleasurable, sometimes awkward, and sometimes not unlike filing papers. Having sex with men is about the same, but not infrequently quite interesting. These powerful men, many of them want to...surrender. They spend their time in charge, making consequential decisions, strong-arming people. Now and then they want to give it all up and have someone else call the shots—in certain very controlled circumstances, of course. Quite a few of them don't even want sex. What they want is to be told that they absolutely must do whatever it is they secretly want to do. So I figure out what that is and play Joan Crawford for a couple hours. Command them to prance around in panties or scrub my floor naked while I watch. Then they pay me a good deal of money and go home."

"They pay you to watch them scrub your floor?"

"Sometimes. Sometimes they pay me to get them all tarted up, help them on with their stockings, do their makeup and nails. And—most importantly—they pay me to know how to get it all off afterward. No pink stains on their fingernails when we're done. But sometimes it's more mundane than that. I bully them, throw my hips around, say mean things, and crack a whip."

The percolator was perking. Lucille poured us each a cup, turned the flame low, and leaned back against the stove with her cup in her hand. "Seeing a new client is the most interesting part. There's something they desperately want you to tell them to do, but they don't want to say it out loud. So you figure it out, by indirection, by little clues here and there. Or by process of elimination. There's an extraordinary power in it. No matter how mundane the activity." She blew on her coffee, sipped, then settled on the dinette's lucky chair.

"As for answering questions, it varies just as much. Depending on who's asking and what they believe they know about me because I do this kind of work. Say, I had a terrible relationship with my father, so I crave attention from every man I meet. Some just think I'm a whore, which I am, but it leads them to dismiss everything else about me. And others figure that if renting my body out for two hours pays my rent for the month, well, it sure beats waitressing."

"So why do you keep the office job?"

"It gives me a safe and reputable place to meet clients. Plus, excellent cover. It's fairly painless work—I'm only there ten to three most days. And it gives me access to a lot of useful information. I'm able to help people out, people the law isn't usually partial to. I like doing favors for people. Just like the mayor does. Only it's different people we're favoring."

"The mayor usually expects some kind of...consideration in return."

Lucille's husky laugh rumbled across the table. "Virtue is its own reward."

Monday at four I was in a corner at Pandora's Box. Two cops swaggered in, just like Madge said, crotches out in front like they were being dragged around by their privates. When the short one went back to take a leak, I moseyed out the front door and around to the alley. It was just a hunch, but as I rounded the corner, muffled sounds told me I was right. He realized I was there when he heard me release the safety as I pressed the gun against his temple.

"Drop it," I said, and felt his gun fall into my hand. I shifted its weight to my pocket, then put my hand on the shoulder of the man kneeling in front of him, the man whose temple his gun had been pressed against. In the shadows of the alley I couldn't tell who it was, but I made my voice confident as I said, "It's okay, Sam, you can stop now." He turned away and retched, dry heaves.

"There's some information I need from you," I said to the cop at the other end of Jimmy's gun, keeping it steady as my voice. "You're gonna give it to me quick so you can get back to your buddy. And after we send you inside, Sam here's gonna be keeping an eye on me. He'll make sure that if anything happens to me in the next week or the next month or the next year, anything unexpected and violent, word of your back alley pleasures will spread faster than a closet queen's ass cheeks. Got it?"

San Francisco's finest nodded slightly. Sam was done with the heaves and stood up. I continued: "Now talk fast. The packet you picked up last week. I'm guessing you opened it, and I'm guessing it didn't have money in it. What was inside?"

"A pair of panties."

I pressed the gun hard against his temple.

"I swear, it was a pair of panties! I don't know what the hell it was about, but they were red, shiny, with a dragon on them. And they were old—faded, the threads all frayed. That's all. That's all I know."

I tried to make sense of it, but realized there'd be time enough later. "So where does the money go?"

"Up."

"Up where?"

"I don't know—just up. I give it to my boss and he gives it to his boss."

"So who's the boss's boss's boss?"

"The chief of police? The mayor, maybe? All of 'em probably take a handful as it goes by."

"I'm going to let you go in just a moment," I said. "But remember about Sam. And Sam's going to tell his friend Ed—so if anything unexpected and violent happens to Sam, word will still spread. And Ed's going to tell his friend Paul. And Paul's got a *lot* of friends, all ready to tell your cop buddies who come in here to haul them off about how you like to spend your time when you go take a leak. Your buddies won't believe it, of course—not the first time they hear it. And they may not believe it the second time. But the third time they'll start to wonder. And when they hear it a dozen times, from a dozen of these faggots you love to beat up, they'll be spreading *your* ass cheeks and ramming a broom handle up them. Your gun will be behind the trash can over there at two a.m. Now go."

He disappeared through the back door of the bar. I felt a tremor in my thigh as I walked to the can and nestled the gun in the grunge behind it.

Chantry welcomed me with his corrosively genial smile, offered me a drink, and invited me to settle into that stiff wooden chair. I declined the drink but accepted the chair, and balanced my hat carelessly on my knee.

"Thank you for connecting me with Frank. He was very helpful."

"I'm pleased to hear that. I assume that means your investigation is proceeding fruitfully," he said mildly, without posing it as a question. I nodded anyway. "Excellent. I trust you'll find your brother very soon."

"Thank you, Mr. Chantry. I won't take up any more of your time." Getting up from my chair, I let my hat slide to the floor, then followed Chantry to the office door. He stepped back to allow me to pass through first. I pretended to remember my hat, fetched it, and came up behind him so he moved ahead of me through the doorway. As I turned to pull the door shut sounds of the bar reached the hallway, and I feigned a surprised look in their direction—eyebrows up, face lit with pleasure. His eyes followed mine, and in that moment I slid a small card between the lock and the jamb as I closed the door. It took both hands, and without any eyes to spare I could only hope I got it in the right place. A quarter-second later he was looking back at me for an explanation of the bright surprise on my face. "Oh, I thought that was a Cole Porter song I love. It's not," I said, feigning disappointment. His eyes looked troubled for a moment, but he bought it, and we walked the short hall together to the bar.

Chantry saw a customer he knew and excused himself. I lingered, eavesdropping, and heard him reassure the customer that there had never, ever, been a raid on the place. Then I took myself to the bar for a jolt of resolve. Chantry was deep in conversation. I headed back down the rear hallway. A woman in a twinset and full skirt left the restroom, and I lingered till she was gone. Then I tried the door of his office. It opened, the card falling to the floor. I scooped it up, slipped inside, and closed the door behind me. The sweat beaded on my forehead as I approached his desk. Its drawers were unlocked. Not much of interest in the shallow ones to the right. The lower left was full of thick files: Elbert Dodson, Peter Dunham, Frederick Fuller, Raul García, Elizabeth Holloway, Adeline Jackson, Rudolph Maynard, Simon Moss, Charles Rutherford, Tyrone Singleton... Engrossed, I suddenly heard voices in the hallway, one of them Chantry's. I slid the drawer closed. I heard the rasp of a key entering a lock. My choices were under the desk or the door behind me. If the door was locked there'd be no time left to heave myself under the desk—but if Chantry sat in his chair, the desk would be no hiding place at all. I reached for the door. The knob turned. Uttering a silent prayer of thanks to the God of Nelly Queens, I threw myself in and squeezed the door shut behind me. Chantry's voice, as he cordially ushered in visitors, was unperturbed.

It was dark behind the door. I felt space behind me and turned slowly. I was in a narrow hall almost as long as a bowling lane, with what looked like amber bars across it at regular intervals, just above waist height. Bewildered, I stared at the bars, and as my eyes adjusted to the darkness I saw dust motes floating in them. They were smoky beams of light. Emanating from the bar.

I crept closer and bumped into something—heard a harsh scrape—froze. The voices from the office continued, an unbroken murmur. Moving more slowly, I ran my hand over what I dimly saw was a wooden chair. It sat below two amber bars, directly across from two small holes drilled through the wall. I was behind the long wall lined with intimate, draped booths. I slid into the chair. Voices from the other side came through with astonishing clarity.

"So then she said..."

"And what did he do?"

The holes, I realized, must be hidden in the decorative painting around the sconces, and the curtains that framed each cozy nook muffled surrounding sounds. Looking to my left, I could make out, amid

173

two more beams of light, another chair. Then another, and another, and two more. One chair for each of the booths.

Suddenly I heard the muffled voices from Chantry's office grow louder, then cease. The sharp clap of a door closing followed. I rose and hustled toward the far end of the corridor, hurling myself to the floor just past the last chair. The door to the corridor opened, then shut. Chantry stepped forward and settled himself in the first chair.

When I could hold my breath no longer I exhaled and sucked in my next lungful, as loud to my ears as a vacuum cleaner hose suctioned to a rug. My heart added a steady beat, subtle as a tympani. I was lying awkwardly on my right arm, my face pressed to the floor, cold and sticky under me. I twisted my neck and raised my head slightly. There, in two amber beams of light and sound, was Chantry: poised, motionless, face inches from the wall, listening. He paid no attention to the twisted body just past the sixth chair.

He sat, attentive, for about a minute and a half. Then he stood, moved to the next chair, and sat again. He remained in chair two for a shorter time, got up impatiently, and perched in chair three. I could see, dimly, the three remaining chairs leading irrevocably toward my body. But Chantry was sitting in the beams of light. His eyes might be affected by the amber glow just beneath them, his vision more hindered than mine. He soon tired of booth three, stood, stepped closer, and sat in chair four.

He was motionless for a minute, then two. He leaned in very slightly. He sat like that, angled forward, for perhaps five minutes, then five more. My right arm was numb, and pains shot through my neck and chest. I couldn't support my head in that position much longer. With excruciating care I turned, settling my cheek to the floor again. Unable to see him, I listened for movement, for any shift in his attention.

A slight sound, and I felt him rise, turn, and move closer, settling in the fifth chair. I began calculating my intimacy with chair six. My head was no more than two inches from its front leg. I saw suddenly that my hat had fallen forward and was resting, just slightly, against it. When he moved to chair six he might knock it with his foot. It was a slight felt hat, a summer fedora: he might not feel it, but if it rolled it would surely catch his eye. I weighed the cost of reaching for it, sliding it slowly back. That motion would be more gradual than the rolling, and he was now further away than he'd be if the hat did roll. But to move at all with him just a chair away seemed reckless. More reckless than not moving?

That's when I realized that any move he made would be subtle. A dramatic scene would only draw the attention of the booth's occupants. He wouldn't risk his entire enterprise on an insignificant bug like me. If he noticed my presence, he'd pretend he hadn't. Go about his business, carry on with the evening, making sure the door of his office was well guarded. Chantry would wait till the bar was closed, the patrons gone, before flipping on the lights and exposing the stiff beetle huddled in a corner at the far end of his narrow parade of lights. Then one of his hulks would crush the cockroach.

I don't know how much time passed. Twenty, then thirty minutes, maybe closer to an hour. I heard no movement and assumed he sat, immersed, in the fifth temple of sound. I wondered what intimate confession he was hearing, what life he was preparing to ruin. I wondered if his dick got hard in those gabardine trousers, if surveillance itself was a kick for him, or if it was simply a business proposition, listening to the agonies of a heart bared: like adding a column of numbers and obeying the sums they produced.

He rose abruptly, then turned swiftly—not toward chair six, but back to his office. He knocked a chair, just slightly, though to my ears the sound was a raucous screech. The door to the office opened, then quickly shut. Perhaps he'd seen me and wanted to smoke me out. But—he'd sat a long time, then left hurriedly. Bumping a chair was unlike him, especially in his sanctum sanctorum. The conversation at booth five must have been significant. He was already formulating the words in his mind, letters to freeze hearts and rupture lives. But he had to know who the voices belonged to. He'd left abruptly only because he had to—because the patrons of booth five were leaving. He'd hurried to catch a glimpse of them, perhaps signal for a tail. If so, his office would be empty for a few minutes—and his door unguarded. I rolled, ignoring the shooting of pins and needles in my arm, slid hands under my torso, and pushed myself up. Squatting, I looked down the long gallery of amber lights. The chairs and I were alone. I limped down the sepulchral corridor, then limped back to collect my hat. My limbs began to loosen by the time I reached the door to his office. I paused, ear against it. Silence. I opened it slowly. The office was empty.

Jerking open the drawer, I rifled through the first file: Elbert Dodson. Addresses—his home, his school—and a list of dates and notes regarding missives sent, money collected. I wildly considered taking the files, but had nothing to conceal them in. I slid the drawer shut and hurried to the door. Listening briefly, I heard only the thudding of my blood. I stepped quickly out and shut the door behind me. I was alone in the hallway. I turned right to find the rear exit, and hurried to the end of the hall. Two doors, opposite the restrooms, were locked. At the end of the hallway, another door: padlocked. The bar had no rear exit. No other way out. I turned back, reentered the bar, eye out for Chantry. He was conferring with the arm. I sauntered toward the front door, saw the bartender's eyes flicker to me. I'd been gone too long to be in the bathroom; no doubt Chantry would hear of it. I reached the curtain at last, passed through it, through the dummy office, past Wide Guy—anticipating his grip on my shoulders—and out to the damp air of the city night. I kept my pace casual as I walked the alley, watching for tails. Reaching the street, I bolted.

Adonis—Judd Nestle—wasn't in those files. Either someone else was blackmailing him or he was a plant sent by Chantry to find out what I knew. There'd been several names in the files I hadn't recognized; of course Chantry was blackmailing more people than Jimmy knew about. If he was getting money from half of them, there was a hell of a lot of velvet in it. Enough to support the bar and a whole lot more. Enough to pay off the police, lavishly. Certainly enough to kill for.

Fog drifted through the streets, obscuring the upper expanses of buildings. Leavenworth was mostly deserted, its gray buildings consenting quietly to their erasure. Midway down Hyde I saw a familiar figure ensconced in an arching granite portico, engaged in some manic solo version of musical chairs. He sat on a ramshackle crate, muttering, then jumped up in a frenzy to perch on another. Considerable arm flailing was required to prevent capsize. "The chair, the chair, the chair is too small!" He launched himself toward another crate, sent it skittering sideways, then grabbed it beneath him and crab-walked back into place. "Too big!" he announced immediately. "The chair is too big! Far too big," he continued, voice turning mournful. Careening to another crate, he sat bolt upright for a moment, then moaned and rocked gently from side to side. "Just right, ooooh, the chair is just right. Just right, the chair." An ecstasy of contentment soothed him. Suddenly his eyes flew open in horror and he shouted, "Too small!" hurling himself to another crate. Occasionally the words changed, from "chair" to "bowl," and from "bowl" to "bed." When he came back around to "chair" I continued on my way, his haunted mutterings following me till they were engulfed by fog.

Mr. Wilkinson smirked as he conveyed the message from Lucille inviting me to dinner, and it was only when I saw the romantic haze cast by her candlelit table that I realized the roses I'd brought were meant to say more than "thank you for helping me find my dead brother." I'd been so busy tending those emotions, I hadn't realized others had ripened.

When it comes to lovers, the charms of experience trump those of innocence, but Lucille didn't hold it against me. After dinner, during which our eyes fell into a slow samba, we retired to the deep burgundy of her living room. She kept the lights low and put on a mellow record. I don't recall what it was that played; my senses were occupied elsewhere, with the curve of her upper lip and her musky scent. We moved toward each other to dance, but as we came close, by silent agreement, we abandoned the pose. She folded her arms around me and I fell against her, feeling the press of all the sordid ugliness and fear of the past weeks. I fended it off as I felt the fullness of her, all the impossibly soft firmness of her breasts pressed against mine. Unconscious as I'd been of what was to come, I'd left off the binding when I dressed, so our breasts were separated only by the thin cotton of my shirt, the thinner silk of hers, and the lace of her brassiere. We moved like that for a long time, each feeling the other's breasts with our own, our mouths exploring each other's depths. She was a fine kisser: knew how to start slowly, tentative and curious, to prepare for the deeper crush to come.

I was lost in her mouth for hours, but when I felt us move toward the couch I persuaded my lips to desert hers in favor of the gorgeously swelling curves below. I laid her gently on the velvet, my hand cradling her head as she murmured something sweet, then made my way across the monumental roundness of each breast. As my cheeks and lips slid across her blouse, as I nuzzled the voluptuous softness of her, I felt her nipples stiffen beneath. I nudged the blouse aside and devoted myself, for a time, to each one, enjoying the tease of the lacy fabric still between us, feeling her rise to meet my mouth, hearing her breath deepen. Eventually there was no lace between us and I took her fully in my mouth, teasing her nipple with my tongue, her throaty moans, at the edge of my consciousness, growing deeper.

I spent eons there, at her breast, and had just begun to hope I'd live forever when my wandering hand discovered the softness of her thigh. Right there, that vast stretch between the top of her stocking and the lace of her filmy panties, there the softness of her flesh, covered with the finest veil of hair, called to me. I heard it call me by name, was surprised that it knew me both as Josie and as Joe. I allowed my lips to graze her plush mound through her panties, but only briefly, as I traveled back and forth between those thighs, feeling her desire, hearing her moaning cries from her faraway mouth.

I moved upward, for a time, determined to explore every nuance of every curve of her gently swelling belly, bringing the softness of my short-cropped hair to meet it, knowing the fuzz of me would entertain the sensitive flesh of her. It did. But I was distracted by finding my way to the zipper at the side of her rustling skirt. I slid the layers off her and her slip followed. The couch was long and I was grateful for the vastness of it, which allowed me to gently spread her legs and run my hands along their length as I buried my face in the tender crevice at their source. I detoured briefly to her mouth, wanting to taste the sweet warmth of her there again before I tasted the tart sweetness of her below, and she welcomed me both places with her wetness, with the softness of swelling lips, and the fullness of her desire.

She was a woman not afraid of her own pleasure, and I held tight as I rode her moans and cries and the thrashing of her hips. She erupted in pleasure, open wide and throbbing, pressing me into her. The second time was slower, a swirling, flickering dance between her clit and my wet lips and tongue. The third time was rough, fierce, both of us demanding full presence as we lost track of whose hands were grabbing fistfuls of whose hair and whose hips were bucking and whose head was crushed between the force of whose legs fiercely wrapped. She roared as she came again. And again and again. Then I heard her voice, languid: "If I'd been keeping track I'd have lost count by now." We collapsed in sweat and laughter, floated for a time in the dimness of the room. As I drifted I heard the rhythmic thp...thp...thp of the record player's needle skipping at the end of the platter.

Lucille stood me up, took my hand, and led me down the hallway. I was still fully dressed, while only a black garter and stockings covered her nakedness. The garter's high arches accentuated the fullness of her ass, each cheek assuming prominence in turn as she walked. If they were cantilevered, no beams were evident.

She led me to a bedroom of dusty rose. The brass bed, centered

below a tall window draped with satin and fringe, assumed the role of throne. Drawing me close to it, she dropped down to slide my shoes and socks off. Then she stood and, reaching up, gently undid my paisley tie. Holding one end in each hand, she used it to pull me toward her, and our mouths met again. As we parted she slid the tie from around my neck and tossed it across the brass headboard. Then she slowly undid each button of my shirt. Before removing it she slid her hands, without gentleness, across my breasts. They were gumdrops compared to hers, but they became firm, hungry gumdrops under her touch. She teased them with her tongue as she slid the shirt off my shoulders and let it drop. She unbuckled my belt, and it joined my tie. As she slid my trousers down past my hips, she looked up at me and murmured, "I am glad you're not stone. Those stone butches, they get so ornery when they're flipped. I spend half the next morning shoring up their bruised egos. Tsk-tsk," she said and smiled, sliding down my boxers, but her eyes were serious. Then she stood, placed her index finger in the center of my chest, and pushed.

I offered no resistance. She nudged till I was centered in the bed. On her knees she crawled up over me and kissed me again. Lost in the kiss, I hardly noticed her hands around my wrists, moving them high above my head and binding them gently with my tie. The metal of the buckle of my belt clinked as it slid across the brass, and I woke from the kiss to find both wrists firmly anchored to the bed.

Straddling my hips, she smiled down at me. Then she roused every inch of my skin, first gently, then roughly, moving across my body like a storm gathering focus. With her fingertips, her lips, her tongue, her hair, she awakened my limbs and reunited them with my torso. No longer mere appendages for walking or eating or holding a gun, they became conduits to every glancing touch that sent waves of sensation cascading up my spine. When she devoted herself to my chest, my belly, my thighs, I felt my splintered body begin to become whole. Bound as I was, released of responsibility, I could only surrender to her touch, and so I laid it all down—Jimmy's murder and his vindication, Lily's murder and her vengeance, the agonies of the blackmailed, the mountain of grief inside me—all that weight seeped out of me as the rising waves of pleasure expanded. I had only a moment to wonder at Lucille's wisdom as she circled the one part of me that remained untouched. Then she dived deep. Joy, which I'd forgotten, suffused me, filled me fully and spilled over, and it was only later, as I surfaced, that I realized the sounds I'd been hearing, of angels moaning and crooning and trilling, were torn from my own throat.

chapter ten

My body was suffused with rapture when I woke the next morning. The tall mirror propped above Lucille's pedestal sink reflected my nakedness from the thighs up. When I looked at my reflection, the pleasures of the previous evening seemed to leach away as though they'd only been a dream. I shut my eyes and the memories stabilized. I gazed at myself again and they shimmered, as though to experience them required some other body—Gary Cooper's, or Errol Flynn's. I followed the arc of the evening in my mind, held fast to its sensations, while I traced the contradictions of my reflection: my cropped hair, my broad shoulders, the modest swelling of my breasts, my angularity, and the slight curve of my hips. This complexity was me. I inhabited Joe, the man who appeared when I was bound and suited, and who some strangers, at least, seemed to believe in. I needed him to move through the world with a minimum of bruises and batterings. But I was Josie, the angular, graceless, capable girl, only now a grown-up version that could no longer rely on "tomboy" for allowances. This body had known pleasures so transcendent they seemed the province of the divine. I held fast to them.

Stretching, Lucille observed with a hoarse laugh, "There are few things as luxurious as a sore throat acquired from moaning in pleasure." It was Sunday, and she had no trouble persuading me to spend the day. She asked me to tell her how I came to be there, in her bed. "From the beginning. And take your time." I was in favor of anything that kept my head cushioned right where it was.

"I got my first inkling of things to come when my best friend invited me for a sleepover. Her parents were chummy at dinner and her mom allowed seconds at dessert. We whispered and giggled for hours, then dared each other to sleep *buck naked*. I was carried away by a delirious sense of luxury—a sleepover with Mary Ann Spivakowski *and* seconds on dessert!—so I crawled from my sleeping bag into her bed, where we snuggled, amazed at how good skin felt against skin. The next morning a hand gripped me like a claw. Mary Ann's mother had a tight smile on her face as she inquired about our sleeping arrangement. Had I gotten cold? Was the floor too hard? Did my sleeping bag itch? When I sleepily said, 'No, it was just yummy,' the grim smile disappeared and she suggested it was time for me to go home. Mary Ann never spoke to me again." Lucille murmured consolingly.

"I felt some terrible kind of wrongness that I couldn't make sense of. I felt it other times, more vaguely. Like one night at supper. Nothing really happened. Father was talking about a neighbor lady, an old spinster who lived with her sister. The conversation became heated and then stopped short when Mother directed a harsh glance from Father to me and back again. I froze, wondering what I'd done wrong, and she punctured the tension with a bright remark about the pot roast. I couldn't figure out what it was about. Then a few years later, in my early teens, I was at the five and dime twirling the wire racks of paperback novels while Mother shopped. A haunting cover caught my eye: two women, one blonde, one brunette, with a world of tension between them. I asked Mother to buy it for me. She took one look at the book, snatched it out of my hand, threw it on the floor, and dragged me out the door. She didn't say a word all the way home—in fact she never said a word about it, but a week later she announced that I was a young woman now and had best start acting like one. That was the last time I wore Jimmy's old jeans past the gate of the farm.

"Several years later all of this took shape in my mind, the way a group of stars suddenly comes into focus as a constellation. I was volunteering at the library, shelving books, and the spine of one sent a shiver up my own. It was marked 'Special Collection': books sequestered in a room behind the librarian's counter, admission granted only by special petition. The librarian had told me to shelve all the books on the cart, so I figured the book in my hand *could* count as permission. Tucking it under my arm, I tiptoed to the room, ducked under the cord that guarded its entrance, and stepped into the mysterious chamber." Lucille thumped a drumroll on her belly.

"The room seemed taller than it was wide. Books loomed above me. The overhead light fixture was filled with corpses of at least a dozen moths. And I heard a sort of crunching, like a thousand tiny worms chomping their way through the glue of a hundred spines. I felt the sudden panic of claustrophobia: I could be banned from the library for life! I shuddered, but the terror passed and I started scanning shelves. Some kind of magnetic force drew me to a volume titled *Psychology of Sex*. No pictures, just strange, convoluted sentences, with phrases like 'prohibitions are incitements.' I wanted to stop and figure that out, but had no time to waste on thinking. I turned the page; the title of the next chapter was 'Homosexuality.'"

Lucille's hand tightened on my arm as I continued. "It read, 'When the sexual impulse is directed toward persons of the same sex, we are in the presence of an aberration variously known as "sexual inversion," "contrary sexual feeling," or "uranism."' Standing in the library's forbidden inner sanctum, I suddenly knew what those strange events had been about—and that there were others like me. The book went on to describe them! The list of creatures 'prone to this deviation' included monkeys and baboons, savage and barbarous peoples, literary and artistic types, and—here my jaw dropped—'hairdressers, waiters, and waitresses.'"

"Oh, my!"

"But just then a thunderous sound rocked me: the book that brought me there slid from my arm to the floor. The librarian's head appeared in the doorway. She *flayed* me with her eyes."

Lucille chuckled softly. "Thus ended your short career as a librarian and began your long career as a homosexual."

"I had mad crushes on various girls in high school, but not much happened till I was seventeen. Jimmy'd been shipped off, and things at home were going downhill fast. One Saturday, in a rare moment of clarity, Father recognized he was too drunk to drive and had me take him into town for a part for the pickup. Toby Summer, town mechanic, had spent the previous weekend in New York and couldn't wait to talk about what he'd seen in the big bad city. I was only half listening when I heard him lower his voice to say, 'You shoulda seen those queers walking around Green Witch Village—in broad daylight, blatant as peacocks. Faces all rouged up, mincing little steps, high-pitched voices. Negro ones too! Crazier than a cow on locoweed.' The next weekend I drove the pickup into New York to find this Green Witch Village. I found a stoop to sit on and a whole pageant appeared: every variety of butch and femme, stud and bulldagger, dandy, drag queen, hustler, and Mary. A Sears catalog of the twilight world!"

"And which would have been on *your* Christmas list?"

"Oh, all of them—but especially the ones who seemed to be partly male and partly female. At first I just wanted to know which was which. Then that gave way to a delirious kind of vertigo."

"Mmmm," Lucille replied.

"I remember a big butch who strode by like a one-man band: sturdy, spiff, in a broad-shouldered double-breasted pinstripe suit. She had a look, like if the whole world burst into flames she'd know exactly what to do and it'd be alright. But butch as she was, she didn't aim for passing: the fullness of her breasts showed through the V of her suit, and I think she wore a touch of lipstick. I about swooned. She was followed by three lithe young men who strutted by with their hands in constant motion as they jostled and spoke over each other in a combination of Spanish and English. Their pompadours were four inches high and their pegged pants ended an inch short of their shoes, flaunting socks that matched their ties. They draped themselves across a stoop a few doors down, and their banter filled the street.

"Next, a louche boy skulked by wearing jeans so tight you could see his next promotion from here. Then a Negro femme who walked like the air was her lover and had waited all day for her to saunter down the street. Soon after that, three motorcycles roared onto the scene and stopped right across the street. Chains rattled in the sudden silence as they locked their bikes. The men all wore stiff leather jackets, heavy boots, and chaps. One of them was bald, with an enormous, bushy beard, like Santa Claus went on the lam and fell in with a bad, bad crowd. The bikers eyed the gaggle in pegged pants. I tensed, and saw other people begin to edge away. Two men just took off running. The whole block held its breath. Then one of the Spanish boys flung his arms wide and shrieked, 'Arthur!' AWOL Santa lumbered over to embrace him, and soon they were all gabbing away. A flock of sailors in their whites strolled by, little hats at a cocky angle, trousers tight across their asses, and the whole group turned to watch.

"A few hours later a brawl did break out. A guy pulled up in a car so big he could've been dating two women and neither would've known. He was square, and he ambled, cocksure, across the street, then disappeared into a building. He came out with a gamine femme on his arm. A tall, boyish butch, about my age, burst out behind them yelling, fists flying, grabbed the guy and slugged him. He slugged back and the femme lunged at him, screaming. The three of them went at it for a while, bystanders egging them on, till the butch's friend, his name was Jack, showed up and dragged her away. A few months later I met that butch—she drove a delivery van for an Italian restaurant. She was a real mensch.

"Toward dawn other figures appeared, with a hungry, wary look in their eyes. Later I found out they were junkies. When a rat the size of a year-old tomcat emerged from a drain and waddled down the gutter, I found the pickup and slept till the heat of the sun woke me. Over the next few months I visited the Village often as I could. It saved my life: if I hadn't been there one weekend about nine months later, I'd have gone with Mother and Father to the annual VFD banquet. On the way home Father misjudged a turn and piloted the car into a large elm. Mother was killed instantly. Father held on for a day, but he was already gone when I returned Sunday evening."

"I'm so sorry. What a tragedy."

"It was tragic, but even at the time it seemed inevitable. My uncle quickly took charge of the farm. He's a sonofabitch who never liked me much and liked me less when I wouldn't say where I was spending my weekends. One night he followed me all the way into the city, and when he found out where I went he told me he didn't want me around the farm anymore. I'd finished high school by then. Jimmy wanted me to move out here with him, but I wanted to be on my own for a while first. I'd do anything to take back that decision now. I had a little money from my parents. I used half of it for first month's rent on an apartment in the Village, shared with two other gay girls. Got a waitressing job, which taught me how to handle myself. In New York, when it comes to tips, a smart mouth can take the place of a short skirt. Even if your views are exactly the opposite of theirs, they want you to have an opinion to stand toe-to-toe with theirs. So I started figuring out what I think and how to say it. And when I'd been there about a year, I fell in love. With a butch. Which meant—I thought—that I *must* be a femme."

"The line between butches and femmes is about as sturdy as that between church and state," Lucille said wryly. "But you must have been quite a lovelorn lamb."

"It didn't feel right, but everything was new and strange to me. That

190

first rocky love affair lasted a little over a year. Next I fell in love with a gorgeous drag queen. That was too preposterous to admit, so I just followed her around, mooning. Helped her dress for shows and ran to the store for more bobby pins. She must have known, but she was gentle and sweet with me. So two years became three, I fell out of love, and three years somehow became four. I was just thinking I'd better move to San Francisco before Cupid strikes again when my birthday came. And Jimmy didn't call. I gave it one day. Then I got the money I'd been saving for my move to San Francisco and got on a bus. And here I am."

"Mmm," Lucille said. "You don't talk much, but when you get going you do all right."

I blushed. "Tell me about you, now."

"What about me?"

"That conversation we had a while ago... You said you know a lot about shame. How'd you come to know so much?"

"What a question," she said, rolling onto her back. Above the bed a small chandelier hung from an elaborate plaster rosette, three feet across, with a woman's head repeated at four points on the circle. Lucille stared at that a while, and then, in her rich, throaty voice, began to talk about sex. I didn't know you could just talk about it.

"In my earliest memory I'm staring up into the dark, fathomless ceiling of a closet, where there's a shelf as far away to me as the man in the moon. Staring, and longing. My mother took my beloved blanket away. She stashed it there because I'd been masturbating with it." I heard the tender smile in Lucille's voice as she continued, "And she thought that would stop me. The dear woman tried valiantly to save me from myself. I'd lie in bed, eyes glued to the narrow elbow of light seeping around the bedroom door, watching for the moment it would suddenly widen to a glaring rectangle when she came to check on me. I persisted, despite the loss of the blanket and the checking, but absorbed the shame she felt about it. Later I learned about shame from words like chippy, slut, nympho. That's the one that cuts most deep for me: nympho. It says my desires are a sickness. That kind of shame isolates you from yourself. It creates a gulf between you and your desires. You and God."

She was silent a while, and when she began again her words were slow, reflective. "For some women sex is a kind of coin, something they trade for things they want or things they need. Whether they spend Friday night on a street corner or in the bosom of their family, sex is a means to an end. They may enjoy it, or they may enjoy using it, but for them sex is always about something else. For other women sex is a kind of dessert: a delectable pleasure, one that tickles the roof of their mouth like buttercream frosting. They only like sex when it's sweet, when it brings their body pleasure." The light, as it fell across her face, heightened the curve of her cheekbones and deepened the ravines of her eyes, creating dark pools of shadow. For a flickering moment she became for me a contour map of the city, its many hills, including Twin Peaks, looming nearby. "Then there are women for whom sex is bread: sustenance. Our need for it is no less real, no less essential, than our need for food. It sustains us, enables us to carry on from one day to the next, one sorrow to the next, one joy to the next. Occasionally we may use it as coin, but rarely, because it's more valuable to us than the things we can trade it for. We often enjoy it like we might enjoy dessert, but that isn't necessary: sex sustains us whether it is sweet or mournful, pleasurable or painful. Its importance doesn't lie solely in the sensations it provides; it's our cord to the current of life itself."

Lucille smoothed the covers over her torso, reached for a cigarette, slipped it between her lips, and handed me the lighter. The flame flared, casting deep shadows around the room. She blew out smoke and resumed. "My mother did her best, bless her heart. Mortified as she was by the subject, she sat me down and explained sex. No one had ever told *her* about it; she learned on her wedding night. Telling me was an enormous endeavor on her part, and an enormous gift." Lucille smiled and inhaled deeply. Smoke curled from her lips and plumed extravagantly. "I remember when I put it together: realized that this way I touched myself, that felt so delicious, *this* was the thing they called sex. Despite the shame, I was secretly proud I'd discovered it all by myself. Got pretty good at it, too, all by myself. My first time with someone else was with the boy who lived upstairs. But his sister had spent a year in reform school, and when she and her friends came around I ascertained that sex with women has three distinct advantages. I can't get pregnant. It lasts much longer." She abandoned her cigarette to the ashtray. Desire thickened her voice as she reached for me, saying, "And it can resume so much sooner."

Later, I slept deeper than I had in months.

When Pearl and I passed under the Chinatown Gate, the streets narrowed and shop signs were written in intricate, angular strokes. Glistening ducks hung in market windows, and a store with wide-open doors offered jar after jar of precious detritus from the soil of another continent. The door to her building was lacquered in glossy red. The steep, narrow stairway turned near the top, where a small window illuminated a hall runner, vivid despite the dim light.

Mrs. Wu gave Pearl a warm welcome, then turned toward me. She tipped her head down to scrutinize me over filigree cat's-eye glasses. Then she nodded and ushered us into her apartment. I smelled coffee. While Mrs. Wu went to the kitchen, I examined the photographs on a side table: a glamor shot of a young Chinese woman in a hairstyle of the thirties, a studio photo of Lily when she was maybe five or six, and another from, I guessed, two or three years ago.

Mrs. Wu returned with a coffeepot of pale green china. "Cream, sugar?" Her voice was raspy, strong but clotted. She settled on the couch and her eyes returned to my face. In this light I saw the red in them.

"I'm so sorry for your loss."

She looked away, then pulled a handkerchief from her pocket and blotted her eyes. "She was so full of life," she said. "I just can't reconcile..."

I saw tears welling up in Pearl's eyes. She waited, then said, as gently as it is possible to say such a thing, "Mrs. Wu, Joe learned something about Lily's murder that I think you need to know. It won't be easy to hear, but it may help us find out who killed her."

Mrs. Wu looked at me, and caution set her jaw. "I don't mean to be rude, but why do you care?"

"I knew Lily, though only slightly. My brother was also murdered, three months ago. He was...like me. Like Lily. Like Pearl and me," I fumbled.

"No need to beat around the bush," she said. "I was a dancer at a nightclub called Forbidden City—a sort of Cotton Club, only Chinese. Some of the boys there were that way. One of the girls, too, my best friend, Marie. It wasn't a secret, not among us anyway. I didn't want that life for my daughter, but when it became clear about Lily, I spoke to Marie, who was her voice teacher. Marie told her about the life. She's a mannish one. Helped Lily buy her first suit, and took her out. I thought it was safer that way, that she wouldn't have to find it all out for herself. Marie taught her how to be..."—her voice caught—"how to be careful. But...then Lily bought that bar..." Her eyes turned haggard.

"Do the police have any leads?"

She shook her head. "They said Lily was out late, alone, in a disreputable part of town. They said she was dressed to draw attention. They told me sex maniacs move to cities, where they blend in with normal people. It could be anyone. Any man, anyway."

"Did they mention any evidence they're working with, anything they're looking into?"

"No. They haven't found any witnesses. They made clear it was a pretty hopeless case."

I spoke carefully. "Madge said Lily was in conflict with the police about protection money. The afternoon before she died, Lily gave them an unusually fat envelope. Did she say anything to you about it?"

"We didn't talk about the bar much. She knew I was unhappy about it—I thought she should focus on her singing. We'd been arguing, lately."

"About the bar?"

She hesitated. "Yes. And other things. I don't know anything about her relations with the police."

"I spoke with the officer who collected the payoff from Lily shortly before she was killed. This is difficult to say to you, but I feel it might be important. The envelope usually held money; this time it contained a pair of red underpants. Silk, with a dragon embroidered on it."

Mrs. Wu sagged, putting her hand over her eyes. She sat that way for some time. When she spoke again, the light had changed and her voice was ragged.

"I said that Lily and I had argued over other things. Personal things. It was about her father. I never married—I use 'Mrs.' because it saves a lot of questions. Lily knew that. I told her that her father was some sailor who went off to war and never came back. But about a month ago she was looking through my old costumes and found a box in the back of my closet. It was locked, but she managed to open it. She found pictures there. He wasn't wearing a sailor suit."

Mrs. Wu dropped her hand from her eyes. "I was very young when we met, at a bar where I danced. This was before Forbidden City—it was just a dive, a hole-in-the-wall with a tiny stage. He'd come and watch me dance. One night he asked to walk me home. Then he'd visit, late, after I got back from work and before his shift began. It wasn't that he wouldn't marry me; he couldn't marry me. Anti-miscegenation laws. California only changed that three years ago. But...I knew, really, that even if he could, given his work, his ambitions... He was just a rookie cop then. It lasted four years between us. Lily came near the end of the second year. And then, suddenly, it was over. We were still in love—I certainly was, and I believe he was too. But he had his ambitions. The woman he married is wealthy, well connected. And white."

She left the room and returned carrying an ornately carved mahogany box with a splintered lid. "He wanted the brassiere, so I gave it to him. I kept the panties. They were in here." She pulled out a photograph and handed it to me. "This was taken before Lily was born. She knew her father was white, but I never wanted her to know who he was, especially when he became so prominent." The photograph was sepia toned, with scalloped edges. The same pretty young woman from the glamor shot on the table stood in the room we were in, near the window, with a burly man. I passed it to Pearl. Mrs. Wu continued. "I also had some newspaper clippings that follow his promotions, from rookie to inspector to sergeant. I stopped clipping them when it was over, but now he's chief of police. Chief Michael Gafferty."

Pearl inhaled sharply.

Mrs. Wu stared at the photo as she spoke. "Lily was furious with me for concealing the fact that her father was still alive, right here in town. She was also furious because of who he is. I begged her to forget it."

"Mrs. Wu, this is difficult to say as well. The same underpants were found...with Lily, when she was murdered."

She looked me in the eye. Her voice regained its strength. "Do you think he killed her?"

I considered her question, trying to place motives and responses. "Since he's her father, he would almost certainly have interpreted the underwear as blackmail. I don't know if that's what Lily meant by it. Maybe she hoped it would get him to lay off about the protection money. Maybe she just wanted to let him know she knew. But given his prominence, he'd have taken it as a threat."

Pearl shook her head. "What doesn't make sense is, it was found with her body."

I nodded. "As if to send a message to someone."

Pearl countered, "But there's no reason to send *her* a message if she's...not alive to receive it."

"Have you had any contact with him recently, Mrs. Wu?"

She shook her head. "I knew nothing about it," she said firmly. "If I had, I would have stopped her."

"He may have assumed she was working with someone else."

"But the underwear—it links him to her murder."

"Yes, but we have no way of proving it was ever in his hands. The cop who told me about it did so under duress. And if he wanted her killed, I don't think Gafferty would have done it himself. People in those positions have others do their dirty work."

"The bastard," she spat, with more venom than I could have imagined from her elegant bearing. "The police never told me about the underwear, never even asked me about it. He must have shut down the investigation. The bastard," she repeated.

We weren't yet on the sidewalk when Pearl said, "We've got to get into his house."

"Gafferty's house?" I yelped.

"Gafferty's house," she confirmed grimly. "There's got to be something there that will incriminate him. Maybe the matching brassiere with a dragon over each nipple. No, he's too smart for that—if he didn't get rid of it before, he would have after he arranged for Lily's murder."

"Records of the payoffs maybe? That wouldn't tie him in directly, but it would establish a clear motive—and it would smear him."

"Right. He wouldn't keep anything like that at police headquarters. Jobs like his are always political, too easy for his enemies to lay hands on things there. If there's anything to find, it'll be in his home. Pick me up tonight after work."

As I watched for Pearl to emerge from the shadow of the club's awning, I wondered whether Jimmy had waited for Bobby here. On the club's towering marquee, a lowercase "f" extended from top to bottom almost two stories high, the top suggestively domed INOCCHIO running vertically alongside. Pearl emerged beneath it with a shiny pink hatbox. As she dodged a car and crossed the street, I wondered if she was thinking of Bobby too.

She slid into the car, kissed me lightly on the cheek, and instructed me to head south first, then west. "You and me don't want to be driving through that neighborhood this time of night. Nobody'd be happy to see either of us there, much less both of us." We didn't talk as we traversed the nearly empty streets. Near her place the lights of after-hours

jazz clubs flooded the car, flashed in the rearview mirror, then vanished. In her apartment Pearl changed into a fuchsia kimono, poured herself a shot of bourbon and me a glass of seltzer, and settled on the loveseat.

"My friend Rose is a maid in Gafferty's neighborhood and knows just about every domestic who works in the area. She rides the bus with Essie Johnson, Gafferty's housekeeper. I spoke with Essie this afternoon. No love lost between them—he's a sonofabitch at home, too—so she was happy to share some information, and I promised nothing would happen while she was at work. Essie couldn't say for certain what happens before seven a.m., that's the earliest she's ever been brought in, but between then and seven at night they tend to be mighty regular. Most days she arrives at one. His wife spends late mornings puttering in the garden, and while she does she keeps the side door unlocked. So getting in may be a piece of cake. Gafferty's den is at the front of the house. Essie said the dust builds up something awful in there because she's only allowed to clean it when he's home—and he's rarely home during the day."

"Pearl, if we're going to do this, I have to be the one to go in. I can't let you risk—"

"Of course not, Joe. You're a far better hero than me," she declared, with just a hint of irony. "I'm in charge of reconnaissance. You do the dirty work."

If this was a different kind of story I'd say it was an eye for an eye and Lily's life was redeemed by the loss of Gafferty's: that Pearl and I rousted him early one morning, shot him point-blank on his front lawn, then rode off together into the sunset. But it didn't happen that way, and not only because the Pacific Ocean is all there is west of San Francisco.

The homes in St. Francis Wood are small mansions inhabiting lots sized for large cottages. Each one, with its pillars and porticoes, haugh-

199

tily ignores the fact that instead of a vast lawn dotted with towering trees, there's another little mansion squatting ten feet away. This was fortunate for me, private dick with all of a couple months' experience, because I could case the joint from Jimmy's car with a pair of binoculars obtained from my friend at the pawnshop. Everything matched what Essie said. Chief Gafferty exited between 8:02 and 8:06 a.m. He picked his newspaper up off the drive, removed his hat, tossed both on the front seat of his dark-blue Packard, and drove off, not to return till between 5:15 and 5:45 p.m. Mrs. Chief was indoors till about eleven, when the sun generally broke through the fog. Then she devoted at least two hours to a sizable cotillion of dahlia shrubs laden with flowers approaching the size of bowling balls. She plucked and pruned, fertilized, debugged, and created vast arrangements that later appeared in the window of what I guessed was the living room. While she worked she left the side door open and the screen door unlocked. She was usually in view of the door, but occasionally knelt in the soil and buried her head in the undergrowth. Slipping out would be dicey: from inside I couldn't know when her attention was elsewhere.

I put in a call to Mr. Dodson and was disappointed to learn that he did not belong to the Northern California Dahlia Society. He was sorely apologetic. "Afraid I'm not fond of dahlias. Two blowsy for me, all those layers of petals, like the underskirts of a can-can dancer. Also quite prone to mites, which invariably move on to neighboring plants," he tsked, and inquired as to my sudden interest in dahlias. I demurred.

The next day, however, I received a call from Mr. García, who wished to see me again. As we were attempting to settle on an evening, he muttered that Thursday wouldn't do, as he had his Dahlia Society soiree. I persuaded him to meet me that afternoon, and there, in the primitives section of the botanical garden, told him what led me to suspect that the police were connected to—at the very least, helping to protect—the blackmailer. Astonishment registered on his face, increasing exponentially when I revealed that I planned a visit to the chief's home.

"The home of the chief of police? Joe, do you think that wise?"

I agreed that it didn't seem at all wise, but it was necessary, and I needed his help to pull it off. His composure cracked. I kept talking. "You'd only need to pay a visit and make sure she doesn't look toward the screen door for a while. There'd be no connection between us—even if I'm caught, you'd just be a visitor who happened to be there when an intruder was found." His alarm turned to skepticism; an improvement, I thought. "Before I consider turning Chantry over to the law, I need to know how high his connections go. If the chief of police is preparing to collect half of what he's demanded from you, the cops are not going to be very helpful."

Mr. García pondered this for a full minute. Then he turned to me and spoke. "Here is what I will do. Those of us in the Society occasionally visit each other to trade specimens. At Thursday's meeting I'll do my best to interest her in a rather rare variety I brought from northern Mexico—a lovely dark burgundy. If she agrees, I'll let you know the date of my visit." He promised to make the appointment in the golden hours between the chief's departure and the housekeeper's arrival.

On Friday I received a message from Mr. Wilkinson: a gentleman who politely declined to give his name said, "Tuesday at eleven." I knew he'd come through; he'd already decided what color bloom to entice her with.

The fog had lifted by the time Mr. García arrived, and they made their way back to the garden. He positioned himself near a shrub with bloodred blossoms so that Mrs. Chief, when she faced him, had her back to the house. I ambled up the driveway and mounted the brick steps to the side door. Only a screen stood between me and the home of Michael Gafferty, chief of police. The door closed on its own with the slightest "whoosh."

Inside was cool and dark. The kitchen windows opened onto the garden, where Mrs. Chief and Mr. García scrutinized a defenseless shrub overburdened with gargantuan flowers. As I skulked toward the front of the house, the lush carpeting felt like a dense, hellish, taupe quicksand. Midway, doors opened onto a dining room and a sitting room with floral chintz far as the eye could see. I continued on to a mildly grand foyer. There, to my right, were French doors, slightly ajar. A faint whiff of cigar issued from the strenuously masculine room: a well-stocked bar, a vast mahogany desk, shelves lined with thick volumes, and dark-green walls sprouting antlers. I entered. A brass clock loudly ticked off the seconds as they progressed toward noon. I headed for the desk.

The leather top had an intricate pattern embossed around the edge, within which sat a desk lamp, a shiny pen set, a telephone, and a deck of cards. The upper-right drawer held a handgun, loaded. The lower-right drawer, sized for file folders, was locked. I ran fingers along the upper shelf of the bookcase, then along the tops of the books on the uppermost shelf. In the hollow between the covers of *Taming the Criminal: Adventures in Penology* was a small key. It fit.

The files were cryptically labeled. Inside "JC" was a list of dates and numbers. Very large numbers. As I skimmed them I heard a car on the street slow. The car pulled into the driveway. I dropped the file and hurried to the window. From behind sheer drapes I saw a dark-blue sedan proceed slowly up the drive. The very short drive. I ran back to the desk, righted the files, locked the drawer, returned the key to its hiding place, and dived behind the bar just as a heavy step approached. Chief Gafferty joined me in his den.

I couldn't see him from where I was, so I hoped he couldn't see me. A drawer opened, then shut. I heard the dialing of a phone, then two sharp raps, followed by a fffffffffffft. The sounds would have unnerved me if I'd had any nerves left. The rapping repeated, then the fluttering, and I realized he was shuffling the deck of cards. A moment later he snarled, "It's me. I waited to let things blow over. Don't think I'm not furious." Rap, rap, fffffffffffft. "Goddammit, Chantry, what the hell happened?!"

The thin, garbled whine from the other end of the wire was placating. The chief interrupted, his voice steely, the rapping and shuffling providing staccato accompaniment: "I told you to lean on her. *Lean on her.* Rough her up a bit. Let her know she damn well better back off. What the hell happened?"

A brief pause, and his words shattered the air: *"Goddammit, what were you thinking?"* Without waiting for a reply, he continued, "You never know *what* he's going to do next—of course he botched it!" Rap rap, ffffffffffft, a pause, then in a sarcastically mincing voice, "'But he's been so much better lately.' You goddam optimist—the world is overrun with goddam optimists handing out second chances like they're candy. Give-him-another-chance optimists." A momentary pause, then he exploded. "Yes, you are! Anyone who takes a crap and ever eats again is a fucking optimist! 'Oh, when he's off the junk he's completely lucid and reliable,'" he jabbered with vicious sarcasm. "Yeah, very reliable: give or take a life or two!" He growled some more, rapping and shuffling. "You'd better clean this thing up, and clean it up good." His voice rising to full fury, he bellowed, *"And don't think he's your eternal bet on a parolee guard!"* and slammed the phone down.

I listened as his breathing slowed, and at first I thought the voices only seemed louder because his breath grew quieter. Then I realized that the voices of Mrs. Chief and Mr. García were inside the house and coming closer. Mr. García's normally modulated tone was almost strident as he announced his pleasure at having the opportunity to meet her husband. He must have heard the car and the yelling and created some pretext to check on my safety. The den couldn't hold the four of us without one of them having a clear sight line to my hiding place. I knew Mr. García would defend me if things got ugly, and I couldn't let him be drawn into it. The voices came closer. They were seconds from the French doors.

There was only one thing left to do.

I stood up.

chapter eleven

W e haven't been introduced," I said. The chief dropped the cards, gawked, then reached toward his desk—whether for the phone or the gun, I didn't have time to find out. I spoke quickly, evenly: "Unless you want to have a conversation about Lily Wu with your wife present, cover for me." At that moment Mr. García and Mrs. Gafferty appeared between the open French doors. The chief muttered, "maggot," as he pasted an amiable expression on his face and rose.

"My dear, you are home early!" chirped Mrs. Gafferty.

"Yes, I'm here with Miss, er, Janet Jennison," he replied, gesturing toward me as I smiled demurely. "Miss Jennison has, er, agreed to act as a witness in an important case, and I brought her here to discuss it. The station's hectic."

Mrs. Chief, who'd definitely punctured a cream puff or two in her day, shot me a sharp glance. Then she smiled, nodded, and turned. "I am delighted to introduce Mr. Raul García, a compatriot of mine in the

Dahlia Society. Mr. García is sharing some wonderful specimens from his native country."

"Glad to know you, García," the chief said, extending his hand. Mr. García shifted bulbous knobs from one hand to the other as dirt sifted to the floor. I apologized silently to Essie.

The chief introduced me, and Mr. García nodded cordially in my direction, saying, "My pleasure, entirely," but his eyes gawked. Not only did I appear to be in with the clover with Gafferty, but I was wearing a frilly dress, a bouffant that added serious altitude to my butch, and white cotton gloves. He wasn't the only one pretending not to swallow a frog. Standing with Mr. García was the woman who, at this proximity, I recognized as the matron in florid headgear at Lily's funeral. There the four of us stood, pretending everything was dandy. We looked at one another, wondering what might happen next.

"Thank you so much, Chief Gafferty," I offered, mustering blithe self-assurance as I extended my hand toward his.

He eyed me grimly, and I saw in them a momentary urge to detain me, but he took my hand and replied, "We appreciate your willingness to come forward, Miss Janetson. Er, Jennison."

"A pleasure making your acquaintance," I said to the other two, and then departed by the front door. I hightailed it to Jimmy's car, sped away from the curb—and nearly drove off the road as a triumphant whoop erupted from the backseat. Pearl's face loomed in the rearview mirror.

"Steady there, Nellie," she cautioned, but when the wheels were again parallel with the street she roared, "His *face* when you stood up! Your *cool* when you stared him down!"

"What the—Pearl?"

"Oh, honey, our friendly neighborhood informer mentioned that dense camellia just outside the den window. So I lurked. I thought it best not to tell you—I was sure you'd be more resourceful if you didn't know I was peering through the screen with this in my hand." She brandished a small revolver inlaid with mother-of-pearl flowers. "And

I was right: I was about ready to lunge through that window when you stood up! But what was that phone call about? He was shuffling so loud I couldn't make out a word."

We sobered as I told Pearl what I'd heard, and what I'd seen in his drawer.

Sleep wouldn't come, so I went out walking. It was that in-between time, after even the after-hours bars and before the early bustle of shop-keepers hosing down sidewalks. Low-lying clouds sank, enshrouding buildings in their mist. When I passed the car lot, Grimace barked halfheartedly, whined, and licked the palm of my hand. I walked on.

At first, all I saw were his feet. Shoeless. Oversized wool socks poking from the crepuscular shadows of a narrow alley. A ragged hole in the left heel exposed gray skin. I wondered where his shoes had gone and whether he was convinced the sky was falling, since in fact, at the moment, it was. He wasn't muttering, singing, or squawking. Perhaps his mind was lost in another fairy tale. Sleeping Beauty awaiting her prince. Or her princess. As I amused myself with that thought I saw his eyes: wide open, unblinking. And the syringe.

His foot was stiff and cold as stone. I found a phone booth and called the police, then waited till they arrived. I told myself it was to make sure whoever had stolen his shoes didn't come back for his coat. They loaded him into an ambulance that drove off with no sirens blaring through the canyon of empty buildings. The police lingered briefly, collecting evidence with less enthusiasm than Grimace expended on barks. Then one of them started toward me. I cursed myself for not taking off before they arrived. He directed his flashlight at my face, blinding me. I put my hand in front of my eyes, and the light moved down to the ground. It was a young cop I'd seen walking the beat. He didn't hassle me much. I asked if he knew the dead man's name.

"Thomas Billing. Been on the street for years. We were supposed to go easy on him; he was a buddy of the chief's, before he went off to war and came back like this. Nutso." The cop scowled and said corrosively, "Junkies all turn up like this in the end. Sometimes the needle's still stuck in their arm." He shook his head in disgust. Then he barked, "Move along, kid."

"Where'd they take him?"

"Indigents go to S.F. General. But we all end up in Colma after that. Now move along."

In the morning I called Mr. García, thanked him for his help, explained what I'd learned in Gafferty's den and how I came to be Janet Jennison. I asked whether there was any chance the chief got my license plate when I drove away. "Oh, no," he said with certainty, "I kept him occupied. There was that deck of cards splayed out over his desk, so I asked his favorite game, then interrogated him on the intricacies of blackjack." I could almost hear him smile with satisfaction as he concluded, "There's more to it than you might think."

San Francisco General Hospital's ornate brick buildings appeared to have been designed for some more opulent purpose. Inside, the toad-eyed coroner's stained jacket prodded my imagination; I trained my eyes on his metal desk. He looked up briefly, returned to his paperwork, and continued writing as he answered my questions.

"Accidental heroin overdose. All junkies overdose sooner or later. The ones who have trouble getting a regular fix, sooner. Tolerance builds up quickly, so they need more and more to get off; but tolerance wears off quickly and they don't realize that, or ignore it because they're so anxious to get off, so they O.D. Junk was almost impossible to get hold of during the war, and when it finally hit the streets again they all overdosed, one after another. Sometimes I'd have three or four in a night. Slowed down since then. But they all overdose eventually. Best thing, really. Puts them out of their misery, gets them out of society's hair."

"How do you know it was accidental?"

"As opposed to suicide, or murder?" He glanced, up, eyed me intently, and replied, "We don't. We don't ever know for sure. Not unless there's a note." He shrugged. "But who'd want to murder a bum?" He stopped and looked embarrassed. "I'm sorry, kid, you a friend a his?"

I shook my head. "Just an acquaintance."

"Well, acquaintances count as friends when it's all they've got. You're the first one come to see about him, and probably the last. You want his personal effects?"

"But I'm not a relative."

"Not likely we're gonna have any of his relatives come visiting." He put down his pen, disappeared behind a heavy door, and returned with a large bag of thick brown paper. He thrust it at me. "Otherwise we just burn it. You gotta fill out a form, though."

I hesitated.

"You wanna have him buried? Otherwise he's going to the potter's field." The cemetery flashed in my mind, Jimmy's mound of naked earth.

I shook my head.

"Well, take the bag anyway. Maybe you'll figure out his secrets."

I set it on the desk. It crackled loudly as I unfolded the top. I pulled out pungent long johns. A shirt and two sweaters, one of which moths had reduced to confetti. Fraying trousers and a length of rope, the one he wore around his waist. His coat, torn at the seams, pockets turned inside out revealing only holes. At the bottom of the bag were his two socks. And two scarves, entangled like snakes, wool skeins snagged, matted. I'd never seen them in the light of day. One of the scarves was chartreuse. The other turquoise.

I heard the bag's thick paper crumpling like distant thunder. The coroner looked at my shuddering hands.

"You okay?"

"If you keep this bag, how long would you keep it for?"

"One month," he said definitively, but looked at me quizzically.

I threw everything back in and thrust it at him. "Please hold on to it for a while."

"You gotta fill out a form, either way," he replied, taking it from me. "So's I can release it to you, or so's we can track you down before we destroy it." He extracted a page from a drawer, turned it around, and slid it in front of me. I filled it out and pushed it back to him.

He squinted at it. "Jeffrey Johnson," he read. "At the Regal Apartments."

I nodded. And fled.

I stopped at Jimmy's garden to sit among the sunflowers he'd watered and weeded but never seen flower. It was a mournful assembly, stalks tilting, blooms spent. Their heads hung, dry and dejected, and the crumpled leaves canted at awkward angles. I sat, chided by birds dissatisfied with the meager remains, and missed him. Then I headed to Mrs. Wu's.

Marie met me at the door. I recognized her from the funeral, a seasoned butch with graying hair and a neatly pressed pocket square. "Call me Marie," she commanded, shaking my hand with a grip nonchalant as a bulldog's jaw. She gestured to a chair, then stalked toward the kitchen, long stride straining her narrow skirt.

Mrs. Wu caught me rubbernecking, and a slight smile lit her mournful face. "Marie's always been that way. When she sang at Forbidden City, Charlie tried everything to get her to walk gracefully: charm school, ballet lessons, rubber bands around her knees. Finally he threw in the towel, dressed her in a tailored suit, and introduced her as 'the Chinese Gladys Bentley.' It flew over the head of most of the crowd, but they loved her anyway."

Marie returned with cups and spoons rattling like a streetcar. She passed me coffee, attentively arranged Mrs. Wu's, then joined her on the couch. When Pearl arrived they listened silently to our news, faces slack with grief.

Mrs. Wu summarized softly, grimly, "It's still all circumstantial."

"It wouldn't convict him," Pearl conceded, "but if it got out, all of it, it would surely implicate him."

Marie concurred. "Lily was his daughter, she refused to pay him off, and she was murdered by an old buddy of his. Anyone can put the pieces together."

"He'd deny it all," Mrs. Wu countered. "Fight like the devil, that's how he is."

"But it would damage him, politically," Marie said firmly. "Maybe enough to bring him down."

Mrs. Wu nodded hesitantly. "Perhaps." She was quiet for a while. Then she lifted her chin and announced, "I'm prepared to tell the papers about my relationship with him. Marie and I have been discussing it: it might force the police to pay more attention to the case." Pearl looked surprised, and Mrs. Wu shrugged her shoulder. "My family disowned me when I became a dancer—in their eyes that was just as reputable as a whore. I've got no reputation to lose. With Lily gone, I have nothing left to lose. But we can't just go to the papers with this, can we?"

Pearl agreed, reluctantly. "The only way to prove the panties left Lily's hands, or landed in Gafferty's, is through the cop who passed them up the line. He's unlikely to volunteer testimony that has him and his boss accepting bribes."

"And the phone conversation I overheard, that's my word against the chief of police. The fact that I was in his home without an invitation wouldn't bolster my credibility."

Marie was undaunted. "Which leaves us with the bit of fluff. If the police wanted to be sure no one knew about it, they'd have tossed it. So they just didn't care enough to notice it. We have to make them see it. And we have to do it before the bag at the coroner's gets tossed."

"But if we say they're ignoring a critical piece of evidence, they'll just make it disappear," Mrs. Wu replied. "We point to the photograph, they'll say it was—I don't know—some lint on the negative. And without it the scarves in the coroner's office don't mean anything."

"We need to get the lint recognized as evidence, first," Marie declared. She stared into her coffee. It seemed as good a strategy as any other, so I stared into mine. I didn't find anything there. But Marie found a plan. It was complicated and it was risky, but it was a plan.

I went to see another bulldog. Madge.

The bar was almost empty that time of day, after lunch but before the evening crowd. Just a few regulars at a corner table, holding one another up while they nursed beers. Madge stood sentry behind the bar with a damp gray towel over her shoulder. She looked about as pleased to see me as a weary rat is to see an alley cat. I said hello. Then I asked her why no one tries to expose the cops for squeezing protection money from the bars.

She looked at me, looked off into space for a while, sighed irritably, and asked, "You seen the big furniture store on The Miracle Mile? The really big one, with that enormous sign three stories up that says Seventeen Reasons Why? You know the one I mean."

I nodded. Supported by a labyrinth of steel scaffolding, jutting up into the sky like there'd never been an earthquake within a thousand miles of the place. "Yeah, I've seen it," I said.

"Well, I got *eighteen* reasons why no one is gonna talk about the payoffs." She cocked her head to one side and counted off heatedly on her fingers. "Reason number one: Who am I gonna go to, the cops? Oh, that's right, *they already know about 'em.* Reason number two: say I bypass the police. Who'm I gonna tell—the *Chronicle?* You think they're not in the pocket of the mayor? Mayor's responsible for the police: if the police look bad, he looks bad. The *Chron*'s never gonna publish anything that damning to his top appointee, the chief of police—not unless there's some seismic shift in power at the top." She blew out air and barreled on.

"Reason number three: let's say I bring it to the *Chron* anyhow—or I up my chances and go to the *Examiner,* just hoping some two-bit reporter's gonna take the bait and try to build his career on a scoop that everyone else thinks is too hot to handle. And let's say my reporter decides that the faster route to fame is getting in good with the cops—who can, just for starters, provide exclusive access to the bloodiest crime scenes for all eternity. So instead of riding *my* story to the Pulitzer, the reporter buys the friendship of the entire police force by mentioning that there's some piddling tight-ass bar owner trying to pass a story about cops taking bribes. What's this bar gonna be worth after that? Every cop on the street'll be on us, raiding the place every night of the week." I put up my hand, but she ignored me.

"Reason number four: let's just say, for the sake of argument, that I do manage, against all odds, to bring these bribes to the public's attention. So it's gonna be my word against the police? Me, degenerate owner of a bar catering to perverts. My word's gonna hold about as much weight as a stiletto with a loose heel. Reason number five: having established that my word holds no weight when stacked against that of the police, I'm never gonna work in this town again. Not as a bar owner, not as a bartender—not as a goddam toilet scrubber. And I'd consider myself lucky if both my kneecaps are still intact." She grabbed one end of the towel and flipped it off her shoulder, slapping it hard on the bar. She was just warming up. "Reason number—where was I? Oh, yeah, reason number six—"

"I get it, Madge, I get it." Her towel spattered little droplets of swampy water on my tie. "But—since we're supposing: let's say you weren't crazy enough to try it, but someone else was. That someone took their chances and told the two-bit reporter when and where a pickup was gonna happen. Anonymously. The bartender wasn't involved in the tip-off, but did happen to appear in the photos that hit the front page the next day. And maybe the bartender helped line up visits to a couple other pickups across town. Just supposing. Would you be that bartender?"

She stared me down. Hard. She slapped her towel on the bar a few more times, watching it smack against the worn wood. My tie kept collecting swampy spots. Then she said, bitterly, "Those fuckers. Yes. For Lily. For what they did to Lily."

That night I retreated to Lucille's body, undressed her slowly, and gave gratitude in pleasure returned. She folded me into her warm nest and kept the dead at bay for a few hours, reminding me there was a world not laced with sinister intent.

I sorted through the library's disorganized stacks of the *Examiner* till I found the paper that reported Lily's murder. Their photograph was taken from a slightly different angle than the *Chron's*. The fluff was there, but only if you knew to look for it. The byline was Danny Carmichael.

"Carmichael here." He had the voice of a man who'd eaten too many steaks. I was hoping for mean and hungry. But then, someone who's eaten a lot of steaks is thinking about the ones he's gonna eat tomorrow. I hung my hope on that instead.

"My name is Charlotte Pearson. I have very sensitive information concerning corruption on the part of the San Francisco Police Department. I'm prepared to make you privy to payoffs extorted from certain establishments by the department. You will have a front-row seat at several pickups. Would you be interested in such information?"

The pause was long. I heard typewriters clacking, someone yelling for coffee, and Carmichael's brain calculating how much beef he could buy with the raise he'd get for the exposé. Versus how much he'd buy with what he got from the police for passing on it. I wondered how he liked his steaks. Man with a voice like that probably liked them well-done. With ketchup.

"I'm very interested in meeting with you, Miss Pearson," he said.

"Mrs.," I corrected him.

"Excuse me. Mrs. Pearson. When can we meet?"

"Tomorrow. Eleven a.m. The coffee shop at the Emporium. I'll be wearing a lavender hat."

"Couldn't we meet at a more discreet location, one that would allow us to talk freely? Your home, perhaps, Mrs. Pearson?"

"No, Mr. Carmichael, we cannot."

"Very well. Please give me your phone number, so I can call you in the event anything unexpected comes up—it does so often in my line of work. I wouldn't want to leave you waiting for me when I was out on a story."

"I think you'll find my information more important than most stories. Goodbye, Mr. Carmichael."

At ten to nine I was outside the Emporium. My companions were ladies wearing hats badly in need of pruning. The coffee shop was quiet, neat linen tablecloths set for tea. Just past it was a hall with a bank of telephone booths guarding the restrooms. I waited till I had the hall to myself, pushed open the door to the phone booth at the far end, and bent down on one knee. The attaché case just fit. With the door open and the light off, the case disappeared in the shadow beneath the seat. With the door closed, the legs of whoever had closed it should obscure the view. It might be overlooked for a couple of hours.

I hightailed it back to Jimmy's room to change. To barter my name to the cops for favors, Carmichael needed to know it. We didn't want him sniffing around the demimonde for me. We aimed to have him searching among ladies who'd clutch their pearls if they saw me in my usual attire. Fortunately, Pearl loves a challenge.

"You're too young for matron, so we'll go for meddling matronette," she mused. "Someone who in ten years'll be organizing campaigns in local high schools to limit how tight girls can wear their sweaters. Campaigns enlisting structural engineers for pro bono studies to measure the tensile stretch of various knits." She was warming to her subject. "Campaigns to strike fear into the hearts of sweater girls who know their finest assets—and induce sleepless nights in those gray-haired engineers, sweating through fantasies of the breaking points of particular knits on nubile chests." At the Goodwill she'd located a dress with a cinched waist and full skirt covered in pink roses. Dismissing the pearl necklaces at the counter—"fake as those rayon stockings they had us wearing during the war"—she loaned me a prim strand of her own, along with a white leather purse and a wig that ended in a demure curl. Then we spent most of the afternoon locating the hat. Five stores, it took, and the money I'd brought for the whole outfit. "Lavender," she said, "Why the hell did you say lavender? In October!" But I had to admit the effect was very Junior League.

She made me practice walking in it. "No, no, no! Not alluring; you want *overbearing*. Authoritative. Busybody! You just know your nose belongs in other people's business. And not in a good way." She showed me how to sit, swiping my hand discreetly down my ass just before I landed, then gently settling the skirt over my knees like I was arranging tissue paper over a fragile gift. "Purse goes on the seat next to you, not on the table. Never on the table! And take your gloves off before you eat or drink. Hey, here's a fake rock. It's a nice fake. I want it back." We worked out my haughty speech and practiced it a dozen times. By evening I was keeping an eye out for wayward sweater girls.

I was ten minutes early for Carmichael. Taking a seat that faced the rear of the cafeteria, I turned back toward the entrance and waited. At two minutes to eleven a cocksure man with a ruddy face stood scanning the cafeteria. I'd been hoping for a hungry rat; instead I got a fox with a luxurious tail and keen eyes.

"Mrs. Pearson?" he inquired.

I extended a gloved hand. "Yes, though it's unlikely you'll find a Charlotte Pearson in the phone book, and if you do, it won't be me. It is an assumed name, Mr. Carmichael."

"Well, thank you for saving me the trouble." His manner was casual, but he studied me closely as the waitress poured our coffees. I removed my gloves, confined myself to one lump, and kept my pinky in the air.

"My husband has a prominent position in this town, and I have reasons of my own for choosing anonymity; suffice it to say, we have a *distant* relative who fell into a sordid underworld. What should concern you is the fact that corruption is permitted and condoned in the current administration. It is an insult to the upstanding citizens of this city that our men in blue, whose salaries we furnish, are susceptible to bribes." I troweled some more sanctimonious bunk his way. "I have the names of three saloons from which the police department exacts payment in exchange for their continued operation. I am prepared to furnish you with these names and the approximate times that officers visit each week. You will have an opportunity to witness and, with the assistance of a discreet cameraman, record the acceptance of bribes on the part of uniformed officials of the San Francisco Police Department. I trust you comprehend the gravity of this information."

"I do indeed, Mrs. Pearson."

"I am pleased to hear that. I will nonetheless point out, Mr. Carmichael, that the information I am to provide you with is worth a great deal to certain people. Its exposure could do considerable damage to the current administration. Its suppression, therefore, could be of extreme interest to those currently in power, the chief of police in particular. Possession of this information, and the means to effectively disseminate it, will therefore place you in a rather ironic position, Mr. Carmichael: one that will enable you to exact considerable compensation for its use or its misuse."

"I follow your implication, Mrs. Pearson. The *San Francisco Examiner* is on the side of integrity and rectitude in governance."

"Those are lovely words, Mr. Carmichael. I hope there will be deeds to substantiate them."

I removed from Pearl's purse a piece of paper and placed it on the table between us. I tapped it several times. Then I slid it across the table to him. I shook out my gloves, slipped one on each hand, and rose. "Good day, Mr. Carmichael."

"Mrs. Pearson, I'm interested in your—"

"I've already said all that I am prepared to say to you, Mr. Carmichael. I entrust you with this information in the hope of saving our fair city from the scourge of corruption. Now, I must excuse myself." I strode to the hallway and entered the last of the phone booths.

Reaching my hand under the seat, I found the handle of the attaché case. I exhaled. I'd kept an eye on the entrance to the hall, so I knew there was one occupant in the men's room. I waited till he left, then stepped quickly out of the booth and into a men's room stall. I set the attaché case on the toilet and snapped it open. Its sharp clicks felt reassuring. I kicked off the pumps, slipped the trousers on, and slid my feet into my pawnshop brogues. I heard the door push open and quickly gathered up the pumps as someone shuffled to the urinals. I tugged off the hat and wig, then the dress, and crumpled them into the case with the pumps. I fished out a shirt and slid it on. The suit jacket was creased, but I shook it out, noticing the handkerchief falling from the pocket—a reminder to wipe off my makeup. Then I flushed, snapping the case closed as the water gushed. I squared my shoulders and stepped out of the stall.

My first glance was to the mirror; it told me I was OK. My second was to my fellow occupant, and it told me Lady Luck was smiling on me. He was an old gent, dapper, but his body listed to the left as though buffeted by a strong wind. We met at the sinks. I complimented him on his fedora, a silver felt with a gray band.

"I purchased it in the haberdashery department here. Quite a fine one, if I do say so myself."

"You know, I'm in need of a hat. I was down by the Ferry Building when a sudden gust took mine into the bay. Where is that department?"

"Why, I'd be happy to show you, young man." We dried our hands and I held the door for him. In the hall I offered my arm. He took it, his weight hardly palpable. I ducked my head as if to hear him better, and asked him how to pick a fine hat. As he explained we strolled through the coffee shop. At the counter was a man in a green trench coat with a sour expression and both eyes on the hall we'd just left. He could be a tail arranged by Carmichael, or a guy waiting for his wife. I accompanied my new friend to the haberdashery, browsed the pricey fedoras, then hit the street.

The pickup at Pandora's Box was Monday afternoon at four o'clock. The other two were on Tuesday, a three o'clock at the Beige Room and a four o'clock at the Chi Chi Club. Tuesday at six I called Carmichael.

"I trust your visits to the locales I suggested were productive, Mr. Carmichael."

"Indeed they were, Mrs. Pearson. I thank you for entrusting me with this information."

"You are most welcome. I will be interested to see how you put it to use."

"Put it to use?"

"Don't be disingenuous, Mr. Carmichael. I want you to know that the information I've provided you with thus far is a canoe capsizing in a lazy river on a sunny afternoon. Whether or not I provide you with the *Titanic* depends on how you handle the canoe. Are you understanding me, Mr. Carmichael?"

"I believe I am, Mrs. Pearson. But how will I—"

"I will contact you again if I find that the information I've given you is used in the manner we discussed. If not, I will take the *Titanic* elsewhere."

That evening, cramps had me nearly bent over. I was falling off the roof, as Mother used to say. A sanitary belt always feels awkward, but it felt more so under men's trousers. It felt...perverse. I'd put on Jimmy's clothes because I was tired of being treated like a little lady, but when I bought my own suits and shirts and ties—I felt right in them. All my beanpole gawkiness seemed to settle down, and it was OK that I wasn't pliant as fresh meringue. With a sanitary belt tangled in the crotch of my boxers, that rightness felt wrong, Jimmy's squirrels-and-peas sermon in the woods seemed off base, and what they say about us rang true: that we are sick, morally twisted, in some inescapable way. That's what they mean when they call us "degenerates": destined to descend, deeper and deeper, into depravity.

A remark I'd read in the paper returned to me that night. Some senator from Nebraska said, "You can't hardly separate homosexuals from subversives." And the same way your tongue worries the crater when a tooth's been lost, my thoughts returned again and again to his claim, seeing it manifest around me, inevitable as fate. As a kid, Jimmy'd gone to boot camp rather than turn in a friend, but he'd last been seen working both sides of the law, an undercover stooge ratting on his friends. For all I knew, Tiny was right: he was in on the blackmail too, finding out what money their victims had left, so he and Chantry could squeeze as much as possible from the lives they'd debauched. My future passed before my eyes, a tunnel at the end of the light. The signs were already there. I was pretending to be someone I wasn't, playing a twisted game with Carmichael, and fixated on death—Jimmy's and Lily's and Bobby's, and now the demise of a lunatic, drug-addicted stranger living on the street. Just a rung or two down from me.

If I fled into Lucille's arms I knew I'd see it all confirmed in her as well—ruinously, irrevocably, I wouldn't be able to stop myself from seeing it and saying it. Huddled in Jimmy's bed, flailing, I reached for a lifeline that didn't lead from me to certain ruin. Remembering Lucille's words, I prayed. I prayed to the God of Nelly Queens— a God, I resolved, with backbone. A God who was loyal, steadfast, incorruptible. A God who would surrender everything to protect friends.

That's when it hit me: when they sang "God Save Us Nelly Queens" at the Black Cat, they followed the melody of "God Save the Queen"— *the same tune as "My Country, 'Tis of Thee."* A tangled morass of reactions flooded me: outrage at their perversion of a song I'd been singing since childhood; acrid appreciation of the irony of that crowd singing to the tune of "sweet land of liberty"; and, finally, a discordant jolt of pride at the depth of the song's subversiveness.

For days I lived in this funk. I walked. I discovered it wasn't at all hard to pull off heartbreak when the sky's high and cobalt. I avoided everyone I knew, afraid I'd see only the worst in them, witness their lives careening toward the kind of fate people like us meet in dime-store novels, the kind Bobby and Jimmy and Lily met. I was haunted, too, by the knowledge that—just like Jimmy before me—I was with-drawing from those I'd thought of as friends.

chapter twelve

The front page of Wednesday's *Examiner* carried, above the fold, three grainy photographs of police officers accepting fat envelopes from bartenders in gloom-clad bars. The chiaroscuro images weren't easily distinguishable from photos of the muck that accumulates in roadside puddles. After considerable study I noted that Madge had gussied herself up and shown some cleavage, which could justifiably be mistaken, in the murky image, for the hind end of a horse. But the headline was crystal clear, a righteously indignant inch and a half tall: "POLICE CORRUPTION EXPOSED."

The article denounced the mayor and the chief of police for cultivating an environment in which police expected payoffs for protection. Carmichael spent considerable time drawing parallels to the corruption scandal that brought down Mayor Eugene Schmitz in 1907; he trumpeted his newspaper's heroic role as a defender of morality and crusader against vice and degeneracy. He paid plenty of attention to Chief Gafferty, including insidious implications regarding the funding of his pet project, the Police Athletic League. The paper's top editorial proclaimed the administration rotten to the core. Even Herb Caen weighed in, between bits on socialite Muffy O'Dair's birthday party and the sage ruminations of a man who worked the corner of Market and Montgomery shining shoes: "And the first shots were fired in next fall's mayoral elections. The Barbary Coast lives up to its reputation... And some people pretend to be surprised..."

The next day the *Chronicle* fired back: "TRUMPED-UP CHARGES MOTIVATED BY POLITICS." The paper denounced false claims against the city's upstanding chief of police and called on the mayor to investigate shady dealings at the *Examiner*. The Police Commission weighed in, professing its "utmost confidence" in Chief Gafferty. I gave Madge a call. She said there'd been no fallout there, but the police had moved their pickups to Wednesdays. The papers slugged it out for the rest of the week. One thing was certain: no one in the City, from Muffy O'Dair to the shoeshine man at Market and Montgomery, could fail to know the name of the chief of police.

"Hello, again, Mr. Carmichael."

"Why, hello, Mrs. Pearson." I'd chosen the same table as last time, but found it harder to play matronette. "Thank you for the fine job you did with the corruption article."

"All in a day's work. Now I'd like to hear about that *Titanic*."

"I have arranged for you to meet with the mother of Lily Wu. Mrs. Wu is prepared to provide you with evidence indicating that Lily Wu was the illegitimate daughter of the chief of police."

Silence.

"You remember the name Lily Wu?"

"That lady bar owner murdered a few weeks back. I covered the story."

"You're going to want to cover this. Her mother has a photo of herself with Gafferty, about thirty years ago."

"Unless it shows the two of them *in flagrante delicto*, a photo doesn't prove anything. The chief's going to deny it."

"Of course he will. But at the same time you're going to show that the department was careless and indifferent in its investigation of her murder. Take a close look at the photographs that accompanied your story. There's a bit of fluff, some threads, hanging from the heel of the shoe that's near her hand. She was defending herself with that shoe. Those threads came from whoever murdered her. The fluff is sitting in a corner of the evidence box. It hasn't even been tagged as evidence. You got a friend in the police department?"

"I know a guy or two," he said, diffident.

"See if he can help you get at those threads. Get them entered as evidence. If you mention them in the papers first, they'll disappear."

"So the police overlooked a few threads in the murder of a lowlife bar owner whose mother claims she's the illegitimate daughter of the chief of police. What the hell kind of story is that?"

"It becomes dynamite when you know the next piece. A veteran who's been living on the streets since the war just died of a drug overdose. Back in the day he was best friends with the chief. This is common knowledge: men on the force had instructions to go easy on him because he used to be Gafferty's buddy. It's an it-can-happen-to-anyone kind of story, a fall from grace."

Carmichael smirked. "Heartwarming."

"Until you look at the personal effects the coroner's office will be holding for exactly three more weeks. And you notice that the fibers in the scarves he wrapped around his neck exactly match the fibers dangling from Lily Wu's shoe."

Carmichael was a sharp guy. "But that's all circumstantial."

"Yeah, and it's all I've got. The chief's position is already weakened by your corruption reports. Linking him to the murder of his daughter— even the murder of someone claimed to be his daughter—looks pretty bad. And since that court case she's resisted paying the cops their accustomed graft, and encouraged other tavern owners to do the same."

Carmichael rubbed his chin, musing. "Hmm... It's seedy, and sensational. The Oriental love child." He perked up like a dog on a scent. "How did the mother meet Gafferty?"

"She was a dancer. At Forbidden City."

He grinned.

"Listen, her daughter was just murdered. Handle her with kid gloves."

He nodded, but he didn't stop grinning.

"Mr. Carmichael, timing is everything. Two pieces of evidence can disappear at any moment: the fluff or the scarves. The chief'll make them disappear if he gets wind of this before it hits the street. He'll claim the fluff in the photo is just a bit of lint on the negative. And who's to know that his old buddy didn't wear gray and brown scarves. Or no scarves at all."

Carmichael was nodding thoughtfully as he lit a cigar. "I'll start with the Lily Wu story. It's a little weak by itself, but after breaking the corruption piece, I'm one up with my editor." He puffed, staring into space as acrid smoke gathered above the table. "My cop friend, he owes me one. I'll tell him I noticed the fluff in the photo and got to wondering about it. Just following up, seeing if there's anything left to the story. Far as they're concerned, it's a dead-end case. So no skin off his back. Piece o' cake. Then we add the mother, and her photo. Salacious. One of her as a dancer, in some skimpy outfit. That'll sell copy. My editor'll love it." He forgot to puff and the ash built up on the end of his cigar. "Then the addict story. The plight of veterans struggling to integrate back into civilian society." He waved the cigar in circles, and ash drifted down to the table.

"I'll get my assistant on it today. Combine it with a few other sad sack stories. Maybe include a guy who manages to turn it around, give it a nice upbeat ending and make it about a bigger issue so the chief doesn't start to sweat. I'll ask his office for comment, give him a chance to make some poignant statement about his buddy's great potential stunted by the violence of war, blah-blah. That'll work." He smiled to himself. "So the chief of police had an illegitimate daughter by a Chinese dancing girl; the degenerate daughter owned a bar catering to perverts and resisted payoffs to the cops; and then she was murdered by an old buddy of the chief's. Perhaps she was blackmailing the chief, perhaps not; either way, her death looks less like a random sex crime and more like an attempt by Gafferty to iron out some shady wrinkles from his past." He looked up at me. "Not bad." The cigar found its way back to his mouth and he clamped moist lips around it. Smoke billowed. I stood. He looked at me, curious. "Say, you get around, don't you?"

"Yeah," I said. "I get around."

"And this Lily Wu. What's your connection to her?"

I scraped together my tired hauteur. "When our, ah, distant relative hit rock bottom in those dens of iniquity, Miss Wu found my husband's card in his pocket and was kind enough to give us a call. Saved the family quite a bit of embarrassment," I sniffed. "And she became a friend."

He pasted a sober expression on his face, like I hadn't just handed him the best story of his career. "I'm sorry for your loss," he said dutifully.

"Like I said, put on your kid gloves when you talk to Mrs. Wu. She's only trying to get some justice for her daughter. This story's gonna cost her. Give her her dignity, will you?"

Carmichael nodded, but I could see his mind was already on those nice steaks. This story'd take him from prime rib to porterhouse.

They tried to drag Mrs. Wu in the dust, but her dignified composure in interviews fortified her account. The chief denied everything; after all, "turquoise and chartreuse were popular colors last year." The mayor was said to be considering his dismissal, but every day Gafferty stayed in his job it became more likely he'd weather the storm. Just a sexual peccadillo, a youthful indiscretion. That link to his old friend: no one controls old friends, especially after they go off the deep end.

Mr. Wilkinson said there was a message from Lucille. "This one's urgent," he added with a wink.

Lucille's voice on the phone was hushed and dead serious. "Word is, someone saw Gabriel Bambino—that cop discharged from the force along with your brother—up in Nevada City. They seem surprised he's alive. The way I heard it, Officer Chet Tully's heading east to find him, soon as he gets off work. Tully's a mean cop. Brawls happen when he's in the vicinity. Keep your distance if you can. About six foot two. Red hair, curly as a pig's tail. Pug nose swarming with freckles."

I found Nevada City on the map in Jimmy's glove compartment. Past Sacramento, north and east, where the lines on the map go from straight as uncooked spaghetti to intricate tendrils that fade out like veins. I filled the tank, put Jimmy's gun in the glove compartment, and drove. After two bridges the buildings gave way to golden, rolling hills studded with scrubby dark-green trees. The gold was radiant, glowing like the earth was lit from within, and I wondered what the forty-niners thought when they saw it. Auspicious, no doubt: a promise, to see hills glowing like that. Then those hills became flat, stubby fields, far as the eye could see. The roads bore bleak names like Mace, Dry Creek, and Winters. Sacramento came and went. I turned north.

Nevada City is a jumble of storefronts clambering steeply up a hill. A western town, right out of the movies, the buildings boasting huge false fronts and plank sidewalks that echo hollowly as you walk. More than half the stores were boarded up. The road in the center was paved, though, and a neon sign in a window said Pie. I gassed up first. A lanky beanpole of a man limped from the garage to take my money. He grunted in place of saying "You're welcome," so I left without asking any questions. Conversing with the wrong person could mean more trouble for Gabe. I parked Jimmy's sedan in front of a tidy cottage with lilacs out front and headed for pie.

It was under glass, on one of those round stands that turn slowly, so I could see from all sides that it was soggy and crestfallen. I ordered coffee. The waitress had a sour smile and watched someone outside the window cross the street while she took my order, so I drank the coffee quickly, paid, and left. In the general store a woman with a tidy bun asked if she could help me. When I said I was looking for a friend who'd moved here several months ago, her eyes turned vague. I bought a pack of gum and moved on. The barber was dozing in his chair, a portly man with eight strands of hair combed across his shiny dome, mouth wide open. He didn't look likely and I didn't need a haircut so I continued on to the hardware store.

The smell of beeswax sweetened my mood as I entered. A polished wooden counter stretched the length of the store. Behind it, a hundred small wooden drawers labeled in spidery script spanned the wall from floor to ceiling. Shelves held the boundless minutiae of hardware stores, meticulously arrayed. Everything gleamed. I heard a throat being cleared, and behind an ornate brass cash register a slight man with a neat mustache and bow tie inclined his head toward me, then continued polishing a large brass hurricane lamp. I fingered a stack of crisply pressed bandanas on the counter, fanned out in alternating red and blue, then turned to him. He set down his lamp and faced me, expectant.

"Lovely town," I began.

He agreed.

"Beautiful shop you have here."

He smiled modestly and thanked me. To give him more time to acquaint himself with my face I removed my hat, lifted my chin, and scratched a nonexistent itch. I looked at the wall of boxes, then the wall of shelves, so he could see my profile from both sides. I said, "I'm looking for a friend." He nodded thoughtfully, so I continued. "He moved up here about three months ago. Italian. Dark hair, olive skin," I added, though I'd never actually seen the man and it added nothing of importance to "Italian." I paused. "He's very fond of opera."

The slender man behind the counter nodded thoughtfully again. He cocked his head slightly to one side, looking concerned. He stroked his

mustache, first the right side, then the left. He cleared his throat before he spoke.

"This friend of yours. Would you be bringing him good news, or bad?"

"Bad news," I said.

After due consideration he observed, "Bad news is generally more essential than good news."

"More urgent, too."

"Hm," he nodded. I'd made a decisive point. "Your friend lives northeast of town." He began to give me complicated directions involving a dilapidated barn, a large scrub oak with a limb that hugged the ground, and not a single road that bore a name. A bell tinkled behind me and the barber walked in.

"Hello, Ed," he said, while I occupied myself with the handkerchiefs. "A pack of razor blades. Went through that last batch mighty quick," he added.

I heard Ed smile as he replied, "Business must be good."

The barber countered pointedly, "Or the blades not as sharp as they should be." Ed let that be. The barber paid and the bell tinkled as he left.

I returned to the counter. Ed was silently drawing a map. When he was done he handed it to me, saying, "You ought to keep that hat on when you can." I nodded. "Tell your friend someone else was looking for him, just an hour or so ago. He flashed a badge." Ed saw the concern on my face. "Not likely anyone in town would have said they knew him. People around here shy away from that. Except maybe Sheriff Tate." He glanced at his watch and his face eased. "It's well past three. Tate's pretty tight by now. Doubtful he'd say much in that state. I saw the man's car heading north."

"Carrot top and freckles?"

Ed nodded.

At a fork in the road the pavement ended. A short length of wood nailed to a tree was hand-lettered with the words THIS WAY and an arrow pointing to the right. Scrawled in a different hand on another piece of wood was THAT WAY, with an arrow pointing to the left. I went That Way, as Ed had directed. The road became rough and curvy. I drove slowly, glad for the irons and spare tire Jimmy left in the trunk. A fainter road, grown high with weeds, broke off to the left and I followed it. When it petered out on a grassy knoll I was twenty feet from a two-story house that had lost all its paint or never had any to begin with. A sagging porch graced the front of the house. On the porch stood a bearded man with a gun pointed at my chest.

I cut the gas and put my hands up where he could see them. My window was down so I called to him. "I'm Jimmy's sister! Brother! Sister." Hell.

"Go away or I'll shoot." The voice was grim.

"I need to talk with you!"

"Go away or I'll shoot!"

"Please," I hollered. "Jimmy's dead. I need to know what happened."

"Go away!" he bellowed.

"Gabe, I need to talk with you. I'm Josie. Jimmy must have mentioned me."

"There's no Gabe here!" he shouted. I waited. I waited some more. The gun was still pointing at me.

"I'm going to open the door now," I called to him. I kept my right hand up as I pulled back the latch, then raised my left again and pushed the door open with my elbow.

"I'm going to get out now," I announced. I made sure he could see my hands all the way.

"My hat's coming off now," I predicted, and knocked it off with my left hand. I was aiming for the front seat, but it fell to the ground and rolled a few feet. I left it there. I looked at him. I kept my hands up.

"Ed, in the hardware store, told me where to find you. I told him you liked opera. He said a man came by an hour or so earlier, looking for you. Ed said he flashed a badge. He didn't tell him anything, and probably no one in town did either. Ed said to tell you that. From the description he gave, I'd say it was Tully."

I waited till my hands started tingling. "My arms are getting tired, Gabe. I'm going to need to let them down. Is it okay if I let them down?" He didn't respond, and I was still looking at the wrong end of his gun. "I'll keep them away from my pockets. I have a gun, Gabe, it's Jimmy's gun, but it's in the glove compartment." No change. "Okay, I'm letting them down now. Please don't shoot me. I just need to talk to you. About Jimmy. I need to know why he died." I kept talking as I slowly lowered my hands. "People are telling me stories about him. That he was working undercover for the cops, as a rat. That he was squealing on people. You know,"—I hesitated—"people like us, Gabe. They say he was squealing on people like us. I can't believe it. Jimmy wasn't like that." My voice broke when I said that. "I need you to talk to me. Please, Gabe."

I waited.

Slowly, the barrel of the gun came down.

"Come on over here," he said, sounding defeated. He was a broad-chested, muscular man with a shaggy black beard that looked like it belonged on someone else's face. His right eye drooped. When he turned and took two steps back to lean his gun against the front of the house, he limped. I waited till he turned back to me, then mounted the stairs with my hand extended. His face was creased with pain. He looked at me with his good eye, took my hand, and shook it gently. Then he pointed to a weathered chair, the only one on the porch. I shook my head and sat on the crate beside it.

"I'm going to get you something to drink," he said, limping down the stairs. He disappeared around the side of the house. Leaving me with the gun. He returned a few minutes later with a dripping metal pitcher.

233

Taking a blue tin cup off the porch rail, he filled it and handed it to me, saying, "Water's good here." I drank, and was suddenly thirsty beyond belief. He refilled the cup, and I gulped some more. Then I set the cup down and waited. He sat. It was a while before he spoke. When he did, his voice was a beautiful baritone, deep and rich, leavened with grief.

"I met your brother my first day on the force. I'd been a cop back east, so I knew the older guys would razz the new ones. They were harsher here, and Jimmy told me which ones to watch out for. He helped me clean peanut butter from the barrel of my gun, and dog shit from my locker. We recognized each other pretty quick. I was new in town so he took me to a couple places. He was cautious, though, and I was too, so we didn't meet much. We were always formal with each other around other cops, like we hadn't already shared our stories."

Gabe gazed out at the grassy yard for a while, watched a dragonfly buzz by, then pondered the trees. I heard his breathing get a little rough just before he resumed.

"When Bobby was killed—you know about Bobby?" I nodded. "When Bobby was killed, Jimmy lost it. He found out who was involved—Tully and some others, but Tully was the ringleader—and met them outside the station after work. I was getting off the same shift, so I was there. Tully came down the steps and Jim just leaped on him, wild, frantic, furious. I tried to intervene and soon there were other cops in the fray, but Jimmy wouldn't stop, just wouldn't stop. We'd get him off Tully and he'd lunge back, again and again—pretend he was calmed down just long enough so everybody'd lay off, then go at him again. Soon it became him and me against everyone else. They heard what he was saying, bawling Bobby's name, so soon enough they were calling us faggot and pervert and queer. I knew it was the end of our days on the force. Got the dismissal very next day.

"Jimmy was so sorry he'd gotten me into it, and he came over to my place to talk. I wasn't too torn up about it, really. I didn't like being a cop, it was what my father did, so I fell into it, and then it was what I knew. Naturally we spent time together, both suddenly unemployed.

He was still all broken up over Bobby. And then he was drinking. You know he couldn't really drink without drinking too much, and when he was drunk he was raw and tender and furious all at once. He got his private dick license and I started working as an usher at the opera. Didn't pay much, but I got to hear the performances, and sometimes they let me in on rehearsals if I cleaned the seats while I listened. One night—almost morning, really—Jimmy came to me high as a kite. I thought he was on something, something serious, but it was just that he was so excited. He'd been at a bar, nursing a beer and seething like he did, when the cops arrived for a raid. Tully was there, strutting around. And Jimmy, right away he says, he knew what he was gonna do. The bar owner had his van parked out back, the one he used for picking up kegs, so Jimmy grabs the keys and starts barking at people to line up single file and head out the rear. He puts on his cop voice and his cop posture, herds a whole line of them out back, loads them into the van, and drives off."

Gabe's face was glowing in the late afternoon light. "He was bursting—he was jubilant, ecstatic, he'd saved them all from jail and bilked that bastard Tully of twelve or fourteen Marys who weren't going to wake up the next day with their lives ruined! He was in North Beach, so he drove them to the top of Telegraph Hill and barked at them to get out of the van, then just drove off, euphoric, howling. What a kick it was, he was so excited—he had to tell someone, and who could he tell but me, who would understand the gravity and the triumph, and his words were just tumbling out of him and his face was all lit up and—he couldn't even sit down, he was dancing around the kitchen, hands up in the air, describing how it happened and how glorious it felt.

"It was infectious, his joy at this thing he'd done, and naturally I wanted to try it too, so we pooled our savings and bought a beat-up old delivery van—and it was crazy. *We* were crazy, but it was that kind of wild, rapturous time for us. We'd go to the bars and just *wait* for a raid, hope for one! It was near the end of the month so we knew we'd get lucky—just like in New York, cops short on arrests get together to fill their quotas, knowing gays are easy targets. We collapse inside and go along meek and quiet because we're so ashamed, so they get to strut and act all Humphrey Bogart. There we'd be at the end of the bar, and when they swaggered in we'd herd a bunch out back and off we'd go. We dropped them at the top of that hill, delivering them from evil like Moses parting the Red Sea, only instead of the Promised Land there was that preposterously phallic tower thrusting into the night sky. We always rode away hooting and hollering. It was glorious! It was dangerous as hell, that was part of it—the rush of emotion when we'd drive off, 'cause we'd done it again and survived." His voice sobered suddenly, and when he spoke again, sorrow suffused it.

"We knew it couldn't last. We even spoke about it. What would happen when we got caught. We knew it'd be serious. But Jimmy—after Bobby—it was like he needed some other huge rush of emotion to get him through to where he could deal with the loss. Neither of us—neither of us ever thought it would be that—that they'd—that they'd kill us over it." He was silent for a long time, studying the trees. "But they did. Tried to, with me. Did this and this," he said, gesturing to his eye and the leg he favored. He was silent again. Then he turned to me, grim.

"They left us both for dead. You're going to want to know who did it. I shouldn't tell you—I shouldn't because I can see you're like him, tough like a dog that's got his jaw around something bigger than him but just holds on, no matter if it's flinging his whole body left and right. You probably know already. It was Tully leading the pack. I don't know how they figured it out, but they were waiting for us one night outside Jimmy's hotel, and they took us to this deserted field. I won't tell you that part, please don't ask me to. And I'm—I'm sorry about before, about trying to scare you off. I just... When I came to, Jimmy was already dead. He was lying there, dead. I'd lost a lot of blood, but I dragged myself to my car and drove, drove away from that city and the horror of it.

"I felt guilty—I felt—I feel—guilty as hell that I didn't stay there and take care of what was left of Jimmy, make sure he got found and got buried, and maybe even try to get them convicted. But I knew the cards were all stacked against me, and if any of them saw me they'd finish the job, and I was so broken up myself, over Jimmy and over everything—it was such a shock, even though we knew it was coming, it was a shock to go from that joy, that glorious feeling of taking these souls who were resigned to losing everything, their jobs and their families and—everything—to take them and leave them there at the top of that hill with the tower and the stars and the lights twinkling off in the bay, and to drive off loving each other for what we'd done together." He looked up at me quickly, then looked away again. "We were, you know. We became lovers, even though Jimmy cried the whole time we made love, every time. We needed each others' bodies, we were—we were living at the edge of every moment, the front edge of it, and we needed each other close to do that, needed to feel the faith in life that loving each other brought."

Gabe surprised me then with a sudden laugh, a deep rumble in his chest. "We called ourselves the Brotherhood of Nelly Queens. He thought of it—I woke up one morning and rolled over to see him smiling in the sunlight, all golden, and he said to me, 'The Brotherhood of Nelly Queens, that's who we are.' And I smiled too, and then quickly, we both sobered. Because we knew The Brotherhood of Nelly Queens couldn't last."

When he spoke again his voice was resolute. "But your brother—you need to know this: your brother, he chose it, he chose to do what he did, and even though neither of us thought it would end the way it did, *I know he'd have done it anyway.* For Bobby, and for the joy it gave him, the glorious heroic joy of saving another van full of queens and gay girls. I know that even if he knew how it'd end, he'd have done it anyway. That's important for you to understand. That's how much it meant to him."

He turned to me again, his brown eyes rimmed with tears. He studied my face and smiled gently. "You have his forehead, and his deep-set eyes. I saw that right away. I knew I had to tell you when you said what they've been saying about him. You had to know, and I'm the only one who could tell you. No one else knew. It was too dangerous to let on. The police do have moles, you know, that part's true. Jimmy wasn't one, but if we told anyone at the bars, the moles might hear of it and we'd be finished. And if we got anyone else involved, when we got caught, they'd be finished too."

We sat awhile, and when I saw the trees around us again they were hooded in shadow. Soon the cicadas began their song, calling to one another across the darkness, matching their rhythms. The hot, dry day cooled quickly. Gabe gestured for me to come inside. He fried some potatoes and one sausage between us for dinner, and we ate at a small table in the kitchen.

I thanked him for sharing his food with me, and for telling me the truth about Jimmy. I said I'd thought Jimmy was murdered because of his blackmail investigation.

Gabe looked up from his plate in surprise. "You know about that?"

"I found his files under the floorboard. And I found the black-mailer."

Fork still poised in the air, he stared at me. "Chantry?"

I nodded.

"All of them?"

I nodded again.

"Jimmy was sure of that, but he couldn't prove it yet."

"You been to the Dollar Bill?" Gabe shook his head. "The place is all swank. The drinks are pricey, but they're not weak. There isn't enough money in it to keep the place swanky *and* protected. There had to be another source of income."

"That's exactly what Jimmy said."

"And Chantry is smart: he never taps the regulars, just the one-tim-ers. He knows if there's the slightest whiff of a rumor about blackmail, his patrons will disappear fast as the nap on a cheap velvet suit."

Gabe put down his fork and leaned forward. "We figured the angles together. Chantry's one of us, so he knows the paranoia from the inside.

We're all jumpy as pigeons on a telephone line. His victims—their fears were already crouched, anticipating the squeeze. It's an easier job, blackmail, when you don't have to convince your victims they deserve to suffer. And the richer we are, the more we have to lose, the less likely we'll tell a soul about it. Try blackmail in a dive bar and someone'll tell someone, word'll get out—hell, someone will *have* to tell someone to borrow enough money to pay the blackmailer! But not the well-heeled ones. No one says anything and they get picked off, one by one. Jimmy even considered starting rumors at the bar, rumors about the blackmail. He knew it would close Chantry down quick, but then he'd squeeze the victims he's already got that much tighter."

I told him about Chantry's listening room behind the booths, and my visit to the chief's den. "Chantry's paying Gafferty directly, so the police will never come down on him. I'm working on Gafferty, though: if he goes down, Chantry might have to close shop. But that won't stop him from bleeding the victims he has."

I told Gabe the rest—about Lily's murder, and everything else. Then he prepared a bed for me on the sagging couch in the front parlor. I heard his slow, uneven gait on the stairs. As I undressed, peeling the binding off my body, layer upon layer of it, I remembered how, when I used to take my brassiere off at night, I would lift it to my nose—that curve just below the breast, there where the sweat gathers, a sweet-sour smell lingered, earthy and musty. It was some kind of comfort to me. It smelled of home. I sniffed the binding. There was no one spot for that essence to gather. I looked down at my chest. The binding left marks crisscrossing my torso. They were still there an hour later as I watched the shadows in Gabe's parlor and thought about him and Jimmy driving down that hill, whooping.

In the morning Gabe made potatoes and eggs, filled a small backpack, and told me to follow him. The forest was brittle, quiet, and tough. After about a mile I heard a rustle that eventually became a roar: we were in a narrow canyon at the edge of a river lined with enormous gray boulders. He led me downstream to a large emerald pool. At first I felt embarrassed when we stripped down to nothing, the spare curves of my body exposed, but I remembered Gabe had been Jimmy's lover. We plunged naked into the freezing water. You couldn't help but feel exhilarated by it—so cold and fresh and wet there in the dryness of those woods—and as my yelp echoed against the narrow canyon walls I thought of Jimmy and him whooping as they drove down Telegraph Hill in a now-empty van. I looked at Gabe and he looked at me with his brown eyes and I knew he was remembering too.

The rocks along the edge were hot from the sun, and they warmed us almost to burning after a plunge. The stone was sculpted by the water, by thousands of springtimes of rushing current, sculpted in some places like muscle and the swell of flesh. I found a crevice that fit my body and settled into it, warm and somehow soft, despite its being stone.

Later I crept out on a spit of rock, a huge boulder that rippled out into the current and then continued, submerged, across the river. A small gully of stone was hallowed out just beneath the surface. As the current flowed over, dark circles appeared on the rock below, spun, and disappeared, and new ones emerged to replace them. It took me a while to figure out that these were the shadows of ripples on the surface of the river. They bloomed and spun for a moment, then disappeared, always replaced by new ones: mesmerizing, perfect discs whirling across stone.

We ate sandwiches he'd packed and drank the cold clear water out of the river, scooping it in his blue tin cup. Then Gabe said to me, hesitantly, "I know you want to know this. I don't want to tell you—it's dangerous as hell, but I think about it when I can't sleep. Agonize over the possibilities. Imagine what I'd do if I ever had the courage to go back."

A powder-blue dragonfly buzzed us. Gabe watched it disappear downstream, then continued. "Everyone knows Tully is a live wire, but there's a code among cops: never rat on a brother in blue. Other cops will line up on his side, provide alibis, threaten witnesses, so there's no way to get him. But there's one cop who might break rank. Elliott Blackstone, everyone calls him Eli. Eli had a partner named Abramowitz. One night they answered a call, a bar fight. Tully responded too, along with a few others. The whole scene turned bad, and the cops were in the thick of it. Tully hurt Abramowitz, hurt him bad. He was yelling 'kike' when he flipped him over a table and broke a chair across his chest. His back never fully recovered, and he had to leave the force, move to lousy low-end security jobs. All the cops there that night kept mum. Eli's hated him ever since."

Gabe looked at me intently. "Eli would love a chance to bring Tully down. But it's dangerous. He'd only try it if he was sure he'd win. To clinch a case like that against a fellow cop, you'd need more than one incident—you'd need a string of 'em. If I was able to find someone who saw Tully beat Bobby to death—it was a Saturday night, the surrounding cells couldn't have been empty—and I testified to Jimmy's murder as well as what they did to me, Eli might just do it. He might initiate an internal investigation. Odds are against it happening, and odds are against them coming down on Tully if it does. But if you want to try it, I'm in."

"I want to try it."

Gabe nodded cautiously. "Remember that we're asking the police to find one of their own guilty. That doesn't happen. And all kinds of bad things happen to people to ensure that it doesn't happen. You won't be able to stay in Jimmy's place. You'll have to find somewhere else—and keep in mind that the cops have every resource at their fingertips to track you. Forget about using Jimmy's car. Don't risk the safety of anyone you care about by letting them know where you'll be. I'll move too. I'll be somewhere else. That way, if they try to beat it out of you, you can tell them exactly how to get to this house. You won't be tempted to play hero."

"How will I get in touch with you?"

"Wherever I end up, I'll find a pay phone. I'll send you a postcard with the number. It'll be in code—count the number of letters in the first word, the number in the second, and so on. And I'll write something about returning by bus at a certain date and time. That's when you should call me. Wait'll you hear from me before talking to Eli. As soon as you talk to him, get yourself settled somewhere else for a while."

We watched the shadows make their way up the other side of the narrow valley, the light, as it came at a slant, revealing the contours of the hills. When darkness settled, bats replaced the dragonflies, fluttering high above us, dipping suddenly, then rising again. Gabe pulled a flashlight from his pack and we slowly made our way back to the house. The next morning he folded me in his broad chest and held me there a while. He asked me to be careful and waited till I agreed before he released me. When he stepped back, Gabe reached into his pocket, then opened his large, weathered hand. On it were three acorns, with mossy chartreuse caps. I put them in my pocket and kept them there through everything that happened next.

I told Lucille the whole story, from the soggy pie I didn't order to the acorns in my pocket. She held my hand and said simply, "You were right about Jimmy." That released me from the fear that it was all a dream. I sobbed. I ached, like I'd lost him all over again. But I'd found him again too.

Then Lucille, who knew me as Josie and as Joe, took me to bed. She caressed all the parts of me, the gangliness, the sharp edges, the spot on my thigh the sanitary belt rubbed raw that previous, bleak week when I'd doubted everything Jimmy had ever done or said. She touched me like I was a natural-born wonder. Lucille's hands restored me. My voice was still thick from crying when I said, "I love that you touch me everywhere." Her mouth hovered near my ear. "Everywhere," she whispered, "and in between." Then she roamed my body like a ship in search of shore.

While I was floating in the sanctuary she cleared for me, I knew that no God I could believe in would instill in me desires and make those desires wrong, grant me such joy and make that joy a sin. Sometimes, even now, I lose hold of my certainty, but I can travel back to it along the silver thread of joy in my body, remembering Jimmy's words and Lucille's hands.

chapter thirteen

Pearl rode the story like a wave, paralyzed when Gabe's gun was pointed at my chest, ecstatic when he and Jimmy careened down Telegraph Hill. When I told her about the Brotherhood of Nelly Queens, she put her hand over her heart and wept.

I knew the fastest way to redeem Jimmy for the rest of the world was to tell Aaron and get out of his way. His mouth hung open when I finished; you could have parked a '49 Chevy in there and had room left for your lawnmower.

Then he shrieked.

"They picked up my friend Bennie! He told me all about it! The paddy wagon pulled away from the bar like a bat outta hell, sent them crashing against the back doors. They drove like crazy, barreled up this steep hill, dumped them out, and drove off. Left them standing in front of that enormous tower. They were free—their names wouldn't be in the paper, they wouldn't lose their jobs—they were free!" Aaron's eyes were wide and jubilant as a theater marquee. "Bennie and the rest of them split up and took off running. And suddenly this flock of huge green birds appeared, screeching. Bennie had, you know"—Aaron looked left and right, pinched two fingers to his lips, and inhaled sharply—"and he was thinking, 'damn, that was some good stuff!' Then he remembered that St. Francis preached to birds, and realized it was *a miraculous intervention—by the patron saint of the city!!* He swore me to secrecy because he was afraid people'd think he was loopy. Everyone *I* told thought it was all a drug-induced hallucination. *But,* the next day, a huge bruise appeared on his right shoulder—he was in the back of the paddy wagon so he slammed into the rear door when it took off—and it was the face of Saint Francis! An *apparition!* He swore to God! He showed it to me, but by that time it was purple and yellow and all you could see was maybe a beard and one bushy eyebrow."

I walked Telegraph Hill, the crazy jutting mound I'd crossed the night I stared into the bay wondering if Jimmy was in its depths. Now I listened for the echo of his jubilant hoots, his ecstatic hollers, the last of his life spreading across its slopes. Ramshackle Victorians cling to the hill's lower stretches, connected by pitched wooden stairways. They give way to dense trees and furtive paths above which a plaza rises, like the top tier of a wedding cake, offering a vast vista of twinkling lights. From there the tower lunges toward the stars.

I stalked the paths, imagining the pounding hearts of those Jimmy and Gabe set free. Married men already regretting the promise they'd made that if God would only get them out of this mess they'd never touch another man again. Drag queens catching each other as they stumbled, wigs askew, hairpins flying. Party boys buzzing with alcohol and reefer, finding visions in the shafts of light that seeped through the trees. Femmes smoothing their hair and vowing revenge on the cops anyway. All of them seeing their futures—which had contracted to the four walls of a jail cell—once again stretch out before their eyes.

I imagined Jimmy's rapture, but could only handle a few seconds of that: it was so tender, the pain so full, when I thought of the moments he gladly lost his life for, touched the joy he felt so deeply that it split the earth open and put him in it. I crisscrossed the hillside with the devotion a child brings to searching the paw of a beloved pet for the splinter causing it to limp. I returned night after night, haunting its hollows, tracing the impromptu trails that wound beneath the trees. When I found myself planted in the center of the plaza, legs apart and arms akimbo, chortling at the obscene member it thrust up into the night sky, I swore not to return. But I did.

The echoes were silent that night. I tried to provoke them, recounting as I paced every word Gabe told me, but the hill remained quiet. Quiet enough for me to hear—to realize with thudding fear—that what I'd thought were the echoes of my own feet were footsteps following me. I stepped off the path into the foliage and the footfalls ceased. I took to the pavement and they resumed. I walked toward them and they receded.

My heart pounded as my mind raced: Gafferty and his minions, Tully and his mates, Chantry and his accomplices—all of them wanted me gone. Tully was the most likely. I remembered his hulking form with fear, and began to run down the hill, toward lights, streets, people. Then I stopped short. There—in the lights, among the people—Tully could shoot me before a crowd of witnesses and he'd be a hero saving the populace from a deranged degenerate. If by some miracle I shot him first, he'd be a martyr and I'd fry for it. Either way, I was dead and he was a hero. For me to have any chance at all it had to end here. I knew the hill intimately. It was my only hope.

I darted down a shadowy trail, mapping the hill in my mind, searching for some snare, some subterfuge, to give me the advantage. The footsteps followed, fell back, came closer. I pulled Jimmy's gun from my pocket and released the safety as I hurried to a dark stretch that offered a clear view of the well-lit path behind. In the transition from light to dark was a fire hydrant overshadowed by shrubbery—about the height I'd be if I crouched low. I tossed my hat onto the hydrant, slipped behind a nearby tree, and turned. A leg stretched into the light but drew back before I could glimpse the body. Just then the wind gusted, a tree arced, a shadow slid, and I saw clearly, for just a moment, the penumbral outline of a figure: no features, just a silhouette and a pose. I knew then, unmistakably: the stalking was a cruising and the cruiser was a queen.

I hooted, one last jubilant whoop of relief for the hill, then descended for what I thought would be the last time.

"*You* got invited to a party at House of Chas? To *the* Halloween party at House of Chas? What's the theme!?"

"Your Mother at a Cocktail Party." His raucous hoot caused heads to turn all across the diner. "Chas encouraged me to bring friends."

Aaron squealed, "Me me me," as his hand shot up in the air.

"Of course."

"Can Pearl come too? She was just saying she's got to start going out again."

"Okay, then, the two of you are my guests."

He wiggled his behind so hard the booth shuddered. "What are ya gonna wear?"

That's when I realized none of the dresses from my mother would work. Over the course of her life she'd consumed enough vodka to float a warship, but she'd done it the old-fashioned way: alone, mostly, or with Father, and without exotic mixers and risqué conversation. I doubt she'd ever been to a cocktail party in her small-town life, and if she had, I didn't have the dress she'd worn to it.

Pearl gloated when she found the magenta crepe sheath with just a few beads missing along the low neckline. I protested as she held it in front of me at the Goodwill mirror, but she insisted: if *she* could pull off "some lovely décolletage," I could as well. Back at her place she produced a pair of sky-high turquoise pumps, a petite pillbox hat with black mesh that fell over my right eye, and the silkiest stockings I'd ever encountered. As I tottered to the mirror she let out a low whistle, and when I saw myself I gasped. I wasn't the girl next door, all sunshine and curves and prettiness; I was chic, sophisticated—and my narrow, angular body, even my broad shoulders, fit the look.

"Go on, honey, strike a pose," Pearl crooned. I put my right foot forward, shifted my weight to the left, turned slightly, and winked. She roared. And suddenly I glimpsed the pleasure of drag: it didn't have to be *me*. Instead of squeezing myself into the narrow tube of Mother's crimson lipstick, I could choose any shade at all. Watching myself in the mirror, I slouched against Pearl's bedpost, pretended to pull a cigarette and lighter out of a purse, and pantomimed lighting up. "Mmm hmmm," Pearl murmured, nodding. I turned to her suddenly.

"Can I ask you a personal question?"

She gave me a broad, warm smile. "You can ask me any kind of question you want, as long as *you* answer it first."

"I was going to ask... Why you wear women's clothing." Her eyebrows went up. Then she fluffed a pillow, reclined, and waited for me to begin.

"At first it was just frustration. Frustration and some whiskey. Traveling alone, trying to find Jimmy, dealing with the police—I couldn't get anywhere without some man hassling me. Staring at my chest or trying to make me or telling me I was talking about etiquette when I just wanted to file a missing persons report. I thought trousers would make things easier. I thought wrong, for the most part. But I kept wearing them because I feel more powerful. Sturdier. Sometimes, though, I also feel a little wrong. Like maybe it's because when I was a kid—"

"Now hold it right there," Pearl interrupted tersely, pointing a long finger at me. "I know where you're headed with that thought. I know *exactly* where you're headed: some serious trauma happened when you were a child, so therefore you like to tromp around in trousers. I'd like to point out that when *I* was a child I flounced around in a dress and *consequently* some serious trauma happened: I got my behind whipped with an elderberry switch. Why are they always saying it's the other way around?" Her vehemence couldn't be contained by the bed. She sprang up and began to pace. "The reason most boys wear pants every

249

day is not some deep dark trauma," she snorted. "It's the terrible trauma they know will happen if they *don't*. That's a tired old story and I won't listen to it." She threw herself back on the bed.

When she spoke again, her voice was patient, generous. "But maybe you mean the more important question, the one that can be answered: where it takes me." She paused. "Are you a singer, honey?" I shook my head. "Now that's too bad," she said with fervor. "When I sing, and when I sing with other people, when my voice resonates with theirs, there's a tremendous feeling of wholeness. I feel complete in myself, and also right in the world—right in relation to other people. As a lady, I manifest that truth and harmony. And that confers on me the fullness of my power. You know what I mean by that? You might feel it when you put on sturdy shoes and trousers: feel the fullness, the truth of yourself, in a way you can't find in a dress and heels."

"I'm not sure," I replied, hesitantly. "I can act more powerful in shoes and trousers. Partly because I know I'll be able to sprint if I need to. And partly because...of the clothes themselves. When they're on, I *am* powerful. And just now, dressing up like this—suddenly I can feel the power in this too, to adopt whatever persona I want. It's a different kind of thing, though."

"That it is," she said soberly. "That was a difference between Bobby and me. Bobby *loved* putting on the ritz. He became another person when he slipped on a beautiful dress. But he was play-acting that person: performing, rather than actually becoming. Over time you'll figure out whether the trousers allow you to become someone else for a while, or whether they *reveal* you. I've even known it to change. My friend Dolores, she performed for years, till one morning she realized that it wasn't a performance anymore. So she didn't go back. You've got to find your own right harmony, and sing it. Now come over here, that hat's slipping."

The streets were full of revelers before nightfall—men dressed as women, women as men, taking advantage of the sole annual night of cross-dressing amnesty. Stray bands of children careened, ghouls, goblins, and hobos. But the preferred costumes of the night were debutante and beau, or wealthy opera-goer.

Pearl carried off a gorgeous cerise dress and lavishly feathered hat, eliciting admiring stares on the streetcar. Aaron, not quite ready for the light of day, carried his outfit in a brown paper bag. It was a warm night, rare in San Francisco, and the party was in full swing when we arrived: windows open, Anita Day wafting to the stars. A man pretty as he was young gestured us toward the wide staircase. On one side, going up, were men carrying suitcases; on the other, coming down, were women in a state of supreme excitement—or hauteur. Their outfits were opulent, their faces ecstatic, like angels in a crèche enacting a scene that had haunted their dreams. Some clutched the railing like a talisman with each tottering step, then looked around for faces to witness their arrival. We obliged.

At the top of the stairs we were ushered into an elegant library, which for this event had become a bar: cocktails sprouted little umbrellas that pierced olives, onions, and fruit. Thus equipped and on the way to sufficiently lubricated, we entered a room in which suits, ties, wing tips, and sock garters littered the floor, ankle-deep. Chas had provided an array of hats, gloves, boas, stockings, lingerie, and stilettos large as small boats. A few of these items hung on a metal rack, but most were draped on the freestanding mirrors or the hefty rack of antlers. Emitting a raucous whoop Aaron leaped into the fray, upended his bag, and tore off clothing. Four other men were in various states of transformation, and we assisted with buttons, hats, and earrings—matters in which, by virtue of Pearl's exquisite taste masquerading as my own, I was assumed to be a proficient.

Zipped into his dress, Aaron balanced on a sweetheart-backed chair in front of a dressing table. Pearl was all business. Perched on the table, she grasped his chin firmly, flicked open a compact, and covered him with gentle pats of a powder puff. A stroke of color and a swipe of darker powder on either side created lovely full apples where his cheeks had

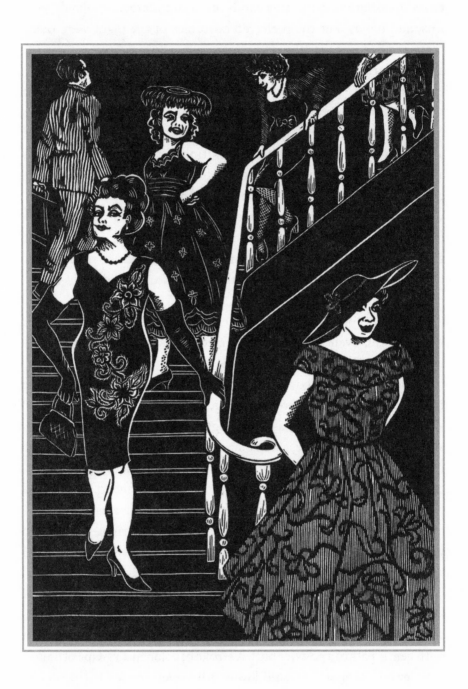

been. Then she applied an impossibly flimsy wisp of false eyelash, with an outermost lash that curled upward, widening his already generous hazel eyes. A little more of this and that, and then the magic: she held up a small gold case with a cloisonné cover, pressed a tiny button, and the top popped open. She paused, case in one hand, brush in the other, and looked sternly at Aaron. He was practicing batting his eyelashes, but caught her seriousness.

"This," she announced dramatically, "is *très chic*. Sent to me by my cousin Camilla in New York, who bought it on Fifth Avenue. It contains tiny flecks of fourteen karat gold. They call it glowing powder, but I call it fairy dust." She dipped the brush into the case, very lightly, and without actually touching his skin, dusted it across his face. I saw the flecks glint in the light as they drifted downward, shimmering.

Aaron exhaled breathily, like an incantation, "Ooooh, fairy dust." When he turned his face up to Pearl it was beatific, glowing with hope. I caught my breath as I realized that Aaron's gushing enthusiasm was a gorgeously irrepressible optimism, and recognized, for the first time, the courage it required. He was a vision.

Pearl put two pinches of fairy dust in a hanky, tied it with a strand of ribbon, slipped it into Aaron's purse, and dragged him from the mirror. As we joined the parade making its way down the stairs, I had a fleeting memory of my fifth birthday: I entered the living room in my birthday gift from Jimmy, a western outfit complete with leather chaps, anticipating the roar of approval that welcomes a cowboy to the ring; instead, I saw Father's face fall. But Chas had anticipated the importance of the moment. We were instructed to write our names on small gold-rimmed cards. These were sent forward, so that as we walked into the ballroom we heard ourselves announced to a flurry of applause. The names varied from "Mrs. Michael Shelby, of Akron, Ohio" to "Miss Ida Mandaman, of the State of Desperation." I'd chewed on the pen for a moment before writing, "Josie, of the Brotherhood of Nelly Queens." When we were all assembled, the manic excitement of the entrances mellowed and everyone behaved with a kind of elaborate courtliness:

the men debonair, the women charmed and charming. A small band played, and dancers twirled around the room, enjoying the hours made all the more precious by the pumpkin waiting for us at midnight. Aaron said the police always added extra patrols to snare stragglers.

We were watching the dancers when he nudged me and whispered loudly, "There's the duchess!" I followed his gaze to a vibrant figure in glittering black lamé. She glanced in our direction and her eyes, sharp coals in the soft wrinkles of her face, brightened. As she sailed toward us she nodded, kissed, and chirped her way through the crowd. Arriving in the port of our threesome, she extended a long, slender arm, a gracefully dropped wrist, and a gloved hand to Pearl.

"Please allow me to be so brazen as to introduce myself, dahling. I am...zee duchess. I witnessed your *outré* performance at The Paper Doll last year, when you emerged from zat *risqué* oyster shell. I do so enjoy being shocked—and it happens so rarely, anymore. Thank you, *ma chérie*."

Pearl introduced Aaron and me in the names we'd chosen for the event. The duchess arched an eyebrow when she heard mine. "You are in fine company, then, Josie—ah, Josephine, *la belle Joséphine*—do you know, I saw the opening performance of your namesake at *le Théâtre des Champs-Élysées. Quelle figure! Quel talent!* And her devotion to France during the war was exemplary. You know she was a spy, *non? Mais oui!* She assisted the French Resistance, smuggling secrets written in *encre invisible* on her sheet music! *Une telle intrigue!* But you are so young, *mon petit Joséphine*. You have not yet been to Europe?"

I shook my head.

"You must go!" the duchess urged, including Aaron with an eloquent swoop of her arm. "Continental attitudes toward *les questions sexuelles* are so expansive by comparison, don't you agree, Pearl—you were there recently on tour, *non?*" Pearl nodded, and the duchess continued ardently, "You *must* experience my country. There is an understanding, there, of the polymorphous nature of desire. Our *perversité* takes many forms, our desires bloom in a vast variety of pleasures. You know, of course, that some individuals take pain as their pleasure—the Marquises de Sade and Sacher Von Masochs of the world seek precisely that which most of us assiduously avoid. But then you must admit that the height of ecstasy, *la petite mort*, as we call it, is shot through with intimations of pain: the intensity of pleasure can itself be painful! It is that which cracks the shell of the world, bursts the *blasé*, awakening us to transcendence in the midst of our most physical perambulations. And so the earthly and the divine meet in the act of love, dahlings. Don't you find it to be true?"

I believe I blinked. The duchess smiled warmly and patted my hand. "Ah, but you shall, *ma chérie*. The stately pleasure dome awaits. Some of us search for love, for a romance to enfold our desire, while others shun the very idea of it, familiarity destroying the charge *érotique*. Some prefer *les plaisirs solo*, or the *ménage à trois*, to the coupled pleasures. Some find pleasure in the hill, others in *la vallée*, and the cleverest among us find it everywhere! But these things are not the color of a petal, or the shape of a leaf—they are not elm trees and oak trees. They are more akin to—what can I say?—to a weed and a crop; or perhaps, an ornamental and a—"

"For rose is a rose is a rose, is it not?"

"*Exactement!*" growled the duchess, her face lighting up as she recognized Tiny, attired in a luxurious tuxedo. When Tiny very solemnly took her hand and gently kissed it, the duchess threw back her head and roared.

"Ah, *ma petite chérie! Tout comme les vieux jours à Paris!* I was just telling these young ones they must go there. Have you met, ahem, *Mademoiselle* Velma Miller the Third," she nodded toward Aaron, "and Josie, of the Brotherhood of Nelly Queens?"

I pretended not to know Tiny and she joined the ruse, elegantly kissing Aaron's hand, then mine, murmuring "*Enchanté.*"

"Tiny and I," the duchess explained, "were in Paris together in the years before the war. What a time that was, yes? *Une époque!*"

"Paris was my favorite lover, ever," Tiny replied. Her face was brilliant, glowing—I saw that nighttime was, indeed, when she lived. "She matched my moods, forgave my every transgression, never minded when I took other lovers. I spent years and years in her arms—and was never told to enter through the service entrance, unless I was providing service." She nodded at Pearl and continued, "That's where I learned to brook no insult to my person, for any reason. There were so many of us there—Josephine, of course, and Langston, Bricktop, Alberta, Mabel, Duke, Fats... Evenings began around midnight, and didn't end till the sun was up. Of course it didn't hurt that there was plenty of money flowing. The place was ankle-deep in it!"

"And in love, as well," the duchess added. "Everyone was sleeping with everyone, everyone tried everything—why not? We were all after love in all its forms!" Her face clouded, and she sighed deeply. "*La société américaine* is in the dark ages here, *l'époque médiévale*. Herds of sheep fearing those who have frightening masks put over their faces, and esteeming those who promise to protect them from the boogeymen. There are populaces around the globe clamoring for democracy, and here you have it—and you would rather find a *fasciste* to follow! *Zut alors*—this is a party, and I have become morose" she amended apologetically. "Please forgive me." Turning to Tiny she smiled and cried, "Come, we'll find you a trumpet," then carried her off toward the band.

At nine thirty I left for the Dollar Bill, hoping the evening's festivities would provide cover for me to get the files. The bar was crowded already, lit by the golden glow of jack-o-lanterns scattered throughout the space. Their distended, manic smiles and wild eyes seemed to mock me. Like a peasant locked outside a feast, the revelry left me cold. But a costume contest was scheduled for eleven, and the crowd was festive. Three witches cackled with Dracula, Snow White, radiant in blue, waltzed by with George Washington, but the evening belonged to the men in gowns, furs, and diamonds. Alcohol was flowing, and as eleven approached the mood became feverish. A large jack-o-lantern between the center booths had collapsed in on itself without extinguishing its candle; light flickered from the solitary eye as it drooped over a contorted smile. Chantry was nowhere in sight.

The band struck up "Somewhere, Over the Rainbow," and a queen in a deep turquoise gown stepped forward to sing. The long corridor behind the wall haunted my awareness; I wondered which chair he occupied, poised to destroy another life. Suddenly a shriek rose above the merriment, followed by bright light flashing across the ceiling, then spreading wildly through a booth. A jack-o-lantern had lit the drapery, transforming fabric to flame. Bodies poured frantically from the booth, cries of pain and bellows of fear, smoke and jagged, searing flashes as another drape caught, and then another. Dracula appeared, whipped off his sweeping cape, and began beating back the flames—but he only fanned them, and they rose and engulfed the next booth, and the next. He kept fanning while shouts rose, ordering him to stop—till Queen Elizabeth grabbed him from behind, holding down his arms. Meanwhile a stampede had begun, a press of bodies crowding toward the entrance. I saw others rushing to the rear of the bar, and shouted "There's no way out there!"—but my voice was lost in the pandemonium. Faces wild with fear returned from the dead-end of the hallway, colliding with those fleeing back, in a crush of confusion.

The barkeeper tried to herd people toward the front of the bar, but the crowd eddied ominously near the entrance. I fought off panic as I remembered that the front door opened inward: the press of bodies could be making it impossible to open. Smoke was surging, and across the room I saw that the booths themselves had caught fire, flames devouring the upholstery. Fire seared across the ceiling in sudden bolts as new arms of the drapery ignited. I joined those in the press toward the front of the building, moving with agonizing slowness, shrieks, and cries. Feeling something soft underfoot, I reached down to grab hold of a hand, and pulled up a shaken, elderly queen, mascara running, the creamy silk of her elegant gown streaked with soot. She was wild-eyed, confused, and I slid my hands under her arms for support.

Then the smoke began to billow and thicken, and, coughing, I shouted, "Get on your knees!" We dropped to the floor where we could breath again, and moved haltingly forward with the bodies around us.

As we approached the heavy velvet curtain, not yet aflame, I turned and saw a slender form in a long, sable gown, with a white stole slanting across the shoulders, emerge from the back hallway, arms filled with files. Pages cascaded to the floor, suddenly catching fire, and the flame shot quickly up the trail of tinder toward her. She flung the files away and ran forward, but slid on the scattered paper, fell to her knees, then forward onto her hands. As she struggled to crawl toward the door, her wig slid down over her face, spilling a tiara that flashed as it tumbled. Another bolt of flame raced across the ceiling, and as she lifted a hand to pull the wig away, I saw the streak of silver above the temple.

Three things happened then, so fast there was hardly an edge between them. I felt a rush of relief, of retribution: Chantry would be dead. I felt a lurch: I should try to save him. And before my heart had the chance to decide, poised on the razor's edge between good and evil, unsure which was which, a heard a fist connect with a jaw and knew the jaw was my own. That's the last I remember. They say someone dragged me out by my legs and disappeared into the night.

When I came to, I heard sirens approaching. I was nearly alone in the alley. Of course no one lingered: the cops would arrive along with the fire department. I have my theories about who that fist belonged to. Someone whose life Chantry had invaded with his poisonous letters, who had a gun and then got lucky: didn't have to pull a trigger, just had to stop some fool from saving his life. Or someone from Chantry's circle, an underworld hood who saw an opportunity to knock off the boss and clear a foothold for himself on the next ledge up. It could have been some dreg of the demimonde tired of seeing a faggot thug get away with being a faggot. I even wonder, sometimes, whether it's possible to knock yourself out. My pet theory: one of Gafferty's henchmen, hired to watch for a chance to rub him out. Perhaps he even helped the flame find the drapery. But I try not to think about it. Most of all I try not to think about that moment on the razor's edge, angel in one ear and devil in the other, trying to decide which was which.

The morning paper reported a warehouse fire in the district. Captain of the SFFD said it was started by a cigarette carelessly thrown in a trash pile. The cigarette belonged to a security guard, who perished in the fire. The Captain offered a stern warning to the public to extinguish cigarettes safely.

Each took the news in their own way. Mr. Dodson smiled at me through his tears. Tiny fumed and stormed. Chas, in his unswerving nonchalance, behaved like he'd been granted a reprieve for a parking ticket. Mr. García clasped my hand in both of his and shook it solemnly for a half-minute, saying, "Thank you, my friend." When I awkwardly pointed out that I hadn't actually stopped the blackmailer myself, he said, "Nonetheless," and continued to cradle my hand. Miss Holloway wept, having already lost everything there was to lose.

Two days later I received a picture postcard of a wizened miner panning for gold. The message was a breezy account of a carefree vacation. I had a week. I got a description of Eli Blackstone from Lucille, and started tailing him home from work.

He stopped at a tavern every night, and spent about an hour there before heading home. It was a neighborhood joint, not friendly to strangers but not hostile either. On the third night I followed him to the entrance, walked around the block once, and went inside. My eyes needed a few seconds to adjust, but my nose had no delay picking up the stench of stale beer soaked into worn wood floors. A green lamp hanging above a pool table created a perfect circle of light on the green felt. Men along its edges looked up from their game and stared. Eli wasn't among them. I eyed the row of mostly empty stools along the bar. He was at the far end. I did my best to saunter, and the pool players returned to their game.

I settled on the stool beside him. A few seconds passed before he turned to look at me. His face was sullen. It turned sour just before he said, "What the hell do *you* want?"

"I'm Jimmy O'Conner's brother. I want to talk about Tully."

The sour expression stayed. His nostrils flared a bit. Then the corners of his mouth sunk lower. The bartender appeared, asking "What'll it be?" I told him I wanted a root beer and his face turned sulky. I have a knack for getting large men to don surly expressions.

I turned back to Eli and spoke low. "Tully hurt your partner and he murdered my brother. I want you to start an internal investigation of both cases. I have a witness willing to testify."

His eyes narrowed.

"Yeah, I could be working for Tully, baiting you, setting you up, but if I was I'd only tell you what you want to hear. I'm going tell you something you don't want to hear: Jimmy had a lo"—I tripped over the word—"a lover. A boyfriend. Bobby. He was beaten to death in a jail cell by Tully. That's where it all started with my brother, why he drank, why he fought, why he poached on bar raids. And why Tully murdered him."

As Eli stared at me, I saw his brain churning, figuring the angles, checking all possibilities, fighting against hope.

"I'm going to find a witness willing to testify in Bobby's murder, too. A pickpocket who was in the opposite cell. That's three cases— four, really: the guy who saw Tully murder Jimmy was hurt bad too, almost died. Lost use of an eye and walks with a limp. With him and Abramowitz, we've got four solid cases."

The bartender brought my root beer, then went away. Eli's brain finished working. I saw a glint in his eye. It wasn't hope, exactly. More like longing. I thought: he's in. But I thought wrong.

"I just want to be clear," he said, face turning rabid, voice bloating with disdain. "I didn't like your brother and I don't like you. Degenerates disgust me. An enemy in common doesn't make us friends. I'm doing this for Abramowitz, not for you or your godforsaken brother."

"Then I'm out," I said, sliding off the barstool. He grabbed me by the arm. I jerked free. "This is too dangerous to be working with someone who despises me." From the bar to the nearest corner I cursed myself for having blown our one chance to get Tully. From the corner to the car I breathed relief at having pulled clear. Agonizing still, I fumbled with the ignition, dropped the key on the floor, then hit my head on the steering wheel as I bent to retrieve it.

When I raised my head no light was coming through the window next to me. Eli's barrel-chested torso loomed. Panic rose in my throat: Gabe was wrong—Eli's with Tully now, and I have the two of them and the whole damn SFPD after me. Then I remembered that I hadn't locked the door. He wasn't hauling me onto the pavement, flaying me there in the street. He was gesturing for me to roll down the window. I did. I saw his eyes. A deep well of pain, tinged with hope.

"I had to be sure," he said. "I'm sorry; I had to be sure."

When I got back to the Chadwick Arms, Mr. Wilkinson beckoned. Call Pearl. Urgent.

"You know about Aaron?" she asked.

"What about him?"

"He started acting strange right after the party. Wasn't at Pandora's or anywhere over the weekend. When I called he said he couldn't talk, that he had a *cockroach* problem. Next time it was *termites*. After that it was an *ant* infestation. I didn't know what the hell he was talking about. Only after he landed in jail—I went to see him and he went on and on about the FBI being after him—I realized he was trying to tell me *he thought his phone was bugged*."

"Aaron's in jail?"

"Yes—he was walking in the park, after dark. A cute guy gave him the eye, and Aaron asked if he wanted to go for a stroll. The guy whips out cuffs and slaps them on him. Aaron's terrified. You think maybe your friend could help?"

Lucille listened intently to the story. "Information's my forte, but I'll see what I can do. He's got to get a lawyer. He may be in for a while.

He's young?" I nodded. "And obvious?" I nodded. She closed her eyes, pressed her lips together, and shook her head.

It was too hot for me to stay in Jimmy's room, but I couldn't leave town yet. I got on a streetcar headed west and took it to the end of the line, out by the ocean, then walked south till I found a hotel too rundown for a phone booth in the lobby, but not so far gone that the doors didn't have sound locks on them. Getting messages was a problem. Lucille and Pearl knew everything—that made it too dangerous for them. I decided to ask The Guardian of the Records, from Jimmy's so-called office. I knew she could be swayed by a handsome face. But Mr. Wilkinson could be swayed by a dollar bill, and they were easier to come by.

I thought I'd seen all the squalid, dead-end alleys of the city. I hadn't. This festering impasse was peopled with nocturnal ghosts in soiled army jackets with yellowed, oozing eyes that were vacant and ravenous at the same time. It stank with urine and despair. Needles littered the ground. A body slanted across the sidewalk, mewling like a newborn kitten.

Lucille had given me the name and likely location of the prisoner who'd been in the cell across from Bobby's the night he was murdered. A junkie pickpocket named Frankie Monroe. Frankie didn't know anything about Bobby's murder till he realized there was money in it. Then he remembered every last freckle on Tully's face. Said he'd testify. I paid him some up front and promised a lot more later.

Eli left a message for me with The Guardian: the internal investigation was underway. I caught a bus south along the coast and took it to the last stop, a little town in the mountains above Santa Cruz where they didn't ask any questions. The motel had a row of tiny red cottages nestled in the duff under the redwoods. I called Eli every couple days to find out where things were, and arranged for Gabe to make it to the hearing.

With help from the lawyer Lucille found for him, Aaron eventually got out of jail. Pearl said he was in bad shape. He was afraid to see me unless I dressed normal; insisted they were still watching him and it was too risky for the both of us. So I put on a wig and a dress and all the rest, and made my way back to the city. We were to meet at a bench on a hill at the top of Dolores Park, near Chas's neighborhood. I was early, so I settled on the bench and waited. Gusts of wind carried laughter from the playground below. A young couple passed, his arm around her shoulder, hers around his waist, whispering in some secret intrigue. Then a man, hunched over, head down. A few seconds later he was standing by the bench, staring at me. I glanced up, annoyed, and my lips were forming icy words instructing him to shove off when Aaron's features emerged from the sallow, despair-shrouded face. A dark gap haunted his mouth where a front tooth was missing. An angry red wound under his left eyebrow seeped, and the eyebrow itself looked askew. He'd always appeared younger than he was, still wet behind the ears; he'd aged a decade.

"Hi Joe. Josephine," he said, in a voice flat as an urban wasteland. I jumped up and reached out to embrace him. He flinched and backed away, looking around nervously. Then he looked at me again, up and down at my wig and my pumps, and collapsed into me with a muffled whine. We fell back together onto the bench. He leaned his large body against me, hard, like he needed not just the support but the assurance of support.

"Aaron, I'm so sorry," I whispered.

He shuddered. "It was awful, awful in there. They were after me, all the time. Whenever the guards weren't looking—in the laundry, the courtyard, even the mess hall. They...they forced me. All different ones. Finally a young guy told me, he said, 'Try to get one of them to like you. If you're his pogue, the rest of 'em'll leave you alone.' So I did. But then that one, he—every time I did something—my voice was wrong, or I walked a certain way, or I moved my hands when I talked—he said he had to punish me. And he did. I had to stop, to stop—the way I walked—the way I stood—the way I said 'hello.' I had to keep doing it and doing it and doing it his way, till I got it right. Or he'd—"

His body trembled against me, but his voice was empty of emotion, like he was reading from a phone book. Then he suddenly pulled away and tilted his face up to mine. "And my job. I lost my job. I loved that job. I was good at that job. The old ladies would let someone go ahead of them in line so they'd get me instead." All his despair was condensed in the area around his eyes. He collapsed against me again. "What am I going to do?" The voice that used to soar and fall like the Himalayas didn't even rise at the end of the question. All his flamboyance, his animation and gushing enthusiasm, were leveled.

"I was fired from my job and I have a police record. How am I ever going to find work, pay rent, live? And... And... And my parents know everything."

There was little I could say to comfort. I held him. I murmured. Then I turned practical. "You could talk to Madge about bar tending for her."

He sat bolt upright. "I can't go to the bars, ever again. Sex deviates fired from the federal government get an FBI file. The FBI is following me. And the local police, too. If they see me in a bar they'll take me in again. I can't go back there. Ever." I could see the world closing in around him.

"Where are you staying now?"

"I'm back in my apartment. The rent is paid through the end of next month. After that, I don't know what I'll do."

"You can stay with me if you want." Then I remembered my own dangerous predicament. "You have so many friends—you can stay with anyone."

He shook his head. "The FBI would find out where I moved, and start following them too. I can't do that to my friends."

"Are you sure about this FBI thing?"

"You don't understand." His face was now a white mask of horror. "Summerfield, the Postmaster General, he's on a crusade against what he calls 'pornographic filth in the family mailbox.' We had to watch for mail with sexual content, especially perverse sexual content. We had a list of local addresses to look for, suspected purveyors or purchasers of pornography. And Summerfield was sure homosexual employees were helping their mail to get through—so they were watching me. It's all part of the Pervert Inquiry. I wasn't randomly picked up in that park. They followed me there, sent that cop out to proposition me. I never should have gone out like that—I knew I shouldn't. But it was late, and I couldn't sleep, and I was nervous, I needed a walk. That cop was so young and sweet, I never would have thought..."

Aaron sobbed against my chest for a while. Then we sat and looked at the view. The park was a full city block in one direction, two in the other, a wide open space, steeply sloped. We hunkered at the upper edge with a vast view across the city, downtown, the sparkling waters of the bay, all the way to Oakland and north to Albany, where Aaron had worked. It was a vast panorama under a high blue sky. It felt cramped and sinister.

The hearing didn't last long. Tully sat through most of it with a malignant smirk. Eli and Abramowitz testified. The pickpocket didn't show; no doubt he'd been bought off by the other side with enough junk to get him all the way to Colma. Gabe took the stand and told the bitter story of his beating and Jimmy's death. I didn't hear it; I honored his wishes and left the room till it was over. It took a long time to be over.

When Tully took the stand he broke down and started bawling about his kid brother. Took a while to make sense of it. Seems his family had a secret spot along the coast where they went abalone diving. One night Tully arrives home for a surprise visit to find that his little brother went off with a friend to dive for a coupla days. Tully gathers his gear and heads out to join them. When he arrives, it's not the deep blue sea little brother's diving into. Tully loses it, lets loose on the friend, killing him, then nearly finishes off his brother too. When the jury hears the story, Tully's off the hook. Little brother survives and the family ships him off to a mental hospital. After a year of shock treatments he's walking around with his eyes dull and his tongue hanging out. Tully's upset about that, but he's mortified that his brother's a queer, and more mortified that he wasn't able to beat it out of him. Bobby, he reminded Tully of his brother's friend, that's why Tully bludgeoned him. And later, Jimmy. And who knows how many before, how many after, and how many more to come. The flinty judge listened impassively and sentenced Tully to two months on desk duty. After that, he'd be back on the beat.

A week later Lucille told me Eli Blackstone was dismissed from duty. Acting on a tip from another cop, they'd found heroin in the bottom drawer of his desk. I called him and we met to talk. His house was up for sale and he was spending his days sitting on a park bench, now and then finding work cleaning gutters.

chapter fourteen

M r. García had told me, "She's the kind of woman people call 'a force of nature.' Grew up in New England, and has that absolute moral rectitude that sometimes comes across as arrogance. She rules the Dahlia Society with an iron fist. You'd be surprised at the dramas that arise in a flower club. She balances competing interests, metes out the little privileges fairly enough to calm petty jealousies. What makes it work is that she doesn't favor anyone: she is exceedingly just. Well-respected, but I wouldn't say well-loved. She keeps a certain distance. Perhaps it is her way of remaining impartial." Armed with that knowledge, I found a phone booth and dialed her number.

"Mrs. Gafferty, my name is...Daphne de Winter." Impromptu pseudonyms always turn alliterative; by the time you realize you've done it, it's too late. I cleared my throat and continued. "We met recently at your home, in your husband's den. He introduced me as...Janet Jennison. I would like to speak with you, privately."

"And this is concerning...?" she demanded imperiously.

"Your husband. And Lily Wu."

When she spoke again, it was quietly. "When do you wish to meet?"

"Tomorrow. In the cafeteria at the Emporium."

"No," she said. She had regained her throne. "I will meet you in the tearoom of Gump's. In one hour." The dial tone startled me.

"Table for two, please."

I didn't know tea rooms had maître d's. He gave me a thorough once-over and sniffed his disapproval. I'd dressed without Pearl's oversight. He bypassed the tables with scenic views and led me to one in a darkish corner. I silently thanked him for the slight. The room was quiet, just a few impeccably dressed couples or trios murmuring as they drank tea. Nothing clashed.

She sailed in under a hat with enough plumage to keep a sizable pot-roast aloft. When she pointed to me as her destination, the maître d' looked dubious and offered her more promising real estate. She declined, demanded a pot of very hot tea, and waved him away. Then she settled herself and turned to me.

"Miss—ah—de Winter, did you say? Any relation to the Manderley de Winters?" she asked archly.

"Only by marriage," I replied. Her laugh was brittle. "I apologize for not giving you my real name," I continued gravely. "It is for my safety, and I mean no disrespect by it."

"No doubt you have your reasons," she said drily.

"I want to lay to rest any concern that this is about blackmail. It is not."

She tilted her head forward and glared fiercely over the rim of her glasses. Then she responded, somewhat subdued, "I will admit, that was foremost in my mind."

The tea arrived. Steam poured out when she lifted the lid. She nodded approvingly, poured us each a cup, then met my gaze. "Well," she announced. "What is it you wish to say to me?"

"You are aware of Lily Wu's relationship to your husband."

"Indeed. That is not news to me. Nor to the citizens of San Francisco, at this point."

"I'm afraid what I have to say may be just as shocking."

"As wife of the chief of police," she replied tersely, "I am quite accustomed to shocking news, and my heart is in excellent health. *Speak.*"

"Your husband instigated Lily Wu's death. They were in a dispute over payment of protection money for her bar, for all the bars. He arranged for her to be frightened—roughed up. The roughing up went too far."

"That is a very serious accusation and I *highly* doubt you have the evidence to back it up. If you had, you'd have gone directly to the police—or to the papers—instead of to me. Yes?"

I had to agree. "The evidence is circumstantial. But I think you will find it no less damning." Her face became a determined mask. "It involves a pair of satin panties. Red satin, with a dragon embroidered on them."

The mask dissolved.

"The coroner found them. Stuffed in Lily's mouth."

Under her rouge, a spot of bright red emerged on each cheek.

"I have here a mimeograph of the coroner's report." I laid it on the table before her. She leaned forward as if to examine it, but her eyes didn't move from left to right. The wrinkles on her face had gathered around her lips. She returned the paper to me. Then she sat back stiffly in her chair and watched the steam rise from her tea.

After a while, she spoke. "For many years there was a locked box in the lower drawer of my husband's desk. A wife has certain prerogatives when it comes to a husband's secrets. I exercised them. In the box was a news clipping from the mother's days at Forbidden City, and a photograph of Lily as a child. I surmised the rest. As soon as I saw the photograph of the child, I knew. She has—she had—his mouth, and something in the angle of her jaw." Her lips tightened to a thin line.

"Also in the box was a red satin brassiere with a dragon embroidered across one breast."

She took a sip of her tea and set the cup down. "My husband is a mercurial man. He talks to me very little about his work. I've learned that if a mood strikes him, I need only watch the newspapers for a few days. The source of his churlish behavior will soon be apparent. Botched evidence in a bank robbery, or the unsolved murder of a prominent citizen. So in early September, when he became quite unbearable, I attended to the news. Cases important enough to upset him usually appear on the front page. But this was on the third. 'Lady Tavern Owner Dead.' I glanced at the photograph, shuddered, and was ready to move on to the crossword when her name caught my eye. I'd never met her, of course. But I felt a certain kinship with her. Well—it was quite literally a kinship of sorts, wasn't it," she said, apparently to herself.

She seemed to gather her strength about her. When she met my eye and spoke, her voice was once again steely. "And your purpose in presenting me with this information? I suppose you expect me to testify against my own husband? To state that the—the garment—was in his possession? Are you really unaware that a wife may legally refuse to provide testimony that might incriminate her husband?"

"I am aware of that. But I believe you are a woman of considerable integrity."

"And you expect *me* to bring him to justice?" she demanded, her voice rising.

I kept mine level. "You misunderstand me. I am not asking you to do anything. I am merely informing you of your husband's role in Lily's death. Your presence at her funeral indicates that you have some personal interest in the matter. What you do, whether you do anything at all, is of course entirely up to you."

She surprised me, then, with the intimacy of her act: she reached across the table, with its bone china and fine linen, and grasped me firmly by the chin. She did so gracefully and without haste, as an elder aunt might fondly chastise a beloved nephew for roguish behavior; not an eye was turned or a brow raised. But her fingers were like pincers as they positioned my face to meet her gaze.

"My husband," she began, with emphasis on each word, "lives for power. Without it he would collapse, as a balloon deprived of helium becomes a flaccid, pointless thing. He has nothing else to play with: no grandchildren, no dedication to noble causes, no fascination with frilly flowers. He is a man devoted to power, and in the absence of it the essence of him would wither and die. What you intend for me to do—deny it though you may—would destroy the man who is my husband." She released my chin, leaving welts that were still visible when I studied my face in the mirror afterward, looking for hints of Jimmy and wondering at what point I might have sealed my own untimely death.

Three days later the papers announced that Michael Gafferty, chief of police, had resigned. He cited personal reasons, but even the *Chronicle* acknowledged it was in response to revelations of corruption as well as a disreputable personal past. In the photograph of the chief making his resignation speech, his wife stood at his side, her steely gaze meeting the camera, her enormous hat trimmed with a blowsy peony. A new chief was sworn in with florid promises of an end to corruption, the elimination of vice and degeneracy, and a return to integrity on the part of men in blue. I spoke with Madge a few days later; she said the pickups had been moved back to Mondays.

All in all, I thought I was pretty clever. Thought I'd stitched the pieces together. But it was Chantry who cut the cloth. Took me a while to figure it out.

It started with that last thing Chief Gafferty said to Chantry on the phone, when he was yelling about optimists and the soon-to-be-dead friend who had murdered Lily. "Don't think he's your eternal bet on a parolee guard," he shouted before slamming down the receiver. I couldn't figure out what the hell he meant by that. I asked Gabe, thinking it might be some police jargon. He shook his head. I discussed it with Pearl. She suggested I ask Tiny. "She's been around the block a few more times than the rest of us. Maybe she can figure out what that bastard meant."

Tiny listened carefully, and sat humming for a while. Then she told me to tell it to her all again, starting with the moment I got into Gafferty's den. About two sentences in she scooted to the front of her chair and demanded, "There was a deck of cards on his desk?"

"Yes."

"Was it a new deck of cards?"

"How would I know?"

She harumphed. "Did it sit there in a neat pile, like it was in an invisible box just its size? Or did the cards sit every which way?"

"They were in a perfect pile."

She waved her hand in the air like she'd just unveiled the meaning of life. "New cards are stiff cards," she concluded.

"Yes," I said tentatively.

"Stiff cards are loud cards," she chided. "He was shuffling a brand new deck of cards—rapping them on the desk, then making that fluttery sound cards make when they come together? New deck, that's a loud sound. Loud sound means you weren't hearing him so well. There isn't much difference between 'parolee guard' and 'très Beauregard' when a brand-new deck of card's being shuffled." She slid back in her chair and continued, reprovingly, "You didn't hear him correctly, child. He didn't say 'bet on a parolee guard.' And he didn't say 'très Beauregard.' He said, 'get outta jail free card.' 'She ain't your eternal get outta jail free card' means: I ain't gonna let you hold Lily's murder over my head forever. Gafferty knew *that murder was no accident*. The next time Chantry went a little too far afield of the law, if the chief didn't agree to cover his ass Chantry would threaten to implicate him in Lily's death. No doubt he had some bit of evidence tucked away connecting Gafferty to the murder. The motive was certainly there: she was his illegitimate wrong-color daughter, refusing to pay graft and encouraging others to do the same. Her murder was something

Chantry could hold over Gafferty's head for a very long time. Didn't matter that he didn't actually do it. Chantry'd just squeeze and hear Gafferty yelp any time he wanted to. And Gafferty knew it: right away, right there on the phone, he felt the tables turn. No doubt he's behind that fire that killed Chantry."

She shook her head slowly. "Lily's life wasn't anything to them, except to be used as a tool. At the funeral a lot of young folks were saying she'd been murdered by the police in retaliation for not paying that hush money. I kept mum—not an easy thing for me to do—but I knew that made no sense. I'm not one to favor the police. But you don't make money off a carnival by shutting down the sideshows. You bleed them, but you keep them going. Terrible thing, that Lily's death. Terrible, terrible thing. But it was no accident. It was too useful to be an accident."

So then I knew. I'd done Chantry's dirty work for him. I'd arranged for his revenge.

"Have you heard?" Pearl asked in a voice grim as fate.

"Heard what?"

"Come over. Now."

She opened the door in a violet kimono and red-rimmed eyes.

"Who?" I asked.

"Aaron," she cried, weeping.

"How?"

She shook her head and led me inside. Hugo made room for me on the couch. A wine bottle and goblets with dregs settling in their bowls littered the table. She filled one and told me to drink up. I obeyed. She poured some more for Hugo, then herself.

Her mouth was moving as though her teeth were chattering, but a quivering moan, rather than chatter, emanated. Hugo sat beside her, with his arm around her. She continued the moan, moving up and down some melancholy scale. Finally she stilled. When she spoke it was slowly and clearly.

"You know he'd been anxious about FBI surveillance. Hadn't been sleeping for a while—that's how he ended up in the park that night to begin with. Since jail he's been afraid to go out at all after dark, afraid they'll set him up again. He said he saw their black car parked right across the street. He was going crazy in his apartment at night, pacing—the downstairs neighbor was rapping on his floor at three a.m. to complain. So he started walking the stairs. The apartment building has one of those grand stairwells with a wrought-iron railing that spirals around and around like a nautilus. He walked them, up and down, up and down. The neighbors must have thought he was insane. He kept going up and found that the door to the roof wasn't locked, and when he was tired of walking he'd lie up there and watch the stars—said it calmed him, that vast expanse of space. He told me he imagined another world out there, one that had room in it for him." She paused, fumbling in her kimono for a balled-up handkerchief. "I could hear in his voice that it calmed him. There was a low wall around the edge of the roof that he said blocked the lights—the city, the bay, all of that disappeared and all he could see were the stars. I was worried about him but he sounded calmer—the stars, he kept talking about the stars and how they made the world seem big enough for him. They soothed him, I heard it in his voice, I did."

"The stars calmed him."

"And that's why I never expected, never thought to think that he'd, that he'd..."

"Jump off the roof?"

She shook her head. "No, the stairwell. They found his body at the bottom of it. We don't know for sure if he jumped or fell, he didn't leave a note, but..." She dropped her chin down on her chest, and her voice grew hoarse. "But the coroner said, the coroner said—Aaron was wearing his uniform from the post office, and he also—he had a dusting of gold powder on his skin. Oh, oh oh oh."

When Mr. Dodson heard what had happened to his former postal boy, he insisted on accompanying me to the funeral. I arrived at his house early for tea.

"Josie," he said as he sat back with his cup, "I'm sorry I spoke so poorly of Aaron. When I spent that night, had that dream with the Datura, something released in me, like the spring of a watch. I realized that I was afraid of him, very afraid, but for all the wrong reasons. I thought if people saw me anywhere near him, they'd realize I was one too. I thought they couldn't help but see the similarity between us. But there *was* no similarity. No similarity at all. My real fear was that if I spent any time near him, *there would be*. Some part of me might... might loosen up, reveal itself... Come undone. And how terrifying that would be."

Everyone was there. Pearl, Luther, Hugo, Madge, Mrs. Wu, Marie, Tiny, José, and multitudes from Pandora's. I even met Bennie of the St. Francis apparition, an obviously kindred spirit, anguished, sobbing. Aaron's father, mother, and brother were there as well: pale, stiff, mortified. They shrank visibly from the condolences of Aaron's friends. Eventually others were warned, before they approached, to let them be.

The casket was open, and Aaron was wearing some kind of military-looking suit, apparently from his high school academy, with a small American flag over the heart. He looked buttoned-down in a way he'd never looked alive, and it surprised me to realize how very normal he appeared; all his obviousness was in his animation, his glorious enthusiasm. Pearl and I knelt together in front of the coffin. I prayed he'd found a world that had room in it for him. Pearl nudged me, then stealthily offered a pinch of her gold powder. As we rose we each released a drift of fairy dust in his direction.

New grief rejuvenates old. I sat with Pearl in Jimmy's diner, wishing I could call it my diner, pushing crescents of pancake around on my plate. When you slide the edge of your fork through a thick pool of syrup, a dry band will appear, an island in the middle of your sticky

275

lake. If you sit back and watch, the thick liquid slowly creeps in, fills up the empty space, seals it over like it never existed. The way life does, on the surface, when you've lost someone. Gradually, over time, the busy-ness of the day to day, this and that, work and play, love and vengeance, fill in, on the surface. But underneath, the gaping hole persists. "It's like losing your religion," I said. "Once you've believed in God, how do you ever fill a space so vast when he's gone? The very idea of him creates a cavern that can't be filled with other things. Nothing is as big, as vast, as the chasm left behind."

Pearl nodded. "Losing Bobby was that for me." She paused, then continued. "Lily—it's more like losing my name." She stared out the window for a while. "When José rouses us to a chorus of 'God Save Us Nelly Queens,' I wonder how long it will be before another like Lily comes along. How many years before we have someone ready to pull off her stiletto and fight back?" I'd asked the same question. Lucille told me it won't be so long. But I think it will be.

We were on our second cups of coffee when Gabe joined us. They eyed each other warily for a moment; the last time Pearl saw Gabe, the whole bar thought he was an undercover cop. But then Pearl stood, opened her arms, and said, "What you and Jimmy did was beautiful." Gabe stepped into her embrace with a shudder, and they held each other. Gabe's hand reached out, collared me, and brought me into the fold. I'm sure all eyes in the diner were on us as we wept. When the waitress loudly asked for Gabe's order, we released each other and set-tled into the booth to talk.

Each of us had lost someone we loved to Chet Tully's fists. All of us knew those fists were going to keep on killing. They'd be aimed at any man who reminded him of his brother's lover: men like Bobby and Jimmy. I knew I had to stay Tully's fists. So we conspired.

When we parted I walked to the Ferry Building, where Gabe said men went when they were looking for other men, especially sailors. "You know how we love our sea food," he said with the hint of a smile. Near the building's toilets stood a bank of phone booths. I wrote Tully's telephone number on the wall, just over a phone. Beside it I scrawled, "Ask me about my big tool."

That night I went to see Lucille. As she led me up the stairs I thanked the God of Nelly Queens for the splendor of her ass. Then she undressed me and took me to bed. We didn't make love right away. Instead we lounged like we usually did afterward, side by side in the near-darkness, intimately close, returning the gaze of the women in the plaster rosette above the bed.

I held my breath for a while. Then I turned to her and said, "I'll be going away."

She nodded gravely. "I thought you might be." She was silent for some time. Then, very seriously, without a hint of complaint, "I'll miss you."

I seized her hand, held it tight. "I'll miss you. Terribly," I said.

We held hands in the near dark. Lights from a passing car slid across the ceiling, briefly lighting the faces of the women above us.

"Be careful," she said.

"Yes," I agreed. "Other towns aren't like San Francisco."

She paused, then said gently, "That's not what I meant."

"What did you mean?" I asked.

"Be careful doing whatever you're going to do that you'll have to leave town after."

I rolled myself into Lucille's arms and clung to her.

Leaving Lucille and Pearl and Gabe tore holes in my heart. That made me realize that I could love again, after Jimmy. I was more careful, in what came next. I wanted to live.

chapter fifteen

As Mr. Dodson and I sat in his little plum house drinking tea, the rest of the world, and our plans for Tully, seemed like a dream. But I told him I had a favor to ask. "It's serious." I reconsidered. "It's very serious."

"Josie," he said cautiously, "there are few things we've discussed that aren't serious. We've never talked about the weather. Or whether you like meatloaf."

I had the sense he was occupying time, allowing his words to take up however many moments he needed to prepare himself. I gave him a few more. "That's true, Mr. Dodson. I have no idea whether you prefer peach pie or key lime."

"Peach," he replied promptly. "I'm not particularly fond of sweet-tart combinations. And you?"

"I have to agree with you on that point. Peach. Though my favorite is banana cream."

"Hm, banana cream," he mused. "Banana cream does have its merits."

I nodded.

He set down his teacup and armed himself with a deep breath. "So, what do want to ask?"

"I would like ten Datura seeds."

After a pause he said, "You aren't planning to grow ten Datura plants."

"I'm not."

"You know that the seeds are dangerous."

"I do."

"Anyone who eats them is likely to have traumatic hallucinations, to see people who aren't really there."

"Like you did."

"Then they may die—but you can't know for sure."

"Yes."

He massaged his forehead for half a minute.

I asked, "Would you like me to tell you what I intend to do with them?"

He considered, tilting his head slightly to the right, then to the left. I wondered which side was pro, which was con. He took a deep breath, then exhaled. "No," he replied with conviction.

"Okay, then. I don't need them today. You can take whatever time you need to think it over."

His eyes found mine. Then he nodded, rose, and trotted over to his Datura. He poked around, pulled something from the plant, then passed by his potting table, where he picked up a tiny envelope. He set a small, prickly orb on the table. "They're supposed to dry on the plant. You're lucky, this one is perfect, hasn't yet split open and spilled them." He carefully broke the seedpod and sorted small brown seeds into the glassine envelope. Then he folded the top over twice and creased it firmly. He held it up for a moment. "You will be careful?"

I nodded.

"They taste bitter, okay?"

I nodded again.

"And Josie, they aren't...for you?"

"I promise, Mr. Dodson: they aren't for me."

He nodded and dropped the envelope into my hand.

I'd spent my evenings tailing Tully after work. He liked to pass an hour or two at a tavern a few blocks from his apartment, a neighborhood place that served food as well as drink. It was low ceilinged and dark, but dull enough to be on the edge of respectability. I still had the knockout threads Pearl found me for Chas's party. I needed another purse—the dainty clutch wouldn't hold Jimmy's gun—so I traded it in at the pawnshop for a large velvet number. I pounded the Datura seeds to a fine powder, returned them to their tiny envelope, and slipped the envelope into my bra. Then I headed to the tavern. I wanted to be there when he arrived.

I was the only unaccompanied skirt in the joint that night. It didn't take long for Tully to move in. I felt him commandeer the barstool to my right, and by the time I turned to say hello he was hovering so close I smelled the soap he used for shaving. My stomach lurched as I wondered whether this was the last scent Jimmy had smelled. Steeling myself against the urge to flee, I smiled anemically. He asked what I was drinking.

"Tom Collins," I said, though it was actually just soda with lemon. I wanted to give him a head start.

"Another Tommy for the lady," he called to the bartender, "and set me up again."

I thanked him with as much charm as I could muster, and we talked. Mostly, he talked. It wasn't necessary to summon a veneer of interest; he assumed it. By the time we'd downed our first round his arm was securely lodged around my shoulder. Every part of me recoiled from his touch, and I had to focus, hard, on being there, in the tavern, to keep from thinking about what this body had done to Bobby's and to Jimmy's and to Gabe's.

I knew he drank boilermakers, downing the shot in one swallow.

I'd spent a lot of time worrying whether he'd notice the powder. But I hadn't realized how difficult it would be to get the powder into his shot glass. He watched his drink like a hawk. I knocked my handbag off the bar; he relinquished my shoulder long enough for me to climb off the barstool and retrieve it. I pointed out something on the tavern's television; he murmured, "Yeah, I know," without twisting around to look. When a friend stopped by he picked up his drink before turning to say hello. I reassured myself that such expertise at guarding his glass must be ingrained habit rather than suspicion of me in particular. I knew he'd have to take a leak eventually. I ordered him a fresh one while he was gone. It didn't arrive till he returned.

When he suggested we head back to his place, the ground seeds were still in my sweaty bra. They'd require at least two hours to take effect: time enough for me to turn from predator to prey. I said I needed a bite first, wondering if there was any food that would mask the bitterness. He was annoyed by the delay, but we ordered chops and another round while we waited. As he picked up his whiskey to down it, another buddy stopped by. This one came with a girl: a girl whose brassiere size rivaled Lucille's. Tully was pretty well pickled by that point. After eyeing her he set his shot back on the bar, freeing up both hands for a very thorough embrace. I felt along the bar for his glass. I was worried his buddy might see, but the buddy was busy watching with distaste as Tully's hands slid over his date's shoulders, lingered at the sides of her breasts, then moseyed to her hips. By the time she extricated herself from Tully's arms, the distaste was becoming anger and the powder was in his whiskey.

As the two of them left Tully grinned at me like we were sharing a great joke. "He's a touchy one," he said snidely. I saw his buddy turn back, ready for a fight, but the girl caught him by the arm and pulled him away. Tully downed the shot, grimaced broadly, pulled something off the tip of his tongue, and turned to his beer. Then he returned his over-friendly attention to me. When the food arrived my hands were still shaking, and I dropped my fork. Twice.

He ate quickly. I forced the food down. When drinks and dinner were almost gone he said again, "Come back to my place." I hesitated. He watched me a moment, then stood up. "C'mon," he commanded, his face dark. I said I needed to powder my nose. My heart pounded and the gun was heavy in my hand as I slipped out the tavern's rear door: I was sure he'd be there, waiting. He wasn't. I checked the time: 7:17.

Gabe and Pearl were waiting, tense, at Pearl's apartment. I changed into trousers. We didn't talk much. We sat, and checked the clock every eight or nine minutes.

At quarter after nine Gabe called Tully and asked him about his big tool. He didn't have to hold the phone in our direction for us to hear the torrent of epithets that followed. Gabe's eyes locked on mine as he returned the phone to his ear and spoke. "You'll beat me with your bare hands? Is that a promise, big boy?" he taunted. He listened a while, then said, "Okay, meet me at the top of Telegraph Hill, beneath the tower. It's the perfect place for you to beat me to a pulp." I flinched.

We took separate cars and parked in different locations around the base of the hill. I made my way, panting, up the Greenwich Street stairs, a tilting, erratic series of rough brick steps winding from Montgomery Street to the tower. I hurried, afraid not to be there with Pearl and Gabe when Tully arrived. At the top, I counted down five steps, knelt, and wound a length of wire from the lower part of the handrail on one side to a craggy brick on the other. I secured it firmly. Then I stepped over the wire and, gasping still, hurried along the path to the plaza.

Pearl and Gabe were waiting. The night was cold, the plaza silent, the stars astonishingly close. The tower menaced, a hulking mass of darkness against the sky. We huddled for a few moments, needing to be near each other's bodies, urging each other to be careful. Then we receded to the shadows of the shrubbery, Pearl to the north, Gabe to the south, and me to the east.

It wasn't long before we heard a car hurtling up the road that circles the hill. It snaked its way around us, rising, then burst onto the plaza. A door flew open before the cab squealed to a halt. Tully's body unfurled itself from the backseat. I heard a man say, "Mister, you want your change?" Silence, then, "Say, thanks, buddy!" and the vehicle screeched away.

Tully's body loomed. He had his back to me, but from where I huddled low in the bushes he seemed huge, rivaling the tower in mass and power. In came the flood of emotion I'd kept at bay when I was beside him in the tavern: these were the hands, these the feet, that had beaten Jimmy to death. My blood ran cold—this is a crazy plan, I thought, reckless, insane—and flimsy, premised on the words of someone Miss Holloway knew who knew someone who worked at the sanatorium where Chet Tully's brother spent his incoherent days muttering, "Chessie, I miss him, Chessie, why, Chessie, why?" for hours at a stretch. I shivered, afraid for Gabe and Pearl and myself, ready to shout, "Let's get out of here!" Then I saw Tully stagger.

He careened, swaying, toward the center of the plaza. So I began.

"Chessie," I called, pitching my voice low. "Chessie, I miss him."

Tully stopped short, lurched upright, spun around toward me, froze. His eyes were huge, dark, dilated, all pupil. He stared at something between us, where I couldn't see anything at all. "Kiddo, is that you?" he cried, pleading, "Is that you Kiddo?" Then his voice changed utterly. "Kiddo, it's you," he cried like a dam broke and all regret rushed out of him.

"It's me, Chessie. But I'm lost, now, and all alone. Why did you do it?" I asked.

Tully's eyes were locked on that spot between us. "I had to, Kiddo, I had to—I had to get rid of him, and I had to beat it out of you, don't you see? There was no other way!"

"No, Chessie, there had to be another way. Now I'm lost and alone."

Tully staggered forward two steps, then threw himself to his knees, wrapping his arms fiercely around legs only he could see. A sob rose from his body. "Forgive me, Kiddo, forgive me please," he begged.

"And what about me?" Pearl's voice arose from across the plaza, haunting, wild as the wind and demanding as the cold. "What about me: the one you left dead on the jailhouse floor?"

Tully's sagging body jolted. He twisted his head from side to side, trying to find the source of the voice, his arms still wound around the legs of Kiddo. Then his face locked on something to the north. "You! You needed to be put out of your misery, you sick pervert!" he bellowed. "You fairy homo! Get away! You have nothing to do with my brother!"

"Yes, Chessie, he does," I crooned. "He was my lover too."

Tully's body shuddered, and he looked up and shouted, "No, Kiddo, no!"

Then Gabe's voice came from across the plaza, haunted, grieving. "And me, you left me for dead. You killed my lover and left me for dead!"

Tully flung himself to the side, falling on his hands, then spread his legs wide and staggered to his feet. He turned in Gabe's direction, raised a hand, pointed, and bellowed, "You! Another one! You pervert, you wop cocksucker pervert, you needed to die! It's you, all of you, that took my brother from me!"

"But he's mine too, Chessie," I called. "He was my lover, too."

Tully whirled back. "No, Kiddo, he's not yours! You're not like him—you're nothing like any of them. It was that sick friend of yours, he perverted you, he seduced you—"

"No, Chessie: I seduced him."

Suddenly Tully was flailing, raging, screaming, "No, they're cocksucker perverts! They're nothing like you!"

Gabe's voice returned, and Pearl's rose, and mine too, our voices surrounding Tully, rising above him to the night sky, and it seemed surely there were other voices now, joining ours, carried on the wind, overlapping, interweaving. Tully turned and twisted frantically, twitching like a bead of water dropped in a hot pan, seeing, somewhere before him, animate bodies giving rise to those voices. Then Gabe's voice rose above the others, a shriek filled with rage and grief.

"You left me for dead. You killed my lover and left me for dead!"

Tully turned toward Gabe's voice and hurled the words into the cold night air, "You! Where are you? *Come out and show yourself!*"

And Gabe did. He emerged from the shadows, leaning on his cane, his face ravaged, his body tilted, holding Tully in his gaze. I saw again Tully's height and his strength, those dark eyes as they watched Gabe, who limped backward a few steps, toward the edge of the plaza. Tully tottered, steadied himself, took a step forward and only slightly sideways, in Gabe's direction. Gabe dawdled a moment, then moved back again, and Tully staggered after him toward the Greenwich Stairs. Eternity passed as they inched toward the steps. I watched, calculating the distance between them, terrified that a sudden burst of lucidity and control would enable Tully to grab Gabe. And then it did: he lunged, and his hands locked on Gabe's shoulders. Gabe struggled to lift his cane and Tully knocked it from him.

I ran from the shadows, across the plaza, shouting, "Chessie, it's me, Kiddo! I'm over here!" I saw Pearl and heard her calling too, taunting, trying to draw Tully's attention, but his eyes and arms were clamped on Gabe.

"Chessie," I shrieked, "come and save me, come and save me *now*, Chessie!"

Tully's body didn't flinch, didn't turn, didn't equivocate. Gabe pulled against his monstrous hands.

I danced near them, shouting and waving my arms. "Chessie, it's me, Kiddo! I miss you, Chessie! *It's me!*"

Tully's face jerked as my body crossed his field of vision. He lurched, grabbing wildly for me—releasing Gabe.

I darted from side to side, serpentine. I hovered and leaped, lingered and flew, using my body as a matador flaunts red satin, shouting his brother's words over and over in the darkness of the night. And slowly, Tully followed. Under the trees and into the darkness, to the top of the stairs. I turned to make sure he was following, then flew down them—grabbing the rail and lifting my body to clear the wire.

Tully followed. I heard the thud behind me, then heard him roll heavily, down and down. His body hitting hard, where the steps turned, was awful in its finality, awful in its relief. He lay there crumpled. Suddenly, there was silence.

"Tully," I whispered. "Tully."

He groaned. He was face down, one leg badly twisted, one arm flung to the side. I was close enough to hear his breathing, rough, labored. I reached down, caught his shoulder, felt his body drenched with sweat, hesitated, then heaved him over. His eyes were enormous, terrified, but not seeing me; staring at something over my left shoulder.

He moaned, "It's you," to the face over my shoulder.

"Yes, it's me," I said. "Jimmy O'Conner's sister."

Confusion, then recognition dawned. "O'Conner? Another one!" His eyes were still fixed to my left.

"Yes, another one," I said.

His upper lip lifted in a snarl. "Another queer O'Conner?" he asked.

"Yes. Another queer O'Conner." I drew a switchblade out and pressed the release. Keeping it from his field of vision, I slid the knife under his chin.

If I'm driving down the road and see an animal's body, broken, lying by the pavement, I always feel a lonely sorrow, and in my head I say a prayer. It's not a prayer-to-God kind of prayer, asking him to open the pearly gates and welcome the dog into his kingdom. My prayer is just to think, for a moment, of that dog or cat or possum when it was alive, bounding on the earth, the blood flowing through its small body and the life force feeling some inexplicable joy in life itself. I pass a moment trying to feel for the crumpled body the obscure elation that I imagine it felt being alive. It comforts me, is what it is, to imagine a fleeting glimpse of that life in the ecstasy of living. I know this doesn't make the dead any less dead. I know it doesn't make killing any less killing. I tell you this just so you know that what I did next wasn't easy. Revenge was not sweet; four murders isn't better than three.

I'd helped Father slaughter pigs on our farm: I knew to pull fast, for mercy, and hard, to get it done. Tully's body bucked as the cold metal touched his skin. I heard a gurgle, and a sickening warmth flooded my fingers. There was so much blood. Blood everywhere. But before I tried to wipe it off, I held up to the light the joy he too must have felt in aliveness, and it came to me in that brief moment that even when he murdered Bobby and murdered Jimmy and murdered God knows how many others on the pavement or the jail cell floor with the protection of his badge, those deeds were for him in some unfathomably obscene and twisted way a manifestation of the urge to live. I didn't dwell there; it was too snarled a mystery for me to untangle. I wiped the handle of the knife for fingerprints and dropped it. They'd know it was me, little chance they wouldn't, but I didn't want to make it easy for them to prove it. I cleaned my hands on my shirt as best I could, and stood. Pearl and Gabe were farther up the stairs, tense, waiting. I nodded. We all took off, then, in different directions. Jimmy's car wasn't far from the base of the steps. I got in and drove, crossing the bridge, leaving the city behind. I knew, when I slid that blade across his throat, I'd made myself an exile.

I headed for Sacramento. Halfway there I stopped and left the bloody shirt in a ditch. I parked Jimmy's car a few blocks from the bus depot and bought a ticket for the next set of wheels heading east. Chicago. I had an hour to wait. I didn't like it, but there was nothing I could do about it. I returned to Jimmy's car. From his glove compartment I pulled a map of the U.S. and that book of postcards from The Mystery Spot. The cards had strange images: two men in plaid trousers standing opposite each other on a tilted stretch of concrete in the woods. The interior of an empty cabin with bizarre angles and a man standing on a shelf attached to a crooked wall. I addressed one to Mr. Dodson. "Sorry I couldn't say goodbye. I'll be all right. Love, Josie." Another to Pearl, even though she already knew: "T. won't be taking any more brothers from this world. Love, Joe." To Lucille: "Gratitude, for everything. Love, J." The ink ran on all of them.

I caught the bus and got off in Cheyenne. From there I caught another heading south. Snaked my way across the country toward New Orleans. My plan was to stay there till the case cooled, then head to Greenwich Village. No one but Lucille knows I spent time there. She'll keep my secret.

Riding in a bus at night through desolate parts of the country, you spend a lot of time staring at your reflection as the dim world outside shimmers through it. I relived that awful moment, the press of his blood against my fingers, the horror of a life ebbing into my hands, and shuddered. Again and again. What I came back to was this: it wasn't about revenge, sweet or otherwise. Jimmy and Bobby were gone, Lily and Aaron too, and nothing I could do would bring them back. I did it for all the young Marys he would have killed, because Tully would have gone on killing. One life instead of a string of gay boys lying dead on the streets of San Francisco, blood oozing onto the concrete. I hit town too late to save my brother, but I saved someone else's. It's not what I came for, but it's something.

I may stay a while. New Orleans suits me. I still wear trousers, but I go by Josie now. People here don't seem to mind much. The city has seen too much history to regard male and female, white and black, straight and queer, or even living and dead as absolutes. The streets are full of in-betweens, and no one is alarmed by the ghosts that live among us. Everyone here knows that the past inhabits the future. For now, I'm home.

h i s t o r i c a l   n o t e s

This is a work of fiction rooted in historical fact. Blackmail, McCarthyism, bar raids, police extortion, gendered rebellion, tavern communities, police brutality, creative resistance, racism, classism, and pulp fiction all form significant threads in the fabric of lesbian, gay, bisexual, and transgender history.

Blackmail targeting Queer people flourished between the World Wars, but its history reaches at least as far back as the late eighteenth century, most famously to Oscar Wilde at the end of the nineteenth. Angus McLaren's *Sexual Blackmail* explores how anti-sodomy laws armed blackmailers, and details the workings of such extortion rings in New York, Atlantic City, and Washington, D.C. In the 1950s the FBI used the purported susceptibility of homosexuals to blackmail to justify hounding out and firing large numbers of us from government service. It was Republican Senator Kenneth Wherry of Nebraska who declared, in a December 1950 interview with the *New York Post*, "You can't hardly separate homosexuals from subversives." Seven months earlier Wherry had announced that 3,750 homosexuals held federal jobs, and soon thereafter the U.S. Senate authorized the official investigation known as "the Pervert Inquiry." The consequences were dramatic: in the years preceding that inquiry, an average of sixty federal employees were dismissed each year following investigations into their sexual histories; by 1951, the rate was sixty per *month*. The Postal Service was among the government agencies that became obsessed with homosexuality. Postmaster General Arthur Summerfield launched a crusade against "pornographic filth in the family mailbox," and the seizure of mail with homoerotic content frequently resulted in FBI surveillance of the recipients. Justin Spring's *Secret Historian: The Life and Times of Samuel Steward, Professor, Tattoo Artist, and Sexual Renegade* discusses the dire impact of the postal service on Queers during this period.

The California Supreme Court ruled in 1951 that bars could not be shut down solely because homosexuals gathered there. Sol Stoumen, the heterosexual owner of the legendary Black Cat Cafe, initiated the case when the Board of Equalization suspended his liquor license because the cafe was "a hangout for persons of homosexual tendencies." While Stoumen initially denied the charge, he hired a lawyer who shifted the focus of the case to civil rights, arguing that homosexuals, too, have a constitutional right to public assembly. The San Francisco Superior Court and the First District Court of Appeals denied this right, but the California Supreme Court agreed to hear the case. In their decision they cite an Oklahoma ruling in which prostitutes were classified as human beings and therefore entitled to such basic human rights as food and shelter, as long as it was not provided for immoral or illegal purposes. Having affirmed that homosexuals are human beings, the court ordered the Black Cat's liquor license restored.

This challenge to the longstanding tradition of bar raids produced a brief flowering of tavern culture, particularly among lesbians, but was quickly eroded by new tactics for surveillance and repression. The police, together with the Alcoholic Beverage Control Board, focused on identifying—and in many cases instigating—illegal acts such as same-sex dancing or a man placing his hand on the knee of another man. They trained their youngest officers and agents to affect "homosexual mannerisms" and to "come on" to bar patrons in order to produce evidence of criminal activity. In 1955 San Francisco's chief of police created a "blueprint of action" to keep "the gathering places of homosexuals under constant pressure." In addition to surveillance and entrapment at bars, beat cops stopped "obvious homosexuals, or the effeminate type," for questioning and, "if warranted," arrest. They provided sex crimes investigators with the names, addresses, and places of employment of individuals questioned or arrested, in order to create a comprehensive list of the city's "known homosexuals." Nan Alamilla Boyd's *Wide-Open Town: A History Of Queer San Francisco to 1965* and Josh Sides' *Erotic City: Sexual Revolutions and the Making of Modern San Francisco* explore the Black Cat legal case and its aftermath.

While the terms *transgender* and *genderqueer* didn't exist in the 1950s, the liminal social space that Joe/Josie and Black Pearl occupy has long been a part of Queer communities, and the distinctions between *transgender* and *gay* or *lesbian* were less defined in the past than they are today. As the SFPD's targeting of "obvious homosexuals" indicates, the more visible members of Queer communities—those who today would likely identify as transgender or genderqueer—often caught the brunt of harassment and violence as they carved out social space for the larger community. Leslie Feinberg's *Stone Butch Blues* is a groundbreaking personal account of this dynamic, and Susan Stryker's *Transgender History* examines it in detail. Stryker's documentary, *Screaming Queens*, explores the 1966 Compton's Cafeteria riot in San Francisco's Tenderloin District. Drag queens and male hustlers battled the police for the right to drink coffee together in public, and won. In the aftermath, they created the National Transsexual Counseling Unit, the first such peer-run advocacy and support group. Readers familiar with the film may recognize the name Elliott Blackstone; I wanted to honor Blackstone, who in the 60s and early 70s resisted the long legacy of police brutality, pioneering as a (heterosexual) police liaison to the transgender community. He was removed from this role after fellow officers planted narcotics in his desk. When Blackstone was asked, at the premier of *Screaming Queens*, why he fought so hard for LGBT rights, he replied, "Because my religion teaches me to love everybody."

Historian and activist Stryker has also helped to preserve the history of Finocchio's, which opened in 1929 as a small bohemian cafe and speakeasy. Finocchio, its owner's real last name, is Italian slang for "pouf" or "pansy," and the "female illusionists" who performed there made it a world-renowned nightspot for decades. Hollywood stars like Tallulah Bankhead and Bette Davis flew in to see themselves impersonated. Finocchio's and other "female impersonation" venues frequently included multiracial casts at a time when the stages of other entertainment venues were racially segregated. Unfortunately, Pearl would not have been able to leave work dressed as she was in my print; to minimize police harassment of the nightclub and to prove that they were "run[ning] the place straight," the owners of Finocchio's required that performers arrive for and leave from work in male attire. A full history of Finocchio's has yet to be written, but J.D. Doyle's website, queermusicheritage.com, provides history, images, and memorabilia from Finocchio's remarkable history.

The character of José Sarria is based on the performer and activist José Sarria, who performed opera and incendiary monologues at the Black Cat Cafe, and ended many an evening with a rousing chorus of "God Save Us Nelly Queens." The real José cofounded several early homophile organizations and in 1961 ran for the San Francisco Board of Supervisors, the first openly gay candidate for public office in the United States. In 1964 he founded the Imperial Court System, which grew into an international association of charitable organizations. José displayed extraordinary elegance and wit in his acts of resistance. In San Francisco and cities throughout the United States, Halloween was the one night when men wearing dresses were generally immune from arrest, but police cracked down at the stroke of midnight, routinely arresting "wagonloads" of men. José created felt patches in the shape of a black cat, inscribed with the words "I am a boy," and attached safety pins to the back so they could be worn like brooches. Because California law prohibited men from wearing women's clothing "with the intent to deceive," José's felt brooches provided immunity for "cross-dressing" revelers: protection from arrest by means of felt, glue, scissors, and safety pins. While the words spoken by the character in this novel are entirely the work of my imagination, the real José's outrageous courage in what can arguably be called the Dark Ages of Queerdom fueled my imagination. You can see José reprise his role conducting "God Save Us Nelly Queens" at a Black Cat reunion in the film *Before Stonewall: the Making of a Gay and Lesbian Community*, directed by Greta Schiller. José died, at 90, in August 2013. His life is chronicled in *The Empress Is A Man: Stories from the Life of José Sarria*, by Michael R. Gorman.

The life of Ada "Bricktop" Smith, the African American performer and self-described saloonkeeper, loosely inspired the character of Tiny. Bricktop owned a series of Paris nightclubs, most notably Chez Bricktop, during the 1920s, 30s, and 40s, where she formed a social circle that included Duke Ellington, Mabel Mercer, Josephine Baker, Cole Porter, Langston Hughes, and F. Scott Fitzgerald. According to one of Baker's children, Baker and Bricktop were briefly lovers early in their careers. Her autobiography, *Bricktop*, written with James Haskins, provides a vivid account of how the relative equality experienced in Europe by expatriates like herself, as well as by Black soldiers during World War II, helped fuel the African American civil rights movement—the gains of which are being eroded today.

The history of the San Francisco Fillmore District informed the characters of Black Pearl, Lily, and Tiny. In 1942, Executive Order 9066 forcibly relocated everyone of Japanese origin to internment camps, and the Fillmore lost a large percentage of its residents. The Great Migration brought African Americans to the neighborhood, where they created an extraordinarily rich jazz scene showcasing performers such as Ella Fitzgerald, Louis Armstrong, John Coltrane, Billie Holliday, Charlie Parker, and Dexter Gordon. This vibrant, racially integrated neighborhood boasted two dozen music venues within its one square mile, along with homes, restaurants, theaters, and many Black-owned businesses. Beginning in 1953 the neighborhood was literally bulldozed in an act of "urban renewal" by San Francisco's Redevelopment Agency, led by Justin Herman. *Harlem of the West: The San Francisco Fillmore Jazz Era*, by Elizabeth Pepin and Lewis Watts, provides a dazzling collection of archival photographs and interviews with those who lived, worked, and performed there.

Arthur Dong's documentary, *Forbidden City, U.S.A.*, about San Francisco's Chinese-themed nightclub, sowed the seeds for the characters of Mrs. Wu, Marie, and Lily. Dong's interviews explore the complex compromises required of the cabaret's singers and dancers, many of them second-generation Americans, who made their living performing as "exotic Orientals." Dong's *Coming Out Under Fire*, co-written with historian Allan Bérubé, explores the astonishingly gratifying and harrowing experiences of Queers in the American Armed Forces during the Second World War. The characters of Miss Holloway and Anne were inspired by a haunting interview in *Before Stonewall* with a woman whose face remains in darkness as she recounts her almost year-long interrogation in the Women's Army Corps at the end of World War II.

The phrase, *A friend of Dorothy*, appears to have emerged during World War II as a coded way for gay men to refer to themselves. It is unclear whether the term originated as a reference to *The Wizard of Oz* or the sharp-tongued Dorothy Parker, but in either case, "Are you a friend of Dorothy?" would sound perfectly innocuous to anyone not in the know, while enabling those wise to the term's implications to identify themselves. It is such a gentle weapon of self defense, crafted in response to extreme repression. My fondness for the term increased exponentially when I learned that it played a role in a Naval investigation of homosexuality in the Chicago area during the early 1980s. As Randy Shilts reports in *Conduct Unbecoming: Gays and Lesbians in the U.S. Military*, upon hearing gay men refer to themselves as friends of Dorothy, intrepid Naval investigators launched a massive womanhunt for this Dorothy, hoping to persuade her to reveal the names of the many gay service members she counted among her friends.

Pandora's Box is a fictional bar, but San Francisco had more lesbian bars in the forties and fifties than it does today. The first lesbian nightclub, Mona's, opened on Union Street in 1934 before moving to 440 Broadway. Mona's featured performers such as Gladys Bentley and anchored a profusion of North Beach lesbian taverns including the

Paper Doll, the Beaded Bag, the Chi-Chi Club, the Tin Angel, and the Anxious Asp. Boyd's *Wide Open Town* explores the evolution of this mid-century lesbian district and the dynamics of increased lesbian public visibility. The role Pandora's plays in the novel was also informed by Elizabeth Kennedy and Madeline Davis' *Boots of Leather, Slippers of Gold*, which argues that lesbian bars served as a "prepolitical" form of resistance, enabling women to find one another, claim public space, and—perhaps most importantly—develop a sense of community. In an era that, for the most part, understood homosexuality as a psychiatric illness afflicting individuals, this was a significant step indeed. I've tried to convey the importance of bars in this ideological transformation, but also the ways racial, ethnic, and class differences complicated community formation, which became a focus of my own graduate work. *Gay Bar: The Fabulous, True Story of a Daring Woman and her Boys in the 1950s*, by Will Fellows and Helen P. Branson, celebrates Branson's role in providing a home for many gay men in Los Angeles; it also illuminates the role of class divisions and the stories that were often told to justify and enforce them.

My graduate research in Yale's American Studies Department involved interviewing lesbians about their lives in the 1940s, 50s, and 60s. More than one life story was anchored by an electrifying moment in a rural podunk's five-and-dime, discovering a lesbian-themed pulp novel. In *Blackmail, My Love*, I stretched the historical record back a bit to suit my imagination: in fact, lesbian pulp fiction was just beginning to appear in 1951, when my novel is set, so it's unlikely that Josie would have found a pulp novel in a dime store several years prior. While there were lesbian-themed novels published in the 1930s, the explosion of lesbian pulp occurred between 1950 and 1969, when hundreds of lesbian-themed pulps were published, some of which sold millions of copies. Tereska Torres' 1950 *Women's Barracks* sold over two million copies in its first five years and was singled out by the House Select Committee on Current Pornographic Materials as an example of how paperback books promoted moral degeneracy. Vin Packer's *Spring Fire* was published in 1952 and reissued by Cleis Press in 2004. Most lesbian pulps were written to titillate heterosexual male readers and offered only tragic endings. Even the positive portrayals, written by lesbians like Ann Bannon and Marijane Meeker, generally ended with insanity, death, or a sudden love affair with a man; because books travelled through the U.S. mail, publishers wary of censorship required that narratives not "proselytize homosexuality." Nonetheless, these books made their way to small towns throughout the country, and encountering them on wire racks was how many lesbians first realized that there were others "like them."

As lesbian pulp fiction demonstrates, oppression and resistance have been intertwined in complicated ways throughout Queer history. Even in the harshest eras, communities and individuals found ways to resist, to celebrate themselves, to create rich and enduring alternative cultures. In *A Restricted Country*, Joan Nestle writes about a lesbian bar in fifties New York City that posted a guard at the bathroom door to ensure that only one lesbian entered at a time; the guard also meted out the allotted amount of toilet paper. An inevitable result was a perpetual line spiraling around the bar. Another inevitable result was a line act: those women swaggered, strutted, preened, and paraded their way along that line, regardless of the urgency they undoubtedly felt about reaching the end of it. As Nestle writes, "We wove our freedoms, our culture, around their obstacles of hatred, but we also paid our price. Every time I took the fistful of toilet paper, I swore eventual liberation. It would be, however, liberation with a memory."

acknowledgements

My gratitude overflows. Renee Mayer, Sandy Rosen, and Cobra Teal midwifed this book: they so gently caught an early draft and lavishly welcomed it into the world, then slapped it on the ass and demanded more of me. Renee graciously allows me to steal her best lines, sweetens my days and nights, and renews the joy of living.

Many people sustained me throughout the writing and the carving. My family embraces and supports me through thick and thin, and there's been plenty of both. Heron Saline provided resonant companionship without which I might never have begun. Margie Cochran and Terry Kelly pushed my thinking on a critical plot point and buoyed my spirits at every turn. Seth Eisen is my comrade in forging relationships with queer ancestors, real and imagined. Dhami Boo generously shared juicy tidbits of oral history. Terry Cavanaugh talked about queers and God. Debora Iyall inspires with her creative boundlessness and perseverance. Dona Taylor is a steadfast and generous supporter of local artists. The volunteers at Under One Roof amaze me with their dedication and make me feel like a rock star. Traci Joy Burleigh invigorates me. Pam Peniston, Jeff Jones, Rudy Lemcke, and the Queer Cultural Center enrich my creative world. The Radical Faeries encourage me to run amuck and come undone.

Special gratitude for encouragement and thoughtful commentary on drafts to Animal Prufrock, Emily Post, Valerie Schlafke, Pam Higley, Ruth Herring, Richard Dodds, Jeff Thomas, Clayton Robbins, Amy Sueyoshi, Seth Eisen, and Debora Iyall. I am thankful for information and guidance from Don Romesburg, Kirk Read, Karl Soehnlein, Carol Queen, and Robert Lawrence. I feel considerable intellectual debts to Audre Lorde, Adrienne Rich, Gayle Rubin, and Leslie Feinberg. I owe deep spiritual debts to the historians, archivists, filmmakers, and hoarders who perform the arduous and underpaid labor of unearthing, constructing, and preserving queer history. In particular I'm thankful to Allan Bérubé, Nan Alamilla Boyd, George Chauncey, Madeline Davis, Arthur Dong, J.D. Doyle, Lillian Faderman, Leslie Feinberg, Michael R. Gorman, Elizabeth Kennedy, Angus McLaren, Joan Nestle, Greta Schiller, Justin Spring, Josh Sides, and Susan Stryker.

I'm grateful to my creative perch, the South of Market Cultural Center, and to my colleagues at SOMArts for keeping alive the spirit of the Neighborhood Arts Program. My students in the Queer Ancestors Project embolden me with their engagement and creativity. My students at Chrysalis Studio make my work a pleasure; special thanks for companionship to Nathan Yergler, Abby Ginsberg, Jeff Thomas, Rob Mitchell, Lucy Irwin, Ethel Mays, and Gina di Grazia. My prints first saw the light of day at City Art Cooperative Gallery, and I'm grateful to the many artists and patrons who have made it a vibrant space for local art. A heart-felt thank you to the intrepid women at Cleis Press who persevere in the perilous fray of publishing, especially the gorgeously enthusiastic Brenda Knight.

While I wrote this novel before joining their order, the Sisters of Perpetual Indulgence provided wildfire inspiration at a point early in its formation. I was returning from a night of performances exploring the fertilely intertwined roots of the Sisters and the Radical Faeries, when I asked myself the essential question: "What Would Sisters do?"—or, what would they have done had they existed in 1951? My dear friend, Insomnia, was visiting and we stayed up late, meditating on the question. The answer inspired the act of resistance by Jimmy at the heart of this novel. Special thanks for love and support to Sisters Penny Costal, Saki Tumi, Zsa Zsa Glamour, Roma, Mary Juanita High, Tilly Comes Again, and Selma Soul.

For my graduate research, generously supported by the Social Science Research Council, I interviewed forty lesbians about their lives during the middle part of the twentieth century. Their experiences animate every page of this novel, and I am profoundly grateful to them for the hours and the intimacies they shared with me. Thank you Addy, Al, Arminta Neal, Barbara Joan Hudson, Bernie, Bess Spears, Donna, Eddie, Jeanette "Jay" Mays, Jo, Karen, Monica, Nellie, Norma Casler, Penny, Shorty, Teddie, and others who chose to remain anonymous. One of these women worked at the Mare Island Navel Base, across San Pablo Bay from San Francisco, during World War II. Returning home from work one night, she was arrested for her mannish appearance and charged with vagrancy despite the employee identification she was wearing on her cap and jacket. The judge sentenced her to six months in prison, suspended "on condition you leave Vallejo within twenty-four hours. We don't want your kind in California." Back home in Wyoming, she tried to commit suicide by driving to the next town drunk, at night, on the wrong side of the road. She didn't meet a single car on the twenty-four-mile drive. Bernie, I'm grateful you lived to share your story. This work is dedicated to our Queer ancestors who survived, and to those who did not.

The artwork in *Blackmail, My Love* is available as signed, limited edition, original linocut prints at katiegilmartin.com.

about the author

KATIE GILMARTIN's checkered past includes stints as a miserable graduate student, buoyant union organizer, bona fide sex researcher, and deeply engaged college professor. She attended Oberlin College and Yale Graduate School, then for over a decade taught cultural studies with an emphasis on the histories of gender and sexuality. For her PhD research Gilmartin interviewed lesbians about their lives in the 1940s, '50s, and '60s. These interviews ignited an enduring passion for not only Queer history, but also pulp fiction. The fifties saw an explosion of pulp novels about lesbians, which made their way into big cities and small towns across the country. Several of the life stories that lesbians shared with Gilmartin were anchored by a riveting moment in a rural podunk's five-and-dime: while browsing the wire racks of pulp novels, a racy cover caught her eye—a haughty brunette, a melting blonde, and a world of tension between them.

Gilmartin studied printmaking at San Francisco's South of Market Cultural Center, and became utterly smitten with the medium as art and as craft. She gradually surrendered her academic life to assume care of Chrysalis Print Studio, where she now teaches linocut and monotype classes. Her prints consistently interweave the visual and the verbal. The Queer Words series explores the multiple meanings of Queer patois—retooled epithets, secret codes, camp, and slang—as a record of creative resistance. Her "Pulps" are faux pulp fiction covers: cover art for novels she's invented that are set in 1950s San Francisco and celebrate the city's history. In writing blurbs for these fabricated novels, Gilmartin engaged more deeply with the aesthetics of pulp fiction and noir. Gradually, the text outgrew the prints and became an actual novel: *Blackmail, My Love*.

Gilmartin founded City Art Cooperative Gallery and the Queer Ancestors Project, which is devoted to forging sturdy relationships between young LGBTQ people and their ancestors. She is also known as Sister Plush Lovebud, of the Sisters of Perpetual Indulgence. *Blackmail, My Love* is her first novel.